FEARIE TALES

Stories of the
Grimm and Gruesome

FEARIE TALES

Stories of the
Grimm and Gruesome

Edited by Stephen Jones
Illustrated by Alan Lee

Jo Fletcher
New York • London

Jo Fletcher Books
An imprint of Quercus
New York • London

Library of Congress Control Number: 2014944403

ISBN 978-1-62365-806-9

Distributed in the United States and Canada by
Hachette Book Group
237 Park Avenue
New York, NY 10017

Manufactured in the United States

2 4 6 8 10 9 7 5 3 1

www.quercus.com

For Dot,
with gratitude.

Contents

INTRODUCTION

Don't Scare the Children

IN THE EARLY years of the nineteenth century, German brothers Jacob (1785–1863) and Wilhelm (1786–1859) Grimm set out to collect folk stories from across Europe in an attempt not only to reflect a German cultural identity in such tales but also to preserve stories that for centuries had been handed down through the generations in the oral tradition.

This had resulted in differing versions of these tales existing from region to region (especially in France), and the Brothers Grimm not only gathered these stories into a coherent manuscript for the first time—after listening to friends, family members, and storytellers, and transcribing the tales they were told—but they also allowed fragments of the old religious beliefs to continue to survive through the telling of these stories.

In this respect, it is not too much of a stretch to consider Jacob and Wilhelm Grimm to be among the first horror anthologists. That is because, despite subsequent editing and rewriting by diverse hands (including Wilhelm himself), many of the original stories contained scenes of gruesome retribution or implied sexuality that early reviewers deemed totally unsuitable for younger readers (who were not in fact the initial audience these tales were aimed at).

Later versions added religious and spiritual motifs to make the stories more uplifting to a middle-class readership, while the cruelty, sexual elements, and anti-Semitism was toned down. In fact, the Brothers Grimm even added an introduction encouraging parents to make sure that their offspring were exposed only to age-appropriate stories.

Culturally at this time the discipline of children was often based on fear, and many of these tales were supposed to be a "warning" to youngsters not to misbehave, lest something terrible befall them (such as being thrown on a fire or eaten alive).

Between 1812 and 1864, *Kinder- und Hausmärchen* (*Children's and Household Tales,* or, as it was later known, *Grimm's Fairy Tales*) went through seventeen printings and was revised many times, with the number of stories included in some larger editions growing from eighty-six to more than two hundred. The book was also widely pirated, and different folktales were often added by other compilers.

Today, just over two centuries since Jacob and Wilhelm first published their seminal collection, fairy tales have probably never been so popular. Although Hollywood (especially Walt Disney Studios) has made liberal use of the Grimm Brothers' work almost since the birth of movies themselves, in recent times we have been bombarded with "reimaginings" such as the werewolf-themed *Red Riding Hood* (2011), *Hansel & Gretel: Witch Hunters* (2013), and *Jack the Giant Slayer* (2013), not to mention various versions of "Snow White," along with such popular TV series as *Once Upon a Time* and *Grimm* (both 2011–).

Over the years, even the Brothers Grimm themselves have been given fictional film biographies (incorporating more than a touch of fantasy) with George Pal's colorful *The Wonderful World of the Brothers Grimm* (1962) and Terry Gilliam's somewhat darker *The Brothers Grimm* (2005).

So, for this volume I invited a number of prominent authors to contribute their own spin on the classic fairy tales, whether inspired by the Grimms or folk stories from other cultures. The only condition I imposed was that, in the end, this was first and foremost a *horror* anthology, as a reflection of those early versions of the stories, before they became overly sanitized.

I am delighted to say that all the writers included in this volume rose to the challenge magnificently, and have produced their own—often unique—spin on some classic tales, while still remaining true to the source material.

Here are some genuinely scary and disturbing stories for the twenty-first century.

In 1884, George Bell and Sons of London published *Grimm's Household Tales*, a new translation of the Brothers' stories by British novelist Margaret Hunt (the mother of supernatural writer Violet Hunt). I have used some of these translations as the basis of those tales interspersed between the original material in this volume.

Not all the stories featured herein have their inspiration in the work of the Brothers Grimm, but I have attempted to include some of their older tales that have either thematic links or served as inspiration for the new fiction that follows them. And, as this *is* a horror anthology, I have also taken the liberty of book-ending those tales with a couple of unfamiliar short ghost stories originally collected by the German siblings.

And so, finally, to echo the warning that Jacob and Wilhelm gave to their readership two hundred years ago: while the stories contained in this volume are based on fairy tales, folktales, and myths, they are perhaps not entirely suitable for children or younger readers.

That is, of course, unless you really want to scare them out of their tiny little minds . . . !

Stephen Jones
London, England
April 2013

The Willful Child

ONCE UPON A time there was a child who was willful, and would not do what her mother wished. For this reason God had no pleasure in her, and let her become ill, and no doctor could do her any good, and in a short time she lay on her death-bed.

When she had been lowered into her grave, and the earth was spread over her, all at once her arm came out again, and stretched upward. And when they had put it in and spread fresh earth over it, it was all to no purpose, for the arm always came out again.

Then the mother herself was obliged to go to the grave, and strike the arm with a rod, and when she had done that, it was drawn in, and then at last the child had rest beneath the ground.

Find My Name

RAMSEY CAMPBELL

DOREEN WAS AWAKE at once and trying to hear why. A dog barked on the far side of the tennis courts, and another yapped from the direction of the golf club, and then she heard noises from Anna's old room. Benjamin was shifting in his crib, a sound both blurred and amplified by the baby monitor. As Doreen prepared to stumble to the next room the sound rustled into silence, and she let her head sink back onto the pillow. Before she closed her eyes she glimpsed midnight on the bedside clock. At the very least she was dozing when she heard a low voice. "You're mine now, Benjamin," it said.

Though she felt as though the night had settled a suffocating weight on her, she managed to open her cumbersome lips. "He never will be. Stay away, Denny, or I'll call the police."

"I'm not the boy's father. His mother had her wish and now it's time for mine."

This had to be a dream—nobody could hear Doreen through the monitor—but she felt pierced by anguish. "What wish did Anna have?"

"Her son till he was a year old."

"And his father abusing her for half of it. You think she'd have wished for that too?"

"That's what she wished away, and I'm the one that made it go. She knew there was a price."

Doreen felt her eyes spill her grief. "She paid for her mistake all right."

"We aren't talking about that." The voice had turned peevish. "Maybe she thought she could cheat me that way," it said. "Nobody swindles me, so don't try it. It's my time."

Doreen couldn't tell if she was struggling to understand or waken. "What time?"

"You've almost had your year of him, so say good-bye while you can, Doreen."

"And what do they call you as long as you know my name?"

"Nobody ever knows." She heard a snigger or the slither of a tongue across the plastic microphone. "I'll see you on his birthday," the voice said. "I'm leaving you a sign."

The dogs began to bark again, and more of them joined in. They were real, and they made her aware that the night was otherwise silent, which allowed her to lapse into sleep. A late April dawn coaxed her awake, and she lay pondering her dream. Was she afraid Benjamin's father would come looking for him while her husband was at the managers' conference? The court had kept Denny away from the child, and if necessary the police would. Perhaps she was uneasy because Benjamin had lost his mother on his only birthday. That ought to be another reason to make his imminent birthday special, and Doreen was thinking of ways when she heard him begin to stir.

His morning ruminations always sounded as if his language was taking time to wake up. "Bid honor revert efforts," she could almost have imagined he was mumbling, not to mention "Font of our reserved birth." Most of thirty years ago she'd enjoyed overhearing Anna's infant monologues, but she tried not to be reminded too much. Now Benjamin was talking to Nosey and Stuffy, the bears that shared his cot. When he started clattering the wooden bars, either playing at percussion or demanding freedom, Doreen made for his room.

He was standing at the bars that faced the door, and she couldn't help being reminded of Anna. His face was almost a miniature of his mother's—blond hair, high forehead, bright blue eyes, small snub nose, full lips, determined chin. In Anna's case the brow had left too much room for brooding, and she'd dyed her hair any number of colors, none of which had placated her partner; apparently few things did. Her eyes had grown dull as stones last year, and the few times Doreen saw her smile it looked more like a plea, even once she'd rid herself of Denny. At least she'd been sufficiently determined to take him to court, but had that left her more afraid of him? Doreen vowed she wouldn't be. "Ready for adventures?" she said to Benjamin.

"Avengers."

"Come on, little parrot," Doreen said, only to falter. The microphone she always planted on top of the blue chest of drawers was lying on the floor. She'd thought the wire was well out of Benjamin's reach, and was dismayed to think she hadn't heard the fall. She felt insufficiently vigilant on his behalf, as if she might be growing too old for the task. As she returned the microphone to the shelf she said "You mustn't do that, Benjamin."

He stuck his lower lip out. "Didn't, Gran."

"Don't tease, now. If you didn't, who did?"

"The man."

"Which man?"

"Comes to see me."

"Who does, Benjamin? Not your—" Nervousness had made her blurt that, and she couldn't avoid adding "Not Daddy. Not your father."

"Not Daddy," the toddler said, and laughed.

Doreen wondered if he was simply repeating her words. "Who then, Benjamin?"

His face grew puzzled before he said "Dark."

"You can't see him, you mean. You know why, don't you? He isn't real. He's just a dream."

"Just agree."

"Sometimes I don't know when you're teasing," Doreen said but didn't really mean.

Surely he could have dislodged the microphone while he was waking up. He put his arms around her neck as she lifted him over the bars. He was warm as sleep, and eager to walk downstairs and run through all the rooms. Doreen caught him in the kitchen, where she helped him off with his sleeping suit. Once she'd praised his potty performance she gave him a hand with dressing while letting him believe he'd done it virtually by himself. She strapped him into the high chair and readied herself for the day, and then she watched him deal with cereal, spilling very little and hardly daubing his face. As she played the game of mopping him while he tried to squirm out of reach she said "What shall we do this morning?"

"See the trains."

He found plenty to chatter about on the half a mile of wide suburban road. "They're jumping for the ball," he said by the tennis courts, and "There's the little hill car" beside the golf course. "Gone in to read," he said beside the deserted schoolyard, so that Doreen knew he was recalling what she'd told him he would do at school. "Robber jugs," he declared outside the antique shop, and she gathered he was thinking of the tale of Ali Baba she'd read him. He called the hairdresser's customers space ladies because of their helmets, and outside the florist's he said "Where the flowers go," which Doreen tried not to find funereal. As they reached the railway she took a firm grip on his small warm trusting hand. "Red bell," he said.

The bells were indeed jangling as the red lights flashed. The traffic halted as the barriers descended on both sides of the level crossing, and Benjamin's fingers wriggled eagerly in Doreen's clasp. When a train left the station she couldn't resist asking "What does it look like?"

"Lots of stamps."

He was still remembering the ones he'd put on envelopes last Christmas—the strips the train windows reminded him of. At his age Anna had loved licking Christmas stamps. These days you peeled them off the backing, and Doreen wondered if the generation after his mightn't even recall that, if every greeting would be sent by computer. Six trains passed, framed by three performances of the barriers, before he was ready to head home.

Doreen saw to lunch and dinner while he had his nap. After lunch they walked past the Conservative Club and the Masonic hall to the Toddling Tiddlers playgroup. "Here's another of our talkers," Dee Maitland cried as he ran to compete with his friend Daisy at garrulousness. While Doreen wouldn't risk entrusting him to a stranger—she'd taken early retirement so as to care for him—she asked Daisy's mother Jonquil to look after him while Doreen made his birthday cake. "There's nobody I'd rather have," Jonquil said, and Doreen was fleetingly reminded of her midnight dream.

She hadn't realized Benjamin had left quite such a mess at home, where toys were scattered through all the downstairs rooms. He helped her clear some of them away before he set about redistributing them, and Doreen reflected that all too soon he would outgrow them. She would even miss his messiness, and after dinner she was in no hurry to finish cleaning his indignant face. She relented when Hubert rang. "How's the man of the house?" he said.

"Being looked after by the woman just now."

"Sorry," Hubert said, sounding surprised if not defensive. "Something's wrong?"

"Just used to having you about."

"I will be on the day that matters most, won't I? You're all right otherwise, both of you."

"Pretty much as you left us." She could tell that was what he hoped if not felt entitled to hear. "You?" she said.

"Not especially looking forward to three more days of hearing how we can improve the public image of the banks. I'd rather just get on with actually improving them if we can," Hubert said loud enough to be heard by colleagues who were audible nearby. "Enough of my grumbles. Shall I say good night to the bedtime boy?"

"He isn't quite that yet," Doreen said as she switched on the loudspeaker. "Who's this, Benjamin?"

"The man." Once Hubert greeted him Benjamin said a good deal more enthusiastically: "Grandad."

"How's the youngest and the best? Only three more nights and you'll be seeing me."

"Free nights."

"That's more or less it, yes. Are you being good for Granny? You look after her and see nothing bad happens to her while I'm at my conference."

For an instant the toddler looked worried. "Nothing bad."

"Nothing's going to," Doreen reassured him. "Better say good night to Grandad now. I can hear he's anxious to relax."

"Good night, Grandad," Benjamin said so enthusiastically that both his grandparents laughed.

He helped tidy up his toys before bath time. "Hot," he said gravely as Doreen tested the water, and then "Not." While she couldn't call herself religious—even less than her parents, which was why her prayers for Anna had seemed so desperate, falling short of defining their goal—whenever Benjamin came out of the bath he looked and felt as she imagined someone newly baptized would. She toweled him and kissed him and vowed to keep him safe as long as she lived, however much that sounded like a fairy tale.

She helped him into his sleeping outfit and laid him down in the cot. She was turning the pages of Anna's battered old book when the title of a story caught her eye. Of course, that had been Anna's childhood favorite. No wonder Doreen had dreamed something of the kind, but she didn't want to read that tale to Benjamin just now. "'Once upon a time,'" she began instead, "'there was a woodcutter and his wife who had children called Hansel and Gretel . . .'"

She omitted the oven and the children's threatened fate. The children were rescued just before Benjamin fell asleep. She turned out the light and took the monitor downstairs, keeping it on the kitchen table while she ate dinner. A day of Benjamin had tired her as usual, not that she would want it to be otherwise, and she was soon in bed.

She wakened to find the zeros of the bedside clock staring out of midnight. She was hoping her body hadn't adopted a routine, having been roused at the same time last night, when she heard the voice. It was so muffled that it could have been inside her skull. "It's you again, is it?" she said or thought. "What do you want this time?"

"What I always get."

"You didn't in the story, did you? Not when they found out your name."

"That old thing? Don't believe everything you read."

"Why, isn't your name Rumpelstiltskin?"

"That's just the tale they told." With a snigger not unlike the rattling of small teeth the voice said "Some of it's true. I know when I'm wanted."

"Then you ought to know you aren't."

"Your girl did when she needed a witness."

"Don't you talk about her," Doreen protested before managing to laugh. "Why am I getting worked up? You're just a dream."

"Still think you're dreaming, do you?" The voice sounded grotesquely resentful. "You'll see," it said, "there'll be another sign," and left her alone.

As far as Doreen was concerned there hadn't previously been one. She found she was trying to remember the witness who'd come forward on Anna's behalf. He'd lived below the apartment she'd shared with Denny, and he'd testified that Denny had abused both her and their child. Despite her efforts Doreen was unable to recall his name or even his appearance, except for an impression of somebody smaller than average, close to dwarfish.

The sun was up by the time Benjamin wakened her. She lay enjoying his soliloquy until she began to wonder why his words were even harder to make out than usual. He couldn't very well be muttering "I drub hens for tot forever," nor yet "Her son for furtive debtor." He sounded oddly distant, that was it—so remote that she could imagine he was being carried away from her. She lurched out of bed and almost fell headlong in her dash to the next room.

The door swung inwards just a few inches before meeting an obstruction. At least Benjamin was in the cot, and gave Doreen a sleepy smile as she edged into the room. The plastic microphone was trapped against the door, yards from where she'd placed it on the shelf and at the limit of its wire. When she picked it up she found her hand was shaking. "Who put this here, Benjamin?" she said as gently as she could.

"The man," he said with a touch of defiance. "Man with all teeth."

"What do you mean?"

"Teeths." As if to demonstrate how plural they could be, the boy opened his mouth wide and dug his fingers into the corners to tug it wider still. "Lots," he said.

Doreen wanted to think he was boasting about his own. "What did I tell you the man was?"

"Comes when I'm asleep."

She was making for the cot when a thought halted her. "Can you climb out for me?"

Benjamin stood up but gave her a reproachful look. "Like you lifting."

That needn't mean he was incapable of clambering out, but when he held up his arms Doreen lifted him. She had to restrain herself from hugging him too fiercely; that wasn't how to protect him. She stayed close to him as he stampeded through the rooms, and found she didn't want to leave him alone at all. Once she'd secured him in the high chair she performed her morning necessities as fast as she could. "What would you like to do today?" she said when she'd recovered her breath.

"Change books."

"That's a good idea," Doreen said, having realized what else she could do.

The library was in the opposite direction from the railway, past the nearest of the parks, which she had to promise Benjamin they would visit later. Doreen signed a petition against closing six libraries and watched him grab books from the table in the children's section. Once he was installed in a miniature chair she hurried to a computer. She could have thought she was growing delusional as the anniversary of her loss came closer, but she found the details for the landlord of Anna's last address.

At home she read three of Benjamin's library books to him before he fell asleep. She succeeded in carrying him upstairs to the cot without rousing him, and took the monitor into her room. She listened to her heartbeats, having keyed the phone number, until a woman said "Wesley Properties."

"I'm trying to find out the name of a tenant of yours."

"We can't give out that information, I'm afraid."

"I see you wouldn't normally, but he was a witness in court for my daughter Anna Marshall. She lived in the same building. She died nearly a year ago."

Doreen heard two more of her urgent heartbeats before the woman said "And you were asking for the gentleman's name because . . ."

"I can't remember it and I need it to help me keep custody of my grandson."

"I'll have to speak to somebody. Please hold on."

Doreen's pulse grew more strident for at least a minute before she was asked to continue holding, after which she heard murmurs that she had to reassure herself weren't in the monitor. More than another minute was measured by her not entirely constant heartbeats, and then a new voice said "Mrs. Marshall, is it? Tony Wesley. Sorry for your loss."

"I still have my grandson, Mr. Wesley."

"So Jane was saying. I do remember your daughter and the sad circumstances. I'd like us to be of assistance."

"Please do."

"As I say, I wish we could be. I can only think we've suffered a small problem with the system. We've no record of the tenancy you were inquiring about."

For several beats her heart was louder in her ears than his voice. "What do you mean, no record?"

"The period of the letting shows up blank. It was only a few weeks while the lady who lived there had moved out and the lady who has the apartment now took up residence."

"But he was there, wasn't he? You know he was there."

"Of course he was." Wesley sounded defensive, however. "You'll forgive us, but nobody here can remember his name," he said. "Not really anything about him."

Doreen felt as if Wesley had robbed her of more than words—of certainty if not worse. She mumbled thanks she didn't feel and held the empty cell in her unsteady hand. Should she phone the court? Suppose there was no official record of the witness? The possibility deterred her more than she understood. Surely she oughtn't to delay, or was her anxiousness just a symptom of age? She hadn't made the call by the time Benjamin left her in no doubt he was awake.

After lunch they walked to the park. In the deserted playground a seesaw was twitching as though someone had sneaked away at their approach. Doreen thought she closed the gate securely, but more than once it proved to be unlatched after she turned her back. A notice said dogs weren't allowed, and she had the distinct impression that one was somewhere nearby, perhaps lying on its belly and baring all its teeth. She pushed Benjamin on one swing after another and bounced him gently on the seesaw and dodged around the climbing frames to be ready if he fell. Far too often she had a sense that a toothy intruder had crawled into or otherwise invaded the playground and was waiting at her back.

When she took Benjamin home she could have fancied that a visitor was lying low somewhere in the house. Perhaps it had curled up in the oven to peer through the glass door, or was poised to poke its head out from behind a piece of furniture. She might be even more dismayed to find it sitting in a chair like an uninvited guest or, worst of all, in Benjamin's high chair. Of course it was nowhere except inside her feverishly buzzing head, but she found herself urging Hubert to call, and almost dropped the phone as she hastened to answer it. "How was your day?" she said as if this might return hers to normal.

"Oh, professional enough."

"What have you had to put up with this time?"

"Plenty of ideas that can be put to good use."

It was plain to Doreen that he didn't want his real thoughts to be overheard. She felt prevented from reaching him, all the more so when he said "And how was yours?"

"Our day?" She couldn't admit to her fears or how they'd caused her to behave. "I'm sure you can imagine it," she said. "Library and park."

"So long as everything's in order," Hubert said, and she heard how much he wanted that. "Shall I speak to the man himself?" When she brought up the loudspeaker he said "Are you looking after Granny for me?"

"Yes, Grandad," Benjamin said so earnestly that Doreen had to suppress a nervous laugh.

"You make sure you carry on, then. Two more nights and I'll take over."

Once he'd gone Doreen said to Benjamin "Would you like to look after Granny a little bit more?"

"Yes," he said more solemnly than ever.

"You can sleep in my room while Grandad's away, then. We'll be company if anyone wakes up."

Was she being too protective? Sometimes she felt she had been with Anna—felt she'd left Anna vulnerable, even helped to cause her death. Nevertheless Doreen dragged the cot into the main bedroom while Benjamin gave it an energetic push. After his bath she lowered him into the cot and sat on the bed to read him Cinderella's tale divested of any ugliness, and then she went downstairs with the monitor.

She couldn't read. She was too aware of the silence in the monitor and throughout the house. Before long she was nervously ready for bed, but she found herself switching on her laptop. Rumpelstiltskin wasn't the only name to figure in versions of the old tale, and she repeated all the names until they were fixed in her head. She felt close to senile for carrying on like that, but would she really rather think she'd neglected some method of protecting Benjamin? When she was certain of recalling the names she tiptoed up to bed.

Benjamin murmured and grew still as she slipped under the quilt. Doreen suspected she would be unable to sleep, but she opened her eyes on the far side of a darkness that had lasted until midnight. As she read the time she heard the voice. "You've been trying to find my name out, have you? Try all you like."

It was closer to her than the cot—perhaps as close as the inside of her head. When she blinked at the dimness, the cot was the only unfamiliar object she could see. "You'll leave us alone if I name you, will you?" she said so softly she could barely hear herself.

"Try me."

"It wouldn't be Whuppity Stoorie, would it?"

"Not in your lifetime," the voice said in a mockingly Scottish falsetto.

"Tom Tit Tot, then."

"Not on your tits and not on your tot."

"Ruidoquedito."

"Not even if you say it right." Having rejected the rest of the names as well, the voice said "Aren't you going to ask them at the court?"

Doreen was instinctively suspicious. "Why would you want me to?"

"Let them see there's no name in their records and maybe they'll have to reopen the hearing."

That was why she'd felt she oughtn't to call, Doreen realized now. "What difference would that make?"

"Maybe they'd have to tell the father and give him another chance."

"Or," Doreen said in a rage that made her reckless, "you could tell him."

"No chance of that. Nobody else can hear me." As Benjamin shifted in his cot—perhaps Doreen's outburst had roused him—the voice said "I'll leave you a sign, though. Or do you think you're doing it all?"

"I don't—" Doreen began without knowing how to continue, only to realize she was talking to herself. Listening for an intruder in the room kept her apprehensively awake, but at some point exhaustion put out her vigilance until she heard Benjamin's morning murmur. She had to waken fully to recall why it was closer than usual, though that didn't help her to grasp what he was mumbling—hardly "Observe or differ on truth" any more than "Run forever, tots, be hid" and still less "Bred introvert, ooh, suffer." He started chatting to her once he met her eyes, but she couldn't help glancing away in search of a sign. Perhaps it hadn't been left in the room, if indeed the threat wasn't just an elderly woman's fearful dream.

She could see nothing wrong downstairs either. Benjamin was eager to walk to the trains again, though he was untypically mute on the way, so that she wondered if he didn't find anything worthy of a comment. Wouldn't he have remarked on a dwarfish shape that seemed to peer over a net in a tennis court before somehow hiding behind the mesh? Perhaps the tuft like greasy unkempt hair that poked above at least one mound on the golf course was too insignificant, but how about the childish shape that dodged out of sight around the school? Doreen wouldn't have expected to glimpse an apparently unaccompanied child in more than one of the shops, but surely these impressions were symptoms of sleeplessness, like the face that glared out of the antique dealer's window before sinking into a vase. "Robber jug," Benjamin said, having found words at last, and Doreen rather wished he hadn't rediscovered those.

The red lights at the level crossing blazed in her eyes while the clangor of the bells jerked her nerves. Though the trains were almost empty, Benjamin kept repeating "He's looking." Surely he meant the toddler on the opposite side of the tracks—a real child, not one of Doreen's fancies, wheeled in a stroller by his mother. All the same, the phrase Benjamin kept parroting worked on Doreen's nerves. Each train reminded her of a strip of film being drawn through a gate, because she could easily imagine that a face was peering over the lower edge of every window—just the top of a face, but the same one. Six trains had to pass before Benjamin had had enough, by which time Doreen certainly had.

Once he was safe in his cot she lay down on the bed. She didn't mean to fall asleep, but she jolted awake to find him at the bars and more than ready for his lunch. As soon as he'd devoured it and she'd cleaned him up she drove to Jonquil's. "Don't worry and don't rush," Jonquil said as he ran to find Daisy. "You take all the time you need with his surprise."

At home Doreen set about making the cake. It wasn't quite enough to distract her from being alone in the house or from recalling how she'd felt last year. She had been on the train to London when her phone had jangled with Anna's final text:

Sorry, Mommy. You won't understand but he'll get in.

Doreen had certainly never understood how Anna could have left Benjamin with a friend and overdosed on drugs she'd obtained somewhere to supplement the ones the doctor had prescribed. Did Doreen understand at last, or was the memory undermining her mind? She left the cake in the oven and went up to lock the wardrobe; she needn't risk Benjamin finding his presents while he was sharing the room.

The stunted figure that peered out of the cot was only one of the bears. She opened the wardrobe to glance at the presents, and her hand clenched on the wood. She'd arranged the wrapped packages along the back of the wardrobe, but now they were piled in a ramshackle stack against the left-hand corner. So this was the sign, or had she done it herself in her sleep, if not in some more distracted state? Suppose instead that the doubts had been planted in her mind as a distraction? She ducked into the wardrobe to line up the presents and made sure the door was locked. She'd begun to think there was something else she needed to recognize.

Though she took her time icing the cake, the middle of the big blue digit on the yellow sugar carapace betrayed an inadvertent shiver. The day was growing dark when she hurried to the car, so that she didn't immediately notice the small figure in the child's seat.

It was all the more unobtrusive for the absence of a head. It was a toy, either a plastic baby or a toddler, and its head had been chewed off; the tooth marks were still glistening. The door was unlocked; perhaps Doreen had been so distracted she'd left it that way. She flung the doll into the rubbish bin on her drive, and once she was able to control her hands she started the car.

Jonquil met her with a momentary frown. "Has everything been all right?" Doreen blurted.

"We've all been having fun. Maybe some of us a bit more than others. He's got a funny notion of hide-and-seek, hasn't he?"

"How funny?" Doreen said without expecting any mirth.

"He kept telling Daisy somebody was doing it. She wasn't too fond, to tell you the truth."

"You mustn't upset Daisy if you want her for your friend." Doreen waited until Benjamin was in the child seat, which she'd vigorously wiped, before she added "Who was hiding, Benjamin?"

"Mr. Toothy."

Doreen did her best to withhold a shiver. "Is that his name?"

"I call him it."

She oughtn't to have bothered asking. It was pointless to expect Benjamin to give her the real name, supposing one even existed—and then, with a jerk of her whole body that made her stall the engine, she knew what she'd been struggling to realize. "Benjamin," she said, "what are those things you've been saying when you wake up?"

"Can't remember." Somewhat indignantly he said "Asleep."

"I mean," Doreen said, praying that she would be able to bring them to mind, "where did you hear them?"

"Don't know. Asleep."

She was almost sure, and she sped the car home. Nobody was waiting in the high chair, and even Benjamin's toys seemed not to have been touched. She played with him and watched him dine and cleared up the remains while her head swarmed with words that tumbled over one another to adopt new shapes. They hadn't revealed anything she would call a secret by the time Hubert phoned. "What are you doing with yourself tonight?" he said.

"Just thinking."

"Try not to miss anyone too much, yes? I'll be with you tomorrow as soon as I can."

"What will you be doing in the meantime?"

"I may take the chance to relax." He sounded apologetic. "I'll see to it you can soon," he said, and when she switched on the loudspeaker: "You take special care of our favorite lady till I'm home, Benjamin."

There was no sign of an intruder in the bathroom, and the wardrobe was still locked. Doreen's mind was chattering with words and unmanageable fragments of words, and she read Benjamin the shortest story in the book, about the emperor who didn't know he was exposed. He looked solemn when she'd finished, even while she gave him a good night kiss and another. As she watched him fall reluctantly asleep she thought of staying upstairs—and then she realized how the clamor in her brain had prevented her from thinking. She fetched the monitor and hurried down to the computer.

Had her inspiration given her false hope? The websites that created anagrams didn't deal with groups of words as long as the ones she was desperate to reshape. Eventually she found a site that did, and typed in one of the sets of words she remembered overhearing. In a few seconds she was shown a rearrangement that made her feel both sickened and triumphant. "That's it," she whispered. "There's still magic somewhere." She tried some of the other bunches of words to be certain, and then she got ready for bed.

She didn't expect to sleep, but in case she did she set the alarm and hid the clock under her pillow. She was wakened by activity that felt as if someone was groping for her face. It was the vibration of the alarm. As she fumbled to turn it off a voice came out of the dark. "Are you ready for me?"

She didn't answer until she had quelled the alarm. "Who are you talking to?"

"Who else but the woman that thinks she knows."

"It could be Benjamin, couldn't it? When you said nobody else could hear, you didn't mean only I could."

"Clever woman. You all think you are."

"It's you that thinks he is," Doreen retorted so fiercely she almost forgot to keep her voice down. "You're worse than a child. You thought you could tease Benjamin—you've got so much contempt for us—but you didn't think he could let me know even if he didn't realize."

"Do you even know what you're talking about? Just listen to yourself. Your mind's gone, Doreen."

"Not while I know my own name. Shall I tell you why nobody knows yours?"

"Amaze me. I'm in no hurry now he's mine."

"Because you haven't got one."

She heard a shrill giggle mixed with a grinding of teeth. "Then you can't tell me and save him."

"I can tell you what you're called, though."

"I'm waiting. I'm all ears except for a mouth."

"Is it hurt for reversion of debt?"

"That's not even a name," the voice said, sounding as sharp as bared teeth.

"I said you've never had one. Do they call you furtive horror? Often beds?"

"You're raving, woman. You're as mad as your daughter."

"Because you and Denny made her." Doreen's grief came close to robbing her of control, but it mustn't while she was protecting Benjamin. "Trove of birth ensured for," she murmured.

"Not even a sentence," the voice scoffed, but it was growing ragged. "I've had enough of you. It's time."

"Yes," Doreen said. "It's my time and my family's." She was tired of taunting him with words the computer had shown her. "They call you devourer of the firstborn," she said.

A shape reared up beside the cot, howling like a beast of prey. While it wasn't much taller than Benjamin, it was as squat as a toad. In the dimness she couldn't distinguish much more, especially about its face, perhaps because it had so little of one. She saw a gaping mouth and the glimmer of far too many teeth, and then the jaws yawned more enormously still. The head split wide as though it was being engulfed by the mouth, and another convulsive gulp made short work of the body. The howl was cut off as though it had imploded, and Benjamin wakened with a cry. As he started whimpering Doreen hurried across the deserted room to hug him. "Happy birthday, Benjamin," she said.

RAMSEY CAMPBELL was born in Liverpool and still lives on Merseyside with his wife, Jenny. His first book, a collection of stories entitled *The Inhabitant of the Lake and Less Welcome Tenants*, was published by August Derleth's legendary Arkham House imprint in 1964; his subsequent novels have included *The Doll Who Ate His Mother, The Face That Must Die, The Nameless, Incarnate, The Hungry Moon, Ancient Images, The Count of Eleven, The Long Lost, Pact of the Fathers, The Darkest Part of the Woods, The Grin of the Dark, Thieving Fear, Creatures of the Pool, The Seven Days of Cain, Ghosts Know, The Kind Folk,* and the movie tie-in *Solomon Kane*. His short fiction has been widely collected and he has edited a number of anthologies. Now well in to his fifth decade as one of the world's most respected authors of horror fiction, Campbell has won multiple World Fantasy Awards, British Fantasy Awards, and Bram Stoker Awards, and is a recipient of the World Horror Convention Grand Master Award, the Horror Writers' Association Lifetime Achievement Award, the Howie Award of the H. P. Lovecraft Film Festival for Lifetime Achievement, and the International Horror Guild's Living Legend Award.

The Singing Bone

IN A CERTAIN country there was once great lamentation over a wild boar that laid waste the farmers' fields, killed the cattle, and ripped up people's bodies with his tusks.

The king promised a large reward to anyone who would free the land from this plague, but the beast was so big and strong that no one dared to go near the forest in which it lived. At last the king gave notice that whosoever should capture or kill the wild boar should have his only daughter to wife.

Now, there lived in the country two brothers, sons of a poor man, who declared themselves willing to undertake the hazardous enterprise—the elder, who was crafty and shrewd, out of pride; the younger, who was innocent and simple, from a kind heart.

The king said, "In order that you may be the more sure of finding the beast, you must go into the forest from opposite sides."

So the elder went in on the west side, and the younger on the east. When the younger had gone a short way, a little man stepped up to him. He held in his hand a black spear and said, "I give you this spear because your heart is pure and good. With this you can boldly attack the wild boar, and it will do you no harm."

He thanked the little man, shouldered the spear, and went on fearlessly.

Before long he saw the beast, which rushed at him, but he held the spear toward it, and in its blind fury it ran so swiftly against it that its heart was cloven in twain. Then he took the monster on his back and went homewards with it to the king.

As he came out at the other side of the wood, there stood at the entrance a house where people were making merry with wine and dancing. His elder brother had gone in there, and, thinking that after all the boar would not run away from him, was going to drink until he felt brave.

But when he saw his young brother coming out of the wood laden with his booty, his envious, evil heart gave him no peace.

He called out to him, "Come in, dear brother—rest and refresh yourself with a cup of wine."

The youth, who suspected no evil, went in and told him about the good little man who had given him the spear wherewith he had slain the boar.

The elder brother kept him there until the evening, and then they went away together. And when in the darkness they came to a bridge over a brook, the elder brother let the other go first; and when he was halfway across he gave him such a blow from behind that he fell down dead.

He buried him beneath the bridge, took the boar, and carried it to the king, pretending that he had killed it, whereupon he obtained the king's daughter in marriage.

And when his younger brother did not come back he said, "The boar must have ripped up his body," and everyone believed it.

But as nothing remains hidden from God, so this black deed also was to come to light.

Years afterward a shepherd was driving his herd across the bridge and saw, lying in the sand beneath, a snow-white little bone. He thought that it would make a good mouth-piece, so he clambered down, picked it up, and cut out of it a mouth-piece for his horn. But when he blew through it for the first time, to his great astonishment, the bone began of its own accord to sing:

"Ah, friend thou blowest upon my bone.
Long have I lain beside the water,
my brother slew me for the boar,
and took for his wife the king's young daughter."

"What a wonderful horn," said the shepherd, "it sings by itself. I must take it to my lord the king."

And when he came with it to the king, the horn again began to sing its little song. The king understood it all, and caused the ground below the bridge to be dug-up, and then the whole skeleton of the murdered man came to light.

The wicked brother could not deny the deed, and was sewn up in a sack and drowned. But the bones of the murdered man were laid to rest in a beautiful tomb in the churchyard.

Down to a Sunless Sea

NEIL GAIMAN

THE THAMES IS a filthy beast: it winds through London like a snake, or a sea serpent. All the rivers flow into it, the Fleet and the Tyburn and the Neckinger, carrying all the filth and scum and waste, the bodies of cats and dogs and the bones of sheep and pigs down into the brown water of the Thames, which carries them east into the estuary and from there into the North Sea and oblivion.

It is raining in London. The rain washes the dirt into the gutters, and it swells streams into rivers, rivers into powerful things. The rain is a noisy thing, splashing and pattering and rattling the rooftops. If it is clean water as it falls from the skies it only needs to touch London to become dirt, to stir dust and make it mud.

Nobody drinks it, neither the rainwater nor the river water. They make jokes about Thames water killing you instantly, and it is not true. There are mudlarks who will dive deep for thrown pennies, then come up again, spout the river water, shiver and hold up their coins. They do not die, of course, or not of that, although there are no mudlarks over fifteen years of age.

The woman does not appear to care about the rain.

She walks the Rotherhithe docks, as she has done for years, for decades: nobody knows how many years, because nobody cares. She walks the docks, or she stares out to sea. She examines the ships as they bob at anchor. She must do something to keep body and soul from dissolving their partnership, but none of the folk of the dock have the foggiest idea what this could be.

You take refuge from the deluge beneath a canvas awning put up by a sailmaker. You believe yourself to be alone under there, at first, for she is like a statue—still and staring out across the water, even though there is nothing to be seen through the curtain of rain. The far side of the Thames has vanished.

And then she sees you. She sees you and she begins to talk, not to you, oh no, but to the gray water that falls from the gray sky into the gray river. She says, "My son wanted to be a sailor," and you do not know what to reply, or how to reply. You would have to shout to make yourself heard over the roar of the rain, but she talks, and you listen. You discover yourself craning and straining to catch her words.

"My son wanted to be a sailor.

"I told him not to go to sea. 'I'm your mother,' I said. 'The sea won't love you like I love you; she's cruel.' But he said, 'Oh, Mother, I need to see the world. I need to see the sun rise in the tropics, and watch the Northern Lights dance in the Arctic sky, and most of all I need to make my fortune and then, when it's made, I will come back to you, and build you a house, and you will have servants, and we will dance, Mother, oh, how we will dance . . .'

"'And what would I do in a fancy house?' I asked him. 'You're a fool with your fine talk.' I told him of his father, who never came back from the sea—some said he was dead and lost overboard, while some swore blind they'd seen him running a whorehouse in Amsterdam.

"It's all the same. The sea took him.

"When he was twelve years old, my boy ran away, down to the docks, and he shipped on the first ship he found, to Flores in the Azores, they told me.

"There's ships of ill omen. Bad ships. They give them a lick of paint after each disaster, and a new name, to fool the unwary.

"Sailors are superstitious. The word gets around. This ship was run aground by its captain, on orders of the owners, to defraud the insurers; and then, all mended and as good as new, it gets taken by pirates; and then it takes a shipment of blankets and becomes a plague ship crewed by the dead, and only three men bring it into port in Harwich . . .

"My son had shipped on a stormcrow ship. It was on the homeward leg of the journey, with him bringing me his wages—for he was too young to have spent them on women and on grog, like his father—that the storm hit.

"He was the smallest one in the lifeboat.

"They said they drew lots fairly, but I do not believe it. He was smaller than them. After eight days adrift in the boat, they were so hungry. And if they did draw lots, they cheated.

"They gnawed his bones clean, one by one, and they gave them to his new mother, the sea. She shed no tears and took them without a word. She's cruel.

"Some nights I wish he had not told me the truth. He could have lied.

"They gave my boy's bones to the sea, but the ship's mate—who had known my husband, and known me too, better than my husband thought he did, if truth were told—he kept a bone, as a keepsake.

"When they got back to land, all of them swearing my boy was lost in the storm that sank the ship, he came in the night, and he told me the truth of it, and he gave me the bone, for the love there had once been between us.

"I said, 'You've done a bad thing, Jack. That was your son that you've eaten.'

"The sea took him too, that night. He walked into her, with his pockets filled with stones, and he kept walking. He'd never learned to swim.

"And I put the bone on a chain to remember them both by, late at night, when the wind crashes the ocean waves and tumbles them onto the sand, when the wind howls around the houses like a baby crying."

The rain is easing, and you think she is done, but now, for the first time, she looks at you and appears to be about to say something. She has pulled something from around her neck and now she is reaching it out to you.

"Here," she says. Her eyes, when they meet yours, are as brown as the Thames. "Would you like to touch it?"

You want to pull it from her neck, to toss it into the river for the mudlarks to find or to lose. But instead you stumble out from under the canvas awning, and the water of the rain runs down your face like someone else's tears.

NEIL GAIMAN has coscripted (with Roger Avary) Robert Zemeckis's motion-capture fantasy film *Beowulf*, while both Matthew Vaughn's *Stardust* and Henry Selick's *Coraline* were based on his novels. Next up, his Newbery Medal–winning children's novel *The Graveyard Book* is being adapted for the movies, with Gaiman on board as one of the producers. The ever-busy author also has out a book of poems, *Blueberry Girl*, illustrated by Charles Vess; *Crazy Hair*, a new picture book with regular collaborator Dave McKean; and the graphic novel compilation *Batman: Whatever Happened to the Caped Crusader?* (with art by Andy Kubert). *The Tales of Odd* is a follow-up to the 2008 children's book *Odd and the Frost Giants,* while *The Absolute Death* and *The Complete Death* from DC/Vertigo feature the character from Gaiman's *Sandman* comic. The author is also working on a nonfiction volume about China, following his visit to that country in 2007.

Rapunzel

THERE WERE ONCE a man and a woman who had long in vain wished for a child. At length the woman hoped that God was about to grant her desire.

These people had a little window at the back of their house from which a splendid garden could be seen, which was full of the most beautiful flowers and herbs. It was, however, surrounded by a high wall, and no one dared to go into it because it belonged to an enchantress, who had great power and was dreaded by all the world.

One day the woman was standing by this window and looking down into the garden, when she saw a bed which was planted with the most beautiful rampion-rapunzel, and it looked so fresh and green that she longed for it, and had the greatest desire to eat some.

This desire increased every day, and as she knew that she could not get any of it, she quite pined away, and began to look pale and miserable.

Then her husband was alarmed, and asked, "What ails you, dear wife?"

"Ah," she replied, "if I can't eat some of the rampion, which is in the garden behind our house, I shall die."

The man, who loved her, thought, *Sooner than let your wife die, bring her some of the rampion yourself, let it cost what it will.*

At twilight, he clambered down over the wall into the garden of the enchantress, hastily clutched a handful of rampion, and took it to his wife.

She at once made herself a salad of it, and ate it greedily. It tasted so good to her—so very good—that the next day she longed for it three times as much as before. If he was to have any rest, her husband must once more descend into the garden.

In the gloom of evening, therefore, he let himself down again. But when he had clambered down the wall he was terribly afraid, for he saw the enchantress standing before him.

"How can you dare," said she with angry look, "descend into my garden and steal my rampion like a thief? You shall suffer for it."

"Ah," answered he, "let mercy take the place of justice, I only made up my mind to do it out of necessity. My wife saw your rampion from the window, and felt such a longing for it that she would have died if she had not got some to eat."

Then the enchantress allowed her anger to be softened, and said to him, "If the case be as you say, I will allow you to take away with you as much rampion as you will, only I make one condition—you must give me the child which your wife will bring into the world. It shall be well-treated, and I will care for it like a mother."

The man in his terror consented to everything. And when the woman was brought to bed, the enchantress appeared at once, gave the child the name of Rapunzel, and took it away with her.

Rapunzel grew into the most beautiful child under the sun.

When she was twelve years old, the enchantress shut her into a tower, which lay in a forest, and had neither stairs nor door, but quite at the top was a little window. When the enchantress wanted to go in, she placed herself beneath it and cried: "Rapunzel, Rapunzel, let down your hair to me."

Rapunzel had magnificent long hair, fine as spun gold, and when she heard the voice of the enchantress she unfastened her braided tresses, wound them around one of the hooks of the window above, and then the hair fell twenty ells down, and the enchantress climbed up by it.

After a year or two, it came to pass that the King's son rode through the forest and passed by the tower. Then he heard a song, which was so charming that he stood still and listened. This was Rapunzel, who in her solitude passed her time in letting her sweet voice resound.

The King's son wanted to climb up to her, and looked for the door of the tower, but none was to be found. He rode home, but the singing had so deeply touched his heart that every day he went out into the forest and listened to it.

Once when he was thus standing behind a tree, he saw that an enchantress came there, and he heard how she cried: "Rapunzel, Rapunzel, let down your hair." Then Rapunzel let down the braids of her hair, and the enchantress climbed up to her.

"If that is the ladder by which one mounts, I too will try my fortune," said he. And the next day when it began to grow dark, he went to the tower and cried: "Rapunzel, Rapunzel, let down your hair."

Immediately the hair fell down and the King's son climbed up.

At first Rapunzel was terribly frightened when a man, such as her eyes had never yet beheld, came to her. But the King's son began to talk to her quite like a friend, and told her that his heart had been so stirred that it had let him have no rest, and he had been forced to see her.

Then Rapunzel lost her fear, and when he asked her if she would take him for her husband, and she saw that he was young and handsome, she thought, *He will love me more than old Dame Gothel does.*

And she said yes, and laid her hand in his. She said, "I will willingly go away with you, but I do not know how to get down. Bring with you a skein of silk every time that you come, and I will weave a ladder with it. And when that is ready, I will descend, and you will take me on your horse."

They agreed that until that time he should come to her every evening, for the old woman came by day.

The enchantress remarked nothing of this, until once Rapunzel said to her, "Tell me, Dame Gothel, how it happens that you are so much heavier for me to draw up than the young King's son—he is with me in a moment?"

"Ah! You wicked child!" cried the enchantress. "What do I hear you say? I thought I had separated you from all the world, and yet you have deceived me." In her anger she clutched Rapunzel's beautiful tresses, wrapped them twice around her left hand, seized a pair of scissors with the right, and *snip, snap,* they were cut off, and the lovely braids lay on the ground. And she was so pitiless that she took poor Rapunzel into a desert, where she had to live in great grief and misery.

On the same day that she cast out Rapunzel, however, the enchantress fastened the braids of hair, which she had cut off, to the hook of the window, and when the King's son came and cried: "Rapunzel, Rapunzel, let down your hair," she let the hair down.

The King's son ascended, but instead of finding his dearest Rapunzel, he found the enchantress, who gazed at him with wicked and venomous looks. "Aha!" she cried mockingly, "you would fetch your dearest, but the beautiful bird sits no longer singing in the nest. The cat has got it, and will scratch out your eyes as well. Rapunzel is lost to you. You will never see her again!"

The King's son was beside himself with pain, and in his despair he leapt down from the tower. He escaped with his life, but the thorns into which he fell pierced his eyes. Then he wandered quite blind about the forest, ate nothing but roots and berries, and did naught but lament and weep over the loss of his dearest wife.

Thus he roamed about in misery for some years, and at length came to the desert where Rapunzel, with the twins to which she had given birth—a boy and a girl—lived in wretchedness.

He heard a voice, and it seemed so familiar to him that he went toward it. And when he approached, Rapunzel knew him and fell on his neck and wept. Two of her tears wetted his eyes and they grew clear again, and he could see with them as before.

He led her to his kingdom, where he was joyfully received, and they lived for a long time afterward, happy and contented.

Open Your Window, Golden Hair

TANITH LEE

AT THE POINT where the trees parted, he saw the tower. It seemed framed in space, standing on a rise, the pines climbing everywhere toward it in swathes, like blue-black fur, but not yet reaching the top of the hill. A strange tower, perhaps, he thought. The stone was ancient and obdurate, in the way of some old things—and these not exclusively inanimate. He could remember an old woman from his youth, that everyone called a witch, crag-like and immovable in both grim attitude and seeming longevity. Someone had said of her that she had never been younger than fifty, and never aged beyond seventy—"But in counted years she's easily ninety by now." The tower was like that.

Brown raised his binoculars and studied it attentively, rather as he had so many landmarks on his excursion through Europe; he did this more as if he should than because he particularly wanted or needed to.

But the tower *was* rather odd. Caught in that mirror-gap of spatial emptiness, only the cloudless sheet of earliest summer sky behind it, turning toward late afternoon, a warmly watery, pale golden blank of light. The tower was nearly in silhouette. Yet something hung down, surely, from the high, narrow window-slits. What was *that*? It had a yellowish effect, strands and eddies—creepers, perhaps.

Should he check the tower in the guidebook? No. He must make on to the little inn which, he had been told, lay just above the road to the west. It would take about half an hour to reach it, and by then the sun would be near setting. He did not fancy the woods after nightfall—at least, not alone.

He was not sure about the inn. They were so welcoming and kindly-spoken he suspected at once they might be planning to rob him, either directly or through the charges they would apply to his bed and board.

But the evening went on comfortably enough, with beer and various types of not unpleasant food. There was a fire lit, too, which was needed, since, with sunfall, a slight but definite chill had seeped into the world. Brown had selected and retained a good seat to one side of the hearth. Here, after his meal, he smoked and wrote up a few brief notes on the day's travel. This exercise was mainly to provide something with which to regale acquaintances on his return. He sensed he would otherwise forget a lot. The general run of things did not often linger very long in his mind. Having, then, made a note on it, he asked the so-genial host about the tower.

"Oh, we do not speak of it," said the host gravely. "It is unlucky."

"For whom?" bantered Brown.

"For any. An old place, once a witch's fortress."

"A witch's, eh?"

The host, having refilled Brown's tankard, straightened and solemnly said, "It is unlucky even to look at it. To go there is most inadvisable." And after this, rather belying his previous assertion that one had better not talk about the tower, he announced, "Long whiles ago, back in times of history, it was said a creature also lived in the tower, the servant of the witch. She had bred it by force on a human woman, they say, and all the while the mother carried this monster-child, the witch fed the woman special liquids and herbs of power from her own uncanny garden. When the baby came forth, the mother, no surprise to us much, died. The creature then grew in the charge of the witch, and did her bidding for evil, and for all manners of ill."

"A fascinating story," said Brown, who thought he was actually quite bored.

"There is more," said the host, now gazing starkly up at the inn's low, smoky rafters. "Men were drawn to the tower, and somehow clambered up there. They were lured by the vision of a lovely young woman with golden hair, who would lean out of the narrow window and flirt with and exhort them. But when they reached the stony place above and crawled in at the window—Ah!" exclaimed the host quite vehemently, making Brown jump and spill some of his beer—perhaps a ploy, so he would have to purchase more—"Ah, sweet Virgin and Lordship Christ, protect and succor us. No one must look at the tower, or venture close. I have said far too much, good mister. Forget what I have uttered."

Brown dreamed. He had gone back to the tower.

However, he was much younger, maybe eighteen or seventeen years of age. And his father was standing over Brown, as so often Mr. Brown senior had done, admonishing his son: "Don't touch it, boy. It isn't to be touched."

Yet surely—it *was*. All that golden floating fluff—like golden feathers escaping from a pillow full of swansdown—which down had come from golden swans.

"But it's so sweet, Father," said Brown.

And frowningly woke in the tiny bedroom up under the roof at the forest inn.

Midnight, harshly if voicelessly, declared his watch.

Now he would be awake all night.

Next moment, Brown was once more fast asleep and dreaming . . .

Treacle goldenly flowed. Of *course* it was *sweet*. He tasted it, licked it up, swallowed and swallowed, could not get enough. He had been deprived of confectionery when a child; his strict father had seen to that.

The only difficulty was that the treacle also spilled all over him. He was covered in the stuff. There would be such trouble later. Better, then, to enjoy himself while he could. Brown opened his mouth wider, and held out both his eager, clutching hands.

*   *   *

The next day dawned bright as any cliché, and Brown got up with the abrupt, rather dreary awareness that he must now go on with his exciting, adventurous journey across Europe. What, after all, was the point, really? Had he been a writer he might have made something of it, some book. Or a playboy would have used the time pretty well, though in a different way and through an unlike agenda. But Brown? What could Brown do with it? Bore people, no doubt, with badly recollected snippets of this and that. Even snippets like the tall tale the inn-host had cooked up last night. It had caused some funny dreams, that. What had they been? Something about sweets, was it, and—gold? Ridiculous.

Brown ate his breakfast in an ordinary silence, which the host respected. If the man felt either embarrassed or scornfully amused at his previous storytelling, one could not be certain. He might even, Brown decided, have forgotten it. Conceivably, he subjected every traveler who spoke of *anything* to some such dramatic recital.

After breakfast, Brown paid his bill, and left the inn.

His next stop was to be a town by a river, both with unpronounceable names. It should take about four hours to reach the unpronounceable town. If everything ran to plan.

Presently, Brown, striding through the sun-splashed blackness of the forest, realized he must have taken the wrong track. For it seemed to him the landscape was familiar. That leaning sapling, for example, and the fallen pine beyond—and then that break in the trees, through which the daylight currently streamed so vividly.

Brown halted, staring out with disfavor and a degree of annoyance. And there, sun-painted now on the sky, stood up again the old tower, with the pines still climbing toward it, and the yellow weeds still hanging down by the windows.

For a long while Brown paused, gazing at the tower. It was not a great distance away, perhaps a couple of miles, or not so much. He noticed a slender path of trodden earth ran down through the forest here, that seemed to lead directly to the foot of the hill, which really, itself, was not significantly steep.

He found he had walked forward without noticing it, and was on the beginnings of the path, descending toward the shallow valley that lay below the hill. See what sheer indolence, mere indifference, could lead to! Did he truly want to go in this direction? Did he *want* to climb up and gape at a nondescript ruin—which probably it *was*, a ruin, when one saw it up close? Then again, why not? It was all the same to him. One more rather pointless episode. *Climbed up to tower,* he mentally penned in his notes: *Nothing much to look at. Perhaps dating from the 15th century; creepers all over it. Not much of a view, as surrounded on all sides by the forest.*

As he had believed, the path and the subsequent climb were not overly taxing for a man who had, so far, mostly walked through two or three countries already.

Well before noon, he had come up and out just below the hilltop, and the stonework loomed in front of him.

Something about the tower was, after all, rather interesting—but what? It was lean, which had made it look taller, though it was not in fact high—perhaps thirty-five feet. It was constructed of a darkish, smoothish stone, polished subsequently by weather, like the carapace of some hard, smooth, rugged sea-creature, possibly. The narrow window-slits appeared quite a way off from the ground, but were, of course, only some twenty-eight or thirty feet up. Nor would they be so narrow, one reasoned, when viewed at their own level. Something he would not be able to do. It was not a tower to climb, not in any way. Nor did he wish to. What, besides, could be up there—an empty stone space?—or else it was full of the wrecked debris from some previous era, only left unthieved because it was so worthless.

But there was a curious and strangely pleasant smell that hung around the tower. It did not resemble the balsamic fragrance of the pines, let alone their other flavors of dryness and wetness, fruition and fading death. On the contrary, the tower had a—what was it? A sort of *honeyed* scent, like the tempting sweetmeats of the Middle East.

Was it the peculiar hanging creepers that gave off this aroma? There seemed to be nothing else that would do so.

Brown was reluctant to go nearer and sniff at them. They were doubtless full of insects, and might even have tiny thorns. One could never tell with alien species. Their color, however, was really after all quite beautiful. Less yellow than a golden effect, a shining *radiant* hue.

There now, despite his caution, he had approached very close. In fact, there seemed nothing remotely injurious about the plant. It was, if anything, extremely *silken*, and totally untangled—as if (fanciful notion) *combed* by careful and loving hands. And yes, the perfume was exuded by these multiple "locks." Irresistibly, Brown leaned forward and drew into his lungs the delicious scent. What *was* it that this recalled for him? *Was* it confectionery—or flowers? Exactly then, something gleamed out above him.

Involuntarily, Brown's neck snapped back. He found he gaped up the stem of the tower at the single window-slit directly above. He noted as he did so that, oddly, the creeper actually seemed, instead of having grown about the stone embrasures, to be extruded from their openings—hung *out* of the windows like some weird and ethereal washing, falling free thereafter down the tower wall.

But what had *that* been meanwhile—that glimpse he had had—something which passed across the slit thirty feet above; something white and vivid and—surely—alive . . . ?

Arrested there, straining his neck, Brown was aware in that moment of a wild memory, the line of some poem, or of a song made from one, a piece by a well-known and respected poet and novelist—Thomas Hardy, was it?—Golden Hair—open your window—Golden Hair—

Something shifted, some loose array of pebbles, or a rock, under the sole of one of Brown's boots. Losing his balance, instinctively he grabbed for the side of the tower. But his hands missed their purchase and met instead the warm waterfall of the creeper. How strong it was, yet exquisitely silky and soft, vibrant with its own aureate and glowing life force. A delight to touch, to hold. And the perfume now, pouring over him, wonderful as some mysterious drug.

He sensed he could fall forward and the creeper would respond. It would catch him and lull him, support and caress him; he need fear nothing. With a startled oath, Brown sprang backward. An icy sweat had burst from every pore of his body. The world rocked beneath him and all about. He was—quite *terrified*. What in God's name had happened?

"Damnation!" Brown exclaimed.

How absurd—the creeper—the creeper had attached itself to him, to his fingers, hands and arms—a rich swathe had folded itself against his chest, nestling there on his clothing, on the skin of his neck, *stuck fast*. For it was *sticky*. Sticky as some ghastly glue—

Struggling, writhing and floundering, he shouted and swore and tore at the encumbrance, trying, exasperated, and next with all his strength, to pull free—how stupid, how *silly*. He was a fool—but how, *how* to release himself? The more he pulled and fought, the more it wrapped itself against, onto and *around* him. Now it had somehow got up into his hair, dislodging his hat, and it had wound about his throat—like an expensive muffler—and the scent, *too* sweet finally, cloying, sickening—he retched, and chokingly bellowed for help to some nonexistent fellow human, to the sky and to the tower itself, to God. None and nothing replied.

Silence then. A hiatus. Brown had ceased to resist, since resistance seemed futile. Through his mind went a jumble of the words of the inn-host: "To go there—inadvisable. Even to look at it—unlucky." So no one would come in this direction, and if they must, they would not look. Nor listen and heed, presumably, should they hear anyone calling or crying out for assistance—

In the name of Heaven, what was he to do?

Brown tried to collect himself together. The situation was fantastic, but had to be rectifiable. He was a grown man, not unstrong. True, he could not reach his pocketknife, the only cutting implement he possessed, aside from his teeth and nails—which would inevitably be inadequate. And the creeper had roped him round very securely. But there must be some way! Stay calm, and *think*.

Thoughts came, but they were no help. He saw himself instead held here for weeks, months, as he slowly died of hunger and thirst, or was poisoned by the stenchful sweetness.

So horrible was this, and so unusually sharply imagined, that for a moment he missed the other, newer sensation.

But then the faint quiver and tensing grew more adamant, and next there was a solid jerk that tipped him off his feet. Tangled in the weedy net he did not, of course, fall. Or rather, he seemed to be falling *upward*—

For several seconds, Brown did not grasp what was happening. But soon enough reality flooded in. It would have been hard to ignore, indeed, as the ground dropped away, the hillside, too, the forested valley, even the lower pines on the surrounding heights. The old stones rubbed slickly against him as he slid. The sky seemed to open, staring eyeless yet intent at his incongruous plight, while the creeper, muscular as the arms of a giant, dragged him without any effort up the stalk of the ancient tower.

Perhaps he lost consciousness for a minute. That was what had happened. He was only dimly aware of the rough tugging and squeezing that shoveled him in at the thin, hard window-slit. His knees and left shoulder were particularly bruised. But they were minor concerns, given the rest.

Spun up in the golden creeper-mass, coughing and retching still, the spasms uncontrollable if intermittent, Brown lay in a knotted ball on a floor of bitterly cold stone. He was not able really to move, for the slightest motion—even the helpless esophageal spasms—seemed to glue and mesh him more, and so confine him further.

The internal atmosphere was dark, though not lightless. The day poured through at the narrow slot and lit his golden chains heartlessly. Here and there patches of light also smudged the stony inner walls. They formed a room, he supposed, a guard-post, one assumed, centuries before. But now nothing was there, only himself, and the restraining weed.

Inadvertently almost, Brown thrust and rolled and kicked at his binding—or attempted to do so. It was, as earlier, to no avail—in fact, again, it made things somewhat worse.

Brown started to sob, but managed to subdue this. If he lost a grip on himself, he would have nothing left. Nothing at all.

Someone had hauled him up here. That much was evident. They had used the creeper, which must have been treated in some bizarre way and had therefore become both lure and trap. Then they had dragged him in like any hapless fish on a line. Soon enough, no doubt, the villain—or villains—would return and hold him to account, maybe requiring a ransom. Brown groaned aloud, thinking of his two maiden aunts, neither wealthy, or the feckless uncle whom Brown had not seen for more than fourteen years. But maybe there would be some other way. Or he might even escape, when once he was unbound.

Brown desperately longed then for his enemy to come back, to free him at least, if only partially, from the net. Presently he called out, in a stern though deliberately nonangry manner, firstly in English, then in the correct local vernacular.

No answer was proffered. There was no sound at all—aside, naturally, from the occasional brush of the breeze beyond the window-slit, the pulse of a bird's wings.

Once he thought he heard a hunter's dog bark two or three times, in the woods below. If only they would come this way—if only he might call again and be heard.

Brown composed himself on the hard, frigid floor, and in his cramped discomfort and bruised pain. He would have to be patient and stoical. Pragmatic.

The spasms had eased. The perfume reek seemed less. Conversely, he sensed the quietly dismal fetor of an enclosed and poorly ventilated place where beasts had died, and too many years stagnated.

He closed his eyes, for the constricted light dazzled, and the contrasting darkness was too full of cobwebs and shadows and *shutness*—except *there*, just beyond where his vision, his head being so constrained from movement, could reach—over *there*, in that wall, something that might be a very low doorway, a sort of arch . . . or maybe not.

*   *   *

Brown's watch had stopped—some knock against the window embrasure. But the clock of the day had gone on, and now the evening arrived. The sky outside the tower was turning a soft, delicate mauve, with vague extinguishing tints of red toward what must be the west. It would be very dark soon. It would be night.

Had anyone come in to inspect their catch? He believed not, though somehow it seemed he had fallen either into a stifled doze or else some kind of trance.

The choking and nausea had passed, but he could not now have moved or struggled, even if the web containing him had permitted it. How curious, Brown mused, deep in his haphazardly self-controlled, near anesthetic misery: a *web*. For was not the creeper very like that: a web? Tempting and beautiful in its own way, but sticky, a snare, and the means to an ultimate capture. And storage.

Should he call out again? If anyone had entered the tower, and was below, they must definitely come up to see to him. There might be threats, or violence, but then, if they wanted him for ransom, at least for a while they would try to keep him in one piece—or so he must hope. If he could talk to them, make promises—however rash or implausible—exhort them to see reason . . . He was not done for yet! He shouted, as loudly and *calmly* as he was able. And, after a minute, again.

And—*yes*. There was at last a faint yet quite distinct movement that he had heard, a little below and behind him. If only he could turn his head. Brown endeavored to, and his neck was spitefully wrenched. He gave out a quickly mastered yelp of physical hurt, protest and frustration.

But the movement, the *sound*, was being repeated, over and over. Steps, he thought, soft, careful, rather shuffling steps, as of a person elderly, or somewhat infirm, climbing up, toward this room.

Thank God, Brown thought. *Thank God.*

"Good evening," said Brown, urbane yet cool, the proper tone, he had judged, in which to greet his lawless captor. The steps had taken a long time to reach him, and once during their progress he had called out again; but now, having spoken, he lay bunched and dumb, tense in every fiber and nerve, awaiting a response—of any kind.

Because he could not turn and *see*, Brown was visualizing a myriad versions of the one who had so astonishingly made a prisoner of him. A bandit, or merely a peasant driven into crime, or some eccentric landowner, a savage *child*—but disabled, certainly, to assess those footfalls; nevertheless obviously dangerous and conceivably lunatic. Brown must proceed very prudently. Yet, even as he speculated on and guessed at all this, he sensed the *other* behind him, not moving now, needing a pause to recover, maybe, from the climb, although there was no noise of labored breathing or other token of distress.

Perhaps some old wound had discommoded him—nothing recent, something to which he was accustomed. And now he only stood at the entry to the room, gloating. Or . . . unsure—could it be *that*? A robber regretting his act, or nervous that his victim, under his shackles, looked far from weak, or himself unable—

"What did you say?" asked Brown. His voice came out far too urgently, and frightened in tone. "I didn't hear you," he added firmly, now much too like a schoolmaster, he thought.

But the visitor had made only one small extra sound. Not a word, no, it had not been conversation. A type of whispering, wheezing *murmur*.

"You'd better," said Brown, "tell me straight out—"

And this was all he had time to say, before the one who had come in moved suddenly forward and was against, and over, and *on* him.

Where he had had a glimpse of something gleaming and white high above, when he stood outside and below the tower, he had the impression now of a mask, pale as marble, yet glistening and streaming with an oily moisture that came from nowhere but itself. Nor was it any mask that resembled a human face.

It was long and snouted and somehow *blind*—and yet—it could see—and there were huge, long, slender needles—that might be teeth—and the large body was stretched out, horizontal, *heavy*, made of flesh but also hard and pale and gleaming-moist, and *stinking,* and there—hands—so many dead-white hands, each with just four fingers, and they flashed, *flashed,* and things tore at Brown, too fast to hurt, and then the hurt came, in long openwork waves, and he screamed and thrashed in the ever-tightening ropes of the golden-yellow web that was like hair, and would not give, or break, but Brown must give and Brown must break, and he gave and broke, and his screaming sank to a dull and mindless whining, and then to nothing at all as the venomous fangs and the thirty-two claws of the creature the witch had raised from the womb on rampion and murder and darkness began to prepare and present and devour its slow and thorough dinner. As already it had done so many, countless times before.

TANITH LEE was born in North London. She did not learn to read—she is dyslectic—until almost age eight, and then only because her father taught her. This opened the world of books to her, and by the following year she was writing stories. She did various jobs, including working as a shop assistant, waitress, librarian, and clerk, before Donald A. Wollheim's DAW Books issued her novel *The Birthgrave* in 1975. The imprint went on to publish a further twenty-six of her novels and collections. Since then Lee has written around ninety books and approaching three hundred short stories. Four of her radio plays have been broadcast by the BBC, and she also scripted two episodes of the cult TV series *Blakes 7*. In 1992 she married the writer-artist-photographer John Kaiine, her companion since 1987. They live on the Sussex Weald, near the sea, in a house full of books and plants, with two black and white overlords called cats.

The Hare's Bride

THERE WAS ONCE a woman and her daughter who lived in a pretty garden with cabbages. And a little hare came into it, and during the wintertime ate all the cabbages.

Then says the mother to the daughter, "Go into the garden, and chase the hare away."

The girl says to the little hare, "Sh-sh, hare, you will be eating all our cabbages."

Says the hare, "Come, maiden, and seat yourself on my little hare's tail, and come with me into my little hare's hut."

The girl will not do it.

Next day the hare comes again and eats the cabbages. Then says the mother to the daughter, "Go into the garden, and drive the hare away."

The girl says to the hare, "Sh-sh, little hare, you will be eating all the cabbages."

The little hare says, "Maiden, seat yourself on my little hare's tail, and come with me into my little hare's hut."

The maiden refuses.

The third day the hare comes again and eats the cabbages. On this the mother says to the daughter, "Go into the garden, and hunt the hare away."

Says the maiden, "Sh-sh, little hare, you will be eating all our cabbages."

Says the little hare, "Come, maiden, seat yourself on my little hare's tail, and come with me into my little hare's hut."

The girl seats herself on the little hare's tail, and then the hare takes her far away to his little hut, and says, "Now cook green cabbage and millet-seed, and I will invite the wedding-guests."

Then all the wedding-guests assembled.

Who were the wedding-guests? That I can tell you as another told it to me. They were all hares, and the crow was there as parson to marry the bride and bridegroom, and the fox as clerk, and the altar was under the rainbow.

The girl, however, was sad, for she was all alone.

The little hare comes and says, "Open the doors! Open the doors! The wedding-guests are merry!"

The bride says nothing, but weeps.

The little hare goes away.

The little hare comes back and says, "Take off the lid! Take off the lid! The wedding-guests are hungry!"

The bride again says nothing, and weeps.

The little hare goes away.

The little hare comes back and says, "Take off the lid! Take off the lid! The wedding-guests are waiting!"

Then the bride says nothing, and the hare goes away. But she dresses a straw-doll in her clothes, and gives her a spoon to stir with, and sets her by the pan with the millet-seed, and goes back to her mother.

The little hare comes once more and says, "Take off the lid! Take off the lid!" and gets up, and strikes the doll on the head so that her cap falls off.

Then the little hare sees that it is not his bride, and goes away and is sorrowful.

Crossing the Line

GARTH NIX

IT WASN'T MUCH of a posse, only six men, all of them old and tired, and Sheriff Bucon himself was pushing sixty and hadn't ridden more than two miles for years. There wouldn't have been a posse at all if it wasn't for Rose Jackson literally dragging the men out of the hotel by shirt collar or waistcoat button, dragging them right out of their comfortable Thursday afternoon poker game and shouting and shaming them onto horses, repeating a similar process that had been enacted on Bucon a half hour before, when Rose had winkled him out of the town's one and only jail cell, where he'd been shutting his eyes for just a moment since earlier that morning.

It was always hard to resist Rose Jackson on the path of her own righteousness, and never more so that day, when she had good reason for it. Her one and only daughter, Laramay, kidnapped by a chancer, a drifter, a man with a strange round-shaped head and eyes two different colors that no one who saw him could agree on, some saying brown and blue, others green and black. He'd ridden in from the east, which was good, and paid for his dinner, whiskey and room with a gold half eagle, which was even better. Said his name was Alhambra, Jayden to his friends, and he was intending to buy property, and would take a look at the two ranches that were always for sale those days, the Double-Double-U and the Star-Circle, the first being for sale on account of its miserableness and general lack of suitability to raise anything but dust, and the second because Broad Bill Jackson had died four years before and his widow, Rose, wanted to take their daughter back east to the big city, to see some doctor on account of Laramay being kind of simple, or maybe because she might catch a better grade of husband, what with her getting close to marrying age and prettier by the month; even if she was shorter and squarer across the shoulders than most considered beautiful, she had a gift of music that made anyone within earshot reconsider her charms.

When Alhambra came to look at the Star-Circle, he didn't do any buying. He saw Laramay singing as she put the sheets through the wringer, singing and turning the big cast-iron wheel, with the soapy water all up her bare arms and the birds themselves coming down to listen, sitting on the line with Laramay's and her mother's clean, wet nightdresses flapping in the wind, and Alhambra just rode on in, picked the girl up in one strong sweep and flung her across his saddlebow, like is often described in tales but is damned hard to do, with many an abduction coming apart with the giving of a girth strap, or a sudden pang to the shoulder. Neither of which occurred this time, and Alhambra was off back up the road with Laramay and almost out of sight before Rose come busting out of the kitchen with her Sharps .50-70 carbine, which she was a dead shot with if the target was close enough and not too risky, neither being the case with Alhambra so distant already and the girl like to be hit as well, or the horse, and her likely to be sore hurt in the fall.

So Alhambra got away, with Rose losing maybe an hour to round up the posse, such as it was, so that the trail was not white-hot, nor even red-hot, but more like that last snowy ash that nevertheless can burn you more than expected, and was certainly warm enough for even old Bucon to follow, who had the experience even if his eyes weren't too good, necessitating a few stops to climb off his horse, get down on hands and knees and inspect the faint, partial crescent mark of a shod horse in the hard dirt, or the angle of a break in the stem of a trampled shrub, and then slowly hoist himself up again, point and declaim, "Thataway," usually followed a few seconds later by "I reckon."

It didn't take more than three hours of pursuit for Bucon at least, and maybe a couple of the others, not including Rose, to figure that

Alhambra wasn't heading for anywhere at all usual, not back to the main road, such as it was, or the mule track over the mountain, or down into Bottle Canyon that opened up into lots of lesser canyons, gorges, ravines and reentrants and was the destination of choice for the local cattle-rustlers and petty thieves.

"He's going for the desert, which don't make sense," announced Bucon as they reined in at the top of the last rise before the said desert, and looked down and ahead about four miles and saw the speck that was a horse bearing two riders, attended closely by a big plume of dust, all heading due west with nothing but flat red rock and drifting white sands ahead. "Least it don't make sense unless . . ."

The sheriff's voice trailed off, and he blinked his tired eyes and then rubbed them a little with the underside of his kerchief, which wasn't so dusty. The other men likewise peered and blinked, and shielded their eyes with their palms, and the horses hung their heads, taking a breather. Rose stood high in her stirrups, her fierce gaze on that plume, which looked to be lessening, the dust falling and growing darker.

"The bastard's stopped," she said, her voice full of a promise that made the menfolk feel uneasy in their parts, like something cold and very unwelcome had suddenly intruded into regions unwanted. "We've got him now."

Bucon wiped his eyes again, and looked at Rose somewhere about her midsection, not wanting to meet her gaze, or get into trouble looking down the top of her shirt, and in fact would have looked at her horse's head if he could have got away with that, only that would have invited trouble as well.

"We ain't got him," he said slowly. "He's crossed the line, gone through."

"Gone through? Gone through where?" Rose snapped out the question, sharp as a gunshot, and Bucon flinched almost like a bullet had whistled past his ear, close enough to feel the angels singing a death in its wake.

"You know," he said. "You know. *There.* She's gone, Rose."

"There ain't no gate," said Rose, but her voice, usually so strident with certainty, was suddenly small and lost. "I never heard of a gate out this way."

"Some says *they* can make gates, when they need 'em," said Bucon. "And there's more around than we can see, for sure. We'd best be getting back. I'd like to make town before sundown. I'm real sorry, Rose."

A frog-chorus of relieved men, guttural and dust-choked, echoed his words as the posse joined in: "Sorry. Sorry. Sorry. Sorry. Sorry—"

"I'm going after her," interrupted Rose. She wheeled her horse to face the posse, a tough woman in her late thirties, still handsome in her looks and doubly so in her character, her once-flaxen hair now a dull gold under her *sombrero cordobés,* which was presumably black underneath the dust. She wore a once-white shirt of heavy cotton, somewhat unbuttoned at the top, below a red and white kerchief that she'd pulled down to speak, and a split riding skirt of soft calf leather lined with pale silk, above a pair of men's boots, big wheel stirrups and all. In addition to the Sharps carbine in the bucket holster by her saddle, she had her husband's Frontier Colt .45 holstered on her right thigh, a knife on her belt, and the eyes and hands to use all these weapons, as had been discovered to their sorrow by various parties over the years, them thinking her husband Broad Bill with the shoulders so wide and the long arms like a gorilla was the dangerous one of the pair.

"I don't expect any of you to come . . . Hell . . . I know it's crazy," she continued. "But she's my daughter!"

"That waterskin full?" asked Bucon. "Got any food? You can't eat or drink nothing there, lest it's given the right way, or you'll never come back."

"There's salt beef and bread in my blanket roll, and the water's full up," said Rose. "I was fixing to ride out to the Pepper Tree this morning, see how Kaleb and the boys were doing with my herd. Got to move 'em on soon. I'd be obliged if you'd tell Kaleb to take them slow over to the Big Hole."

"I'll tell him," said Bucon. "Rose . . ."

He hesitated, and fidgeted with the sheathed knife he wore on a leather thong around his neck: a small thing, ivory-handled, more like a letter-opener than a proper piece of steel, sort of unfitting for a sheriff. People had noted it before, one of them often enough and in the wrong way, so it ended with him having its razor-sharp blade drawn across the back of his hand as a reminder about manners and suchlike.

"What?" asked Rose. "You got something to say, Bucon, say it. I ain't got time to waste."

The sheriff chewed his mustache a little, showing yellow teeth, looked ahead, then lifted the knife over his head and flicked it to Rose. She caught it by the leather thong and looked at it with some puzzlement.

"I got a knife," she said. "I don't need some little razor to trim my mustache."

"You need this knife," said Bucon, glancing at the other men, who stared in fascination. This was even better than Laramay's kidnapping, since it didn't look like it would entail them being involved in anything dark and dangerous and could be talked about for months or even years.

"I bin there," said the sheriff, real quiet, so everyone leaned forward in their saddles, even the horses going quiet as if they knew a matter of import was to be discussed. "I bin there, a long time ago, when I was a younger man . . . and . . . not righteous. I was riding with some bad fellows, and with one thing and another . . . we had to cross the line. Within a couple of days, I was the only one left, death coming for us thick and fast, every which way, creatures I ain't never seen and never wish to see again, and things happening, the very ground against us. I was set to die, when I got helped out by a man who come upon me, in my extremities. He got me out and set me on my right path. He gave me this knife and said if ever I had to go there again, for some good reason that couldn't, simply couldn't be gone against, then I should stick this here knife in the first tree I see. Ask first, and stick it gentle, just like you might skinning, when you want to take it in your hand again in a moment, because the trees ain't always trees. Leave it there and just say some words about being in need of help. So you take it, Rose, and do that, and maybe he will come."

"We talking forty years ago or more," sniffed Rose. "And how does sticking a knife in a tree do anything?"

"Things are different there, Rose," said Bucon. "Time is different too. Tell me you'll do as I say and use the knife."

Rose slipped her hat back and put the thong over her head, the knife resting down about her stomach, a little below her breasts. Bucon looked away and cleared his throat.

"I'll do it," said Rose. "I'll be seeing you, boys. With my Laramay."

With that, she dug in her knees and chirruped to her horse, named Darcy, a rig who had been gelded wrong so he still had one testicle, and acted like a stallion. He was named after the gelder, who left Rose's employ precipitately, fearing for his own equipment when she discovered he'd been drunk and botched the business with half a dozen mounts. The other horses had been fixed proper, but Rose had come to like the bit of fire that Darcy the horse retained, so he was left as he was, neither full stallion nor gelding.

"Good luck, Rose," said Bucon. He took off his hat and waved it after her, the rest of the posse doing likewise, though there were no catcalls or hurrahs. It had the feel of a permanent parting, and not a happy one.

Rose rode down toward the desert, the ground beneath changing under Darcy's hooves, the red rock sinking under the blowing sands that came from the desert, the stunted salt bushes giving up even their lackluster hold, till there was nothing but sand and some mighty stones that still protruded here and there, like swimmers breasting an unlovely sea, sure to drown before too long.

And after some hard riding, there was the gate. Rose knew it at once, though she had never seen one, and those who had were generally loath to talk about it. It simply couldn't be anything else, a sunken roadway in the sand that descended twenty feet in twenty yards, with sheer, unsupported walls all along and the end of it an archway that was not sand but a shimmering pattern somewhat like a chance-caught glimpse of a rough-cut opal by a candle flame, stone and light and color swirling and shimmering.

A saddle and harness lay at the entrance to the ramp, and to Rose's surprise the skeleton of a horse, shreds of fresh flesh sticking off of it as if it had been sucked almost clean by some giant glutton. A pair of saddlebags lay nearby, open, their contents strewn as if they had been hurriedly ransacked for wanted items; the things left behind that immediately caught Rose's eye were wrapped food packets, water bottles, ammunition boxes and even a canvas bag of the kind used to carry a considerable sum of gold. The rifle she had seen at Alhambra's side was also there, thrown away as if it could not serve him beyond the gate.

Perhaps that was true, she thought, but she rested her hand on the worn, skin-smoothed bird's-head grip of her own Colt, trusting to its power that she knew well. The horse bones troubled her more than the other abandoned stuff, because the skeleton was so fresh, and it had to be the round-headed man's mount. But what had he done to it, how and why?

She encouraged Darcy forward to descend the ramp, but he balked, answering neither knee nor even the prick of her spurs, tilting his head back and showing the whites of his eyes, though he made no sound of protest, as if scared even beyond that. She backed him a little, and had to hold him hard to stop him bolting away. Eventually he answered to pressure of leg and rein, but she knew she could not even lead him through the gate. Dismounting, she took off gear and saddle, bridle and bit, and stacked them neatly on the ground, somewhat away from the ramp.

"Go home," she said to Darcy, and smacked him on the rump. He took off fast, straight as an arrow back toward the ridge. She had no idea if he would go home, all the way to the ranch, but like as not he would follow the posse's horses, and get back to town at least. Bucon would keep him for her, for a while . . .

It was quiet without the horse's movement and breath, and the air was still. It felt cooler than it should, Rose thought, and shivered.

The desert heat was absent by the ramp, though there was no shade. She set her mind on her daughter, and took a tin box of bullets from her saddlebag and wrapped it with the bread and meat in her blanket roll, which went over her shoulder with the waterskin. Cradling the Sharps in her arms, she set off down the ramp toward the gate of twisting colors—and without hesitation strode straight into and through it, disappearing from the regular world as if she had never been there.

Rose came out in a forested high glade, partway up a small mountain, tall trees above and below and the sun that got through the puzzle of piney branches significantly less warm than would be right for anything within five hundred miles of the Star-Circle Ranch. It could well even snow a little higher up, Rose adjudged, and shivered. She shivered again as she slowly spun around, hands tight on the Sharps, finger tapping the trigger guard till she willed it to stop. There was no gate behind her, no shimmering colors, nothing but the slope of downward-marching pines, littered beneath with fallen pinecones and small branches.

She began to look around for trail signs, bending close to examine the forest floor. As she leaned, the small knife around her neck swung out, almost as if it was reminding her of Bucon's instructions.

"Nothing to lose by it, I expect," she whispered to herself, not wanting to admit that she felt cowed by the strange place she had entered. Even the trees didn't seem quite right, not exactly any kind of pine she had ever known. The cones, seen up close, had barbs, and the stiff green bristles on the fallen branches wound around like tight, thin springs.

She unsheathed the knife and addressed the nearest tree, feeling not at all abashed as she might have done back on the other side. She hoped no one or nothing *was* watching, but that wasn't for fear of embarrassment. That was just plain old-fashioned fear, simple, pure and strong.

"Begging your pardon, tree," she said. "I've got to stick this here knife in you just a tiny fraction, enough to get a hold."

She stabbed as she spoke, the point of the blade breaking through the tough bark. Sap spewed out, amber-colored and strong-smelling, but again, not the pine-smell she was used to.

Rose stood up and addressed the knife. "I need help all right, so I'm hoping whoever gave this blade to old Bucon can come along and help me and my daughter. Thank you, sir."

Nothing happened, save that a breeze began to tickle the treetops above and a few more of the barbed pinecones fell, one narrowly missing Rose's head. She ignored the falling tree debris and began to cast about in a wider circle, looking for evidence of the passage of Alhambra and Laramay. When she found it, a small tear cropped up, to be immediately blinked away, because the boot-heel mark and the slipper-print were side by side, and that meant Laramay was walking along willing, like, or at least easy, something Rose had always feared. Laramay was a good girl, but she'd always been kind of absent, going along with whatever anyone told her to do. Mostly the teller was Rose, and things worked out fine, but with a kidnapper of uncertain morals, and now, given their whereabouts, uncertain humanity, the case was much different and more dire. The only saving grace, and the slightest of comforts to Rose, was the knowledge that Laramay probably wasn't even affrighted, thinking herself on a picnic or some gambol.

She began to follow the tracks, trying to stay quiet herself, though that was difficult, with the forest floor so strewn with sticks and cones, and the ground underneath it damp and slippery. Not mud, not quite, but clear indication that it had rained recently, and would again, though Rose couldn't see much cloud at present, when she got a clear glimpse of the sky through the thick weave of the pine branches above. Rose got warm climbing the slope, but it was the kind of sticky warmth that was only temporary, and she knew it would freeze on her later. As far as she could gauge, it was past four in the afternoon, and once the sun set in a few hours, it would be very cold.

Maybe a mile along and a few hundred feet up from where she'd come through, still following boot- and slipper-prints, Rose realized that for some time now she'd been hearing something else beside the scuff and slip of her own footsteps, the *choof* of her breath, now steaming out her mouth as the air cooled around, and the beat of her working heart. There was another sound, a stealthier, nastier sound, someone or something sneaking up behind her . . .

She turned, carbine ready, and fired one shot before the thing was upon her, so fast and strange that she couldn't fix her eye and mind on what it was, save hairy and fanged and twice the size of any dog, its dimensions all awry anyway, too long in the back and the legs uneven and the snout wide like a fan, with teeth every which way, and she was working the lever to get another round up the spout when it hit her and she had to flick the carbine diagonally across its huge mouth to hold it off, and it threw her back, chewing and whittling on the weapon, and she knew she'd hit it the first time and it hadn't done a thing and she brought her foot up and kicked it in the guts, shouting out words that the Mothers' Club would have expelled her for, if they'd ever let her join in the first place, but the kicks didn't daunt it and then it spat out the carbine and raised its foul head to let out a roar that blew her hat off, the roar being a mistake because in that moment Rose dropped the carbine, drew her knife that had been Broad Bill's and plunged it right up to the cross-hilt in the puffy, less hairy flesh under the great jaw that she figured was the critter's throat, twisted it twice, and pulled it out again.

Black, steaming, vile-smelling blood spewed out like a train venting steam, Rose dodging it as she stumbled backward, colliding with the trunk of one of the pines, which was as richly decorated with tiny barbs as the cones. The creature, wolf-weasel-widemouth, whatever it was, turned in a circle like a cat settling and then went straight down in a heap, the blood gushing from under its head running down the slope in an ugly rivulet.

"That's a mighty fine display of knife-work," said an admiring male voice a little ways up the mountain. Rose whirled around. Already holding the knife, she turned the Colt on her right sideways in its holster and drew it with her left hand, a move she'd learned from a friend of her late husband's, a gunslinger called Lefty Truss, who carried on his right but drew with his left and not a cross-draw neither, which when it worked confused and dismayed his enemies, but as he eventually found out was slower and less effective than sticking to the basics.

The man who had spoken held his palms out and open by his sides as Rose drew a bead on his chest. Metal glinted on the breast of his oat-colored coat, a star within a circle, with some writing around the circle's edge that Rose didn't need to even read, she just instantly recognized the pattern and knew it said U.S. MARSHAL.

Rose lowered the Colt, not all the way to pointing it at the ground, because you never knew for sure, and a metal badge could come unstuck and get put on someone different, particularly when the rightful bearer was dead. And this was across the line, through the gate, over the border . . . It paid to take extra care.

They took stock of each other for a moment or two. Rose saw a very tall, lean, good-looking man, about fifty, maybe even older, with plenty of sun-lines around his eyes under his pale Stetson, and though clean-shaven within the past day or so, the stubble on his chin was white and he didn't look to have a lot of hair beneath the hat. He was well covered against the cold, his coat lined with fleece, though he had it unbuttoned and open at the front, showing a leather waistcoat and the big silver buckle of his belt, a broad swath of odd-looking bullets through the loops, silver at the tip, and a revolver on either side, older guns than Rose's—Remingtons, she thought, like her father had favored.

"Name's Thornton," said the man. "You did real well there, ma'am, figuring so fast a bullet wouldn't work."

"What was that thing?" asked Rose, but she didn't take her gaze away or holster the pistol. She liked the look of the man—he seemed straight enough, and civil—but . . .

"I don't think it rightly knew itself," said Thornton. "I call that kind of mix-up a scarum. Not too troublesome, but they can't be killed with plain lead or a steel blade. They need the silver-death, like a lot of the critters here, and some of the folk as well."

"The silver-death?" asked Rose and this time she did look away, at the knife she held, in the same instant knowing it for a bad mistake and then in another instant feeling an intense relief as she snapped back and Thornton hadn't moved, smiling down at her peaceably with a glint in his eye that told her those weren't all sun-lines creasing up his face: the man had a sense of humor as well.

"Your knife has a silver wash over the blade," said Thornton. "Speaking of knives, if you'd allow me to dip into my pocket without plugging me . . ."

"Go on," said Rose.

Thornton reached under his coat and drew out the slender knife Bucon had given Rose. Holding it up, he said, "I gave this to a feller a long time ago, told him how to use it if he had to come this way and needed help. Seems to me he gave it to someone else, on account of it was a woman's voice I heard whispered through the trees this morning. So I was wondering, you being the first lady I've seen in some time around these parts, if it was you used the knife, requesting the assistance of the duly constituted authority of this part of the border, meaning myself."

"Yes," said Rose. She let some of the tension out of her body, starting to feel a bit tremblesome, the shock of the attack, the weight of her weapons. "Sheriff Bucon gave me that knife, and I used it. He didn't tell me how it would work, or that a marshal would come."

"*Sheriff* Bucon?" asked Thornton. "How about that? I wasn't sure what direction that boy would go. Now, as I said, being the duly constituted authority around here, marshal and warden, both ways and both sides, afore I *can* help you I need to be sure you ain't up to no good yourself. Why did you come through the desert gate?"

"I came after Laramay, my daughter!" protested Rose. "Kidnapped and taken from my ranch by a man called Alhambra, who rode straight for that gate, and what else could any mother do but follow?"

"Alhambra?" asked Thornton. "Kind of funny-looking, head too round?"

"Yep," said Rose. "Now, you happy with my bonafides? Because I want to get after him before something happens to my Laramay and I ain't got time to stand around jawing with you!"

"True enough," said Thornton. "We had best get after them. Alhambra's a Carver, and if he can get enough meat, he'll be at work before sundown. By the bye, I missed your name before, ma'am, when we was doing introductions."

"Rose Jackson. What's a Carver? What's that about meat? His horse, he left it . . . a skeleton fresh outside the gate, the meat stripped from its bones—"

Thornton whistled, a rueful whistle that suddenly gave Rose cause to register that she hadn't heard a single bird since she'd come through the gate. Not a one, and none seen neither, which made the whole place seem even more unnatural, all over again.

"That's bad, Mrs. Jackson," he said, turning on his heel and taking a couple of lanky strides up the slope before pausing to half-turn back and beckon her on. She noted that he had a real long knife in a scabbard tied diagonal across his back, almost a sword, though broader in the blade than the cavalry sabers she'd had a swing with from time to time. "Real bad. I've an inkling where he's headed, but we have to catch him before sundown. Come on!"

Rose holstered her pistol, bent quickly and wiped her knife clean on a big broad-leafed weed, both sides, real fast, sliding it back home before she started to scramble on. She left the Sharps, seeing at once it was bent beyond use.

She caught up with the marshal ten yards on, him crashing along without any attempt to be quiet, clear indication that speed really was of the essence.

"What's a Carver?" panted Rose, skipping over a slippery patch where Thornton's heavier step had cut through to bare the mud below.

"Guess you'd best understand it as a kind of demon, an evil spirit," said Thornton, talking out the side of his mouth as his clear blue eyes watched ahead, flickering across and up and side to side as he chose the best way between the trees. "They ain't got human bodies as such: they have to make their own from time to time, gather up a lot of meat and carve one out. Only they ain't got an eye for it neither, so they waste a lot of flesh; that'd be why he stripped a whole horse . . . and they need what you might call an artistic model to get it even halfway right."

"An artistic model? My Laramay? She's kind of short."

"But I'm guessing she's pretty; they like to try for the best, even if they can't reproduce it too well."

"She's pretty," said Rose grimly. "Can't we go any faster?"

"Maybe a little," allowed the marshal, and stepped up his pace, leaning forward with his long, loose limbs so that within a minute Rose was very hard put to keep up and Thornton, without saying anything, slowed down a little again.

"What . . . what'll they do with their . . . models?" panted Rose.

"They kill 'em," said Thornton. "To finish the piece. They hope to take in their talents that way, though it hardly ever works. Your Laramay got any talents?"

"She sings," said Rose. "Prettier than anything you ever heard. Brings the birds right down from the trees."

"Sings the birds down?" asked Thornton, with a quizzical backward glance. "What's your husband's name, ma'am?"

"He was Broad Bill Jackson, may he rest in peace," said Rose. "But Bill couldn't sing worth spit, nor me neither. I don't know where Laramay gets her music from."

"Broad Bill, huh? If he was the feller I'm thinking of, it'd be his mother had the music, and it's a good thing, because it might mean a little extra help for your daughter, ma'am, and when we see her, you yell out to her to sing, straight off, don't wait for nothing else."

"I will," said Rose. "But I figured more on shooting that Alhambra than shouting at my daughter."

"Carvers are mighty difficult to kill," said Thornton. "Need silver-death and plenty of it, so don't waste your lead. Singing can be a powerful thing here, and if I'm right in my recollections, might serve your Laramay well. You call out to her while I keep that Alhambra distracted. I doubt they're more than five minutes ahead, judging by the signs. You be ready now: we'll come out of the trees, they'll be right ahead, by the big stone in the clear place."

"I'm ready," said Rose, though she didn't know what to be ready for, and she couldn't believe that they were going to come out of the trees, for the pines were as thick and tall as ever, and no clear sky above or sun coming through where the forest might be winnowing, but then all of a sudden there was sunshine, not warm, but bright on her face, and she squinted hard, refusing to blink in case in that moment she missed the chance to do something, and they burst from the tree line like gophers smoked out of their holes and there was a great flat stretch of tableland ahead, of short grass and dotted saplings and right in front a stone the size of the Star-Circle's bunkhouse, only up on its end, gray and stark and casting a shadow sharp and dark like some evil finger, and at its very point in the sunshine there was Laramay sitting on the grass, picking the little blue wildflowers, and across from her was Alhambra wielding a mirror-bright knife, a-cutting at a great hunk of horsemeat, this way and that, up and down and across, blood and gobbets flying though nothing touched the girl.

"Sing, Laramay, sing!" shouted Rose, running behind her words as fast as she could, almost overtaking them in her urgency, and beside her one of the big Remingtons boomed as the marshal ran forward too, firing as he went, fanning the hammer, dropping the first gun as it emptied and drawing the next, and Rose saw the silver bullets hitting home, heard them strike with a sound like a boiled pudding dropped in a big pot of steaming water, but Alhambra didn't fall back or seem even indisposed. He lifted his bright knife and ran straight for Thornton, who drew that big knife of his own and the two met in a clash of blades and fury, and Rose ran past to Laramay, who was smiling prettily at her ma and the show the men-folk were putting on and *wasn't* singing.

"Sing!" screamed Rose, reaching her daughter and dashing the flowers from her hand. "Sing something, Laramay!"

Laramay opened her mouth obediently and began to sing. Rose whirled to see what was happening with Thornton and Alhambra, seeing them slash and feint and stab, jumping and twisting, turn-ing this way and that, like no knife-fight she'd ever seen, not least because it was still going and no blood to see, whereas normally by now there'd be someone on the ground with gore all over, maybe both parties down, and plenty of screaming and sobbing and last regrets; but all that could be heard here was Laramay's voice, warm, clear and bright like the first full sun of the day, so it was no wonder the birds themselves came down from the sky to listen.

Only here it wasn't the birds that came. Something came *up* from the ground near the girl's feet: an intense blue flame busting out in a spume of dirt, with a shadowed, vaguely human-shaped figure at its core. Laramay laughed and became a blue flame too, still singing, and swung out her arms so that a trailing edge of fire brushed Rose's face, not hot at all, but warm, so warm and kind that it made her laugh with a surprised joy that brought hot tears and a flush of warmth through her whole body, exiting through toes that jangled as if they'd never been fully alive before.

The two flame-wrapped figures bent together, the shadows within falling into an embrace, Laramay's voice still singing high and clear, Rose only just then realizing that her daughter wasn't singing words in any language either of them had ever spoke before.

"No!" roared Alhambra, leaving his fight to rush toward the shining two, but as he sped the marshal leaped after him, swinging his knife at that fat neck and *snicker-snack* the over-round head came tumbling off and rolled across the ground, the body flailing onwards till it ran smack into the big stone and tumbled over, kicking and bucking like a swatted bug.

The head kept rolling, straight toward Laramay, till Thornton caught up with it and stamped down with his foot, pinning it under his boot-heel. The mouth was working, teeth gnashing, tongue lashing, but only a hissing sound came out. The different-colored eyes were open and unclouded, and looked to Rose as alive as ever.

"I got to be going, Ma," said Laramay. Her voice sounded different. More direct, not dreamy like normal, as if she was all present for once, and not half somewhere else.

"Go where?" asked Rose desperately. All the sudden happiness she'd felt was gone in an instant, replaced by dread. Her daughter lost after all? She shielded her face with her arm and tried to look at Laramay, but the girl was too bright, too close. "I ain't come all this way to let some bright critter carry you off like that Alhambra tried to do!"

"I got too big a part of Pa's family in me to live right on the regular side," said Laramay. "More of the old blood than he did, just waiting to be woken. You knew where he came from, didn't you, Ma?"

"I s'pose I did," said Rose. "We didn't talk about it, but . . . I knew."

"Pa would've brought me across the line if he could've," said Laramay. "Soon as I was of age. That Alhambra just hurried things up a few months, is all."

"So that's it?" asked Rose, drawing herself up, sniffing back whatever was itching at her nose, and blinking back a little irritation that was forming in her eyes. "You go off with this here candle flame and I never see you again?"

Fingers clicked inside the flames and the bright blue fire went out, leaving an unassuming young man with a strong physical resemblance to Broad Bill Jackson, though perhaps only one and a half ax handles across the shoulders rather than two complete, and almost exactly the same height as Laramay. He was dressed foreign, in a shirt of iron rings over a kind of nightdress, and his legs were wrapped in leather cords above boots that looked to be also iron, and danged uncomfortable.

"Pleased to meet you, Mrs. Jackson," said the young man. "Guess you can call me . . . Robert's close enough. I'm a kind of cousin of your husband's; I had the honor to be nearest when Laramay called. She will be very welcome amongst our kin and be held in honor, for it is long since we have had such a singer in our hall."

"And of course you'll see me, Ma, if you want to. This side of the line."

"Easier said than done," muttered Rose.

"You were going to take me east," said Laramay. "To some hospital or such. It is far better I be here, where I was always meant to be."

"I weren't going to leave you in a hospital!" snapped Rose, but she did not dispute the fact further. This was a new Laramay to her, one that could put some thoughts together about the future and suchlike. "Besides, that's neither—"

"You got a silver dollar on you, Mrs. Jackson?" interrupted Thornton. "This here head is getting restless."

Rose looked over to where the marshal was having trouble keeping Alhambra's head in place. It kept trying to rise up off the ground, as if propelled by an invisible body, and Thornton had to put all his weight onto his boot to keep it down. She felt in the pockets of her skirt and, sure enough, there was a silver dollar in one of them. She took it out, wondering what he wanted it for.

Alhambra's head seemed to know. It made a sudden lunge and got out from under Thornton's boot, streaking into the air with a thin scream of hatred. Rose watched it climb, higher and higher, and even before it faltered and slowed a couple of hundred feet up she knew it was going to come back down, fast and deadly.

"Throw the dollar!" shouted Thornton. "Shoot it into the head!"

Alhambra screamed again and dropped like a hawk upon its prey, straight down, mouth gaping open wider than wide. Rose flicked the silver dollar up, a flash tumbling end over end as it rose, head and coin accelerating together as she drew the Colt and fired, bullet striking the coin, the coin driving into the strangely round head, right between the eyes, Rose stepping aside as the head smacked into the ground and burst like an overripe pumpkin too long forgotten after Halloween.

"Good shooting," said Thornton.

"Thanks," said Rose. She wrinkled her nose at the ugly remains, but truth to tell it didn't look so much like a crushed head as just a pile of old scraps of meat, like you might feed to a hog, there being nothing left of its roundness, or any human features, not even eyes, matching or otherwise.

"Now, young lady—" she started to say, but there was no young lady there, nor a young man neither, just the great standing stone and its shadow, and the marshal with the sun beginning to set behind him, all red and bloody, and the chill of the night coming on.

"Guess they couldn't wait to tell the rest of the family the good news," said Thornton. "That's young folks, always in a hurry."

"But . . . but . . . I'm her mother! Where did they go?"

The marshal pointed at the ground.

"Like she said, she takes after your husband. Mountain-folk can go where we can't, that's the truth of it. And the fact is, you can't stay this side too long anyhow, not all at once. If you allow me, ma'am, I'll just pick up my pistol and I'll walk you home."

"I'll have something to say to that girl when I see her next!" snapped Rose, following after him. "The ingratitude, after all I've done!"

"It's the natural order of things," said Thornton, carefully reloading both pistols from his belt. "Here *and* the other side. Still, I expect she'll have other things to talk about next time you do see her. A wedding, like as not, or maybe grandchildren. Time runs strange when you cross the line."

Rose was silent, thinking about this, putting all her thoughts in order, setting them down like sorting a larder after a trip into town. She'd always been one to make her dinner from what she had, rather than dreaming about what she didn't. If that meant a griddle cake and a cup of water because that's all there was, she saw no point drooling after steak and bacon pie and coffee.

"He looked a good lad," she acknowledged as Thornton offered her his arm.

"And she's a fine-looking young woman," said Thornton. "Though I'd have to say not a patch on her ma."

"You'd say that to an old widow-woman, would you?" asked Rose. She looked ahead to the empty ground and added, "And where are we going, anyway? Ain't the gate back down the mountain?"

"There's gates a-plenty, if you know how to see them," said Thornton. "Means that for a feller in the know, or a woman, say, it ain't that much a matter to cross the line. Not so dangerous neither, if you choose when and where. So if there's call to be visiting, either here or there, it can be arranged."

"Well, that's something to think on," said Rose. "But didn't you say something when we first run together about needing a reason to go crossing the line? So there'd only be visiting there, not here?"

"Well, I don't know," said Thornton. "I was thinking when you knifed that scarum, and another one when you shot that dollar so straight, that I couldn't do better myself, and that being the case, and me the duly constituted authority on both sides, marshal and warden, that I might be looking at someone else of the same nature."

Rose stopped, turned in toward Thornton and flipped back the brim of her hat a little, to see him clear. He was fumbling in his waistcoat pocket, this time not for the little knife but a shiny metal star. This one was not a star in a circle, and the writing on it was not English and did not say U.S. MARSHAL, but she knew it was kin to the one Thornton wore, in nature if not in name. She stood very straight as he pinned it on her shirt, the backs of his fingers touching her bare skin just below the collarbone, so that they both shivered, not from the cold, which the man and woman had not felt for some time.

"You going to walk me all the way home to the Star-Circle, Marshal?" asked Rose, linking her arm once again through his, but not too tight, because she might need room to draw, though she was already thinking ahead about carrying on the left, and practicing her off-hand shooting.

"Reckon so," said Thornton.

GARTH NIX lives with his wife and son in Sydney, Australia. He is the best-selling author of the young adult fantasy series The Old Kingdom, The Seventh Tower, and The Keys to the Kingdom. A former sales rep, publicist, and senior editor in the publishing industry, his other novels include *The Ragwitch, Shade's Children, A Confusion of Princes,* and the Troubletwisters trilogy (with Sean Williams). He has also written a number of scenarios for role-playing games and articles on information technology. Often asked if his name is actually a pseudonym, he is happy to confirm that it is not.

Hansel and Gretel

HARD BY A great forest dwelled a poor wood-cutter with his wife and his two children. The boy was called Hansel and the girl Gretel. He had little to bite and to break, and once when great dearth fell upon the land, he could no longer procure even daily bread.

Now when he thought over this by night in his bed, and tossed about in his anxiety, he groaned and said to his wife, "What is to become of us? How are we to feed our poor children, when we no longer have anything even for ourselves?"

"I'll tell you what, husband," answered the woman, "early tomorrow morning we will take the children out into the forest to where it is the thickest. There we will light a fire for them, and give each of them one more piece of bread, and then we will go to our work and leave them alone. They will not find the way home again, and we shall be rid of them."

"No, wife," said the man, "I will not do that. How can I bear to leave my children alone in the forest? The wild animals would soon come tear them to pieces."

"Oh you fool," said she, "then we must all four die of hunger; you may as well plane the planks for our coffins," and she left him no peace until he consented.

"But I feel very sorry for the poor children, all the same," said the man.

The two children had also not been able to sleep for hunger, and had heard what their stepmother had said to their father. Gretel wept bitter tears, and said to Hansel, "Now all is over with us."

"Be quiet, Gretel," said Hansel, "do not distress yourself. I will soon find a way to help us."

And when the old folks had fallen asleep, he got up, put on his little coat, opened the door below, and crept outside. The moon shone brightly, and the white pebbles which lay in front of the house glittered like real silver pennies. Hansel stooped and stuffed the little pocket of his coat with as many as he could get in. Then he went back and said to Gretel, "Be comforted, dear little sister, and sleep in peace. God will not forsake us," and he lay down again in his bed.

When day dawned, but before the sun had risen, the woman came and awoke the two children, saying, "Get up, you sluggards. We are going into the forest to fetch wood." She gave each a little piece of bread, and said, "There is something for your dinner, but do not eat it up before then, for you will get nothing else."

Gretel took the bread under her apron, as Hansel had the pebbles in his pocket.

Then they all set out together on the way to the forest. When they had walked a short time, Hansel stood still and peeped back at the house, and did so again and again.

His father said, "Hansel, what are you looking at there and staying behind for? Pay attention, and do not forget how to use your legs."

"Ah, Father," said Hansel, "I am looking at my little white cat, which is sitting up on the roof, and wants to say good-bye to me."

The wife said, "Fool, that is not your little cat, that is the morning sun which is shining on the chimneys."

Hansel, however, had not been looking back at the cat, but had been constantly throwing one of the white pebble-stones out of his pocket onto the road.

When they had reached the middle of the forest, the father said, "Now, children, pile up some wood, and I will light a fire that you may not be cold."

Hansel and Gretel gathered brushwood together, as high as a little hill. The brushwood was lighted, and when the flames were burning very high, the woman said, "Now, children, lay yourselves down by the fire and rest; we will go into the forest and cut some wood. When we have done, we will come back and fetch you away."

Hansel and Gretel sat by the fire, and when noon came, each ate a little piece of bread, and as they heard the strokes of the wood-ax they believed that their father was near. It was not the ax, however, but a branch which he had fastened to a withered tree which the wind was blowing backward and forward.

And as they had been sitting such a long time, their eyes closed with fatigue, and they fell fast asleep. When at last they awoke, it was already dark night.

Gretel began to cry and said, "How are we to get out of the forest now?"

But Hansel comforted her and said, "Just wait a little, until the moon has risen, and then we will soon find the way."

And when the full moon had risen, Hansel took his little sister by the hand, and followed the pebbles, which shone like newly-coined silver pieces, and showed them the way.

They walked the whole night long, and by break of day came once more to their father's house. They knocked at the door, and when the woman opened it and saw that it was Hansel and Gretel, she said, "You naughty children, why have you slept so long in the forest? We thought you were never coming back at all."

The father, however, rejoiced, for it had cut him to the heart to leave them behind alone.

Not long afterward, there was once more great dearth throughout the land, and the children heard their mother saying at night to their father: "Everything is eaten again, we have one half-loaf left, and that is the end. The children must go; we will take them farther into the wood, so that they will not find their way out again. There is no other means of saving ourselves."

The man's heart was heavy, and he thought, *It would be better for you to share the last mouthful with your children.* The woman, however, would listen to nothing that he had to say, but scolded and reproached him. He who says A must say B, likewise, and as he had yielded the first time, he had to do so a second time also.

The children, however, were still awake and had heard the conversation. When the old folks were asleep, Hansel again got up, and wanted to go out and pick up pebbles as he had done before, but the woman had locked the door, and Hansel could not get out.

Nevertheless he comforted his little sister, and said, "Do not cry, Gretel, go to sleep quietly, the good God will help us."

Early in the morning came the woman, and took the children out of their beds. Their piece of bread was given to them, but it was still smaller than the time before. On the way into the forest Hansel crumbled his in his pocket, and often stood still and threw a morsel on the ground.

"Hansel, why do you stop and look around?" said the father. "Go on."

"I am looking back at my little pigeon which is sitting on the roof, and wants to say good-bye to me," answered Hansel.

"Fool," said the woman, "that is not your little pigeon, that is the morning sun that is shining on the chimney."

Hansel, however, little by little, threw all the crumbs on the path.

The woman led the children still deeper into the forest, where they had never in their lives been before. Then a great fire was again made, and the mother said, "Just sit there, you children, and when you are tired you may sleep a little. We are going into the forest to cut wood, and in the evening when we are done, we will come fetch you away."

When it was noon, Gretel shared her piece of bread with Hansel, who had scattered his by the way. Then they fell asleep and evening passed, but no one came to the poor children.

They did not awake until it was dark night, and Hansel comforted his little sister and said, "Just wait, Gretel, until the moon rises, and then we shall see the crumbs of bread which I have strewn about: they will show us our way home again."

When the moon came they set out, but they found no crumbs, for the many thousands of birds which fly about in the woods and fields had picked them all up.

Hansel said to Gretel, "We shall soon find the way," but they did not find it.

They walked the whole night and all the next day too from morning till evening, but they did not get out of the forest. And were very hungry, for they had nothing to eat but two or three berries, which grew on the ground. And as they were so weary that their legs would carry them no longer, they lay down beneath a tree and fell asleep.

It was now three mornings since they had left their father's house. They began to walk again, but they always came deeper into the forest, and if help did not come soon, they must die of hunger and weariness.

When it was midday, they saw a beautiful snow-white bird sitting on a bough, which sang so delightfully that they stood still and listened to it. And when its song was over, it spread its wings and flew away before them, and they followed it until they reached a little house, on the roof of which it alighted. And when they approached the little house they saw that it was built of bread and covered with cakes, but that the windows were of clear sugar.

"We will set to work on that," said Hansel, "and have a good meal. I will eat a bit of the roof, and you, Gretel, can eat some of the window; it will taste sweet."

Hansel reached up above, and broke off a little of the roof to try how it tasted, and Gretel leaned against the window and nibbled at the panes.

Then a soft voice cried from the parlor: "Nibble, nibble, gnaw, who is nibbling at my little house?"

The children answered: "The wind, the wind, the heaven-born wind," and went on eating without disturbing themselves.

Hansel, who liked the taste of the roof, tore down a great piece of it, and Gretel pushed out the whole of one round window-pane, sat down, and enjoyed herself with it.

Suddenly the door opened, and a woman as old as the hills, who supported herself on crutches, came creeping out. Hansel and

Gretel were so terribly frightened that they let fall what they had in their hands. The old woman, however, nodded her head, and said, "Oh, you dear children, who has brought you here? Do come in, and stay with me. No harm shall happen to you."

She took them both by the hand, and led them into her little house. Then good food was set before them, milk and pancakes, with sugar, apples, and nuts. Afterward two pretty little beds were covered with clean white linen, and Hansel and Gretel lay down in them, and thought they were in Heaven.

The old woman had only pretended to be so kind. She was in reality a wicked witch, who lay in wait for children, and had only built the little house of bread in order to entice them there. When a child fell into her power, she killed it, cooked it, and ate it, and that was a feast day with her.

Witches have red eyes, and cannot see far, but they have a keen scent like the beasts, and are aware when human beings draw near. When Hansel and Gretel came into her neighborhood, she laughed with malice, and said mockingly, "I have them; they shall not escape me again."

Early in the morning before the children were awake, she was already up, and when she saw both of them sleeping and looking so pretty, with their plump and rosy cheeks, she muttered to herself that they would be a dainty mouthful.

Then she seized Hansel with her shriveled hand, carried him into a little stable, and locked him in behind a grated door. Scream as he might, it would not help him. Then she went to Gretel, shook her till she awoke, and cried, "Get up, lazy thing! Fetch some water, and cook something good for your brother—he is in the stable outside, and is to be made fat. When he is fat, I will eat him."

Gretel began to weep bitterly, but it was all in vain, for she was forced to do what the wicked witch commanded.

And now the best food was cooked for poor Hansel, but Gretel got nothing but crab-shells. Every morning the woman crept to the little stable, and cried, "Hansel, stretch out your finger that I may feel if you will soon be fat."

Hansel, however, stretched out a little bone to her, and the old woman, who had dim eyes, could not see it, and thought it was Hansel's finger, and was astonished that there was no way of fattening him.

When four weeks had gone by, and Hansel still remained thin, she was seized with impatience and would not wait any longer. "Now, then, Gretel," she cried to the girl, "stir yourself, and bring some water. Let Hansel be fat or lean, tomorrow I will kill him, and cook him."

Ah, how the poor little sister did lament when she had to fetch the water, and how her tears did flow down her cheeks. "Dear God, do help us!" she cried. "If the wild beasts in the forest had but devoured us, we should at any rate have died together."

"Just keep your noise to yourself," said the old woman, "it won't help you at all."

Early in the morning, Gretel had to go out and hang up the cauldron with the water, and light the fire.

"We will bake first," said the old woman. "I have already heated the oven, and kneaded the dough." She pushed poor Gretel out to the oven, from which flames of fire were already darting. "Creep in," said the witch, "and see if it is properly heated, so that we can put the bread in." And once Gretel was inside, she intended to shut the oven and let her bake in it, and then she would eat her, too.

But Gretel saw what she had in mind, and said, "I do not know how I am to do it. How do I get in?"

"Silly goose," said the old woman, "the door is big enough. Just look, I can get in myself," and she crept up and thrust her head into the oven.

Then Gretel gave her a push that drove her far into it, and shut the iron door, and fastened the bolt. Oh, then she began to howl quite horribly, but Gretel ran away, and the godless witch was miserably burned to death.

Gretel, however, ran like lightning to Hansel, opened his little stable, and cried, "Hansel, we are saved! The old witch is dead!"

Then Hansel sprang like a bird from its cage when the door is opened. How they did rejoice and embrace each other, and dance about and kiss each other. And as they had no longer any need to fear her, they went into the witch's house, and in every corner there stood chests full of pearls and jewels.

"These are far better than pebbles," said Hansel, and thrust into his pockets whatever could be got in.

And Gretel said, "I, too, will take something home with me," and filled her pinafore full.

"But now we must be off," said Hansel, "that we may get out of the witch's forest."

When they had walked for two hours, they came to a great stretch of water. "We cannot cross," said Hansel. "I see no foot-plank, and no bridge."

"And there is also no ferry," answered Gretel, "but a white duck is swimming there. If I ask her, she will help us over." Then she cried: "Little duck, little duck, dost thou see, Hansel and Gretel are waiting for thee. There's never a plank, or bridge in sight, take us across on thy back so white."

The duck came to them, and Hansel seated himself on its back, and told his sister to sit by him. "No," replied Gretel, "that will be too heavy for the little duck. She shall take us across, one after the other."

The good little duck did so, and when they were once safely across and had walked for a short time, the forest seemed to be more and more familiar to them, and at length they saw from afar their father's house. Then they began to run, rushed into the parlor, and threw themselves around their father's neck.

The man had not known one happy hour since he had left the children in the forest. The woman, however, was dead.

Gretel emptied her pinafore until pearls and precious stones ran about the room, and Hansel threw one handful after another out of his pocket to add to them. Then all anxiety was at an end, and they lived together in perfect happiness.

My tale is done, there runs a mouse, whosoever catches it may make himself a big fur cap out of it.

Peckish

ROBERT SHEARMAN

THERE WAS NEVER any scandal in the Von Zieten family. The Von Zietens did not approve of scandal. Sieglinde knew that there had been a Von Zieten in the war once and that he had done something very bad—she didn't know which war, and by now it was probably too late to tell; he had either been cowardly when he should have been heroic, or had been heroic when the tide of public opinion had turned against heroism, and discretion would have been the more sensible option. It had been most embarrassing. But Captain Von Zieten had made amends by taking his own life—he'd shot himself with his service revolver—and the family had grimly forgiven him.

And sometimes at parties, sometimes if Uncle Otto got drunk, Sieglinde heard muttered tales about an Aunt Ilse who had harbored an amorous fascination for goats. Otherwise, nothing; the Von Zietens were respectable and decent and clean.

So when the scandal broke around Grossmutti Greta, everyone was surprised, and privately even a little pleased. It gave them someone new to condemn.

It took Sieglinde a few days to find out what the scandal was. She was still a child, they said, and so everyone's voices dropped when she came into the room. But at last she was told by her mother, on the pretext that it was for her moral education. She was sat down with all due solemnity, but Sieglinde noticed how excited her mother sounded, how her eyes sparkled and how fast she talked, how much she reveled in Grossmutti Greta's wickedness.

And it was this: that after more than sixty years of marriage, Greta now wanted a divorce. "More than sixty years!" Mother said, and that as far as the Von Zietens could tell, it had been a happy marriage too—certainly the family had never seen reason for complaint. It wasn't as if Greta had anything she could do with her remaining years—she was at least eighty, and there was precious little point in Greta causing a scandal now for a few last gasps of independence. Greta hadn't given a reason for divorce, or, at least, Grossvatti Gunther had said he'd not been given one; everyone felt a bit sorry for Grossvatti Gunther, and that was uncomfortable in itself: Grossvatti was a sturdy man of no fixed emotion; feeling sorry for him was just wrong somehow. The family wondered whether Greta had simply gone mad. That would make sense—might even mitigate somewhat in her favor. But surely, if she had to go mad, it would have been better to have done so quietly without drawing attention to herself.

Sieglinde had been taught to avoid scandal, and had always done her best. Here she was, a few months shy of sixteen, and she still wasn't allowed to see Klaus without a chaperone—even though the family knew the two would one day get married—even though the family had chosen him in the first place! Sieglinde knew she should ask no further questions about her grandmother and her heinous ways. But she liked Grossmutti Greta. She was the favorite of all her grandparents, probably—Greta was a little stern, but then, they were all a little stern. And sometimes when Sieglinde went to visit, especially when she'd been a little girl, Greta had made her the most wonderful gingerbread men. Sieglinde had never tasted anything as good as those gingerbread men. Sieglinde never knew what special ingredients there must be in them.

She knew that if she asked her parents whether she could visit her grandmother, they would say no. So she didn't ask. One afternoon, when Father was in his study, and Mother was busy in the kitchen, Sieglinde sneaked away. She didn't want to go to her grandmother's empty-handed, and so spent her pocket money at the baker's, buying a bag full of brioches; some of them had chocolate in the middle.

Her grandmother didn't seem surprised to see her. "There you are," she said. "Good. You can help me find a suitcase."

"I brought brioches," said Sieglinde.

"I have eaten my last brioche," said Grossmutti Greta.

"Some of them have chocolate inside."

"The same for chocolate," said Grossmutti Greta.

"So, it's true, then? You're really leaving?"

"Yes," said Grossmutti Greta.

"Are you mad? Everyone thinks you've gone mad."

"I haven't gone mad," said Greta. "Or if I am mad, I am as mad as I was before. I have just decided to stop pretending. All the pretense, I am so tired of it. I have baked some gingerbread men, my very last batch. We shall eat gingerbread men and talk."

Sieglinde agreed. She hadn't tasted one of her grandmother's gingerbread men for a long time, and had rather assumed she was now too old for them.

"Ach, nonsense," said Greta. "You're the perfect age for my gingerbread men. All the other men you've eaten, that was just practice. Now, at last, you can eat the real thing. But first," she added, "we find my suitcase, yes?"

They went up to the attic. There was no light up there. "Your grandfather," said Greta, "he always said he'd fix the electrics, but he never did; it was always 'Tomorrow, tomorrow, you'll have your lightbulbs tomorrow.'"

Sieglinde asked if that was why she was leaving him. "All in good time," said Greta as she poked around in the dark, and then she said, "Yes, yes, here it is," and she was pulling a suitcase out of the shadows. It was big and brown and had brass buckles on it. "Good," she said. "Now we talk."

The gingerbread men were fresh from the oven; they smelled moist, they smelled *juicy*, somehow, even though Sieglinde knew there was no juice in gingerbread. She felt her mouth water. Greta picked up the bag of brioches, opened it, recoiled, then dropped it unceremoniously into the swingbin.

"Do you really have to go away, Grossmutti?" asked Sieglinde, and tears pricked at her eyes, and that was strange, for she was not a sentimental girl—sentiment was frowned upon in the Von Zieten house.

"Now, now," said Grossmutti, and she tapped at Sieglinde's hand sympathetically, and she wasn't used to acts of sentiment either, and she did it too hard and too awkwardly, and it felt like being comforted by a wrinkly bag of onions. "I shall tell you the story, the same as I told my husband. And you shall eat."

Sieglinde bit into the gingerbread man. It tasted good.

"I came from a poor family, much poorer than yours. I had a brother called Hans, a father who cut wood, and, for a little while, I had a mother. Then the mother died. And my father married again. The stepmother didn't like us much."

"Was she a cruel stepmother?" asked Sieglinde.

"I don't think she was particularly cruel, or any crueler to me than my own mother was. Stepmothers have a bad time of it. It's hard enough to love your own flesh and blood, and I should know. It's almost impossible to love someone else's. Ach, this is not a story about wicked stepmothers."

"*All right.*"

"You're as bad as your grandfather. No more interruptions."

"*Sorry.*"

"Stepmother didn't want us home. She tried to smile at us when we were there, but Hans and I could see through them: there was effort in those smiles; it was like she had toothache. We played in the forest. Deeper and deeper we'd go; every day we'd dare ourselves to get to the very heart of it. And one day out playing, Hans said to me, 'Well, we've done it now, Sister, we're well and truly lost. Home could be miles away, and in any direction. We could walk around for the rest of our lives and never find it. Might as well face it, we're going to die out here—if starvation doesn't get us first, the cold and the wolves will'—and he had a tear, for my brother was an unnaturally sensitive boy.

"We laid ourselves down to die, and we were resigned to it; we didn't used to struggle so much against death as people do now. But before we expired we found an old woman was standing over us. I say she was old; she was probably not old, but I was of the age when I thought that anyone with gray hair and missing teeth and pockmarks was old. She said, 'You poor children, you must be hungry. Let me take you to a place where there is food, all is food. My pantries are filled to bursting, and the bricks of my walls are made of fresh soft bread, the cement is warm chocolate fudge, the roof is thatched with licorice sticks. Will you come with me? It isn't far.'

"Hans was my brother; I always did what Hans said. Hans said, 'Okay.' And I wondered whether this woman could be our new mother. I asked for her name, and she said she hadn't got a name, or if she'd had one, she'd lost it. I began to tell her our names, and she stopped me, and she said she didn't think we would have that kind of relationship.

"And so it turned out to be. We entered her house and she locked the door behind us with a big key. 'I'm so sorry, my dears,' she said, and to be fair, she looked very sorry too, and we couldn't be angry with her. She said, 'As you can see, the bricks are made of brick, the cement is just some cement, the thatch has largely blown away, but when it was there it was very far indeed from looking like licorice. This is a house of food—but the food is you—you are it—by which I mean, I'm going to eat you both up, are you following me? It's inside you, your kidneys and your hearts and your chitterlings: you walk about carrying all that tasty grub wrapped up in thin sausage skin, and it's a waste, and we're going to let it out."

"She snapped off one of Hans's fingers and ate it. Then she snapped off one of mine, chewed at it thoughtfully. Because, as you know, the fingers are the best way of determining whether a child is ripe or not. 'Not quite ready yet,' she said, 'but not long to go, and what a feast you'll make! And in the meantime, I promise you, I'll be kind to you, and nice; I'll be a mother to you—it's the least I can do. I really am most terribly sorry, but you must understand, I really am most terribly hungry as well."

"She had to fatten us up. And that wasn't easy, since there was no food in the house. She would stand us upright in the bathtub, naked, and scrub away at us with a loofah, one of those big loofahs with the hard bristles, you know? And all the dead skin would come peeling off, and she'd gather it all up, every last wormy strand, and she'd fry it, and tell us to eat—and that skin smelled so good, it was like onions, it'd sizzle so invitingly in the pan. And yet she never ate a morsel, no matter how hungry she got—'No, no,' she'd say, 'this is a treat for you kids, don't you worry about me, I'll get my dinner soon enough'—but sometimes she would watch us eat and she couldn't help it, the sight of it would make her tummy gurgle, and she would cry. We'd beg her, 'Eat, please eat.' We'd say, 'Take another of our fingers, snap them off, have them as a snack.' One day she did that, and she put them in her mouth and she winced and said we still weren't ripe—and we'd caused her to *waste* two perfectly good fingers before they were ready, that was very selfish of us. She was angry, I think, for the only time we knew her, and she sent us to bed without any supper. Which, in those days of starvation, was pretty much par for the course.

"One morning, over breakfast, as Hans and I gorged ourselves on the dead skin leftovers, the woman said she couldn't wait any longer. She was starving; she would be dead from starvation within the hour; then where would we all be? She'd have to eat us both right now. And if we weren't ripe enough yet, well, she'd just have to put up with any resultant indigestion. She was too weak to prepare the oven, so Hans and I did it all for her, and we did our very best, but somehow we made a mistake: we ended up cooking her instead of ourselves. I kept saying to Hans, 'Are you sure we're doing this right?' as we folded the woman's arms together and tucked them underneath her belly so she'd fit through the oven door, and he told me not to worry about it. The woman didn't blame us. She said, 'Oh, well, either way, here's an end to my suffering'—and I suppose it was.

"We took the key and opened the front door and went out into the forest, and oh, the air tasted so fresh, it was almost good enough to eat. And we were free. And we set off home."

"I don't like that suitcase."

"Sorry?" said Sieglinde. "What about the suitcase?"

"I don't like it," said Grossmutti Greta. "All those big brass buckles! Such ostentation! So shameless! Ach, when you're lugging a suitcase about, with nowhere you can call home to take it, you don't need brass buckles weighing you down. No. We go back to the attic. Come on. Back to the attic; we find a better suitcase."

Sieglinde thought that the dark of the attic seemed even darker than before, and that was impossible, surely—but the black made Sieglinde's eyes hurt. "Stay here," said Grossmutti Greta, and then she plunged into the blackness, and Sieglinde knew she wouldn't be able to see a thing—Sieglinde's eyes were still young and untainted; how much weaker must Greta's be, ancient as she was!

And she heard Greta grunt with effort, as if she were wrestling with something, as if she were wrestling with the dark itself. And Sieglinde felt the sudden certainty that she would never see her grandmother again, that she'd be lost within the dark, that she'd die—and that the only way she could save her would be if she too jumped into the blackness and put herself at the mercy of whatever was inside and begged for her grandmother's life—and she hadn't got the courage, she realized, and what was worse, she hadn't got the *inclination*.

And then Greta emerged, and her hands were tight around another suitcase—this one bigger, grayer, and free of all offending buckles. And she looked calm, and matter-of-fact, as if she hadn't tussled with the monsters in the black, as if she hadn't confronted death itself—and maybe she hadn't. "Some tea," she said, "that's what we need, and you can have another gingerbread man, yes? Come along, come along."

In the kitchen Sieglinde said, "I won't have another gingerbread man, thank you."

Grossmutti Greta said, "Why not?"

Sieglinde explained she didn't want to get fat.

Grossmutti Greta said, "There was a time when we didn't worry about such stupid things. It was good to be fat. It meant we might survive the winter."

Sieglinde said that had been a long time ago, and now it wasn't good to be fat, and that Klaus wouldn't want her if she put on weight—he'd told her he didn't fancy girls with big thighs.

Greta said, "That Klaus of yours is an idiot," and she said, "and your thighs are not fat, and believe me, I am an expert, I feel they could do with a lot more fattening. Now, eat another gingerbread man, or you will offend me and we shan't part as friends." And Sieglinde didn't want that, and besides, she did like the gingerbread men: they really were quite delicious.

"Won't you have one?" asked Sieglinde as she bit off a leg, and Greta waved the offer aside and instead clasped hold of her teacup, and Sieglinde noticed that there were indeed fingers missing from Greta's hand, and she'd never seen that before; how strange.

"I liked your story, Granny," said Sieglinde. "But I don't understand why you're leaving Grossvatti."

"That's because the story isn't finished yet," said Grossmutti Greta. "Now be quiet, blood of my blood, and listen."

"I said that the air tasted so fresh that it was good enough to eat. Well, you couldn't. And though Hans and I enjoyed our freedom, and thought we'd escaped certain death at the hands of the old woman, in truth we were still in danger. We walked through the forest as hungry as before, and as lost. We walked for hours and our feet hurt and our stomachs hurt, and Hans said, 'It's no good, my sister, we were better off as we were. At least before there was a *reason* for our deaths: another would have lived through our sacrifice, and she would have buried our bones, and she would have remembered us, and in the darkness of the night when she was all alone she might have patted her belly for company.' Hans shed a tear, because, as I say, he was very sensitive.

"Still we walked on, and it was with our last remaining strength that we dragged ourselves to a house. And only as we reached the door did we realize we knew this house—we had spent all this time walking in a circle. We had returned to the cottage where we had been imprisoned, and the bricks were not made of bread, and the cement not made of fudge, but nevertheless something inside smelled very tasty. And we opened the door, and there, of course, was the woman—just as we'd left her, and cooked to an absolute tee.

"Oh, how my tummy cried out for that meat. 'We have no choice,' said Hans, and from the oven he took the roast dinner, and broke off one of the woman's arms, and began to gnaw at it. The woman stared at us through eyes that had browned in the heat and looked like fried eggs. 'At least close them,' I said, and Hans did one better: he tore off her face altogether and threw it into the fire. 'You have to eat,' he said. 'My dear sister, you know we can't afford to be picky with our food now.'

"And I said, 'Could you find me a piece of meat that isn't too meaty—something that won't look too much like it's from a corpse?' And he had a rummage, and then produced something that looked a little like chicken, and I put it in my mouth, and I swallowed.

"And oh! It was good. My stomach roared with approval—so much so, in fact, that at first it sent the meat right back up again, and I had to swallow it once more, more slowly, to prove to it it wasn't dreaming. We had a feast that night. I soon overcame my scruples—what else was there for it, when I had the evidence of my own senses? The body had such a *variety* of tastes—the heart, the lungs, the kidneys, the flesh: not a single one bland, not a single one without subtle flavors all its own. We are meant to be eaten—we are *designed* that way. Pretty soon I even fished the woman's face out of the fire, and we ate that too. And do you know, the eyes did taste a little like eggs, if you closed your own and pretended.

"I said that the food would give us the strength to find our way home the next day, and Hans agreed. And that night we slept with full bellies—so full that we couldn't sleep on them; so full that we kept rolling right off our bellies and onto our sides. And in the morning Hans said, 'But why leave? This can be our house now. And we can eat the fruits of the forest. Because the forest is full of children, all the children of the world play here at some time, and most will come too far and too unwisely; there are a million cruel stepmothers to escape from, there are a million million kindly woodcutters who don't take enough care.'

"I remember the first child we caught. It looked up at us with such idiot relief. It said it thought it was going to die alone. Hans said, 'Not alone'—and he broke its jaw fast, because the woman had been right, it was better the child didn't give its name; you didn't want to get too attached to the livestock. We broke off a finger each, and sucked on them, and they seemed ripe enough to us, but what did we know? Then we hung the child upside down and it was bawling all the while, and then it stopped bawling and its sobbing was so quiet, and we slit its throat, and then even the sobbing stopped.

"Childmeat is the best meat of all: it lifts straight off the bone and melts in your mouth—and it tastes of death, and the taste of death is good. You can *survive* on vegetables but you can't enjoy them, and feasting on death gives even for a moment the sense we have risen above death, we are gods, we will live forever.

"And this went on for some years. And we were never cruel to the children—they never suffered unnecessarily—and that was good too, because an unripe child may taste a little sour, but a suffering child tastes sourer still. And we forgot the face of our father. And we didn't care—I thought we didn't care.

"One day we found a little girl sleeping under the bushes. She was just outside the house, no more than a few feet away—it was as if she'd been left there as a gift. At first I thought she was already dead, and there is little worth in a child who is already dead— it's edible, but where's the fun in eating the leftovers of crows and worms? Hans turned it over with his foot, and she opened her eyes, and blinked at us, and smiled. She smiled. Hans said, 'We are going to eat you.' And the girl said, 'I know the way out of the forest. I know the way home.'

"I said to Hans, 'This is it, this is our chance to escape.' And Hans said, 'There is no escape for us. We are what we are, and we can never be anything else. We prey upon the weak and the defenseless, and if that makes us evil, why, then, so we are evil, but we do our evil honestly. There is no home out there for us, Greta.'

"And he shed a tear, but by now I was sick of my brother's sentiment. I said, 'This is not what I wanted my life to be. To eat and pretend what we eat is something else. To shit and pretend what comes out is not what we have eaten. To fuck and pretend you're not my brother. There has to be more to life than that.'

"And Hans said, 'That is all life has *ever* been.'

"And the child. The child never stopped smiling. I swear to you, if the child had caved in, if it had begun to cry like all the others, if it had struggled or begged for its life, I'd have given in to my hunger and eaten it raw right there on the spot. But it smiled. So what else could I do?

"I said to Hans, 'I'm leaving.'

"And he said, 'If you leave, we will never meet again.'

"And I said, 'So be it. Will you let us go?'

"Because he held his knife. And we were starving—it had been a cold winter, and the children had been playing safe. And I thought he might eat the girl regardless. And I thought he might eat me too.

"And we stood there for a while, all three of us, my brother, me, and the smiling girl. And then my brother turned around and went back to the house and went indoors.

"'Come on,' said the girl, and she took my hand. And I held on tight, and I tell you, I was blinking back tears, and I don't know whether it was because someone had rescued me at last or because I had lost my brother. 'Come on,' she said, 'I'll get you home.'

"And we walked right out of the forest. I got a job in a department store, selling hosiery. That is where I met your grandfather. He was working there as an accountant. He took pity on me. He didn't mind my coarse ways. He married me, he smoothed off my rough edges. Ach, he took me to his bed, and I gave him children. One of them was your father."

Sieglinde asked, "What happened to the little girl?"

"And the family accepted me for his sake. Or if they did not accept me, they tolerated me. They tolerated me to my face. And we lived happily ever after. I never ate another child—I need you to know that. I need you to understand. I never hurt anyone ever again, not after I had left the forest. I paid that price."

"What happened to the little girl?"

"This suitcase does not suit! Look at this suitcase. It is too big. What is the use of such big suitcases? Who needs to carry so much?"

(And for a moment Sieglinde thought her grandmother was going to ignore her question, and then Grossmutti Greta sighed, and looked straight at Sieglinde, and said . . .)

"It was a very large forest."

Greta offered Sieglinde another gingerbread man, and Sieglinde didn't want one, and her grandmother told her not to be silly. Sieglinde said, "What is the special ingredient?" And Grossmutti Greta looked shocked for a moment, and saw that Sieglinde was in earnest, and that she was even shaking a little, and shaking with fear of all things; and she laughed, and said it was cinnamon, just cinnamon.

And Sieglinde bit into the head, and now she knew, of course, it was obvious it was cinnamon, but she couldn't help but taste something fleshy there too. Her grandmother was watching her. Her grandmother would be disappointed if she didn't finish. She didn't want that. She wolfed the whole man down, every last scrap of him.

"It was a very large forest. The girl had told me she could find her way out of it, and I don't think that she was lying to me, or if she was, she was lying to herself. We got lost. It was dark. It began to rain. We were hungry. We slept for hours, sometimes complete days, because we were too tired to move. And I said to her, 'You or I have to eat the other. It's the only way one of us even stands a chance of survival.' And I said to the girl, 'I think you've got a whole life ahead of you, and it's still sweet and untainted, and you haven't made any mistakes yet, or if you have, they weren't of your making. You should be the one who lives. It should be you.' I said to her, 'Eat me.'

"And the little girl said, 'No.' And I told her there was no choice, and I told her it wasn't hard. And I ran my finger down my breasts and down my thighs, and showed her the best meat she could get from them, and how thinly she should slice, and exactly how long over an open flame she should cook for the most appetizing results. I told her there was nothing to it. I told her that I had done it, and so had my brother, and we were nothing special. Not like her. Not like she could be.

"And she begged me. She begged me not to make her go through with it.

"'Eat me,' she said. 'Eat me. Because you know just what to do. You'll enjoy the meat so much more than I will. Don't waste your chitterlings on a palate as weakly sensitized as mine.' And she said, 'Eat me knowing that I give myself to you in full cooperation, I give myself to you as a present; feast on me, and enjoy, and know that I'll be in Heaven looking on. Eat me, and let your last meal of child be the best meal of child you've ever had, let me be the apotheosis of all who have gone before, let me be the reason you can stop afterward, because there'll never be a child as succulent as me.'"

"And I said, 'All right.'

"And then she told me her name. Her proper name. And I let her."

Sieglinde asked, "What was it?"

"Ach, what does it matter now?"

"Did she ask you your name?"

"Yes."

"Did you give it?"

"No. What good would it have done her? I was about to hang her on a tree upside down and slit her throat. I gave her a name—a made-up name. It was a perfectly good name."

"Is that what really happened?"

"It's the way that I remember it."

Sieglinde said quietly, "And was she succulent?"

"Oh, yes."

The grandmother leaned forward, and Sieglinde thought she was going to impart some terrible secret, something that would be so dreadful that it would taint her even to hear it. And she leaned forward too—she wanted to hear it, she knew she wanted her innocence destroyed. *Let it be now,* she thought, *let it be now.* Grossmutti Greta smiled. And said, softly, "Shall we go up and find that suitcase, once and for all?"

The dark of the attic was now solid, like a wall; the light from the staircase touched it and died. "You can't go in there," Sieglinde said to Greta, and Greta agreed.

"No, my dear, now it's your turn. You go into the attic and fetch for me the best suitcase you can."

And Sieglinde thought it would be impossible—that that solid darkness would knock her back—and she looked at her grandmother's face, and it was so old, and she saw now how close it was to death. Sieglinde stepped forward, and the darkness pooled around her, and all the light was gone, all the light was gone completely.

There were things there, in the dark—things that feed off the dark, that aren't afraid of it, that need the pitch-black to survive. She felt something leathery, like a bat, but it was too scaly for a bat; something tickled against her hand—a spider? But it was too large for a spider. And the blackness was thick like syrup, and it was pouring out all over her, into every last corner of her body—a syrup—and she could bite into it if she chose; she could eat it; if she didn't eat it, it would eat her, she knew. But she didn't want to eat it.

She heard her grandmother's voice. There was an echo to it. As if it came from a long way away.

"Don't panic," she said. "Just listen to my voice. Listen to me, and all will be well."

And Sieglinde knew nothing would be well again—that she would never more be able to see, or speak, or feel—because if she opened her mouth to speak, the darkness would swim down her throat; if she dared to feel, then the darkness would feel at her right back. But she listened to her grandmother's voice, and to her surprise it worked—her heart steadied, she stopped shaking, she began to calm.

"You think you now know why I'm leaving your grandfather? Yes? You think it is guilt? It is not guilt.

"Oh, I feel guilt enough. But not for the children I've killed. I feel guilt because I married a man I did not love and have never loved, not one day in all these sixty years. I feel guilt because I never loved my children. I kept popping them out, just to see whether I'd produce a single one I might feel some affection toward. I didn't. I hate them all. Your father, he's an especially cold fish. He deserves that bitch of a mother of yours. You do know your mother is a bitch, my dear? And that she has never cared for you?"

Sieglinde didn't open her mouth to answer. But, yes, she thought. She hadn't realized it before, and now that she did, it didn't much seem to matter.

"I have spent so many years trying to be what I am not. The scent of childmeat clings to me. I taste it in everything I cook. Just a hint, mocking me, telling me that out there is something tastier, richer, better. And I will be dead soon. And I must not waste another day on this little excuse for a life.

"I need to eat the flesh of innocents again. I was wrong. All these years, I was wrong. I should never have left my brother. I will go to him. I will go, and see whether he will take me back. I shall fall into his arms and apologize and beg his forgiveness. He may not recognize me. If he doesn't recognize me, he will eat me. But if so, ach, well, then, there's an end to this suffering.

"I am so hungry. I am so hungry. I am so hungry.

"Now, get me a suitcase. Come out of the darkness, and bring the best you can find."

Sieglinde thought she would stay in the dark. It might be safer in the dark, after all. But the dark began to drain away from her and she tried to cling on to it, she reached her arms out and grabbed— onto the bat, onto the spider—and then she saw she was clutching on to a suitcase, a nice, neat little suitcase, and the bat-leather was its shell and the spider-legs were its straps.

Grossmutti Greta took it out of the hands. She looked it over. "Yes," she said. "Yes, good choice." She held it against Sieglinde's body as if measuring it against her.

And Sieglinde knew that she was going to be put into the suitcase. And then her grandmother would take her into the forest, and she would find her brother, and together they would hang Sieglinde upside down and gut her and eat her.

"Please don't kill me," said Sieglinde.

And it was as if Sieglinde had slapped her grandmother. It made her step backward.

"You think I would eat you?" said Greta. "Oh, my darling. Oh, blood of my blood. I could never hurt you. Because you're like me. You're just like me. All these years, I've been waiting to find someone in this family I could love. And it is you. Don't be afraid. Be afraid of everyone, but never of me."

And Sieglinde saw her grandmother was crying, and realized she was crying too.

"The suitcase," said Greta, "is for you."

"I don't understand," said Sieglinde.

"Ach, you think I need a suitcase? At my time of life? What would I want with a suitcase where I am going? But you. My darling, my blood. You will leave. You will leave this place, thank God, because you cannot stay here with these people, with these passionless people. And when you do, this suitcase is for you."

She gave it back to her granddaughter.

Sieglinde weighed it in her hand, and it felt right. Not too heavy, the right size, none of those annoying buckles. The strap fitted snugly in her fist.

"There is no forest anymore, Granny," said Sieglinde. "They chopped it down. Father said they chopped it down years ago. There are factories there now."

"I know where my forest is," said Greta. She bent down, kissed Sieglinde on the cheek. It still felt awkward, uncomfortable, like being brushed by a wrinkled bag of onions.

Greta walked into the attic. The darkness swallowed her.

Sieglinde waited to see whether she would come out. She didn't. Sieglinde went home.

Sieglinde tried to think of an excuse to explain where she'd been. But when she got home, Father was still in the study, Mother was still in the kitchen and they hadn't even noticed she'd gone. They hadn't cared.

She phoned Klaus. He wasn't in, she got the answering machine. She told him she had never loved him. She told him she would never see him again.

She took the suitcase up to her bedroom, opened it. It seemed so big inside, you could fit a whole world in there, a whole future. She opened up her wardrobes and closets, worked out what she wanted to take with her. There was nothing. She needed none of it. So she closed up the suitcase again and carried it down the stairs and out of the house and into her new life.

She would fill it up along the way.

ROBERT SHEARMAN is an award-winning writer for stage, television and radio. He was resident playwright at the Northcott Theater in Exeter, and regular writer for Alan Ayckbourn at the Stephen Joseph Theater in Scarborough. He is a recurrent contributor to BBC Radio 4's afternoon play slot, but he is probably best known for his work on TV's *Doctor Who,* bringing the Daleks back to the screen in the BAFTA-winning first series of the revival in an episode nominated for a Hugo Award. His first collection of short stories, *Tiny Deaths,* was published by Comma Press in 2007 and won the World Fantasy Award. His second collection, *Love Songs for the Shy and Cynical,* published by Big Finish Productions, won the British Fantasy Award and the Edge Hill Readers' Prize, and was joint winner of the Shirley Jackson Award. A third, *Everyone's Just So So Special,* won the British Fantasy Award. In 2012, the best of his horror fiction—half taken from these previous collections and half new work— was published by ChiZine as *Remember Why You Fear Me.*

The Three Little Men in the Wood

THERE WAS ONCE a man whose wife died, and a woman whose husband died, and the man had a daughter, and the woman also had a daughter.

The girls were acquainted with each other, and went out walking together, and afterward came to the woman in her house. Then said she to the man's daughter, "Listen, tell your father that I would like to marry him. And then you shall wash yourself in milk every morning, and drink wine. But my own daughter shall wash herself in water and drink water."

The girl went home, and told her father what the woman had said. The man said, "What shall I do? Marriage is a joy and also a torment."

At length, as he could come to no decision, he pulled off his boot, and said, "Take this boot, it has a hole in the sole of it. Go with it up to the loft, hang it on the big nail, and then pour water into it. If it hold the water, then I will again take a wife, but if it run through, I will not."

The girl did as she was bid, but the water drew the hole together and the boot became full to the top.

She informed her father how it had turned out. Then he himself went up, and when he saw that she was right, he went to the widow and wooed her, and the wedding was celebrated.

The next morning, when the two girls got up, there stood before the man's daughter milk for her to wash in and wine for her to drink, but before the woman's daughter stood water to wash herself with and water for drinking.

On the second morning, stood water for washing and water for drinking before the man's daughter as well as before the woman's daughter.

And on the third morning stood water for washing and water for drinking before the man's daughter, and milk for washing and wine for drinking before the woman's daughter. And so it continued.

The woman became her step-daughter's bitterest enemy, and day by day did her best to treat her still worse. She was also envious because her step-daughter was beautiful and loveable, and her own daughter ugly and repulsive.

Once, in winter, when everything was frozen as hard as a stone, and hill and vale lay covered with snow, the woman made a frock of paper, called her step-daughter, and said, "Here, put on this dress and go out into the wood, and fetch me a little basketful of strawberries—I have a fancy for some."

"Good heavens," said the girl, "no strawberries grow in winter. The ground is frozen, and besides, the snow has covered everything. And why am I to go in this paper frock? It is so cold outside that one's very breath freezes. The wind will blow through the frock, and the thorns tear it off my body."

"Will you contradict me?" said the step-mother. "See that you go, and do not show your face again until you have the basketful of strawberries." Then she gave her a little piece of hard bread, and said, "This will last you the day," and thought, *You will die of cold and hunger outside, and will never be seen again by me.*

Then the maiden was obedient, and put on the paper frock, and went out with the basket. Far and wide there was nothing but snow, and not a green blade to be seen.

When she got into the wood she saw a small house out of which peeped three little men. She wished them good day, and knocked modestly at the door. They cried, "Come in!" and she entered the room and seated herself on the bench by the stove, where she began to warm herself and eat her breakfast.

The little men said, "Give us some of it, too."

"Willingly," she said, and divided her piece of bread in two and gave them the half.

They asked, "What do you here in the forest in the winter time, in your thin dress?"

"Ah," she answered, "I am to look for a basketful of strawberries, and am not to go home until I can take them with me."

When she had eaten her bread, they gave her a broom and said, "Sweep away the snow at the back door." But when she was outside, the three little men said to each other, "What shall we give her as she is so good, and has shared her bread with us?"

Then said the first, "My gift is, that she shall every day grow more beautiful."

The second said, "My gift is, that gold pieces shall fall out of her mouth every time she speaks."

The third said, "My gift is, that a king shall come and take her to wife."

The girl, however, did as the little men had bidden her, swept away the snow behind the little house with the broom. And what did she find but real ripe strawberries, which came up quite dark-red out of the snow. In her joy she hastily gathered her basket full, thanked the little men, shook hands with each of them, and ran home to take her step-mother what she had longed for so much.

When she went in and said good-evening, a piece of gold at once fell out of her mouth. Thereupon she related what had happened to her in the wood. But with every word she spoke, gold pieces fell from her mouth, until very soon the whole room was covered with them.

"Now look at her arrogance!" cried the step-sister, "to throw about gold in that way." But she was secretly envious of it, and wanted to go into the forest also to seek strawberries.

The mother said, "No, my dear little daughter, it is too cold. You might freeze to death." However, as her daughter let her have no peace, the mother at last yielded, made her a magnificent coat of fur, which she was obliged to put on, and gave her bread-and-butter and cake for her journey.

The girl went into the forest and straight up to the little house. The three little men peeped out again, but she did not greet them. And without looking round at them and without speaking to them, she went awkwardly into the room, seated herself by the stove, and began to eat her bread-and-butter and cake.

"Give us some of it," cried the little men.

But she replied, "There is not enough for myself, so how can I give it away to other people?"

When she had finished eating, they said, "There is a broom for you, sweep it all clean in front of the back-door."

"Sweep for yourselves," she answered, "I am not your servant."

When she saw that they were not going to give her anything, she went out by the door.

Then the little men said to each other, "What shall we give her as she is so naughty, and has a wicked, envious heart that will never let her do a good turn to anyone?"

The first said, "I grant that she may grow uglier every day."

The second said, "I grant that at every word she says, a toad shall spring out of her mouth."

The third said, "I grant that she may die a miserable death."

The maiden looked for strawberries outside, but as she found none, she went angrily home.

And when she opened her mouth, and was about to tell her mother what had happened to her in the wood, with every word she said, a toad sprang out of her mouth, so that everyone was seized with horror of her.

Then the step-mother was still more enraged, and thought of nothing but how to do every possible injury to the man's daughter, whose beauty, however, grew daily greater. At length she took a cauldron, set it on the fire, and boiled yarn in it. When it was boiled, she flung it on the poor girl's shoulder, and gave her an ax in order that she might go on the frozen river, cut a hole in the ice, and rinse the yarn.

She was obedient, went thither and cut a hole in the ice. And while she was in the midst of her cutting, a splendid carriage came driving up, in which sat the King.

The carriage stopped, and the King asked, "My child, who are you, and what are you doing here?"

"I am a poor girl, and I am rinsing yarn."

Then the King felt compassion, and when he saw that she was so very beautiful, he said to her, "Will you go away with me?"

"Ah, yes, with all my heart," she answered, for she was glad to get away from the mother and sister.

So she got into the carriage and drove away with the King. And when they arrived at his palace, the wedding was celebrated with great pomp, as the little men had granted to the maiden.

When a year was over, the young Queen bore a son. And as the step-mother had heard of her great good-fortune, she came with her daughter to the palace and pretended that she wanted to pay her a visit.

But, when the King had gone out, and no one else was present, the wicked woman seized the Queen by the head, and her daughter seized her by the feet, and they lifted her out of the bed, and threw her out of the window into the stream which flowed by.

Then the ugly daughter laid herself in the bed, and the old woman covered her up over her head.

When the King came home again and wanted to speak to his wife, the old woman cried, "Hush, hush. That can't be now, she is lying in a violent sweat. You must let her rest today."

The King suspected no evil, and did not come back again till next morning. And as he talked with his wife and she answered him, with every word a toad leaped out, whereas formerly a piece of gold had fallen.

Then he asked what that could be, but the old woman said that she had got that from the violent sweat, and would soon lose it again.

During the night, however, the scullion saw a duck come swimming up the gutter, and it said, "King, what art thou doing now? Sleepest thou, or wakest thou?"

And as he returned no answer, it said, "And my guests, what may they do?"

The scullion said, "They are sleeping soundly, too."

Then it asked again, "What does little baby mine?"

He answered, "Sleepeth in her cradle fine."

Then she went upstairs in the form of the Queen, nursed the baby, shook up its little bed, covered it over, and then swam away again down the gutter in the shape of a duck.

She came thus for two nights. On the third, she said to the scullion, "Go and tell the King to take his sword and swing it three times over me on the threshold."

Then the scullion ran and told this to the King, who came with his sword and swung it thrice over the spirit, and at the third time, his wife stood before him strong, living, and healthy as she had been before.

Thereupon the King was full of great joy, but he kept the Queen hidden in a chamber until the Sunday, when the baby was to be christened.

And when it was christened he said, "What does a person deserve who drags another out of bed and throws him in the water?"

"The wretch deserves nothing better," answered the old woman, "than to be taken and put in a barrel stuck full of nails, and rolled downhill into the water."

"Then," said the King, "you have pronounced your own sentence." And he ordered such a barrel to be brought, and the old woman to be put into it with her daughter. And then the top was hammered on, and the barrel rolled downhill until it went into the river.

Look Inside

MICHAEL MARSHALL SMITH

I'M GOING TO tell a little fib to start off with. Don't worry—I'll let you know what it was, later on. What I leave you with will be the truth. I promise.

But I'll tell you the other stuff first.

And I'm pregnant.

When it started, I'd been out for the evening. A work dinner, which meant a few hours in an Italian restaurant in Soho while my boss rambled over the challenges facing his company in these tough economic times, and was fairly good about not glancing down my blouse. He's not a bad guy and he's married and I know he wants to stay that way, so I let the looks pass. I'm sure that the sisterhood—or the sleek academics and marketable malcontents that pass for it these days—would argue that I should give him a hard time about it, preferably in public and accompanied by a brisk slap upside the head, but I can't be bothered. Men have been sneaking peeks at women's bodies (and vice versa, let's speak true, our waiter had a butt you could have bounced a sugar lump off) since we were covered in a pelt of fur, and I don't see the practice dying out any day soon. It's all very well for the sisterhood. They work in free-range all-female collectives where the issue doesn't arise or else sit preening in universities where the guys are all so weedy and beardy and institutionalized that they don't dare step out of line. Try pulling that Camille Paglia shit in the real world and you'll wind up quickly unemployed, not to mention notoriously single.

It wasn't a long dinner, and even after tubing back I was still home by half past nine. I own a very small house in an area of North London called Kentish Town, not far from the station and the main road. Kentish Town is basically now an interstice between the nicer and more expensive neighborhoods of Hampstead, Highgate and Camden, but before it was subsumed into urban sprawl it had been a place of slight note, open country enlivened by the attractive river Fleet—sourced in springs up on Hampstead Heath but long-ago so snarled and polluted that it was eventually lost, paved over for its entire length and redirected into an underground sewer.

My narrow little house stands close to where it once ran, in the middle of a short mid-Victorian terrace, and is three (and a bit) stories high with a scrap of garden out back, halved in size by a galley-kitchen extension put in by the previous owner. Originally, so I was told by said owner, the homes were built to house the families of men working on the railway line, and it's remarkably unremarkable except for the fact that one side of my garden is bounded by an old stone wall, inset into which is a badly weathered stone plaque mentioning St. John's College. A little research turned up the fact that hundreds of years before the land that these houses were built on— and a chunk of Kentish Town itself—had belonged to the College, part of Cambridge University. Why a college would have owned a garden a hundred miles away is beyond me, but then, I've never understood the appeal of reality television or Colin Firth, either, so it's possible I'm just a bit dim.

Here endeth the tour.

It's a very small house but I'm lucky to have it at all, given London's lunatic house prices. Well—not *just* lucky. Oh, how my friends took the piss when I bought my first apartment and shackled myself with a mortgage straight out of university, but now that I've been able to swap up to a place with an actual staircase and they're still renting crappy two-bed apartments in excessively multicultural neighborhoods, it's not so damn funny, it appears (except to me, of course).

Once indoors I hung up my coat, kicked off my shoes and undid the top button of my skirt in an effort to increase my physical comfort in a postpasta universe. Thus civilianized, I wandered through the living room (an epic journey of exactly five paces) and into the kitchen, where I zoned out while waiting for the kettle to boil. I'd drunk only two glasses of wine but I was tired, and the combination put me into a fuzzy trance.

Then, for no reason I was conscious of, I turned and looked out into the living room.

The kettle had just finished boiling, sending a cloud of steam up around my face, and yet there was a cold spot on the back of my neck.

Someone's been in my house.

I knew it without doubt. Or felt I did, anyway. I've always believed it a romantic notion (in the sense of "sweet, but deluded") that you would somehow know if someone had been in your house—that the intrusion of a stranger would leave some tangible psychic trace; that your dwelling is your friend and will tattle on an interloper.

A house is nothing more than walls and a roof and a collection of furnishings and objects—most chosen on the grounds of economy, not with boundless attention or existential rigor—and the only difference between you and every other person on the planet is that you're entitled by law to be there. And yet I knew it.

I knew someone had been in my house.

What if he's still here?

The kitchen extension has a side door—my back door, I guess—which leads into the garden. I could open it, slip out that way. I couldn't get far, though, as the neighbors' gardens are the other side of high fences (in one case built upon the remains of that old wall). I didn't like the idea for other reasons, too.

It was my fucking house and I didn't want to flee from it, not to mention I'd feel an utter fool if I was discovered trying to shin my way over a fence into a neighbor's garden on the basis of a "feeling." That's exactly the kind of feeble shit that gives us chicks a bad name.

I reached out to the door, however. I turned the handle, gently, and discovered . . . it was unlocked.

I knew the *front* door had been locked, too—I'd unlocked it on my return from dinner. All the windows in the kitchen were closed and locked, and from where I stood, still frozen in place, I could see the big window at the front of the living room was locked, too.

There was, in other words, only one possible way in which someone could have got into the house—and that was if I'd left the back door unlocked when I left the house that morning.

I didn't know anything about the tactics of housebreaking, but suspected that you'd leave your point of entry open (or at least ajar) while you were on the premises, to make it easier to effect a rapid exit if the householder returned home. You wouldn't close it.

My back door had been closed. Which meant hopefully he wasn't still on the premises.

I relaxed, just a little.

I tiptoed back through the living room to the bottom of the stairs and peered up them, listening hard. I couldn't hear anything, and I know from experience that the wooden floors up there are impossible to traverse without setting off a cavalcade of creaks—that sometimes the damned things will creak in the dead of night even if there's no one treading on them, especially the ones on the very top floor.

"Hello?"

I held my breath, listening for movement from above. Nothing. Absolute silence.

So I went on a cautious tour of the house. The bathroom and so-called guest room on the first floor; the bedroom and clothes-storage-pit on the next; and finally the minuscule "attic" room at the very top, situated up its own stunted little flight of five stairs. According to the previous owner, this would originally have been intended for a housemaid. She'd have needed to be a tiny fucking housemaid, I'd always thought.

The space was so small that any normal-sized person would have to sleep curled up in a ball. She wouldn't have been able to stand up in the space, either, as I'd confirmed only the day before. I'd finally got round to hoicking out and charity-shopping a few old boxes of crap that had been languishing in there since I moved in. During the process I straightened at one point without thinking, banging my head on the dusty old beam hard enough to break the skin, causing a drop or two of blood to fall to the wooden floorboards.

I could still see where they'd fallen, but at least the tiny room was tidy now.

And empty, along with all the other rooms.

The whole house looked exactly as it had when I'd left that morning, i.e., like the lair of a twenty-eight-year-old professional woman who—while not a total slattern—isn't obsessed with tidiness. Nothing out of place, nothing missing, nothing moved. Nobody there.

And there never *had* been, of course. The sense I believed I'd had, the feeling that someone had been inside, was simply wrong.

That's all.

By the time I reached the ground floor again I was wondering whether I was actually going to watch television (my previously intended course of action) or if I should have a bath and go to bed instead. Or maybe just go straight to bed, with a book. Or magazine. I couldn't quite settle on a plan.

Then I thought of something else.

I shook my head, decided it was silly, but wearily tromped toward the kitchen. Might as well check.

I flicked the kettle back on to make a cuppa for bed (having decided on the way it was now late enough without spending an hour half-watching crap television, and showering tomorrow morning would do just fine, given the emptiness of my bed). Once a teabag was in the cup waiting, I turned my attention to the bread bin.

My mother gave this to me, a moving-in present when I bought the house. It's fashioned in an overtly rustic style and would look simply fabulous if placed within easy reach of an AGA in a country kitchen (which my mother has, and would like me to have too, preferably soon and in the company of an only moderately boring young man who would commute from there to a well-paid job in the City while also helping me to start popping out children at a steady clip). In my current abode the bread bin merely looks unfeasibly large.

I don't actually eat bread either, or not often, as it gives me the bloat something chronic. I was therefore confident that it should be empty of baked goods but for a few crumbs and maybe a rock-hard croissant.

Nonetheless this is what I had come to check.

I lifted the handle on the front, releasing a faint scent of long-ago sliced bread. Then I let out a small shriek, and jumped back.

The front of the bin dropped with a clatter which sounded very loud. I opened it again and blinked at the interior, then cautiously reached out.

Inside my bread bin was a note. I took it out.

It said:

It's very pretty. And so are you

I need to backtrack a little here.

Years ago, in the summer after I left college, I went on a trip to America. I can't really describe it as "traveling," as I rented a car and stayed in motels most of the time—rather than heroically hitchhiking and bunking down in vile hostels or camping in the woods, dodging psycho killers, poison oak and ticks full to bursting with Lyme disease—but it was me out there on my own for two months, and so it qualifies for the word "trip" in my book.

In the middle of it I lodged for five days with some old friends of my parents, a genteel couple called Brian and Randall who lived in decaying grandeur in an old house in a small town near the Adirondack Mountains of New York State, the name of which escapes me. It was a pleasant interval, during which I learned that Mozart is not all bad, that my mother had once vomited for two hours after an evening sampling port wines, and that you can perk up cottage cheese no end by stirring some fresh dill into it. Fact.

I noticed something the first night I was there. Randall had gone upstairs to bed. Brian, by a slender margin the more butch of the two, sat up with me awhile longer, conferring advice on sights in the locale that were worth a detour (almost none, according to him).

As we said good night in the kitchen, I noticed that he checked the house's back door was shut (without locking it, however), and hesitated for a moment in front of a small wooden box affixed to the wall immediately opposite it before giving it a little tap.

The next morning I was up early and as I made myself a cup of tea (Brian and Randall were fierce Anglophiles, having spent several years living in Oxford, and had a bewildering array of hard-core teas to choose from) I drifted over and took a look at the wooden box.

It was small, about two inches deep, nine inches wide and six inches tall. There was a hinged lid on the top and upon this had been painted the words LOOK INSIDE!

I didn't feel that I could or should, however, and it was a couple of days later—after I'd seen Brian go through his late-night ritual twice more—that I finally asked him about it. He rolled his eyes.

"Silly idea," he muttered. He gestured for me to come over. "See what it says?"

"'Look Inside,'" I said.

"What does that make you want to do?"

"Well . . . look inside."

He smiled. "Good. Go ahead."

I opened the little box. Inside was an envelope. I looked at Brian. "Go on," he said.

I pulled it out. The envelope was unsealed. I removed from it a cheerful greetings card which had the words WELCOME, FRIEND printed clearly on the front. Inside was another envelope, a little smaller than the first. I let this be for a moment and read the message which had been inscribed in the card:

Dear Uninvited Visitor.

Welcome to this house. We have called it ours for a long time now, and we like it very much. We hope you will find good use for what is in this card, and that it will be sufficient incentive for you to go on your way, without further loss or damage to our dear home. If so, you leave with our thanks, and our very best wishes.

    Regards,

    Randall & Brian

I frowned, and looked up at Brian.

"Look inside the second envelope," he said.

I put the card down and opened the envelope. Inside, held together by a large paper clip with a smiley face on it, were bills totaling two hundred and sixty dollars.

"We started with a hundred," Brian said. "And have raised it by twenty every year. So it must be seven years, now, I suppose. No, eight. Time does trot along, doesn't it?" He gestured vaguely to indicate the house as a whole. "Nobody's going to break in through the front door," he said. "It's right on Main Street, and in a town this small, people tend to keep a friendly eye on each other's properties. Someone could come around the side, but breaking windows is such a chore, and prone to be noisy. So we always leave the back door unlocked."

"What? Why?"

"Otherwise that would be the obvious way to break in, my dear, and a broken door alone would cost several hundred dollars to put right, never mind the time and inconvenience—and who knows what they'd steal or damage once they'd gained entrance? The way it stands now, someone can simply open the door and come straight in, and once you're in the kitchen the very first thing you see is that box. Hard to resist, don't you think?"

I was smiling, charmed by the idea. "And does it work?"

"No idea," Brian said. "I have never once risen from my slumbers—nor returned from promenading during the day—to discover the envelope gone. The whole thing was Randall's idea, to be honest. I generally find it's best to let the old fool have his way. Except when it comes to the proper method for making a nice, silky hollandaise, of course, with regard to which he is . . . so *very* wrong."

A couple of days later I got back into my rental car and set off to wherever I went next (a vague trawl through the Carolinas, I believe, though as my route was completely without form, and void, it all gets a bit mixed up in my mind now). I evidently brought Randall's idea back home with me to London, however—buried beneath the levels of conscious recall until I moved into this house.

In my previous apartment it wouldn't have made a lot of sense, what with it being on the third floor. Quite soon after I moved into my house in Kentish Town, however, I saw a little wall-box in a local knickknack store and the idea popped back into my head as if it had been waiting patiently for attention all along.

I bought the box and picked a spot on the wall, about six feet up the corridor from my front door. I spent a happy evening rather painstakingly painting the words LOOK INSIDE! onto the lid. You'd have to be charitable to describe the result as artistic, but it was legible. When I'd finished, however, and hung the result on a nail, I felt foolish.

Not because I'd done it—I was still charmed by the notion—but at stealing the fruits of someone else's personality. This was Randall's idea, not mine. In the house he shared with Brian (the latter sheepishly colluding, out of love) it was a song of individuality, like the mandatory dill stirred into their cottage cheese. If I did the same thing, I was merely a copycat.

So I changed it a little. Instead of putting an envelope of cash in the box on the wall, I left a note there telling them to look . . .

In the bread bin, in the kitchen.

And I didn't make an offering of cash. I left a piece of jewelry there instead. It wasn't a piece that meant the world to me, admittedly, but it wasn't without emotional value, either. I'd found it in Brighton years before, paid more than I could afford at the time and had real affection for it. I chose it for the offering on the grounds that a genuine sacrifice could not be made without cost. It was probably worth about a hundred quid too, or at least that's what I imagined you could get for it, should you show it discreetly around one of the area's less reputable pubs.

Like Brian, I'd never yet woken or returned to find evidence that the note in the box in the hallway had been found.

Never, that is, until now.

I walked quickly back out into the hallway. I stopped when I was a few feet from the box and approached cautiously.

It looked the same as always, though to be honest I'd stopped noticing it some time ago. I looked inside.

The envelope there had been opened.

Of course it had. It had to have been. Without reading the message I'd written on the card—almost the same as the one Randall had concocted—the person wouldn't have known to look inside the bread bin and find what was there and leave me the note.

Suddenly all the strength seemed to go from my legs, and I tottered into the living room and sat down on the sofa just in time.

The house was still empty, of course. I'd already established that, and what I'd just discovered made no difference. There was nothing to be frightened about. Nothing in the present situation, anyway.

But . . . yes, there was.

I'd been right after all. Someone *had* been in the house. They'd prowled around, found the box in the hallway and the note and then the jewelry in the bread bin, left a note and then . . . Gone.

What should I do? Call the police?

Well, obviously I should. Someone had been in the house and taken something. Though it *was* something I'd invited them to take, of course.

Unless . . .

I did another quick tour of the house and couldn't find anything else missing. My iPod, iPad and iLaptop were all where they should be, along with my near-worthless television and DVD player. So was my other jewelry, the stuff I didn't store in the bread bin. I even dug out my underused checkbook from the bedside drawer and established there were no checks missing from the middle (a cunning ruse I'd read about in some magazine or other—steal a few from the middle, rather than the whole book, and nobody notices they're gone until it's too late). I'm not sure even thieves use checks much anymore, though, and apart from a few knickknacks of purely sentimental value, there was nothing else worth nicking in the entire house. And none of it had been nicked anyway.

But someone still shouldn't have come into my place, even if their only score was a piece of jewelry I'd effectively offered to them.

I grabbed my phone and went back into the kitchen to retrieve the note from the counter, to have it to hand over when the police arrived. Did one dial 999 in these nonurgent circumstances, or were you supposed to look up the number of the local station? I had no idea.

I hesitated, and put the phone down.

The next day at work was hectic and slightly bizarre, as the woman who shares my office appeared to have a teeny tiny mental breakdown in the late morning and stormed out, never to return. I'd always thought she was a bit bonkers and so I wasn't totally surprised, though I was impressed by how much chaos she left in her wake.

My boss took the event admirably in his stride. He looked dispiritedly around at the mess she'd made, told me to leave it for now but asked if I'd mind answering her calls until she either came back or he could hire a replacement. This meant I was busy as hell all afternoon, but I prefer it that way. The working day slips by far more quickly when you don't have time to think, and I'd already spent more than enough time screwing about on the Internet during the morning.

I had time to think on the tube journey home, however, and of course what I mainly thought about was what had happened the night before.

I hadn't called the police, in the end. It was late and I was tired and although the event had freaked me out a little, I couldn't face dealing with them.

Also . . . I just thought, *Well, that's the end of it.* The police wouldn't be able to find the thief (who wasn't even technically a thief, of course; I suppose "intruder" is all I could legitimately say he'd been), and so it'd end up in a dusty log in the local police station and they'd give me a crime number which I could use in dealing with the insurance company if I chose to try to claim something back for the piece of jewelry.

Before I'd gone to sleep the night before I'd tidied the event away in my mind, electing not to think any more about it, and I rein-forced this on the tube and throughout the five-minute walk in the freezing rain from the station—during which, wanton hedonist that I am, I also stopped at the corner shop to buy a frozen ready-meal to zap in the microwave for my tea. Plus a small tub of ice cream. And some biscuits.

This time, however, it was obvious that something was wrong the minute I stepped through the door.

One of the advantages of living by yourself is that you get to be in sole charge of certain types of decision. The central heating, for example. My father is a total miser when it comes to gas bills, and my parents' house is so cold in winter that it's just as well my mother *does* have an AGA, so she and I can go huddle around it when Dad's not looking. Living by myself means no man gets a say in how warmly I spend my evenings. I have the heating set to come on midafternoon, so the place is nice and toasty when I get home. As soon as you close the door behind you, you're enveloped.

Not tonight, however. The heating was on, as I could tell from touching my hand against the radiator in the hallway, but the house was chilly.

I went into the living room. The windows were all shut, but through one of them, I could see why the house wasn't as warm as it should be.

The back door was wide-open.

It had been both closed and locked when I left for work that morning.

I *thought* so, anyway. I knew it had been closed, at least, but I hadn't actually checked that it had been locked. Hadn't even checked the key, for I knew it was in its normal place, stuck there in its lock.

I remembered my thought of the day before, that an intruder would be likely to leave a means of escape open if he was on the premises, and found my eyes drifting warily upward, to the living room ceiling and the floors beyond.

What if he was still here this time?

I got out my phone. I dialed 999, but did not press the call button.

"Is somebody here?" I called up the stairs, backing into the hallway and toward the front door. "If so, you should know that I'm calling the police. Right now."

There was no sound from above. I knew that if there was someone in the house and he chose to get violent, I could be a bloody and broken mess in the corner of the living room before the local cops had got halfway here through the traffic on Kentish Town Road.

So I opened the front door a little and walked back to the bottom of the stairs. "The front door's open," I said. "I'm going to get out of your way. I'll . . . go in the kitchen, so I won't see you."

Was this a good idea? Or a really stupid one?

Stupid, I decided.

"Or," I said, "here's another plan. *I'm* going to leave. I'm going to go back out of the house and stand around the corner. I won't look this way. Shut the back door to let me know you've gone."

And that's what I did. I went out of the front door, closing it behind me, my finger still hovering over the call button on my phone. I walked quickly to the corner.

I waited ten minutes. I didn't see anybody come out of the house. The front, anyway.

I walked back. I let myself back in, cautiously.

The back door was now closed.

I quickly ran up to the next floor, making as much noise as possible, and found it empty. Then I went right to the top, including poking my head into the tiny attic room. Nobody anywhere. No sign of anything disturbed.

When I made it back down to the kitchen, however, I realized that the back door wasn't actually shut. The intruder had pulled it to when he left, but hadn't closed it properly.

I pushed it open and stepped out into the garden, on impulse, even though I knew he could still be out there.

To the side of my kitchen there's a tiny concrete patio. Beyond that is my "lawn"—a scrappy patch of grass that would be about ten feet square if it was actually a square; in fact it's a kind of parallelogram, barely six feet wide at the far end. Because of the high hedges that surround it, the grass rarely gets much light even in summer, and it's ragged and muddy in the winter.

And soggy enough this evening, I thought, that you should be able to see the foot marks of a departing intruder, indents from shoes or boots.

There were none.

Something else caught my eye, though, and I stepped gingerly on to the grass to have a closer look.

The garden gets its shape from the fact the left-hand wall slopes radically toward the back, and it's this that's made of stone and features the faded old plaque. The plaque's low down, as if to be at child-height, not very large and made of the same basic stone as the rest of the wall. I'd been in the house for nine months before I'd ever realized it was there. All it says is—

[. . .] GARDEN
ST. JOHN'S COLLEGE

—the first word is so weather-worn and chipped that it's unreadable. The wall must predate the buildings that now overshadow it by several hundred years, this scrap of it left by early Victorian developers because it happened to more or less coincide with the layout of the minuscule back gardens they were affording these somewhat perfunctory workingmen's cottages.

Something was lying on the grass, close to the point in the wall where the plaque is.

It was my piece of jewelry.

Half an hour later I was in the living room with a cup of tea. The brooch was on the coffee table in front of me. The house was nice and warm now that the back door had been shut for a while.

It was my brooch, without doubt. It had a distinctive triangular design, capped at each point with a dot of some green semiprecious stone. When I'd found it in the antique store years before, I hadn't been convinced it was even an antique. The shape was so minimalist—literally a triangle, albeit one of unequal sides and with a slight curve to all the lines—that it had looked pretty modern to my admittedly untutored eye.

It looked different now. When I'd got it back to the apartment I was living in at the time, I'd intended to have a go at cleaning it. I realized I rather liked the tarnish, however, and decided to leave it be. Over the years since, it had become darker and darker, and when I'd put it in the bread bin months and months ago, the metal had been a very dark gray indeed.

Now it shone. The silver—and there was no doubt that's what it was made of, which meant I'd probably got more of a bargain than I'd realized—was so shiny it seemed almost white.

It didn't merely look clean—it looked fresh-minted.

Whatever process had brought this about had revealed something else, too. There were designs all over it. Etched very lightly into the silver was an incredibly fine and detailed series of lines and curves and interlocking Celtic shapes. At first glance it seemed chaotic, but the more I looked—and I'd been sitting there for quite a while—the more I sensed there was a pattern that I hadn't yet been able to establish. It looked beautiful, and otherworldly, and extremely old.

The problem was I was pretty convinced that the pattern hadn't been there before.

Yes, it had been tarnished when I got it, as discussed—but in the early stages of oxidation you'll often find that any engravings (or imperfections) in metal are more, rather than less, obvious. It's easier to spot hallmarks, for example. You'll *glimpse* a pattern, at least, especially when looking at something as closely as you do when you're considering blowing hard-earned cash on it. I hadn't seen any such thing.

So what was it doing there now?

I belatedly realized I hadn't done anything about my shopping from the corner shop and had dropped my shopping bag in the middle of the room, when I'd seen the back door hanging open. I hurried over and grabbed the bag. The tub of ice cream was glistening in that way that says it's well on the way to melting, courtesy of my generous central heating policy. I carried it to the kitchen, still worrying at the problem of the design on the brooch, and stowed the contents in the freezer of my poxy little fridge.

When I straightened, my eyes were directly in line with the bread bin. Something, I'm not sure what, made me reach out and open it.

The same smell of old bread greeted me again, though it seemed stronger this time, which made no sense.

There was a piece of paper in there, too.

I knew it couldn't be the one I'd found the night before, as I'd put that one in the drawer of the bureau in the living room (an old and cheerless piece of crap that belonged to my grandmother).

I picked the paper up and read it.

I hope you like what I have made on it

I didn't need to compare the handwriting on it to the other paper. It was clearly the same.

But then I realized there was another line of writing, an inch further down the page. Why hadn't I spotted that right away? Because it was much fainter. Not as if faded, however—in fact the opposite.

As I watched, feeling the hairs rise on the back of my neck, the writing, at first so faint it was barely visible, gradually strengthened until it was as distinct as the line above.

It said—

I have designs upon you, too

No, I didn't call the police. I could have. Probably should have. I could have told them that both lines of the message had been visible when I found the piece of paper, and I didn't have to tell them it had been left in my bread bin. I didn't have to say that I was convinced someone had somehow etched a faint and intricate design on an old piece of jewelry so that it looked as though it had always been there.

The problem was if I wasn't truthful about these things, I wouldn't be conveying the reality of the situation. They'd assume some local miscreant was making a habit of breaking in, and I already knew that wasn't what was going on. I'd known this, or at least suspected it—and now I must finally start to be honest—since the beginning. Since I told my fib.

It was a small fib, but significant.

When I came home the night I had dinner with my boss, and first had the intuition that someone had been in my house, and checked the back door, it was unlocked. That's what I told you, anyhow.

But it wasn't true.

The back door was *locked*.

It was locked, from the inside. So were all the windows, on all the floors. So had the front door been too until I unlocked it on my way in. Nobody could have got into the house from outside to find my note in the box in the hallway and then the brooch in the kitchen.

Whoever did these things had already been inside.

I don't know for how long. Perhaps always. That's what I've come to suspect. At least since the house was built, upon land that had once been a garden meadow on a little hill, near woodland and a pretty stream now trammeled far underground.

Before the day went pear-shaped—after my coworker went sweeping out of the office and saddled me with all her work—I'd spent an hour covertly using the Internet, doing some digging I probably should have done long before. I'd always assumed that the missing word on the stone plaque on the wall in my garden was MEMORIAL—the sign put there to cordon off a patch of garden where people came to remember those now dead.

I could find no reference to such a thing in the area, however, even though the records for this part of London are pretty good, and I'd never understood why the plaque was positioned so low, as if for the eyes of people well below normal height.

I did find a single mention of an "Offering Garden." An uncited reference on a rather amateur-looking local history site, claiming that the old stretch of open countryside belonging to St. John's College had featured an example of the long-forgotten practice of securely walling off a portion of any meadow or hillside or forest that had a reputation for being home or playground to wood-nixies or elementals, coinhabitants of our world that could not be seen, the idea being, apparently, that any such creatures would remain within such walls. Forever.

The people who eventually developed the area, several hundred years later, would not have known this. The practices and the beliefs supporting it had long ago died out. They could not have been expected to notice, either, or to care, that the weathering on the plaque was very uneven, almost as if someone had chipped away at the first word in order to obscure the wall's original purpose.

Just before my ex-colleague had her meltdown and I had to stop looking, I finally tracked down a website with a very old map of this part of Kentish Town. It had been badly reproduced and was hard to make out, but seemed to show a small, boundaried portion within a fifty-acre parcel belonging to a Cambridge college. The circumscribed area was not named or labeled, but by superimposing it upon a modern-day Ordnance Survey map of my street, I was able to establish both that the plaque must have been placed on the *inside* of the wall, and that the area it had encompassed had not been very large.

Just big enough to include my house.

I eventually microwaved my dinner and ate it in front of the television, turning it up loud. The frozen curry tasted a lot better than I expected. The ice cream was really good too, and I finished the entire pack of biscuits. My appetite was greater than usual, despite an odd tickle of nervousness in the pit of my stomach.

I had a bath. As I dried myself afterward I thought I noticed some very fine lines on the skin of my shoulders, not quite random, and when I went up to bed I discovered the room smelled faintly of new bread.

Not quite of bread, in fact. Though the odor was reminiscent of a fresh-baked loaf, now that it was divorced from the bread bin in the kitchen I realized it was actually closer to the smell of healthy grass, warmed by a summer sun. Warm grass or recently opened flowers, perhaps. Something vital, but secret.

Something very old.

I saw that the cover on my bed had been folded back. Neatly, as if in hopeful invitation. A piece of paper lay in the area that had been revealed—

Soon, pretty one

—was all it said at first.

As I watched, however, another line revealed itself. It was delivered to me slowly, as if brought to life by the moonlight coming in through the window.

All I need is a little more blood

It was then that I heard the first faint creaks, like small feet on very old floorboards, coming from the little attic room above.

Though it turns out he's not so small.

If you know what I mean.

MICHAEL MARSHALL SMITH was born in Knutsford, Cheshire, and grew up in the United States, South Africa, and Australia. He currently lives in Santa Cruz, California, with his wife and son. Smith's short fiction has appeared in numerous magazines and anthologies and, under his full name, he has published the modern SF novels *Only Forward*, *Spares*, and *One of Us*. He is the only person to have won the British Fantasy Award for Best Short Story four times—along with the August Derleth, International Horror Guild, and Philip K. Dick awards. Writing as Michael Marshal, he has published six international best-selling novels of suspense, including *The Straw Men* and *The Intruders*, currently in development with the BBC. His most recent novels are *Killer Move* and *The Forgotten*.

The Story of a Youth Who Went Forth to Learn What Fear Was

A CERTAIN FATHER HAD two sons, the elder of whom was smart and sensible, and could do everything, but the younger was stupid and could neither learn nor understand anything. And when people saw him they said, "There's a fellow who will give his father some trouble."

When anything had to be done, it was always the elder who was forced to do it, but if his father bade him fetch anything when it was late, or in the nighttime, and the way led through the churchyard, or any other dismal place, he answered, "Oh, no, Father, I'll not go there, it makes me shudder." For he was afraid.

Or when stories were told by the fire at night which made the flesh creep, the listeners sometimes said, "Oh, it makes us shudder." The younger sat in a corner and listened with the rest of them, and could not imagine what they could mean.

"They are always saying 'It makes me shudder, it makes me shudder'; it does not make me shudder," thought he. "That, too, must be an art of which I understand nothing."

Now it came to pass that his father said to him one day, "Hearken to me, you fellow in the corner there, you are growing tall and strong, and you too must learn something by which you can earn your bread. Look how your brother works, but you do not even earn your salt."

"Well, Father," he replied, "I am quite willing to learn something—indeed, if it could but be managed, I should like to learn how to shudder. I don't understand that at all yet."

The elder brother smiled when he heard that, and thought to himself, "Good God, what a blockhead that brother of mine is. He will never be good for anything as long as he lives. He who wants to be a sickle must bend himself betimes."

The father sighed, and answered him, "You shall soon learn what it is to shudder, but you will not earn your bread by that."

Soon after this the Sexton came to the house on a visit, and the father bewailed his trouble, and told him how his younger son was so backward in every respect that he knew nothing and learned nothing. "Just think, said he, 'when I asked him how he was going to earn his bread, he actually wanted to learn to shudder.'"

"If that be all," replied the Sexton, "he can learn that with me. Send him to me, and I will soon polish him."

The father was glad to do it, for he thought, *It will train the boy a little.*

The Sexton therefore took him into his house, and he had to ring the church bell. After a day or two, the Sexton awoke him at midnight, and bade him arise and go up into the church tower and ring the bell. *You shall soon learn what shuddering is,* thought he, and secretly went there before him, and when the boy was at the top of the tower and turned around, and was just going to take hold of the bell rope, he saw a white figure standing on the stairs opposite the sounding hole.

"Who is there?" cried he, but the figure made no reply, and did not move or stir. "Give an answer," cried the boy, "or take yourself off, you have no business here at night."

The Sexton, however, remained standing motionless that the boy might think he was a ghost. The boy cried a second time: "What do you want here? Speak if you are an honest fellow, or I will throw you down the steps."

The Sexton thought, *He can't mean to be as bad as his words,* uttered no sound and stood as if he were made of stone.

Then the boy called to him for the third time and, as that was also to no purpose, he ran against him and pushed the ghost down the stairs, so that it fell down ten steps and remained lying there in a corner.

Thereupon he rang the bell, went home, and without saying a word went to bed, and fell asleep.

The Sexton's wife waited a long time for her husband, but he did not come back. At length she became uneasy, and wakened the boy, and asked, "Do you not know where my husband is? He climbed up the tower before you did."

"No, I don't know," replied the boy, "but someone was standing by the sounding hole on the other side of the steps, and as he would neither give an answer nor go away, I took him for a scoundrel, and threw him downstairs. Just go there and you will see if it was he. I should be sorry if it were."

The woman ran away and found her husband, who was lying moaning in the corner, and had broken his leg.

She carried him down, and then with loud screams she hastened to the boy's father. "Your boy," cried she, "has been the cause of a great misfortune. He has thrown my husband down the steps so that he broke his leg. Take the good-for-nothing fellow out of our house."

The father was terrified, and ran thither and scolded the boy. "What wicked tricks are these?" said he. "The Devil must have put them into your head."

"Father," he replied, "do listen to me. I am quite innocent. He was standing there by night like one intent on doing evil. I did not know who it was, and I entreated him three times either to speak or to go away."

"Ah," said the father, "I have nothing but unhappiness with you. Go out of my sight. I will see you no more."

"Yes, Father, right willingly. Wait only until it is day. Then will I go forth and learn how to shudder, and then I shall, at any rate, understand one art which will support me."

"Learn what you will," spoke the father, "it is all the same to me. Here are fifty talers for you. Take these and go into the wide world, and tell no one from whence you come, and who is your father, for I have reason to be ashamed of you."

"Yes, Father, it shall be as you will. If you desire nothing more than that, I can easily keep it in mind."

When day dawned, therefore, the boy put his fifty talers into his pocket, and went forth on the great highway, and continually said to himself, "If I could but shudder. If I could but shudder."

Then a man approached who heard this conversation which the youth was holding with himself, and when they had walked a little farther to where they could see the gallows, the man said to him, "Look, there is the tree where seven men have married the rope-maker's daughter, and are now learning how to fly. Sit down beneath it, and wait till night comes, and you will soon learn how to shudder."

"If that is all that is wanted," answered the youth, "it is easily done. But if I learn how to shudder as fast as that, you shall have my fifty talers. Just come back to me early in the morning."

Then the youth went to the gallows, sat down beneath it, and waited till evening came. And as he was cold, he lighted himself a fire. But at midnight the wind blew so sharply that, in spite of his fire, he could not get warm. And as the wind knocked the hanged men against each other, and they moved backward and forward, he thought to himself, *If you shiver below by the fire, how those up above must freeze and suffer.*

And as he felt pity for them, he raised the ladder, and climbed up, unbound one of them after the other, and brought down all seven. Then he stoked the fire, blew it, and set them all round it to warm themselves. But they sat there and did not stir, and the fire caught their clothes.

So he said, "Take care, or I will hang you up again." The dead men, however, did not hear, but were quite silent, and let their rags go on burning. At this he grew angry, and said, "If you will not take care, I cannot help you. I will not be burned with you," and he hung them up again each in his turn. Then he sat down by his fire and fell asleep.

And the next morning the man came to him and wanted to have the fifty talers, and said, "Well, do you know how to shudder?"

"No," answered he, "how should I know? Those fellows up there did not open their mouths, and were so stupid that they let the few old rags which they had on their bodies get burned."

Then the man saw that he would not get the fifty talers that day, and went away saying, "Such a youth has never come my way before."

The youth likewise went his way, and once more began to mutter to himself, "Ah, if I could but shudder. Ah, if I could but shudder."

A wagoner who was striding behind him heard this and asked, "Who are you?"

"I don't know," answered the youth.

Then the wagoner asked, "From whence do you come?"

"I know not."

"Who is your father?"

"That I may not tell you."

"What is it that you are always muttering between your teeth?"

"Ah," replied the youth, "I do so wish I could shudder, but no one can teach me how."

"Enough of your foolish chatter," said the wagoner. "Come, go with me, I will see about a place for you."

The youth went with the wagoner, and in the evening they arrived at an inn where they wished to pass the night. Then at the entrance of the parlor the youth again said quite loudly, "If I could but shudder. If I could but shudder."

The host who heard this, laughed and said, "If that is your desire, there ought to be a good opportunity for you here."

"Ah, be silent," said the hostess. "So many prying persons have already lost their lives, it would be a pity and a shame if such beautiful eyes as these should never see the daylight again."

But the youth said, "However difficult it may be, I will learn it. For this purpose indeed have I journeyed forth."

He let the host have no rest, until the latter told him that, not far from thence, stood a haunted castle where anyone could very easily learn what shuddering was, if he would but watch in it for three nights. The King had promised that he who would venture there should have his daughter to wife, and she was the most beautiful maiden the sun shone on. Likewise in the castle lay great treasures, which were guarded by evil spirits, and these treasures would then be freed, and would make a poor man rich enough. Already many men had gone into the castle, but as yet none had come out again.

Then the youth went next morning to the King and said, "If it be allowed, I will willingly watch three nights in the haunted castle."

The King looked at him, and as the youth pleased him, he said, "You may ask for three things to take into the castle with you, but they must be things without life."

Then he answered, "Then I ask for a fire, a turning-lathe, and a cutting-board with the knife."

The King had these things carried into the castle for him during the day.

When night was drawing near, the youth went up and made himself a bright fire in one of the rooms, placed the cutting-board and knife beside it, and seated himself by the turning-lathe. "Ah, if I could but shudder," said he, "but I shall not learn it here either."

Toward midnight he was about to poke his fire, and as he was blowing it, something cried suddenly from one corner, "*Au, miau!* How cold we are."

"You fools," cried he, "what are you crying about? If you are cold, come take a seat by the fire and warm yourselves."

And when he had said that, two great black cats came with one tremendous leap and sat down on each side of him, and looked savagely at him with their fiery eyes. After a short time, when they had warmed themselves, they said, "Comrade, shall we have a game of cards?"

"Why not," he replied, "but just show me your paws."

Then they stretched out their claws. "Oh," said he, "what long nails you have. Wait, I must first cut them for you."

Thereupon he seized them by the throats, put them on the cutting-board and screwed their feet fast. "I have looked at your fingers," said he, "and my fancy for card-playing has gone." And he struck them dead and threw them out into the water.

But when he had made away with these two, and was about to sit down again by his fire, out from every hole and corner came black cats and black dogs with red-hot chains. And more and more of them came until he could no longer move, and they yelled horribly, and got on his fire, pulled it to pieces, and tried to put it out.

He watched them for a while quietly, but at last when they were going too far, he seized his cutting-knife, and cried, "Away with you, vermin!" and began to cut them down. Some of them ran away, the others he killed, and threw out into the fish-pond.

When he came back he fanned the embers of his fire again and warmed himself. And as he thus sat, his eyes would keep open no longer, and he felt a desire to sleep.

Then he looked around and saw a great bed in the corner. "That is the very thing for me," said he, and got into it. When he was just going to shut his eyes, however, the bed began to move of its own accord, and went over the whole of the castle. "That's right," said he, "but go faster."

Then the bed rolled on as if six horses were harnessed to it, up and down, over thresholds and stairs, but suddenly *hop, hop,* it turned over upside down, and lay on him like a mountain. But he threw quilts and pillows up in the air, got out and said, "Now any-one who likes, may drive," and lay down by his fire, and slept till it was day.

In the morning the King came, and when he saw him lying there on the ground, he thought the evil spirits had killed him and he was dead. Then said he, "After all it is a pity, for so handsome a man."

The youth heard it, got up, and said, "It has not come to that yet."

Then the King was astonished, but very glad, and asked how he had fared.

"Very well indeed," answered he. "One night is past, the two others will pass likewise."

Then he went to the innkeeper, who opened his eyes very wide, and said, "I never expected to see you alive again. Have you learned how to shudder yet?"

"No," said he, "it is all in vain. If someone would but tell me."

The second night he again went up into the old castle, sat down by the fire, and once more began his old song: "If I could but shudder."

When midnight came, an uproar and noise of tumbling about was heard. At first it was low, but it grew louder and louder. Then it was quiet for a while, and at length with a loud scream, half a man came down the chimney and fell before him.

"Hullo," cried he. "Another half belongs to this. This is not enough." Then the uproar began again, there was a roaring and howling, and the other half fell down likewise.

"Wait," said he, "I will just stoke up the fire a little for you." When he had done that and looked round again, the two pieces were joined together, and a hideous man was sitting in his place.

"That is no part of our bargain," said the youth. "The bench is mine."

The man wanted to push him away. The youth, however, would not allow that, but thrust him off with all his strength, and seated himself again in his own place.

Then still more men fell down. One after the other, they brought nine dead men's legs and two skulls, and set them up and played at nine-pins with them.

The youth also wanted to play and said, "Listen you, can I join you?"

"Yes, if you have any money."

"Money enough," replied he, "but your balls are not quite round." Then he took the skulls and put them in the lathe and turned them till they were round. "There, now they will roll better," said he. "Hurrah! Now we'll have fun."

He played with them and lost some of his money, but when it struck twelve, everything vanished from his sight. He lay down and quietly fell asleep.

Next morning the King came to inquire after him. "How has it fared with you this time?" asked he.

"I have been playing at nine-pins," he answered, "and have lost a couple of farthings."

"Have you not shuddered, then?"

"What?" said he. "I have had a wonderful time. If I did but know what it was to shudder."

The third night he sat down again on his bench and said quite sadly, "If I could but shudder."

When it grew late, six tall men came in and brought a coffin. Then said he, "Ha-ha, that is certainly my little cousin, who died only a few days ago." And he beckoned with his finger, and cried, "Come, little cousin, come."

They placed the coffin on the ground, but he went to it and took the lid off, and a dead man lay therein. He felt his face, but it was cold as ice. "Wait," said he, "I will warm you a little, and went to the fire and warmed his hand and laid it on the dead man's face, but he remained cold."

Then he took him out, and sat down by the fire and laid him on his breast and rubbed his arms that the blood might circulate again. As this also did no good, he thought to himself, *When two people lie in bed together, they warm each other,* and carried him to the bed, covered him over and lay down by him.

After a short time the dead man became warm too, and began to move. Then said the youth, "See, little cousin, have I not warmed you?"

The dead man, however, got up and cried, "Now will I strangle you!"

"What?" said he. "Is that the way you thank me? You shall at once go into your coffin again. And he took him up, threw him into it, and shut the lid. Then came the six men and carried him away again."

"I cannot manage to shudder," said he. "I shall never learn it here as long as I live."

Then a man entered who was taller than all others, and looked terrible. He was old, however, and had a long white beard. "You wretch!" cried he, "you shall soon learn what it is to shudder, for you shall die!"

"Not so fast," replied the youth. "If I am to die, I shall have to have a say in it."

"I will soon seize you," said the fiend.

"Softly, softly, do not talk so big. I am as strong as you are, and perhaps even stronger."

"We shall see," said the old man. "If you are stronger, I will let you go—come, we will try."

Then he led him by dark passages to a smith's forge, took an ax, and with one blow struck an anvil into the ground.

"I can do better than that," said the youth, and went to the other anvil. The old man placed himself near and wanted to look on, and his white beard hung down. Then the youth seized the ax, split the anvil with one blow, and in it caught the old man's beard. "Now I have you," said the youth. "Now it is your turn to die." Then he seized an iron bar and beat the old man till he moaned and entreated him to stop, when he would give him great riches.

The youth drew out the ax and let him go.

The old man led him back into the castle, and in a cellar showed him three chests full of gold. "Of these," said he, "one part is for the poor, the other for the King, the third yours."

In the meantime it struck twelve, and the spirit disappeared, so that the youth stood in darkness. "I shall still be able to find my way out," said he and felt about, found the way into the room, and slept there by his fire.

Next morning the King came and said, "Now you must have learned what shuddering is?"

"No," he answered. "What can it be? My dead cousin was here, and a bearded man came and showed me a great deal of money down below, but no one told me what it was to shudder."

"Then," said the King, "you have saved the castle, and shall marry my daughter."

"That is all very well," said he, "but still I do not know what it is to shudder."

Then the gold was brought up and the wedding celebrated, but howsoever much the young King loved his wife, and however happy he was, he still said always, "If I could but shudder, if I could but shudder." And this at last angered her.

Her waiting-maid said, "I will find a cure for him, he shall soon learn what it is to shudder." She went out to the stream which flowed through the garden, and had a whole bucketful of gudgeons brought to her.

At night when the young King was sleeping, his wife was to draw the clothes off him and empty the bucketful of cold water with the gudgeons in it over him, so that the little fishes would sprawl about him.

Then he woke up and cried, "Oh, what makes me shudder so? What makes me shudder so, dear wife? Ah, now I know what it is to shudder!"

Fräulein Fearnot

MARKUS HEITZ

Translated by Sheelagh Alabaster

Homburg, Saarland, Germany

AND SO IT was that Asa came upon the beast up on its hind legs, a foot and a half taller than she was herself. Its sharp fangs were each as long as her little finger and the eyes glowed red and evil. From the depths of its throat the werewolf growled as it stared hungrily down at the brown-haired girl, pointed claws opening and closing in greedy anticipation, saliva dripping from its jaws.

Asa had quite different problems to cope with, werewolf or no werewolf.

She glanced up at the roof of the sandstone cave where she and the werewolf stood. It looked as if the stonework just above Tinkerbell—Tinkerbell the Lycanthrope, her favorite—was going to crash down any moment now. Tinkerbell had four processors to control movement, brilliant red eyes, real fur and a shockingly convincing snout. On the press of a button, gobs of slobber and stage blood came shooting out.

Asa picked up her radio. "Martin, we've got a problem on Level Eight in the Throne Room," she reported. "The rock face has got to be glued back pronto or the whole lot's going to come down on top of Tinkerbell."

"How bad is it?"

"I really think it should be dealt with tonight." She turned back to the werewolf, burying her fingers in its fur to find the switch at the side of its neck. She pressed it, and the creature's growling ceased and the red eyes stopped flashing. "Good werewolf," she grinned, patting it.

"Okay. I'll let the boss know. Are you coming out now?"

"Not yet. I've got some stuff to do on Goldilocks. See you in the morning."

"Don't know the meaning of sleep, do you?"

"Nope."

"And you don't know the meaning of fear, either," he retorted. "What's a nice young girl like you doing here with all these—"

She laughed. "Piss off, Martin." She switched the radio off and left the cave they called the Throne Room. The soft sand under her feet silenced her steps.

Altogether there were twelve levels in the Schlossberg, Europe's largest sandstone cave system. A wealthy investor had turned it into a massive horror attraction. Hundreds of years ago the quartz sand here had been dug out for the manufacture of glass, and now people came here in droves to get scared out of their wits. Each level had its own theme: from werewolves to vampires, ghosts, demons, serial killers, execution scenes and torture chambers. There were actors to boost the effects of the motorized figures, ensuring terrified screams from the punters.

But the whole place reeked of history, and some said the mountain itself was properly haunted. Visitors had reported seeing strange things on parts of the tour where there were no show installations at all. And Martin, one of the staff, claimed to have experienced it himself.

Asa wasn't just a splendid technician; she would dress up in costume like the actors and steal round corners, creeping up on the paying public to terrify the life out of them.

She'd give anything to catch sight of one of the real ghosts herself.

She thought of herself as being a kind of phantom. Her boss hadn't ever put her on the books—he paid her in cash—and she didn't have a fixed address.

What did she need an address for? She could live wherever she wanted to.

Her breath was like white fog in the air. The temperature in these caves was a steady 10°C, which wasn't necessarily very good for the valuable figures, so it was vital to carry out regular maintenance.

Asa reached her workshop at the back of Level Ten and surveyed Goldilocks: a seven-foot-tall zombie, its body in an advanced state of decay, but very muscular and cleverly airbrush-finished in an aggressive pose—enough to make weak hearts falter any time it came whizzing out from a side corridor, groaning horribly.

The girl fastened back her longish brown hair with a quick movement and started up the gas turbine heating. She took off her coat, displaying the neat body that she mostly kept concealed under a black roll-neck sweater and dark cargo pants. On her feet she wore Doc Martens, which helped insulate her feet from the cold.

Asa began the intricate repair work on the zombie, resoldering a few points on the motherboard before checking the programming.

In general people called her a geek, and thought her reserved and difficult to get on with. Others assumed that she was highly gifted. Now thirty, she'd never completed any apprenticeship or course of study, but she was good at anything she cared to turn her hand to. If you didn't know her and had never seen her work you might think she was a bit dim—but in fact she had an inquiring mind and wasn't afraid of anything—all good qualities for a research scientist, really.

Asa didn't give a damn what other people thought of her. She had her little sweeties, her own created monsters—and nothing shocked or disgusted her. Why would it?

A faint sound issued from the corridor.

Asa put down the soldering iron and cocked her head to listen.

Another rustle—something was being dragged along on the sand.

She glanced at the time. Could it be the technicians, off to the Throne Room to mend that precarious roof?

Then there was a clink, followed by a noise she couldn't identify, but it sounded a little like sobbing. A high voice started begging desperately, "Don't! Please don't—please don't—"

That was definitely not the tech-crew. Asa picked the hammer up from the bench and started toward the noise. She was thrilled to think it might be real ghosts.

Stepping out into the long corridor, she saw a dark figure swish past. A ghoulish laugh reverberated off the walls. "This is our mountain," a voice breathed in her ear. "Get out of here, human, or we will kill you!"

"Hey—stop!" She raced off, hammer in hand, toward Tinkerbell's cave.

The emergency lighting gave the sandstone a fascinating, magical appearance. The werewolf looked like a living creature frozen by a sorcerer's spell. But where was the fog coming from? Asa had no idea. She'd never noticed that phenomenon here before.

Her heart was thumping in anticipation. "Who are you?"

"The souls of dead mine workers," came the whispers from all sides, out of the drifting mist.

She took another step and grinned with delight. "Then show yourselves—I want to see you!"

"Go away, get out of our mines," came the hissed warning, "or you will forfeit your life."

"Let me get a look at you." She forced her way through the damp mist. "This is so much better than my mechanical creations—"

"We warned you, woman," came the thundering, angry voice behind her. "Now you shall die!"

Asa spun round and saw a sketchy figure with long, skeleton-like fingers reaching for her—and she lashed out with the hammer.

The tip of the weapon hit home, demolishing the face. The ghost spun back, screaming.

"Not so fast," Asa shouted as she followed through and swung the iron hammer at the phantom again, forcing it to flee, stumbling, back into the protection of the mist.

Then something grabbed Asa's shoulder.

"I'll show you, you stupid ghost," she cried as she twisted herself skillfully out of the phantom's grasp and slammed the hammer into the lost soul's skull. "I'm not going to let you kill me—"

The blunt end of the hammer burst through the cranium and the metal was now stuck fast, deep inside the skull. The figure collapsed with a gurgling sound and lay convulsing at Asa's feet, blood gushing out over the tips of her shoes and sinking into the sand.

Asa realized something wasn't quite right. "What the hell—?" She bent down to examine the ghost.

The fog lifted slowly and it became clear that the figure collapsed at her feet was no ghost, but a human in disguise. The man had transformed himself into a ghoul by means of an elaborate costume.

She pulled the fabric away and saw the shattered bone where the hammer was lodged. It was Martin, her coworker; the microphone he'd used to activate the loudspeaker at his waist had distorted his voice. Now it hung, broken, on his jaw. There was little point in checking for a pulse.

Asa began to realize that the other figure hadn't been a ghost, either. It, too, was human, and decidedly mortal.

Dismayed, she rushed back to the spot where she had beaten off her first attacker. She did not have to search for long. The girl could see from the scuffs and blood splatters that the other victim must have dragged himself a few yards further on. He lay in the sand, smashed face upward, with splinters of bone piercing the skin. The battered features looked grotesque, inhuman. There was blood streaming from the ears and the nose, and one eye had burst open. The man's headset mouthpiece had been slammed right into his teeth, and there were broken stumps showing.

It could be Bernard, one of Martin's buddies, the sound techie for the Ghost Ride, but there was so much blood that Asa couldn't be sure. She remembered he'd once threatened to play a trick on her—he'd said he wanted to make her so afraid she'd crap herself.

Looked like it had all gone disastrously wrong, for him and for Martin.

"Hell." She glanced at her filthy sweater, her bloodied hands and the glistening hammer with strands of hair still sticking to it— Martin's hair.

Nobody was ever going to believe her.

At the very least she'd be banged up for ages in custody while they tried to fathom exactly what had happened. And her boss would be in trouble, too, for employing her illegally. Perhaps he'd be so scared that he'd just deny he'd ever met her . . .

Asa decided to take the simple way out. It was the easiest thing in the world for someone who didn't officially exist and who had no fixed address to just disappear.

She sent her boss a quick text, explaining and apologizing for everything, expressing her distress at the two deaths, then she collected her things and set off.

She'd been working on the Ghost Ride for such a long time, and now, thanks to her and to a misunderstanding, the show sported a couple of genuine lost souls.

Ten kilometers south of Hannover, Germany

"So, do you do this a lot, bombing up the autobahn in the dead of night?" Asa was hitchhiking again, as she'd so often done in the past. She was enjoying the luxury of stretching her legs out in the roomy limo. Her kit was stowed in the trunk of the car, and Angelika, a blond in a bright red business suit, turned out to be a film director, and really easy to talk to. She'd picked Asa up at the last motorway service station, offering to take her to Hannover. It wouldn't be far to Hamburg from there.

Angelika nodded. "It's always easier driving at night. There's no traffic on the autobahn and the Merc does a cool 220 k.p.h., no bother. You cover the distances in no time at all."

"That's quite a lifestyle."

"Yup, always fast and dangerous."

"Dangerous?" Asa asked with a grin. "Why?"

"Well, a tire blow-out at 220 and you've had it." Angelika gave her a sidelong glance. "Doesn't the thought scare you?"

"No—it's exciting. How about going a bit faster?" She grinned.

Asa had never been afraid of taking lifts with strangers. So far there had been only two disconcerting situations. Once there'd been a young student who was high as a kite and really not fit to drive at all, and then another time the guy had insisted on sex as payment for the ride. But Asa knew how to look after herself—the many and varied jobs she'd done had given her quick reactions, and in spite of her slim build she was strong and used to defending herself. The guy who tried to get it on with her got his comeuppance with a few sharp jabs high and a well-aimed blow lower down. He'd even ended up giving her 500 euros not to go to the police about him.

Angelika laughed. "I don't get passengers saying that very often."

"Do you give rides to hitchhikers a lot?" Asa was loving watching the landscape fly past. The speedometer showed 181 k.p.h.

"From time to time." The woman nodded to the sign for the motorway junction. "Nearly there. Do you need a hotel?"

Asa hesitated. "I . . ." Her finances weren't looking great.

Angelika must have been reading her thoughts. "If you like, you can stay with me," came the surprise offer. "I've got a spare room. Then tomorrow, shower, breakfast and on your way to Hamburg."

"Oh, that's really nice of you!" Asa jumped at the opportunity. "Tell me, what's your most recent film?"

"*Night of the Corpses, Part 11*," Angelika replied proudly. "DVD production, a classic splatter-horror. We sold 150,000 copies and it's in all the video shops." She took the exit to Hannover into an obviously well-to-do suburb. "A lot of it was filmed at my house, in the cellar."

"Really? What fun!"

"That's what I thought. There are still a few extras hanging around. They sort of suit the place. You never know when you might need them again." Angelika pulled up in front of an impressive-looking mansion and got out of the car.

She led the way into the building, where it was as silent as the sandstone caves had always been after the last visitor had left. Asa was still upset about the way Martin and Bernard had died, but it hadn't been her fault. Unsurprisingly, her boss had not responded to her text.

Angelika switched on the light. "Welcome!"

The spotlights in the hallway picked out gruesome specimens displayed in niches or on pedestals; there were glass jars containing human and animal remains: malformed fetuses, hydrocephalic brains, the embryo stages of Siamese twins, misshapen body parts. And no fewer than four skeletons—one of them giant-size, one of them tiny, one twisted and another one bent nearly double—stood in huge display cabinets. It looked as if the doors would open any second for the bones of the dead to hurl themselves out onto the living.

Asa put down her duffel bag and clapped her hands with glee. "Wow! What a collection. Where did you get it all?"

Angelika blinked in astonishment. "Aren't you even a little bit . . . well, taken aback?"

"No. Should I be?"

The horror film director gave a loud laugh. It sounded cruel, like an archetypal film villain. "Well, in that case, I've got an idea. What would you think of spending the night in the room we made the films in?"

"Why not?" Asa took a look around, drinking in her impressions. This would all have been great for a new level at the Ghost Ride, but of course, unfortunately . . . It occurred to her that one day, maybe, she might open her own Horror Park—one with a built-in heart attack warning.

"It might be horrible."

"Doesn't bother me."

Angelika folded her arms and all of a sudden her eyes grew ice-cold and murderous. "Let's say, if you stick it out till morning, I'll give you 1,000 euros."

Asa regarded her hostess with surprise. "I'll win that bet at all events—unless there's something down there that's going to kill me."

Angelika shook her head and led her through the lobby, going past the glass displays to the back of the hall where there was a heavy metal door secured with an electronic lock. She tapped in the code and the door swung open. Neon lighting clicked on automatically and the stairs became visible. There were splashes of blood on the steps, and a sickly-sweet smell—like the smell of decay. Warm air streamed up, and there was a distant roar, as if from a huge fire.

Asa was reminded of the gas burners in the workshop. "It looks as if your cleaners haven't been very thorough," she murmured, and she went down the steps, her duffel bag over her shoulder. "See you in the morning. Bacon and eggs."

"What?"

"For my breakfast." Asa turned round, grinning. "I'll be hungry."

Angelika looked at her in surprise, one hand playing with the pendant that hung around her neck. The metal door clanged shut and the locking mechanism clicked into place.

The brown-haired girl went down slowly, noting how the smell of decay increased with each step she took. There were even more bloodstains down here. It looked as if someone had chucked a load of intestines down the stairs—or people, perhaps, with open wounds. Otherwise Asa couldn't explain the mess. The smell was appalling.

When she reached the tiled area at the bottom of the stairs the sight took her breath away: in the cold neon light she saw eleven naked corpses in various stages of decay hanging from the ceiling. Some were strung up, as if on a gallows, and some had been suspended, skewered on sharp meat-hooks.

The dead bodies twisted slowly as they hung there, blind eyes fixed on the young woman below. Their gray flesh showed deep cuts and ax wounds and was covered in mold. Coagulated blood that had dripped down was black and sticky, like jam; bellies were bloated with the expanding internal gases and some had even burst open. Evil-smelling fluids seeped down the legs, forming stinking puddles on the floor.

Asa sighed. That made clear where the awful smell was coming from. She'd never be able to sleep with that stink.

But between the hanging cadavers she could see a bed, made up with clean fresh linen. It was worth a try.

The girl put her duffel bag down on the duvet cover and investigated her surroundings.

She soon found where the roaring sound was coming from: there was a central-heating furnace in the next room. It was computer-operated, but there was a large drop-door that could be opened to shovel in coal.

In the tiled room Asa found a tap, a wide roll of heavy-duty cling-film, a hosepipe and some cleaning fluid. The detergent didn't smell bad at all.

She soon had a plan. She estimated the time at her disposal. It was shortly before midnight now; if she put her back into it, she'd be finished in an hour and could get a good night's sleep. She hadn't made any promises to the film producer about not altering the state of the room. The deal was whether she could stick it out down there all night. She wouldn't be losing that bet.

Asa took the cling-film and wrapped herself up in it, clothes and all, as protection against the noxious fluids from the corpses. One-by-one she lifted the dead bodies down from the ceiling. She assumed Angelika must have stolen them from a cemetery. Weirdo horror-film-woman freak.

She didn't find it hard to drag the bodies, male and female, over to the furnace. One cadaver at a time was pushed into the roaring fire to roast in the flames. The ghastly smell in the cellar lessened.

As she was heaving the last of the corpses in through the furnace door, the young man turned his head. His blinded eyes were fixed on Asa.

"Thank you for letting us all find rest," he said, speaking through cracked and blackened lips oozing dark blood like thick oil. "Avenge us, and you will receive a greater reward still."

The man's legs were already alight and flames were licking up at the rest of the body that Asa was still carrying. She was holding a ghost in her arms: a real live dead ghost—no imitation this time. Fantastic! It was so exciting, such a turn-on. "What do you mean?"

"Angelika murdered us—we were all hitchhikers, like you. She took us home and made films with us, horrible films. We were tortured to death. Then she used what was left of us as props for her next films," the dead man said. "Kill her—or you'll suffer the same fate!"

Fire spread, crackling, over the rotten flesh, consuming it. The corpse uttered one long last cry before Asa dropped him into the inferno. She clanged the furnace door shut.

She didn't succumb to panic, or rush around like a headless chicken. The important thing was to get some sleep now so that she'd be strong enough to stand up to the film director in the morning.

She quickly set about hosing the juices from the rotten cadavers down the drain, then she took off her cling-film protection and hurled it into the furnace. After that she dispensed cleaning fluid liberally into every corner of the room, filling the whole place with the fragrance of oranges.

For her own security she took a length of nylon thread out of her kit and used the meat-hooks to fasten it like a tripwire across the stairs. She hung the rest of the sharpened S-shaped hooks off the bed-rail.

Satisfied, Asa lay down, in a clean, warm environment that smelled of citrus.

A loud crash woke her.

She sat bolt upright, and saw Angelika getting up from where she'd tripped over the nylon thread. There was a shattered video camera on the tiles, and a case containing knives and surgical instruments had burst open, shedding its wickedly-sharp contents all over the floor.

The film director was wearing a long butcher's apron and metal-ringed gloves, the sort used to protect against slipping knives when working with carcasses.

Angelika pushed herself to her feet with a curse and grabbed a meat cleaver and a scalpel. When she fell, her pendant had slipped outside the apron: it was oval, made of gold, with a symbol engraved upon it. Asa knew at once that the dead man had not lied to her. She indeed was to have been the next victim.

She jumped up from the bed, seizing the hammer she'd concealed under her pillow. "It was bacon and eggs I ordered for breakfast," she said in greeting. "Not my own execution."

"What have you done with my corpses?" The film director was baffled. "And why is everything so *clean*?"

Asa gestured toward the furnace with the hammer. "I cremated them, and then I tidied up. Otherwise I couldn't have got any sleep. They told me you'd killed them—hitchhikers, like me." She twirled the hammer in her hand, her heart beating faster. The sight of those deadly blades coming at her was a stronger stimulus than any espresso.

"But I needed them to make *Night of the Corpses, Part 12!*" shrieked Angelika, leaping toward Asa.

The girl swerved out of her attacker's path, fending off the chopper blow with her hammer. The sound of metal clashing against metal was exaggerated by the tiled surfaces of the killing room.

Angelika stabbed and chopped, fast as lightning, but Asa stayed unruffled, parrying or avoiding blows with agility, skillfully turning aside to snatch up a meat-hook, which she rammed into her opponent's wrist. She did not let go of the other end.

The other woman screamed out, dropping the scalpel, and in the same instant she was hurled backward by a powerful kick in the chest. As she was still attached by the meat-hook, she did not travel far.

Asa dropped, dragging the film director down and over, rolling on top of her and driving the free end of the giant meat-hook into the woman's back so that her right arm was anchored to her own body, the cleaver dropped by her nerveless fingers.

"Going to kill me, were you?" The girl hammered repeatedly at the woman's left shoulder until it cracked. "I'll teach you—"

Angelika screamed in pain.

Using half a dozen of the meat-hooks, Asa neatly fixed her opponent's legs together and clamped her arms to her body. Blood flowed from where the sharp ends of the hooks had been driven into the woman's torn flesh, but Asa was not overly sympathetic. "I'll give the police a tip-off," she announced. "I'm sure they'll soon get the picture. They'll find all the evidence they need."

"Let me go," whimpered the filmmaker. "Please—I've got money—"

"I'll be taking that anyway. And the ghosts promised me a further reward." Asa forced the ends of two more hooks through the skin under the woman's collarbones, making Angelika moan in agony. "You wait here for the police." With surprising strength, Asa dragged the woman over to the bed and from there attached her to one of the ceiling fixtures from which the corpses had been suspended.

Angelika screamed at the top of her lungs, spinning on the hooks, blood flowing down over her shoes from all the incisions and forming a sticky puddle on the freshly cleaned floor.

Asa shouldered her duffel bag and left the cellar. She conducted a thorough search of the mansion and pocketed several thousand euros in cash she found in a desk drawer.

As she was crossing the lobby, passing the display cases and the glass jars of curiosities, one of the containers started to glow, and then shifted, as if moved by an unseen hand.

The jar crashed to the ground in front of the girl, revealing a human rib cage; in the middle of the bones something shimmered metallically.

Is this the ghosts' reward for me? Asa bent down and picked up two silver brass knuckles, each with beautifully engraved patterns. The business edge of each weapon was encrusted with sharp-edged, skin-splitting diamond fragments.

She couldn't understand the symbols, but she was sure this was indeed her gift from the dead. She wiped the artifacts clean and put them in her pocket. These would be more use to her than a hammer.

The girl disguised her voice to call the police and then hurried away from the ghoulish mansion.

It would just be Angelika's bad luck if the police did not open the cellar door in time to find and arrest her while she was still alive.

The murder victims would all be rubbing their ghostly hands with glee.

Germany, two kilometers south of Hamburg

". . . so her soul will still be hanging around in the cellar as we speak, suspended on those pointy meat-hooks." Asa wound up the horror story she had improvised to entertain the long-distance truck driver she was sitting next to in the cab of his thirty-two-ton truck. She was in her element.

"Epic! That's some story!" Charon, as he'd said he liked to be known, shouted with laughter and slammed out a double fanfare on the truck's horn in appreciation.

He was old enough to be her father, and looked like Lemmy from Motörhead, except just a little more debauched. His arms and throat were covered in tattoos indicating a penchant for violence and an interest in the occult. It didn't bother Asa.

"You're a tough one," he crowed, laughing. "You know what? If it'd been me in that cellar, I'd've shit meself."

"Not me." She reached behind her and grabbed a sandwich out of her lunch pack: tasty wholemeal bread and a can of Coke, courtesy of the last service station.

"You mean, you really weren't frightened?" Charon gaped. "Any normal person would have been scared witless!"

"Not me," Asa insisted with a grin.

"Show-off!"

"No, really. That's just how I am. I'm never scared at all, whether it's bungee jumping or white-water rafting or being face-to-face with a poisonous snake or if someone dares me to eat blowfish. It used to drive my parents mad. I was always plunging headlong into the next adventure." She politely suppressed a burp the Coke had given her. "I just think it's all . . . exciting. My brother, on the other hand—he's the quiet one. He runs an upmarket restaurant in Hamburg—it's called Chagall. Ever been there?"

"Do I look like I go to fancy restaurants?" Charon glanced over at her. His expression had changed and he had a nasty look about him. "Right, then, Fräulein Fearless—what if I held a knife to your throat and raped you?" The lights in the cab dimmed.

"I'd smash your face in." Asa grinned. "You planning on it?" She finished her last mouthful of sandwich and wiped her hands clean on her trouser-legs. "Okay, so are you going to try?"

Charon's eyes took on a yellowish gleam and the tattoos grew brighter, as if burning into his flesh. One of the ink designs was exactly like the symbol on Angelika's pendant. The pattern became more prominent. His skinny fingers clutched the steering wheel, bonier than ever, as the fingernails started to sprout. "I'll violate your body and I'll swallow up your soul," he growled.

The truck with its cargo of chemicals was plowing up the autobahn at a good 100 k.p.h., heading straight at the truck in front.

Asa grimaced. "Keep your eyes on the road, or you'll have nobody left to violate."

Charon gave a dirty laugh. Blue flames shot from out of his mouth and played around Asa, surrounding her, but not burning. "I'll fuck you so hard you won't know what's—"

Asa did not intend to end her days by crashing into the backend of some random vehicle. She slipped one of the brass knuckles over her fingers and hit Charon full in the face, breaking his nose. He screeched like a stuck pig as dark-red blood spurted out of the ruined flesh of his face. Suddenly the tattoos all went pale.

She gave him a second blow to be on the safe side, just so he'd know who he was dealing with, this time on the mouth, driving back those blue flames.

Charon fell back, half-conscious.

"There you are, you see." Asa leaned over and grabbed the wheel. She indicated as per the Highway Code and pulled out into the fast lane to overtake the slower vehicle. "That's exactly what would happen if you tried anything," she explained with a laugh as she wiped the bloodied knuckle-duster clean on his shirt.

Charon gave a hesitant nod and pulled himself together, once again taking control of the wheel and driving on as if nothing had happened. But he was bleeding heavily, all over his shirt, his pants and the nice seat cover. It took a long time for the wound to start to heal, but eventually he looked like a normal man again.

Asa did not worry about the blue flames, the glowing eyes and the strange thing that had happened to the tattoos. Stuff like that happened to her occasionally. She seemed to imagine these things sometimes. *Must have been working on the Ghost Ride too long,* she said to herself.

Charon set her down when they got to the container port in Hamburg. As he pulled away, Asa noticed he was talking into his cell phone while quickly glancing her way. He was probably telling another truck driver about some girl who meant what she said when her answer was no.

Asa had the address of her brother's Hamburg restaurant memorized. He'd be glad to see her after all these years—and she had sufficient cash in her pocket to treat them both to the most expensive items on the menu and still have enough left over for a generous tip for the staff. Imagine their faces! This was going to be some evening.

It was just after three o'clock in the afternoon, so she thought it might be a good idea to find a hotel near the restaurant before she splashed out on the evening meal.

She sauntered off, looking for the nearest subway station, or perhaps a taxi. She passed a snack bar, and decided she fancied a coffee.

She entered the empty café and ordered a double espresso, some mineral water and, because they looked so good, a doughnut with chocolate filling.

As the machine got to work and churned out the coffee. Asa smiled at the man behind the counter, pushing the strands of brown hair out of her face. "Always as quiet as this?"

"Everyone's at work," he replied. "It'll fill up at five."

"I see." Asa looked round in surprise and couldn't really believe it. "So you'll take a break?"

The young man merely sniffed.

Asa took a seat in the corner with a view of the port, relishing the sight of all the big ships. It made her want to go on a long journey. Perhaps she'd stow away, go to a foreign land; that would be exciting—a real challenge. China—that'd be the place.

But that would have to wait till after the meal in Chagall with her brother.

Somebody came to sit near her—she could hear the rustle of a jacket as whoever it was moved closer.

Asa stopped looking at the huge barges in the port and turned in surprise to the two uninvited guests, then she looked around the café. Music was coming out of the loudspeakers, but the place was as empty as ever. There was no earthly reason for this older man and his younger female companion to sit at her table. There was plenty of room elsewhere, so there was certainly no excuse for their pushing up so close.

"If you'd just let me by?" she asked politely, getting to her feet. "I'll find somewhere else to sit."

The man sitting opposite her produced a chilly smile and did not move. He was wearing an expensive pin-striped suit and his aristocratic features were framed by an elegant beard. His hands were in glacé leather gloves, revealing the bones of his fingers; in his right hand he held a cane which bore a picture of a glowing-eyed dragon embossed on the head.

The black-haired woman with him, about Asa's own age, did not move, either. She wore a pleasant perfume—a warm, spicy fragrance, which for some reason reminded Asa of a fiery smithy. Her clothing was light; she was dressed in red and black, very stylish— her shapely figure and impressive breasts were shown off to advantage. Her face was flawless, the lips full and curved. For a kiss from those lips men would surely have braved any danger, any battlefield. But most normal people would have been repelled by the cold light in her eyes. Asa, on the contrary, was enchanted by her gaze—it was like love at first sight.

Asa sat down again.

She was in no mood for an argument and the doughnut looked delicious, so she stayed where she was and started to sip her espresso. She took a bite from the doughnut. The mysterious visitors would let her know what they wanted in due course. Or perhaps they were the local crazies, on the lookout for their next victim.

But the filling was coagulated blood, oozing out of the dough-nut, and it tasted foul.

Revolted, Asa spat out what she was eating and went to rinse her mouth out with coffee—but again all she tasted was blood. She spat the liquid back into the cup.

The man sitting opposite gave a quiet laugh. "If you want to complain to the manager, look no further. That's me." He sketched a polite bow in her direction. "Barabbas Prince."

Asa was considering whether to try the mineral water, but she supposed it would probably taste of urine. "Now I know why no one comes here." She put the doughnut back down on the plate.

The woman gave a low, enticing laugh, and Asa caught herself wondering what it would be like to kiss that full mouth. She had never before felt such a strong attraction, either for a man or a woman. "She's got a sense of humor, Father."

"Not really. I'm just making deductions." Asa put her hand in her pocket and slipped the silver brass knuckles on, in case the situation escalated.

Barabbas Prince laid his arm along the upholstered back of the bench, then leaned forward in a lordly and condescending manner. "You are a girl who knows no fear, I understand."

Asa shrugged. She saw the man had a pin in the lapel of his jacket with the same design she had noticed in the trucker's tattoos and on the film director's pendant. They must all belong to the same organization, though probably not all at the same level of membership. This man Prince would surely have platinum status. "Who says so?"

"Truck drivers you've had rides with. And directors whose cellars you've slept in," he answered, a touch of amusement in his voice. "You will do me a favor." Prince's snakelike eyes narrowed. "No, three favors. But the rewards are high. Fearless as you are, you should be able to cope with these tasks easily."

"No. Why should I?"

"Because otherwise he'll kill your brother," the young woman broke in.

"There are not many restaurant managers in the Chagall who look a lot like you," the man added as his companion held out a cell phone to Asa. On the display she could see her brother, bound and gagged.

"My father is generous if his wishes are met," whispered the raven-haired beauty. "All the gold you could wish for."

Asa looked at the photos and surreptitiously removed the brass knuckles from her hands. She believed every word Barabbas Prince was saying. There would be no reason for him to lie. Also no point in her offering resistance to these two without first knowing where they were keeping her brother. "Three favors," she repeated. "Go on."

The man laughed and twirled his walking cane so that the eyes of the embossed dragon on its head shimmered. "We'll fly you to Leipzig in a private jet. There you'll spend three days in different locations. My daughter will give you your instructions."

"You're to spend the night in each of these places," the woman put in.

"And I'll be doing what, exactly?" Asa felt confused.

"Nothing. All you have to do is stay there. And survive." Prince looked her up and down. "If you succeed, you'll be the first to do so."

"Why is that?"

"The others all died." The daughter stared at Asa intently, the corners of her mouth lifting slightly. Then she stopped. Perhaps she had been watching for Asa to react, one way or another. Her expression changed to one of surprise and curiosity. "Of fear," she added as an afterthought.

"Ah." Asa's mouth still held the disgusting taste of blood. "And what guarantee do I have that you won't kill my brother while I'm there? Or afterward?"

Barabbas stopped twirling his cane and the embossed dragon's head pointed directly at Asa. "There's the snag. You'll have to accept my word of honor, won't you?"

Asa looked at his daughter. "She goes with me. She's my security." Asa stretched out her hand. "Agreed?"

The black-haired woman laughed out loud. "No way—!"

"Done," said Barabbas, silencing his astonished daughter's outburst. "She will remain at your side, as far as this is practicable." He shook Asa's hand.

"I'll come up with something. She gets whatever happens to my brother."

"Father!" exclaimed the black-haired woman in protest.

But the man got to his feet. The deal had been done. "I'll take you both to the airport. When you are in Leipzig, you'll be in charge."

The woman jumped up and grabbed his arm. "But, Father," she implored, "how can you—?"

There was no warning when he struck out with his cane. The heavy dragon-head struck her a calculated, glancing blow on the left cheek, enough to make her cry out and stagger back, her black hair flying up round her head in a dark corona.

Asa caught the young woman in her arms and breathed in the heady fragrance.

Barabbas pointed the end of the cane at his daughter's stomach. "Obey me, Bathseda! Soon we shall have reached our goal, after a thousand long years. Have a care to remember that you serve a higher cause than your own vanity." With that he left them and went over to the door—and seemed to dissolve into thin air as he left the café.

All of a sudden a limousine with smoked-glass windows appeared as if from nowhere.

Bathseda straightened up and shook off Asa's hands. "Let's go," she hissed, and the sound of her voice made the server at the counter give a strangled cry as he fell to the floor in a faint. Again she looked at Asa in surprise, because the girl appeared to be completely unaffected. Bathseda opened her mouth, but said nothing.

I can't help it! Asa stepped forward and to her own astonishment planted a kiss full on those tantalizing lips. The taste was amazing—it was certainly a thrill to kiss Bathseda. A feeling like static electricity coursed through Asa's body.

With a shattering crash all the windows in the café imploded as jagged glass splinters flew through the air, just missing the two women and burying themselves in the upholstery or into the walls.

Bathseda pushed Asa away. "How dare you—?" She stumbled backward, then staggered blindly toward the doorway to leave the building, not realizing that, with all the glass gone, she could have exited anywhere.

Asa felt like she had wings on her heels; she had superpowers—she could do *anything*. She would master the tasks they set her, and she would save her brother. As she picked up her duffel bag and got into the car next to the fascinating ebony-haired woman, it occurred to her that she was only having this adventure because she had killed a couple of people by mistake. What else could possibly happen to her?

Leipzig, Germany

"This is where you're going to spend the night." Bathseda pointed to a floodlit monstrosity of a building positioned in front of a large rectangular pool. It reared up into the darkening sky like some dire threat made manifest.

The two young women were standing at the far end of the water basin, about two hundred yards away from the building.

Asa had to admit that it was impressive. There were enormous stone sculptures at the top of the memorial, of warriors leaning on huge swords. The whole place had a martial air and epitomized the aesthetic of a bygone era, but this did not detract from the powerful visual effect.

Asa had seen the monument once before, but could not remember what it was for. "What is that?"

"The Völkerschlachtdenkmal—it commemorates the dead of the Battle of Leipzig." Bathseda was wearing a black coat with red stripes down the sides, which only emphasized her slim figure. "It is dedicated to those who died in the Battle of the Nations. Austria, Prussia, Russia and Sweden formed an alliance to combat the French. Napoleon's troops suffered a bitter defeat here." She gazed at the monument in respect. "This pool is known as the Lake of Tears for the Fallen. The building itself serves as the funeral urn for all their lost souls."

"An urn?"

"The souls of the fallen soldiers are housed here. It is their receptacle, since they are prevented from entering either Heaven or Hell."

"How many lost souls are we talking about here?"

"A hundred and twenty thousand. None of them was innocent enough or cruel enough to be assigned to one side or the other. That is the irony of mediocrity—you get nothing." Bathseda moved off. "Come on. You have to be there before midnight."

"Because?"

"Because that's when the transformation begins, and the dead take over the halls. Your task is to spend the night there. In the crypt. I know a secret entrance."

Asa followed the other girl, walking along the narrow path at the edge of the pool. She was aware they were alone there. This was certainly not a coincidence. She looked up at the monument again, guessing its height to be about three hundred feet. "Where's the way in?"

"By the steps. You press a certain area on the stonework of the archangel Michael and a hidden door opens." Bathseda had reached the platform in front of the statue. The figure, portrayed as a medieval knight complete with sword and shield, towered above them, as if defending the monument, or perhaps preventing the souls of the dead from escaping. To the right and to the left there was a pair of carved reliefs, three feet square, showing the archangel in a chariot on the battlefield surrounded by warring Furies. There was a door set into the base of the statue, but this did not appear to be the secret entrance.

Asa stopped short at the top of the steps leading to the Lake of Tears. "I assume you're not coming in with me?"

"No. I don't want to die." Bathseda grinned and her icy-blue eyes radiated an attraction Asa found irresistible. Against all odds, this must be the thing called love.

"But I'm afraid I can't leave you unsupervised. You're my security hostage."

"If you don't get inside right now, you won't complete the task and your brother will die," Bathseda countered. "That's what's known as a dilemma." In a feat of superhuman strength she catapulted herself up from where she was standing to land on the statue's shoulder, her coattails fluttering out behind her. She pressed down on the lower half of the grim-faced figure's visor and there was a loud click, revealing a narrow opening in the wall behind the archangel's shield.

"Go through! And stay in the crypt until sunrise," came the instruction, before Bathseda leaped back down from the angel's shoulder, landing at Asa's feet.

"Is that all?"

"That's all."

Asa grasped Bathseda's wrist. "Wait for me while I tackle the first task."

Bathseda chuckled, covering her mouth with her free hand, unable to hide her amusement. Then she burst out laughing. "And why would I do that?"

"Because I say so. And because your father agreed."

"I couldn't care less."

"Then I'll have to make you."

The other woman suddenly looked deadly earnest, and her eyes took on that expression that Asa was so drawn to. "You have no idea who or what I am," she whispered. "Nothing can stop me. There is nothing that can force me to do anything!"

Asa, without being seen, had managed to slip one of the brass knuckles onto her right hand and she now dealt the black-haired girl a sudden blow to the cheek, finely calculated in strength and not violent enough to kill.

Bathseda gave a cry of surprise; the engravings on the weapon glowed brightly and she fell unconscious into Asa's waiting arms. The power of the magical artifact had proved stronger than she was.

Asa laid the other girl down gently in a sheltered corner and placed her own coat over the inert figure. Then she clambered up the statue to enter the monument. The narrow door behind the shield gave on to steps that led down to the waiting crypt of the Völkerschlachtdenkmal.

* * *

The girl passed through a hidden entranceway into the Hall of the Dead. Behind her the door slid into place and then disappeared as if it had never existed.

Asa looked around the vaults of this symbolic grave with its mysterious illumination. In the center of the hall there was a bronze memorial plate set into the floor. Stone warriors stood guard around the chamber walls, their heads bowed. The figures stood in eight groups of two, their sculpted faces earnest and dignified.

Every step Asa took made a sound that echoed back from the roof. The dome of the chamber was far above her. She did not know what was in the gigantic room above the crypt, but she thought she could make out even larger sculptures up there in the shadows.

There was no escape. The proper entrance was locked and the stairs up to the Hall of Fame above the crypt were blocked off.

Asa sat down in the center of the room, on the memorial plate, closed her eyes and waited. She was ready for her confrontation with one hundred and twenty thousand souls.

It was not in her nature to feel any unease. On the contrary, she wanted to know everything they could tell her—how they had lived their lives, what it was like living on as a cursed soul. She was bursting with curiosity. So many different fates, so many individual stories!

And if the souls were not prepared to behave themselves, well— for that circumstance she always had her special brass knuckles . . .

Whistling quietly to herself the next morning, Asa strode past the astonished security guard who was just unlocking and opening up the steel doors to the memorial. She left the crypt feeling more alive and invigorated and happy than she had for a long time.

"Excuse me. Where have you just come from?" asked the man in surprise.

"You can see where I've been," she answered blithely.

He took a look inside the circular crypt, noticing that the stone figures seemed to have lost their usual mournful appearance. He was also aware of a change in the atmosphere in the room. "You spent the night in here?" Asa nodded. "But . . . the ghosts? The one hundred and twenty lost souls?"

"Oh, so you've heard of them?" She stopped and smiled at him. "I don't know what's supposed to be so terrible about them. We talked all night and they were delighted I was so interested in what they had to say. They were all really nice. And when they'd had a chance to tell their stories they just melted away. We managed to get through everyone's tales by the time the sun came up. My ears are still buzzing."

The guard, a man of about fifty dressed in a cheap gray uniform suit, scratched his head. His expression wavered between surprise and alarm. "Then . . . in that case, the first spell is broken!"

Asa plunged her hands into her pockets. This was getting even more exciting. "What spell is that?"

He leaned forward slightly. "Only a few people are initiated into the secret. The whole town has been under a curse since Doctor Faustus made his pact with Mephistopheles. The town can only be freed from the curse if . . . if a hero turns up, able to complete all the tasks set for them. In my time I've removed several dead bodies from this crypt. None of them managed to get past the first hurdle." He looked the young woman up and down. "Can it be that you are the hero we've been waiting for?"

"Possibly—what do I need to know in order to complete the other two tasks?" She had a vague memory of having read something about Faustus. Wasn't it a play by Goethe? A tragedy? That was all she could remember.

The security guard shrugged. "Nobody knows that. But I'll pray for you. Good-bye for now, although I feel we'll meet again."

Asa thanked him and stepped out of the monument that was now no longer a refuge for lost souls. She hurried down the steps to where Bathseda was still unconscious in the corner.

She awakened the raven-haired beauty with a gentle kiss on the lips.

Bathseda opened her eyes and stared up at her, perplexed.

"Right. What's next?" asked Asa.

"You're . . . still *alive*?" The young woman rubbed her face in amazement, briefly fingering the place where Asa's knuckle-duster had grazed her cheek. "And you knocked me out? How could you possibly do that? No normal human being could do that!"

Asa simply smiled and helped the girl to her feet. "So, what's the next thing I have to do to free my brother?"

Bathseda gave her a long, searching look as if she were struggling to make sense of a thousand wild thoughts, then she grasped Asa's hand and pulled her along. "I'll show you."

They took the limousine back into town, past houses that had seen better days and splendid buildings that had been restored; past dazzling, brightly lit palaces of glass and stubbornly defiant ruins that harked back to darker times. Asa sensed that they were headed into the very heart of Leipzig.

The vehicle suddenly stopped and they got out. The smoked-glass windows gave no clue as to who or what was actually their driver.

Asa and Bethseda made their way through the streets under an already darkening sky, past ancient façades, stone statues and lofty towers, until they arrived at the magnificent entrance to an impressive-looking shopping mall.

Everything was bright: there were cafés and shops full of glittering luxury goods, but the black-haired girl took Asa past a group of figures cast in bronze and down some steep steps leading to Auerbachs Keller.

Instead of going through the main door, Bathseda chose a side entrance giving onto a smallish room which contained only a large wine barrel against the wall and a table and some chairs.

"Wait here for midnight," she instructed. "I'm eager to know whether we'll meet again in the morning."

"What's going to happen?"

Bathseda looked at her. "I don't know. I didn't set the tasks." She turned around, all set to leave.

"What's the story with you and your father?" Asa saw her words had rooted the young woman to the spot.

"What do you mean?" she asked without turning.

"You both behave very strangely," Asa announced. "You can do peculiar things and I feel very odd when you're near me. Then there's the hint you gave—that no normal person could best you in a fight."

Bathseda glanced back provocatively over her shoulder. "If you can work it out, then I am yours." That was all she said. The girl lowered her eyes, and then left the dark room.

Asa looked around and then, with no further ado, made herself comfortable on the table, using her jacket as a pillow. She closed her eyes, needing to recover from an eventful night.

The stories she had been told were still buzzing around in her head. The ghosts had related many different fates, and they had all been speaking at once. It had been very loud and confused, but somehow every single tale had registered in her brain. She could well understand how any normal person would have died of fright.

Asa was not sure, but she had the impression that she had allowed those ghosts to find their rest, although Bathseda had maintained that there was no place for them in either Heaven or Hell.

"She has traveled far, her journey long. Her strange apparel—she looks all wrong." This was said in a loud masculine voice, and it was followed by a chorus of laughter.

Asa thought it best to pretend that she was still asleep. She must have nodded off.

"In truth, my friend, how right you are! The things you see in Leipzig nowadays! We're just like Paris, and our people so cultured," came a second voice, mocking the previous speaker.

"Who do you suppose this stranger is?" asked another.

Asa lay still upon the table, her eyes tight shut. Let these newcomers chatter if they wanted to.

The antiquated manner of their speech indicated these might be more ghosts from a very long time ago. So far as she could work it out, there were four of them, and she soon picked up their names: Frosch, Siebel, Altmayer and Brandner. From the sound of their voices she thought they must be young men.

And suddenly she remembered: they were in Goethe's play! The bronzes she had passed on her way down to Auerbachs Keller had been the students in *Faust*! Could they have been real people, not just invented characters in a drama? Her pulse was now racing with excitement.

Asa opened her eyes and sat up, stretching and pretending she had just woken up.

She looked about and saw four figures gathered around the table. They looked real enough, of flesh and blood, unlike the misty phantoms from the crypt beneath the Völkerschlacht monument.

The quartet were wearing clothes which had been fashionable centuries ago, and they had very odd-looking haircuts, although possibly quite the height of style in their day.

"Wake up, good lady," Brandner called encouragingly. "You shall be our guest—let us offer you a drink!"

"Many are the guests that come, yet most in fear take flight when they of us catch sight," added Frosch.

Brandner helped her down from the table, and Altmayer held out a chair for her. She sat down and smiled at the four students. She was surprised to see a wine-tap set into the table at each of their places, as if the furniture itself was a wine barrel filled with the fermented juices of the vine.

"My thanks. What do you have to offer?"

"Here I have the finest Rhenish wine," announced Frosch, raising his goblet.

Brandner laughed at him. "Champagne is mine! Foaming, sparkling, tastes divine!" He indicated the tap nearest his own seat.

Siebel gave a dismissive gesture. "Fair Fräulein, I offer you Tokaji, Hungary's very best."

Altmayer broke into contemptuous laughter. "The wine I pour will never tire. It's any taste you may desire."

Asa was beginning to realize what her next challenge was going to be—a peculiar kind of wine-tasting. As soon as she removed any of the bungs, one of the various wines described would fill the cup she apparently now held.

The girl quickly racked her brains to consider what the dangers might be, apart from getting really drunk and having a major hangover.

"I can't refuse?"

"No, we insist!" the spirits chorused.

Frosch got up first, offering Asa his seat. "Now, dear lady. Take the cup. You must not spill a single drop."

The other three chuckled, eyeing her expectantly.

Asa stepped over, sat down and held out her goblet. The tap was level with her navel. She hoped the wine would not come shooting out at high pressure, or else it would soak her.

The expressions on the students' faces made her wary. One of them licked his lips, and they all watched her hungrily. Were they waiting for her to make a mistake? Would they attack her if she did?

Asa was excited and in high spirits. She loosened the first bung carefully. "Tell me, friends dear, how long you've been residing here?" She had to grin when she realized she was mimicking their way of speaking.

"Oh, ever since Doctor Faustus and his friend deigned to honor us with their company," answered Brandner, not taking his eyes off her for a second.

"It is as if it were but yesterday," added Altmayer.

"But yet, a whole eternity," sighed Siebel. "How I wish I might return to my own home."

Asa held the cup in position, removed the plug and caught the wine carefully without spilling a drop.

"Go on, go on—fill the goblet to the brim," Frosch whispered in an ugly tone. "To the brim!"

"If you let it spill, with you it will go ill!" warned Siebel with a cruel laugh.

Asa nodded, filled the cup right up and closed off the tap, lifting the wine. "And with you!" Taking long, slow drafts, she drained the alcohol. It wasn't bad at all, but very strong, with an intense aftertaste.

Altmayer looked disappointed. "They nearly all succeed the first time round."

"Let's pop the next cork!" Brandner moved to make way for Asa. "Champagne!"

The students crowded around her as Asa heaved herself with some difficulty into the next chair. Her limbs were heavy and she could already feel the effect of the alcohol. She did not usually have this problem. Ghost wine was apparently strong stuff.

She took more care this time as she attempted to open the champagne. The cup filled with foaming liquid and this time, too, she managed to avoid any spillage. The four ghostly beings were starting to look annoyed.

Despite her efforts, some of the champagne bubbled over the edge of the goblet, flowing down the side and wetting her thumb.

Asa drew in her breath sharply at the dreadful pain. The skin on her thumb went black and a brownish smoke curled up from the wound. The wine had burned her flesh right through to the bone. She nearly wobbled, risking the loss of more of the cup's contents, which would surely have caused grave injury.

Frosch giggled maliciously. "There you are! Burns like hellfire, don't it?"

"We did warn you." Brandner had a diabolical grin on his face. "Now drink it down, all in one go. Inside your throat it won't hurt so."

Asa was very drunk by the time she slammed the empty cup down onto the table. In order not to stumble as she changed seats once more, she held fast to the edge and slid herself along to get to where Siebel was.

She was having difficulty focusing; the four figures looked demon-like. Asa thought it was all getting very intriguing.

What made her furious was that the drink was making her hands shake. This could all get very dangerous. Hadn't the wine in Goethe's play turned to fire when it touched the floor? That meant that if she let a single drop fall, she would be engulfed in flames like a human torch.

Asa fiddled clumsily with the next bung as her fingers slipped, but finally it popped out and she managed to catch the wine in her cup.

The four students were bent over laughing at her. However, their high-spirited enjoyment had an evil, malevolent side—they were hoping that she would fail.

Asa drank down the Tokaji wine, then crawled over the table while the young men screamed with laughter as she fell off the other side, landing with her face under the final wine-tap. She was gasping for breath and felt nauseous, but she reckoned this accursed wine would turn into hellfire if she was sick.

"Now," Altmayer bent down, grabbed her by the hair and pulled her up. "The final cup. *Drink!*"

"And what if I can't?" Asa's words were slurred.

"*Then you will die!*" all four of them roared in unison, laughing hysterically.

"Not nearly ready to do that yet." She hiccoughed, screwed up her eyes and struggled with the last bung. Guessing rather than seeing where the liquid was going, she caught it in the goblet while the ghouls howled and shrieked with anger.

But suddenly she could not drink any more. The stuff smelled like vinegar and she found it abominable.

"That's not . . . wine," she stammered, about to put down her cup in disgust. "You've tricked me."

"No, there's no deceit here, my tap dispenses any drink, my dear," Altmayer contradicted her. "You must have been wishing for vinegar, I think, so now that cupful you must drink."

"Or you fail the whole," Siebel hissed, "and that means the end for you!"

Brandner started a rhythmic slow hand-clap. "Drink, Fräulein, *drink!*" Now they were all egging her on. She could barely bring herself to set the cup to her lips. But there was no choice, unless she wanted to die. And if she died, that would mean death for her brother as well.

Asa shut her eyes and stood up, and though she staggered around in circles, she drank the revolting liquid, though it ran sour down her throat. Mouthful by mouthful, she swallowed it, right up to the last ghastly drop.

"She's done it," screamed Frosch in horror. "That's the Devil's own work!"

"It can't be true," howled Altmayer, pulling out his knife. "It shan't be true. My knife will make short work of you!"

Asa forced her eyes open and hurled the goblet at the wall with a laugh. It broke into pieces. She stuck her hands into her pockets and none too elegantly slipped the brass knuckles onto her fingers. "I have passed the test," she called out in a muffled voice. She could hardly feel her own tongue. That must have been the vinegar. "Now it's your turn to drink my wine. See how you like what I'm going to serve you."

Asa whirled round and crashed both her fists down onto the tabletop.

The diamonds embedded in the silver brass knuckles flared up, and under the mystic strength of the twin artifacts, the piece of furniture shattered into four segments. Wine gushed out of the ruined wood, flooding the little chamber. It was as if an immense dam had suddenly burst.

Miraculously, the torrents of wine spared the young woman, but they caught hold of the four ghostly students, spinning them around and forcing them beneath the surface, so that they all drowned.

"Drink up!" Asa staggered and fell into a chair, laughing, as the maelstrom swirled past with its four ghoulish victims. "Drink up, you rotten . . ." She toppled over in an alcoholic haze and passed out.

By the time that Asa woke up again in that room—lying on the floor this time—there was no sign of the students and not even a puddle of wine to be seen. The shattered table, however, was evidence enough that the events of the night had not been entirely normal.

She got to her feet and found she had neither a raging thirst nor a hangover. The only thing that bothered her was the nasty taste of vinegar that she still had in her mouth.

"Now tell me not to believe in miracles," she quoted from *Faust*, the only line she remembered. She pulled off the sparkling brass knuckles and put them in her pocket as she left the room.

To her surprise she saw the guard from the Völkerschlacht memorial waiting outside for her. He was still in uniform. "I don't believe it!" he exclaimed in delight. "You've broken the second spell!"

"You're stalking me." Asa walked past him. It was Bathseda's face she had wanted to see, not his.

"No, I'm following you," he corrected swiftly, grasping her arm. "People are saying that you've taken up the challenge to remove the curse that Faust and Mephistopheles laid upon the town. You've no idea how long we've all been waiting for this!"

Asa stopped and looked him up and down. "I must get on—to the third test."

The guard nodded eagerly. "Of course! I won't hold you up. My best wishes go with you. All of us, the whole town, we're all rooting for you." Asa was about to walk on, but he stopped her once more. "Tell me one thing. How did you come to take up this challenge?"

"I was forced into doing it," she replied, giving an honest answer.

He looked at her in shock. "How could anyone force you to do anything when you are afraid of nothing?"

"My brother has been kidnapped and I'm to carry out the tasks in exchange for his life."

"Oh, no! I have a terrible feeling—" The guard blanched and took two steps backward. "Would the kidnapper's name be . . . Barabbas Prince?" She gave no answer, but the truth must have been written all over her face. The man wore a horrified expression. "So that devil has found a way—"

His words were interrupted by the arrival of Bathseda.

The man staggered back with a cry as he saw the black-haired woman, and when she turned her gaze on him, he collapsed into a whimpering heap.

"Come, Asa," she said, her voice cold as the North Wind. "We have things to do."

"But he—"

"Don't worry about him." Bathseda looked at Asa, and this time her face showed relief rather than surprise. She was glad to see the brown-haired girl alive. "We'll solve the third test."

In silence they left Auerbachs Keller, walking up the steps and passing the bronze statues portraying Faustus, Mephistopheles and the students.

Asa noticed that the sculptor had omitted one of the students. Brandner, Altmayer and Frosch were all represented, larger-than-life and condemned to live on in metal, if not as ghosts, but Siebel had been omitted.

Bathseda led her out of the shopping mall to where the car was waiting. They climbed into the backseat.

Without exchanging a word they started off, out of the pedestrian zone, through the center of Leipzig and away from the town.

Asa's eyes kept closing. The events of the previous night were demanding their rightful tribute—but suddenly she felt warm soft lips touching her own. She knew, she could smell, that it was Bathseda kissing her. The attraction was now mutual, and Asa gave herself up to the other girl's caresses.

"I've never met anyone like you before," the raven-haired beauty whispered tenderly. "You have won my heart, Asa. Now you must win the last test."

"Will your father honor his part of the bargain?"

Bathseda hesitated. "I suppose so. I am still your hostage."

"Does he value you highly enough?"

Again the other girl hesitated.

That was enough of a response for Asa, before she slipped into deep slumber, broken only by her companion's kisses.

Toward evening Asa opened her eyes and stared out of the car window. The limousine was parked at the edge of a lake. A floodlit church tower rose up from the water, and a floating platform surrounded by railings had been erected around the exterior of the building.

Bathseda was waiting on the pebble-strewn beach, and nearby a motorboat rocked on the rippling waves. The car was buffeted by a strong wind whistling through the surrounding trees, and it caught Bathseda's jet-black hair.

Asa already had an idea what the next challenge was to be—to spend the night in the drowned church.

She stepped out of the car and walked over to Bathseda, who took her hand at once. "This is the Störmthaler See," the girl explained softly. "Once upon a time they quarried coal here. Many villages were sacrificed to the mining, the houses demolished and the people evacuated. That's the story, anyway."

"It's not true?"

"No. The ground here opened up and swallowed the villages, killing everyone. The authorities started the myth about mining. They brought in excavators and diggers to explain the hole. Many years later they flooded the whole blighted region."

"Nobody asked questions about the people who used to live here?"

"No. All sorts of lies were made up to cover their disappearance."

Bathseda pointed to the artificial island. "That's where the parish of Magdeborn originally had their church. It was the first building to go. What you see here is a monument to mark the place where the disaster began." She gave Asa a long kiss, placing a hand gently on the nape of the other girl's neck to pull her closer. "Survive the night. But be warned—there's a terrible monster that lives in the lake. It is the reason that the ground around here opened up in the first place. Even today it sometimes swallows the occasional careless swimmer, or a fisherman along with his boat."

Asa nodded and strode over to the motorboat, the wind tugging at her body and whipping her hair across her face.

Stepping in to the small craft, she started the outboard motor and was quickly chugging across the choppy surface. The increasingly powerful waves crashed against the hull of the boat and spray hit her face, blinding her momentarily. Asa imagined the monster hidden by the murky waters and creeping along the lakebed beneath her fragile nutshell of a craft. The idea gave her a thrill.

She was getting closer to the dark island with its fake bell tower. It was about forty-five feet tall, a floating construction made of wood and plaster anchored by chains to the bed of the lake.

Asa brought the boat alongside the platform and tied up to the railings. She stepped quickly across the wooden boards and entered the tower.

Immediately she noticed wet footprints on the dusty floor. Then the darker patches.

Turning around, she saw the guard from the memorial lying out of breath and exhausted among upturned chairs. His suit was dripping wet—he must have swum over to the island. There was blood pouring from a gaping wound in his side.

She hurried over and knelt down next to the badly injured man. "What on earth—?"

"You must not succeed in this final test," he groaned, obviously in intense pain. "Faust's curse is as nothing compared to what will happen if you do."

"But my brother and I will die if—"

"Your lives are not important," the guard interrupted her, clinging hard to her arm. "Whatever happens, Barabbas must not gain control of Leipzig."

"Just who is he?"

"You don't recognize the name? He is one of the criminals Pontius Pilate set free in place of Jesus. He is under a curse and cannot die. He's condemned to roam the earth for eternity, doing evil." The man's words came quickly and were difficult to understand. Asa had to concentrate to make sense of what he was saying. "Over the centuries he has made many pacts with fellow demons, but he always broke his promises, and sometimes he was tricked by the devils, too. Mephistopheles is his arch-enemy. If Barabbas were to break the Faustian spell and take control of the town, it would be his greatest triumph."

Asa suddenly wondered just how old Bathseda was. "He and his daughter—"

"She is the daughter of Mephistopheles," the guard interrupted her. "He has tricked her into remaining with him and she has no choice but to keep up the charade." The man coughed and convulsed with pain. "Barabbas will raze Leipzig to the ground to celebrate his victory. Everyone will perish!" His grip on Asa's arm was growing painful. "Fail in this last test, or the whole town and all its people will be destroyed!" A final gasp of breath left his lips and his eyes rolled back.

Asa loosened the dead fingers from her arm. "What shall I do?" she murmured.

Searching through the pockets of the dead man, she found nothing to indicate how the guard had been so well-informed.

The hour of midnight struck above her.

The wind dropped abruptly and the sudden deathly quiet was like that following a disaster, or the final scream of a murder victim.

Asa stepped outside, eager to find out what spectacle might await her.

The whole lake was a luminous jade-green, glowing from below as if the sun had set in a sea of ink. Coils of mist rose and floated over the surface, making her head spin, but she did not waver. She held fast to the platform's railings.

Suddenly the waters divided.

A gargantuan creature shot up from the depths, half-fish, half-monstrosity; something Asa had never even seen in any book before. It displaced the shimmering waters of the lake. Seven ice-gray eyes stared down out of an ugly visage forty feet above her. The jaws opened, revealing rows of long, sharp teeth.

"You dare to measure your strength against mine, wretched human?" the creature thundered.

"Yes, I dare." Asa smiled, even though its booming voice hurt her ears. This was quite some monster—awesome!

"And you are prepared to risk death, worthless worm?" The monstrosity lifted its tentacles and whipped the surface of the lake, sending clouds of spray over her, soaking her through. Waves washed over the boards of the platform.

Yet Asa stood firm. "Yes."

"The cruelest of deaths? The sharpest pain and the worst of tortures?" The monster opened its mouth wider and displayed teeth that were certainly strong enough to crunch through wood.

"If need be."

"You might end up between my fangs. Or I might swallow you whole and you'll rot away in my stomach." The creature was enjoying itself. "And I'll—"

Asa interrupted the beast. "You're wasting my precious time." She was sizzling with excitement. "Get to the point."

The monster rose up further still out of the bubbling water, much taller even than the Völkerschlachtdenkmal. "So you really and truly are willing to risk life and soul in combat with me?" it screamed out. "This is my last warning, puny human!"

Asa nodded firmly, though she had no idea what would happen next. She spat out the lake water she'd had to swallow while being splashed. Not yet loosening her grip on the railings, she slipped the silver brass knuckles onto her fingers. Given the size of the monster, they would probably be too small to have any effect anyway. *Let him swallow me up. I'll punch my way out of his belly!* she thought.

Amazingly, the creature sank back down in front of her very eyes, turning and twisting in the water and sending up huge waves that swamped the man-made island. The tentacles lashed the air close by her, but she kept a tight hold on the railings and stood her ground despite the raging floodwater.

Screaming at the top of its voice, the creature thrashed around in the glowing jade-green waters, sending up more violent waves. It opened its gaping mouth wide to release a ghastly sound, together with the stink of rotting fish and fetid water.

Asa was expecting it to attack her at any second, and she wiped the spray out of her eyes to be ready for it. "Bring it on!" she yelled, competing with the creature's mighty roar.

"I'm going to eat you up!" boomed the monster, racing through the turbulent waves toward her, fast as a torpedo.

Asa could hardly believe her eyes, but . . . the closer her monstrous opponent came, the smaller it appeared to be.

It shrank and shrank until eventually it was the size of a small fish, which catapulted itself out of the lake and landed, flapping wildly, at her feet.

Asa wasted no time, but stamped her foot down on the ridiculously helpless monster, crushing it to slime beneath her heel.

Abruptly the windows of the church tower streamed with brilliant light and the air was filled with the ringing of what sounded like a hundred cathedral bells.

The lake monster fed purely on its victims' fear! Since Asa had never been afraid, not even for a second, the beast had had no power over her and had ceased to exist.

All three ordeals had been successfully withstood!

She jumped into the small boat and started back to dry land, where she hoped to find Bathseda waiting for her.

When she reached the shore she found not only her darling girl but also Barabbas Prince.

He smiled and lifted his cane in greeting, sketching a bow. "How could I ever have doubted you or your love for your brother?" he said sarcastically.

"I carried out all the tasks. Now give him back to me." Asa put her hands in her pockets and was able to slip the brass knuckles on without being observed.

"Oh, I shall. As soon as you've left here," the man replied with a malicious grin. "I can't have anyone near me as bold and fearless as you."

"That's not the deal we made. But I've been told you have a reputation for always breaking your word." Asa approached her startled opponent, pulling her hands out of her pockets and hitting him hard with the magical artifacts. "It's time to teach you some manners!"

Try as he might to avoid her blows, the immortal criminal could not match her strength!

His dragon-headed cane snapped under the girl's violent attack, his bones fractured, piercing him from the inside, and his flesh was slashed by the sharp edges of the jewels. Finally, even his skull burst open as Asa directed ferocious blows to both temples simultaneously. Blood gushed out of his nose and ears and he uttered a ghastly cry.

"I'm not going to let you take over the town!" Asa punched both fists into his face. "This time you will not escape your punishment!"

The sharp diamond tips of the brass knuckles gouged into his eye sockets—and then, with an enormous thunderclap, Barabbas Prince exploded in a puff of smoke! His immortality had suddenly run out, and all that remained were his bloodstained clothes and the broken cane, lying amongst the pebbles beside the lake. The dragon's eyes on the cane glowed with fire for a final time before growing dark.

Asa looked at Bathseda. There was another spell that now needed to be broken. "And as for you," she said, "you promised that you would stay with me if I named your true identity."

The black-haired girl surveyed the pile of bloodied rags and splintered cane in astonishment. "But you know who I am."

"No. He was not your father. You are really the daughter of Mephistopheles."

With a cry of delighted astonishment, Bathseda immediately flung her arms around Asa's neck and covered her companion with kisses. "You have released me!" she cried joyfully. "The curse has finally been lifted!"

Asa embraced her. "And will you still come with me?"

"Yes, yes, yes and three times yes," she answered happily. "Let me tell you this: I have never met anyone braver than you." Bathseda took both Asa's hands in hers. "Now all Barabbas's fortune belongs to you. I can take you to where he hoarded all his treasure—he was immensely rich. You can buy yourself everything you've ever dreamed of—all your wishes can come true!"

Asa only had the one wish. "Do you know where he has been keeping my brother?"

Bathseda nodded. "Of course. We can go there and free him this very instant."

And off they went, together.

* * *

Now listen here to how the story goes:

So this was how the fearless young Asa freed the town of Leipzig from the dreadful curse laid on it by Doctor Faustus and Mephistopheles; how she destroyed the immortal demon Barabbas Prince; how she won the heart of the beautiful Bethseda and, last but not least, how she saved her brother's life.

On top of these successes Asa was heaped with riches and rewards, enough to open her very own Horror Park, in which the main attractions, thanks to the splendid connections she made through Bethseda, were genuine ghosts and demons and monsters, who respected Asa as their mistress because she never for a single moment showed any fear.

Her brother was made the manager of the attraction and visitors came from far and wide to experience the ultimate in bloodcurdling, spine-chilling frights.

Asa's Horror Park soon gained a worldwide reputation for being the most scary place on earth.

But you should also know this: there was a very simple reason why Asa was never afraid.

In fact, she suffered from Urbach-Wiethe syndrome—a very rare brain disease affecting the area known as the amygdala or *corpus amygdaloideum*. And the amygdala, of course, is the seat of fear.

So everything she experienced that would have driven any normal person insane with fear, she experienced as hugely exciting—and very entertaining.

However hard her brother and Bathseda tried to show Asa what it was like to feel fear, they had no earthly chance of success.

But one day, many years later, Asa happened to glance in a mirror—and suddenly she realized: she couldn't live with Bathseda forever. As a mortal woman, she would die someday, she must die someday, some hour, suddenly or slowly, suffering or without warning.

I will die, Asa thought. *And lose my love.*

She shook with horror, and her skin was covered in goose bumps. She gasped and felt as though her heart would burst. Quivering all over, she was nearly sick, she was so upset.

What a revelation—so this was what fear was like!

Then Asa realized that nothing could be more terrible, nothing more cruel, nothing more indescribably awful, than losing the love of her life.

MARKUS HEITZ was born in 1971 and lives in Homburg/Saar, Germany. His debut novel, *Schatten über Ulldart* (the first in an epic fantasy series), won the Deutscher Phantastik Preis (German Fantasy Award) in 2003. Since then, he has won the GFA ten times, more than any other writer. The author of more than thirty novels (seventeen bestsellers in Germany) in all genres, along with two children's books, Heitz's popular series Die Zwerge (The Dwarves) includes *Der Krieg der Zwerge* (*The War of the Dwarves*) and *Die Rache der Zwerge* (*The Revenge of the Dwarves*) and established him amongst Germany's most successful fantasy writers. The series is now translated all over the world, including in Russia, Japan, and China. He is the editor of the science fiction series *Justifiers*, based on the RPG of the same name, and he also wrote the libretto of the musical *Timm Thaler* (aka *The Legend of Tim Tyler: The Boy Who Lost His Laugh*) and produces the German ambient-Gothic band Lambda.

Cinderella

THE WIFE OF a rich man fell sick, and as she felt that her end was drawing near, she called her only daughter to her bedside and said, "Dear child, be good and pious, and then the good God will always protect you, and I will look down on you from Heaven and be near you." Thereupon she closed her eyes and departed.

Every day the maiden went out to her mother's grave, and wept, and she remained pious and good.

When winter came the snow spread a white sheet over the grave, and by the time the spring sun had drawn it off again, the man had taken another wife.

The woman had brought with her into the house two daughters, who were beautiful and fair of face, but vile and black of heart. Now began a bad time for the poor step-child.

"Is the stupid goose to sit in the parlor with us?" they said. "He who wants to eat bread must earn it. Out with the kitchen-wench!" They took her pretty clothes away from her, put an old gray bed-gown on her, and gave her wooden shoes. "Just look at the proud princess, how decked out she is!" they cried, and laughed, and led her into the kitchen.

There she had to do hard work from morning till night, get up before daybreak, carry water, light fires, cook and wash. Besides this, the sisters did her every imaginable injury—they mocked her and emptied her peas and lentils into the ashes, so that she was forced to sit and pick them out again. In the evening, when she had worked till she was weary, she had no bed to go to, but had to sleep by the hearth in the cinders. And as on that account she always looked dusty and dirty, they called her Cinderella.

It happened that the father was once going to the fair, and he asked his two step-daughters what he should bring back for them.

"Beautiful dresses," said one.

"Pearls and jewels," said the second.

"And you, Cinderella," said he, "what will you have?"

"Father, break off for me the first branch which knocks against your hat on your way home."

So he bought beautiful dresses, pearls and jewels for his two step-daughters, and on his way home, as he was riding through a green thicket, a hazel twig brushed against him and knocked off his hat. Then he broke off the branch and took it with him. When he reached home he gave his step-daughters the things which they had wished for, and to Cinderella he gave the branch from the hazel-bush.

Cinderella thanked him, went to her mother's grave and planted the branch on it, and wept so much that the tears fell down on it and watered it. And it grew and became a handsome tree.

Thrice a day Cinderella went and sat beneath it, and wept and prayed, and a little white bird always came on the tree. And if Cinderella expressed a wish, the bird threw down to her what she had wished for.

It happened, however, that the King gave orders for a festival which was to last three days, and to which all the beautiful young girls in the country were invited, in order that his son might choose himself a bride.

When the two step-sisters heard that they too were to appear among the number, they were delighted, called Cinderella and said, "Comb our hair for us, brush our shoes and fasten our buckles, for we are going to the wedding at the King's palace."

Cinderella obeyed, but wept, because she too would have liked to go with them to the dance, and begged her step-mother to allow her to do so.

"*You* go, Cinderella?" said she. "Covered in dust and dirt as you are, and would go to the festival? You have no clothes and shoes, and yet would dance?"

As, however, Cinderella went on asking, the step-mother said at last, "I have emptied a dish of lentils into the ashes for you, if you have picked them out again in two hours, you shall go with us."

The maiden went through the back-door into the garden, and called, "You tame pigeons, you turtle-doves, and all you birds beneath the sky, come help me to pick the good into the pot, the bad into the crop."

Then two white pigeons came in by the kitchen window, and afterward the turtle-doves, and at last all the birds beneath the sky came whirring and crowding in, and alighted amongst the ashes. And the pigeons nodded with their heads and began *pick, pick, pick, pick,* and the rest began also *pick, pick, pick, pick,* and gathered all the good grains into the dish. Hardly had one hour passed before they had finished, and all flew out again.

Then the girl took the dish to her step-mother, and was glad, and believed that now she would be allowed to go with them to the festival.

But the step-mother said, "No, Cinderella, you have no clothes and you cannot dance. You would only be laughed at."

And as Cinderella wept at this, the step-mother said, "If you can pick two dishes of lentils out of the ashes for me in one hour, you shall go with us." And she thought to herself, *That she most certainly cannot do again.*

When the step-mother had emptied the two dishes of lentils amongst the ashes, the maiden went through the back-door into the garden and cried, "You tame pigeons, you turtle-doves, and all you birds beneath the sky, come help me to pick the good into the pot, the bad into the crop."

Then two white pigeons came in by the kitchen-window, and afterward the turtle-doves, and at length all the birds beneath the sky came whirring and crowding in, and alighted amongst the ashes. And the doves nodded with their heads and began *pick, pick, pick, pick,* and the others began also *pick, pick, pick, pick,* and gathered all the good seeds into the dishes. And before half-an-hour was over they had already finished, and all flew out again.

Then the maiden was delighted, and believed that she might now go with them to the wedding. But the step-mother said, "All this will not help. You cannot go with us, for you have no clothes and cannot dance. We should be ashamed of you."

On this she turned her back on Cinderella, and hurried away with her two proud daughters.

As no one was now at home, Cinderella went to her mother's grave beneath the hazel-tree, and cried: "Shiver and quiver, little tree, silver and gold throw down over me!" Then the bird threw a gold and silver dress down to her, and slippers embroidered with silk and silver. She put on the dress with all speed, and went to the festival.

Her step-sisters and the step-mother however did not know her, and thought she must be a foreign princess, for she looked so beautiful in the golden dress. They never once thought of Cinderella, and believed that she was sitting at home in the dirt, picking lentils out of the ashes.

The Prince approached her, took her by the hand and danced with her. He would dance with no other maiden, and never let loose of her hand. And if anyone else came to invite her, he said, "This is my partner."

She danced till it was evening, and then she wanted to go home. But the King's son said, "I will go with you and bear you company," for he wished to see to whom the beautiful maiden belonged.

She escaped from him, however, and sprang into the pigeon-house. The King's son waited until her father came, and then he told him that the unknown maiden had leapt into the pigeon-house. The old man thought, *Can it be Cinderella?*

And they had to bring him an ax and a pickax that he might hew the pigeon-house to pieces, but no one was inside it.

And when they got home Cinderella lay in her dirty clothes among the ashes, and a dim little oil-lamp was burning on the mantle-piece. For Cinderella had jumped quickly down from the back of the pigeon-house and had run to the little hazel-tree, and there she had taken off her beautiful clothes and laid them on the grave. And the bird had taken them away again, and then she had seated herself in the kitchen amongst the ashes in her gray gown.

Next day when the festival began afresh, and her parents and the step-sisters had gone once more, Cinderella went to the hazel-tree and said, "Shiver and quiver, my little tree, silver and gold throw down over me."

Then the bird threw down a much more beautiful dress than on the preceding day. And when Cinderella appeared at the festival in this dress, everyone was astonished at her beauty.

The King's son had waited until she came, and instantly took her by the hand and danced with no one but her. When others came and invited her, he said, "This is my partner."

When evening came she wished to leave, and the King's son followed her and wanted to see into which house she went. But she sprang away from him, and into the garden behind the house. Therein stood a beautiful tall tree on which hung the most magnificent pears. She clambered so nimbly between the branches like a squirrel that the King's son did not know where she was gone. He waited until her father came, and said to him, "The unknown maiden has escaped from me, and I believe she has climbed up the pear-tree." The father thought, *Can it be Cinderella?* and had an ax brought and cut the tree down, but no one was on it.

And when they got into the kitchen, Cinderella lay there among the ashes, as usual, for she had jumped down on the other side of the tree, had taken the beautiful dress to the bird on the little hazel-tree, and put on her gray gown.

On the third day, when the parents and sisters had gone away, Cinderella went once more to her mother's grave and said to the little tree, "Shiver and quiver, my little tree, silver and gold throw down over me."

And now the bird threw down to her a dress which was more splendid and magnificent than any she had yet had, and the slippers were golden.

And when she went to the festival in the dress, no one knew how to speak for astonishment. The King's son danced with her only, and if anyone invited her to dance, he said, "This is my partner."

When evening came, Cinderella wished to leave, and the King's son was anxious to go with her, but she escaped from him so quickly that he could not follow her. The King's son, however, had employed a ruse, and had caused the whole staircase to be smeared with pitch. And there, when she ran down, had the maiden's left slipper remained stuck. The King's son picked it up, and it was small and dainty, and all golden.

Next morning, he went with it to the father, and said to him, "No one shall be my wife but she whose foot this golden slipper fits."

Then were the two sisters glad, for they had pretty feet.

The eldest went with the shoe into her room and wanted to try it on, and her mother stood by. But she could not get her big toe into it, and the shoe was too small for her. Then her mother gave her a knife and said, "Cut the toe off. When you are Queen you will have no more need to go on foot."

The maiden cut the toe off, forced the foot into the shoe, swallowed the pain, and went out to the King's son.

Then he took her on his horse as his bride and rode away with her. They were obliged, however, to pass the grave, and there, on the hazel-tree, sat the two pigeons and cried: "Turn and peep, turn and peep, there's blood within the shoe. The shoe it is too small for her, the true bride waits for you!"

Then he looked at her foot and saw how the blood was trickling from it. He turned his horse around and took the false bride home again, and said she was not the true one, and that the other sister was to put the shoe on.

Then this one went into her chamber and got her toes safely into the shoe, but her heel was too large. So her mother gave her a knife and said, "Cut a bit off your heel. When you are Queen you will have no more need to go on foot."

The maiden cut a bit off her heel, forced her foot into the shoe, swallowed the pain, and went out to the King's son.

He took her on his horse as his bride, and rode away with her. But when they passed by the hazel-tree, the two pigeons sat on it and cried: "Turn and peep, turn and peep, there's blood within the shoe. The shoe it is too small for her, the true bride waits for you!"

He looked down at her foot and saw how the blood was running out of her shoe, and how it had stained her white stocking quite red. Then he turned his horse and took the false bride home again.

"This also is not the right one," said he. "Have you no other daughter?"

"No," said the man. "There is still a little stunted kitchen-wench which my late wife left behind her, but she cannot possibly be the bride."

The King's son said he was to send her up to him, but the mother answered, "Oh, no, she is much too dirty. She cannot show herself."

But he absolutely insisted on it, and Cinderella had to be called.

She first washed her hands and face clean, and then went and bowed down before the King's son, who gave her the golden shoe.

Then she seated herself on a stool, drew her foot out of the heavy wooden shoe, and put it into the slipper, which fitted like a glove. And when she rose up and the King's son looked at her face, he recognized the beautiful maiden who had danced with him and cried: "That is the true bride!"

The step-mother and the two sisters were horrified and became pale with rage. He, however, took Cinderella on his horse and rode away with her. As they passed by the hazel-tree, the two white doves cried: "Turn and peep, turn and peep, no blood is in the shoe. The shoe is not too small for her, the true bride rides with you."

And when they had cried that, the two came flying down and placed themselves on Cinderella's shoulders, one on the right, the other on the left, and remained sitting there.

*   *   *

When the wedding with the King's son was to be celebrated, the two false sisters came and wanted to get into favor with Cinderella and share her good fortune. When the betrothed couple went to church, the elder was at the right side and the younger at the left, and the pigeons pecked out one eye from each of them. Afterward, as they came back, the elder was at the left, and the younger at the right, and then the pigeons pecked out the other eye from each.

And thus, for their wickedness and falsehood, they were punished with blindness all their days.

The Ash-Boy

CHRISTOPHER FOWLER

"ONCE UPON A time in a far-off land there was a rich merchant who had two children, a boy and a girl born a year apart. The boy was called Peter and the girl was called Elizabeth. Their lives were happy, and they were as close as brother and sister could be. But a terrible sickness swept through the region and touched nearly every family. Elizabeth lost her mother and her beloved brother, and watched in the town square as their bodies were burned, for it was the only sure way of stopping the plague from spreading. Then, with the smell of her loved ones' cinders still in her clothes, she returned home to tend to her grief-stricken father.

"Elizabeth planted a hazel tree in her mother's memory, and its branches filled with ravens that kept watch over her. She returned to the marketplace and scooped up some of her brother's ashes, and took them to the scullery fireplace, where she fashioned an image of her brother from the ashes, so he would glow there in the grate and in her heart every time the fire was lit to warm the merchant's house.

"Just as Elizabeth was reaching maturity—which is to say that her body had changed and she could now be expected to perform all the duties of adults—her father resolved to find her a new mother, in order to provide her with the guidance that a man could not.

"The unwed townswomen looked upon the merchant with fresh eyes, for they saw a fellow with a fortune and only his daughter on which to spend it (it was common in this town to have six or seven children at least), and although the merchant was fat and ungainly and rather dull, he soon acquired a great number of eligible women seeking his hand in marriage.

"The rich merchant chose unwisely from their number, for he was no match for feminine guile. The woman he selected (or rather, who selected him) was fair of face but severe in temperament, and she brought with her two plain daughters from her last marriage, her husband having died of exhaustion and disappointment brought on by his wife's bitter ministrations.

"The two daughters were versions of their mother, but with their most inherited features attenuated, so that they were more mean-spirited, more selfish and more shallow. They had trouble following conversations that were not about themselves, and one had a pitch to her laugh that could shock birds from the trees, while the other spoke in such an uninteresting manner that she put listeners to sleep. They resented their new father's beautiful daughter, who could charm the fruit to ripen, and took away the nice clothes she had made for herself and sent her down to work in the scullery, washing and cleaning and tending the fire, which she was warned to never let go out (for this was in a mountain region the sun hardly ever touched, where frost bristled the skin even at the height of summer).

"The sisters refused to call the merchant's daughter any other name than Cinder-Ella, and promptly forgot about her, except when they needed her to perform some unpleasant duty. The merchant was busy working to maintain his fortune, and his new wife passed her days visiting other wealthy ladies in the nearby towns. The sisters did very little beyond brushing their hair, painting their toenails, gossiping about the townsfolk, checking the local gazette for dinners and dances and screaming at each other over the perception of slights."

"One day they heard of a handsome prince who was coming to visit. He was to be given a grand ball at the Mayor's palatial mansion in the verdant green hills above the town, the only part of the valley that the sun ever touched. The Mayor was after political favors and the Prince was still unwed, and as the town was filled with single women (too many beaux having succumbed to woodland overwork or plague), it was thought that a series of lavish parties might work to the satisfaction of both sides.

"Everyone who cared about such things was to be there, and the sisters begged their mother to petition for invitations. Gold-edged cards were duly sent out to every female between the ages of fourteen and twenty-one, and the merchant's family were able, through their connections, to obtain these coveted invitations, despite the fact that the stepsisters were visibly beyond the required age-range.

"The ungainly pair could not resist bragging about the ball to Cinder-Ella. 'Perhaps I could come too?' asked Cinder-Ella hopefully. 'After all, I am of an eligible age.'

"'You?' laughed one of the sisters, batting the gold-edged invitation before her bony-white face. 'But, my dear, just look at yourself, so filthy and ragged and uncouth. How could you possibly attend a ball held for a man so finely bred as the Prince? Besides, you must stay here to ensure that the embers never burn out. There's ice upon the windowpane and you can't allow the house to grow cold, for we cannot afford to appear before the Prince with red noses.' Laughing gaily, they went off to town to have their hair dyed and twisted into shapes that might please a minor member of royalty.

"That night the rest of the family set off for the Mayor's palatial home, leaving their stepsister to tend the great fire. 'It's so unfair,' thought Cinder-Ella as she gathered more logs. 'Why should I be forced to work when they go to the ball seeking to marry a handsome prince? And under false pretenses, at that.'

"But then she realized that she couldn't go anyway, for she had no invitation. The fire was growing low and the burned logs had exposed the glowing shape of the Ash-Boy, her lost brother, Peter, and she took comfort from his image. Her tears dripped onto his crimson form with a hiss, and as they did so she thought she heard a voice that said, 'But you *can* go to the ball, Cinder-Ella, for a ticket was delivered for every eligible female member of the household.

Your stepsisters threw your invitation into the fire, but I placed my cold ash hand over it and refused to allow it to burn.'

"And with that Ash-Peter raised his ash hand and revealed the unscorched card, and Cinder-Ella fished it from the fire intact.

"'Thank you, Ash-Peter,' said Cinder-Ella, 'but this is no good by itself, for I have nothing to wear.'

"'You made your own clothes before our father remarried,' whispered Ash-Peter, 'and although they were not made of silks and satins, nor covered in diamonds and rubies, they were as lovely as the trees, as flowing as the streams, as graceful as the breeze.'

"And, inspired by his words, she went out to the little woodshed where she and her brother had always kept their meager belongings and she returned with some bundles of cloth, some emerald grass and sapphire moon-dew, and her deft fingers darted so quickly that soon she had sewn a dress that shone with all the colors of the night. Cinder-Ella was good with a needle.

"She quickly washed and dressed, and dared to admire herself in the looking glass; she was quite beautiful enough to dazzle a prince. She made herself a tiara woven from hazel twigs and pinched her cheeks to make them pink, and poured rosewater into her hair. She even carved a pair of dainty little shoes from bark and painted them silver with the frost from the meadow.

"'Your natural beauty will outshine those painted, corseted slatterns,' Ash-Peter told her. 'Now you can go to the ball, but you'll have to take the carthorse. You can leave him at the end of the drive.'

"And so Cinder-Ella galloped to the ball."

"The great house in the hills was lit in every window like a great golden chandelier. When she arrived, her entrance, breathless and unaccompanied, down the winding stone staircase of the Mayor's mansion killed all conversation in the ballroom below. Nobody ever entered alone—such a thing broke every rule of etiquette, and the townsfolk always insisted on doing everything by the book, for they were in truth rather provincial—but Cinder-Ella's natural beauty swept aside any possible complaint. Although she was quickly surrounded by suitors, she refused them all until the Prince himself, dressed in white and gold, approached her.

"They danced so gracefully together that gradually the floor emptied out and the other guests moved to the edges, watching the couple in awe and admiration. The Prince was light on his feet and loved to dance and whirled Cinder-Ella around until she was quite exhausted. She knew that her sisters would return home soon after midnight, so she kept a watchful eye on the clock above the staircase.

"Her own family failed to recognize her, such was her transformation into a beauty. The Prince ignored every other girl in the room, and danced only with Cinder-Ella, so that she lost all track of time. It was only when she looked around and saw her stepsisters leaving in disgust that she knew it was time to go. Breaking free of the Prince just as he asked her name, she ran to the steps and beat them out of the door. But in her rush she lost one of the silver-twig shoes, and it was this that the Prince found after she had gone.

"Of course nobody knew the identity of the Prince's dancing partner, and although the entire ballroom was agog with gossip they could not help the Prince discover who she was. She had appeared from nowhere and had vanished into the freezing night.

"The Prince announced that he would search the town for her the next morning, and so it came to pass that he and his chief of guards began knocking on every door, asking to meet every female in the house.

"When he reached the merchant's home, Cinder-Ella's stepmother answered the door and summoned her own daughters, but nobody else. The stepsisters simpered and mewled about the Prince while his guard produced the silver shoe. They each tried it on in turn, but it fitted neither foot because they were at least three sizes too big for such a pretty little slipper. The stepmother took her daughters aside and urged them to cut off their ugly toes to fit the shoe. So while their mother engaged the Prince in conversation about the weather, they went out to the woodshed and each took turns with an ax to hack off the toes of their right feet. Soon their stumps were bleeding so badly that they looked like bony nubs of butchers' shop gristle, and they were in so much pain when they limped back that the Prince was put off of letting them try on the slipper and sent them away, as he hated the sight of blood.

"'Are you sure there is no one else here at all?' asked the Prince's guard.

"'No, there is no one here,' said the stepmother. But one of the ravens from the hazel tree alighted on the guard and clawed at his clothes, and as he was batting the bird away he glanced through the scullery window, and there he saw smut-faced Cinder-Ella tending to the burning grate.

"'What about her?' he asked.

"'She is nobody, just a scullery-maid,' sniffed the stepmother.

"'Nevertheless I must meet her,' said the Prince. 'Bring her to me.'

"Cinder-Ella shyly tried on the shoe and of course it fitted perfectly.

"'Wonderful!' the Prince cried. 'You are surely the girl I danced with.'

"'I am, sire,' she replied, lowering her head in his regal presence.

"'Then I shall return to the Mayor's house tonight and we shall continue to dance merrily, and I shall marry you and dress you up and show you off to the entire nation, and you will be my pretty little dancing doll forever, as befits a Prince. Until tonight, then.' He shook her hand politely and rode off with his guard.

"The stepsisters were furious. They hobbled toward Cinder-Ella, leaving a bloody trail, and pushed her back into the scullery, further and further, until she was on top of the roaring fire. 'If we can't have him, you shall not have him,' hissed one of them, and grabbing a poker she shoved it at Cinder-Ella, pushing her into the flames. The other twisted her arm and bent her back over the flames until she could no longer remain upright. They rammed her onto the burning coals and held her in place with pokers until the flames set fire to her clothes and her hair and singed her flesh until it was black. Lying below the burning logs, Ash-Peter could hear his sister's desperate cries, but could not rise up to save her.

"And so poor Cinder-Ella perished in dreadful agony. Her blood and her tears put out the fire and turned the embers to cold ashes as the sisters went off to prepare for another ball, where they hoped once more to turn the head of the Prince.

"There was nothing left of Cinder-Ella except her dainty right foot, which had been thrust beyond the edge of the grate. Ash-Peter roared with fury, and as he did so his anger ignited the coals again and he rose up, and the Ash-Boy stepped out of the great fireplace into the scullery. He stood before the fire and dusted off his gray ashes and found himself whole once more, and he swore revenge for his sister's terrible death.

"That night, the Ash-Boy waited for the rest of the family to leave the house. Being roughly the same size as his sister, and most alike in complexion and deportment, he donned her ball gown, gloves and tiara. Luckily the Prince had left the other twig-slipper, so he still had a matching pair. Then he slipped out to find the cart horse and rode off to the Mayor's house.

"At the expected hour Ash-Peter arrived at the top of the grand staircase in his dead sister's raiments. He was worried that the guests might spot the difference, but the room was lit with candles so nobody noticed and indeed, they were so very similar in height and bearing and even beauty that nobody thought it odd at all.

"As soon as the Prince saw Ash-Peter dressed in his sister's finery he rushed over, and if he saw the difference he did not show it, for the moment the orchestra started to play he picked Ash-Peter up and whisked him to the dance floor, and once again he waltzed the night away. This time, though, the Prince's partner did not rush off before the stroke of midnight, but stayed to dance until even the Prince needed to catch his breath, and led Ash-Peter to his private balcony, where they kissed in shadows.

"As the guests dispersed, the Prince led Ash-Peter upstairs to the suite the Mayor had given him (for his own castle was several days' ride away) and carried his bride-to-be toward his bed. He blew out the candles and undressed his prize and throughout that night he displayed all the manly prowess that might be expected of a Prince.

"The next morning his maids and servants brought him break-fast and found him in bed with a slender young man curled beneath him. They pretended not to notice and scurried from the room, but a whisper was started that became a scandal that quickly spread throughout the entire town, so that when the Prince awoke and appeared at his bedroom door, ready for his morning bath, the Mayor and the *Bürgermeister* and all of the town's officials were there to point the finger of accusation at him, for this, as I mentioned earlier, was a very provincial town.

"After a few minutes' deliberation, and despite a rather unbelievable plea of total ignorance from the Prince, the Mayor's soldiers took their guest out to the courtyard and hanged him until his heels stopped kicking.

"While all this commotion was occurring, Ash-Peter slipped out of the grounds, found his horse and returned to the merchant's house."

"It was snowing hard when he arrived, and the family was starting to freeze because Cinder-Ella's blood and tears had put out the fire, and nobody could make it stay alight. The merchant tried burning newspapers and his wife tried lighting twigs, and even her daughters tried blowing on matches, but nothing would make the fire catch, so they crept off to their chambers to cover themselves in blankets and huddle together in the deepening cold.

"Ash-Peter saw himself in the looking glass and knew he could not stay in human form for much longer, so he took the cold ashes from the fireplace and smeared them all over his face and body and said: 'Now I must once again be what I became before, an Ash-Boy,' and it was true for he was already losing the softness that made him human. He looked like an angry warrior who had risen from the grate to take revenge for his sister's cruel fate.

"He told the ravens in the hazel tree to peck out his stepsisters' eyes, but they stared at him blankly, for they were just birds and had attacked the Prince's guard because they feared he was threatening their nest. The only magic in the household had come from the

fireplace where Cinder-Ella had lovingly tended the flame that held
her brother's form.

"So Ash-Peter took the ax from the woodshed, and sharpened
its blade on a stone until it had a razor edge, then went upstairs to
find his stepsisters. They were wrapped in blankets in their bed-
chambers, shaking with the cold, and when they saw the fearsome
Ash-Boy walking toward them, dragging his ax so that it sparked
against the flint floor, they screamed in terror.

"'So you would cut off your toes to win your Prince, would
you?' he said. 'Perhaps you would have a better chance if you fitted
Cinder-Ella's gloves.' And he chopped off their fingers one by one
until their hands were just trowels of bloody flesh. The stepsisters
screamed and howled and shook, but nobody came to rescue them.
'And perhaps the Prince would marry you if you fitted Cinder-Ella's
dress,' Ash-Peter cried, hacking pieces of flesh off their sides until
their limbs were lopped from their bodies and their innards fell
from beneath their ribs. 'And perhaps you would have been wed if
you'd worn Cinder-Ella's fine tiara,' he said as he brought the sharp
blade of the ax down across their pates, and with their silly skulls
split they expired in dreadful agonies.

"He was about to head for his father's room when he heard
Cinder-Ella's voice in his ear. 'Please,' she said, 'do not punish our
family any more, for they have no children left to comfort them in
their cold old age and surely that is punishment enough.'

"Ash-Peter saw that she was right. By now the house was
freezing. The bread and meat in the kitchen had turned hard as
rock, and so there was nothing for the merchant and his wife to
eat. The water had solidified in the taps, so there was nothing for
them to drink. The floors and the doors were crusted in thicken-
ing ice, and warmth would never come here again. And so he left
the selfish merchant and his shrewish wife and returned to the
scullery.

"Scooping out the remains of his sister's ashes, he took them to
the little woodshed at the end of the garden and lit a fire with them
the very first time he tried, and he stayed warm in the wooden box

while the frost cracked the windows of his father's house and icicles like great glass spears formed along the edges of the roof.

"He waited. Soon enough, his father and stepmother spotted the glowing light of the woodshed from their window and hurried, shivering, from the house. He heard his stepmother say, 'Someone is warming themselves on our land, and they shall pay. We'll kick them out into the cold and take the fire for ourselves.' But as she slammed the front door behind them, the icicles on the roof cracked loose and fell, spearing each of them clean through the heart.

"Ash-Peter emerged from his woodshed and checked that they were dead. Then he returned to his fire and climbed into his sister's flames and danced and danced, quite mad in grief and victory, until the furnace consumed him and there were only his ashes left.

"And they mingled with his sister's ashes, and the icy wind blew them away to the farthest corners of the kingdom, where they warmed the deserving and froze only those with bitter hearts.

"The End."

He closed the book and lowered it, studying his daughter's face.

For the last five minutes she had hardly stopped crying long enough to draw breath. "So you see," he said, tenderly wiping away her tears with his sleeve, "there are fairy tales where the beautiful girl gets the Prince and there are ones like real life, where nothing ends as you expect it."

And as his daughter started to cry once more, he threw aside the book and went downstairs to find something sharp before resuming the fight with his wife.

CHRISTOPHER FOWLER is the multi-award–winning author of more than thirty novels and twelve short story collections, including *Roofworld, Spanky, Disturbia, Paperboy,* and *Hell Train.* He has also written eleven Bryant & May mystery novels so far, the latest being *Bryant & May and the Bleeding Heart.* These follow the adventures of two elderly detectives who investigate impossible crimes in London. The cases are filled with dark humor and often gory, bizarre deaths. PS Publishing recently issued *Red Gloves,* a collection of twenty-five new horror stories by the author to mark a quarter century in print, and he scripted the *War of the Worlds* video game featuring Sir Patrick Stewart. He currently writes a column in the *Independent on Sunday* and reviews for the *Financial Times.* His latest books are *Invisible Ink: How 100 Great Authors Vanished,* the graphic novel *The Casebook of Bryant & May,* the sinister comedy-thriller *Plastic,* and a memoir, *Film Freak.*

The Elves #1

ACERTAIN MOTHER HAD her child taken out of its cradle by the elves, and a changeling with a large head and staring eyes, which would do nothing but eat and drink, lay in its place.

In her trouble she went to her neighbor, and asked her advice.

The neighbor said that she was to carry the changeling into the kitchen, set it down on the hearth, light a fire, and boil some water in two egg-shells, which would make the changeling laugh. And if he laughed, all would be over with him.

The woman did everything that her neighbor bade her.

When she put the egg-shells with water on the fire, goggle-eyes said, "I am as old now as the wester forest, but never yet have I seen anyone boil anything in an egg-shell." And he began to laugh at it.

While he was laughing, suddenly came a host of little elves, who brought the right child, set it down on the hearth, and took the changeling away with them.

The Changeling

BRIAN LUMLEY

THE SUN WAS beginning to set as I finned lazily into the shallows, thrust my speargun before me and laid it to rest in six inches of still water, then turned over and sat facing the sea. Removing my face mask, snorkel and fins, I tossed them onto the fine yellow sand at the water's edge behind me. I wasn't at all concerned that my things might drift off, carried away by a wave and lost to the current; for this was the so-called tideless sea—the Mediterranean—and I couldn't possibly lose my gear to surf or current on an evening as calm and still as this one, when the only ripples worth mentioning were the ones I had left in my wake, only now catching up with me and beginning to lap at the beach.

When I had gone into the water maybe forty-five minutes earlier, a handful of people—British tourists—had been leaving, commencing a two-mile trek back to the crowded resort on a jutting promontory that was completely out of sight and sound of this small, cliff-guarded bay. This secret-seeming place was no more than a hundred yards wide end-to-end, like a mere bite—or bight?—that the ocean had sculpted from the bleached-yellow cliffs. With its soft sand and secluded—one might even say isolated—location, its crystal-clear water and sunken rocks that formed a shallow, reef-like bottom no more than sixty or so feet out from the beach, the bay set a scene which conjured a single word: "idyllic." Little wonder that artists love to paint in the perfect light of the Greek islands, with their dramatic, sometimes lush, sometimes sparse, frequently parched or calcined scenery.

And yet again, as when I had first set eyes on this lonely place while descending the rough-hewn path down the face of the shallow cliffs, I wondered about the absence of commercial activity in what was apparently a virtual haven of peace and quiet. Indeed, I had dreamed of such places—my main reason for coming to Greece in the first place; yes, dreamed of bays such as this, and more especially of the tranquil waters that lapped their shores.

But where was the seemingly inevitable, almost compulsory *taverna*? Where the stacked sunbeds and parasol sunshades—not to mention the bronzed attendant with his purse and clinking drawstring bag of drachmae? Nowhere in sight! Not a bit of it!

Oh, there had been at least one attempt at some sort of industry, and possibly more than one. The steps down the cliff, for instance: someone had cut them. And there, near the eastern extreme of the bay—where, upon my arrival in the midafternoon, I had settled myself down—that single circular concrete base whose central hole had once accommodated the stem of just such a parasol as now was nowhere evident . . . unless a rusting skeleton cage minus its canopy, half-buried in the sand at the foot of the cliffs, was all that remained of it.

Of course, the resort's owners might well have discouraged any such attempts by an outsider at building a gainful business enterprise here, especially one that could detract from its own profitability. But then, why not adopt and adapt this place for its own, perhaps supplementing its earnings and easing the crowding on its own rather small beach? There again, as an outsider myself, I had no knowledge of local Greek land rights. It wasn't at all unlikely that this tiny bay was under some sort of protective government order; why, it might even be privately owned! Then again, being in my own right the proprietor of a small numismatic business in England where I dealt in collectible coins, on the one hand I considered the failure to put this marvelous location to use a lost opportunity and even a waste; on the other—perhaps contrarily or selfishly—I was glad that the bay had managed to stay as it was and exactly as nature intended. At any rate, for the duration of my stay.

No one had told me of this secret place, as I now in earnest considered it; if I had not escaped from the crowd, to wander and explore on my own, I would never have discovered it. But after lunch I had decided to leave the resort, go off in an easterly direction through the scrub, pines, a few brambles and tortured olives—a route which a locally produced chart of the region displayed as a blank, uninspiring expanse of yellow land and azure blue ocean—to see what I might see. And then, if sticking close to the sea, I should come across a way down to a beach or a rocky shelf from which I might swim and fish . . .

. . . which was precisely what had happened.

Earlier, after my first snorkeling swim to check out the scene underwater—especially the reef—I returned to dry land to find a youth (one of the double handful of tourists along the beach) standing near my belongings, looking at but in no way interfering with my equipment bag and other possessions. He seemed particularly interested in my rubber-powered speargun, which I'd left behind while I reconnoitered the reef in flippers and mask.

The spot where I had settled myself, making it my base of operations, was, as I have said, close to the bay's eastern extremity, where in wilder seasons the ocean had worked to undercut the cliffs. Tumbled from those layered heights, a number of huge flat slabs of rock had half-buried themselves in the sand, where one of them made a fine horizontal bench facing the sea. And it was there, directly in front of this great slab—where some unknown person had planted that previously mentioned concrete anchor for a long-since-disused, dilapidated and discarded sunshade—that the English youth stood waiting for me.

I had seen him earlier as I came down the cliff path. He and another youth of a like age, maybe sixteen or seventeen years, had been trying to drag a great knotted driftwood log—in fact the seven- or eight-foot trunk of what had looked like an ancient, gnarled olive tree—from where it had washed ashore back down the beach to the sea. Hauling first on one end of the log, then on the other, their determined efforts had left a helix-like scar in the sand, like the trail of a monstrously huge sidewinder. Odd, because that had been some fifty or more yards west of my present location, in the middle of the bay; yet now I saw similar scuff marks in the sand right here, just a few paces from where I was gathering up my swim gear.

So, perhaps there had been another old log which I hadn't noticed . . . but likewise odd that I had failed to notice it when the boys were working on it. There again, I had been chiefly interested in the sea; my thoughts had been centered on what I might find in the reef's cracks and crannies, the secret lairs of fishes that might be hiding under its shallow submarine shelves . . .

I had asked the youth if there was anything I could do for him and found that I was correct: he told me he had seen my speargun as I came down the cliff path and was interested. So I had shown him the safety catch and explained how the gun was loaded, then *un*loaded it and put it down under my towel: out of sight, out of mind. And finally I had asked him about the party he was with—how had they found their way here?

They were a two-family party he told me, neighbors back home in England who sometimes vacationed together. A local taxi driver at the resort had told them about the little bay, how it was a nice place to picnic—but it wasn't a good idea to stay too late, not on an evening. It was a very "special" place, and lonely. And he'd heard it was frequented, on certain rare occasions, by "foreigners." Which was all he would say about it; but he had also asked them not to tell other tourists about it: the resort might lose money, while an overly talkative taxi driver could find himself unwelcome there, unemployed and losing money of his own!

Well, that was okay: they certainly wouldn't mention this place to anyone else; unfortunately this was to be their last day here. Bright and early tomorrow morning they would be gone, off to the airport on the far side of the island and back home to spend the rest of a doubtless dreary summer in England.

And that had been that. The lad had set off back along the beach to where his party was camped beneath a nest of sunshades they had obviously brought with them, and I had been left on my own to eat an orange and my egg-and-tomato sandwiches and drink a small warm beer straight from its bottle. While I didn't have the luxury of a sunshade, at least there was *some* shade cast by the layered cliffs looming on my left . . .

That had been then and this was now. Still dripping brine, I gathered up my things and headed up the beach toward the huge flat rock where I had left my equipment bag, towel and small heap of clothing. And that was when I saw my uninvited guest.

The way his black robe, a cassock, probably—it was hard to tell in the gradually failing evening light, with salt water dripping from my hair and forehead into my stinging eyes—but the way that robe was spread out voluminously all around him on the great rock bench where he was seated within arm's length of my property, well, at first glance I had understandably taken him for a priest from the island's Orthodox Greek church. Until, moving closer, I quickly discovered my mistake— that in fact he was simply an aging, possibly eccentric local.

"Hello there!" I said, taking my towel and backing away as I began to dry myself.

Nodding his large head, he replied in a cultured but paradoxically guttural, phlegmy-sounding voice, "And a good evening to you, sir."

And with that . . . well, that was it. It was in that voice, in the air, in the sudden absence of the previously congenial atmosphere. What had been—whatever it had been—was no more. Now I was just a little cold inside; I thought I felt a shiver in there, and I wondered what in the world there could be in a mere presence and its voice that could do that to me.

Still backing off, my legs came up against a smaller flat-topped boulder, which caused me to sit down abruptly facing the stranger. And suddenly wary, I let my flippers, mask and snorkel fall to the soft sand and stood my speargun on its pistol grip close to hand, leaning it against my seat.

As for possible reasons for my nervousness, they were several. For one thing, I had remembered what that taxi driver had told the tourists: that it would be inadvisable to picnic or party here in the evening; that the little bay was somehow special; and that odd, foreign folk were known to sometimes frequent the place.

My first thoughts on that had been: But weren't the majority of guests at the resort, including the British, foreigners of a sort? And now I thought: Ah! But then there's foreign and there's *foreign* . . . a term in common usage which might also mean outlandish, alien or simply peculiar. And right now "outlandish" appeared to fit this uninvited one just perfectly.

As to why that was so, and some of the other reasons for my apparent nervousness:

There was this smell that I hadn't noticed before; a smell which seemed that much stronger in the stranger's immediate vicinity. It had been more than noticeable—I might even say unavoidable— when I had approached him closely to reach for my towel: the smell of the dried-out, weedy tidemark on a shore at low tide . . . the shore of an ocean that *has* a tide, that is.

Then there was his overall look, his decidedly odd appearance. His unseen body would have to be gross, even obese, under that flowing, all-enveloping cloak, cassock, mantle . . . whatever the garment was; gross and probably unwashed, which might possibly account for the smell. And as for his face—

—but his face was in the shade of a hooded extension to the rear of his cloak, that dark garment which I now saw seemed to have a purplish tint in the oh-so-slowly failing light. And despite that, out of common decency—which is to say, in consideration of what this poor fellow must recognize as the anomalies of his own weird features, and be embarrassed by them—despite that, for this reason I hesitated to study his face for too long or too intently, still I found it fascinating. And to my own discomfort I felt compelled to stare at it.

"I seem to have disturbed you," he observed in that guttural swampy croak of a voice. "You didn't expect to come across me here. Well, I apologize for my . . . presence. But this is a place—one might even say a private place—which I sometimes enjoy to visit. And so, just as I would seem to have, er, *interfered* with your privacy, so you have interfered with mine."

Before I could reply—perhaps to protest, possibly to excuse myself, but in any case failing to find the right words—he shrugged, which caused his cloak to gently billow or ripple, its purplish tints flaring up and momentarily intensifying, and went on: "But no harm done, and in a little while I shall be on my way. A pity, really . . ."

"A pity?" (That he would soon be moving on? Not from where I was sitting!) But what he had said was true enough: this lost, lonely place had seemed very private—to me as well as to him—but now even its ambience was lost, its genius loci, its spirit-of-place; and strangely, it felt like and *was* more surely his place now, no longer mine at all.

"Yes," he said, nodding—scowling, I thought, though his expression in the shade of his cowl was difficult to interpret—and squirming under his billowing cloak as if uncomfortable, agitated or disappointed. "A great pity, for I think I might have enjoyed a little conversation. I note that you are an Englishman and, I would hazard a guess, decently educated? In recent decades I have only rarely come into close contact with men of any learning whatsoever. Men who might more readily understand and marvel at a life—an *existence*—such as mine: its origin, various stages of mutation and evolution before . . . before it engendered the likes of me. And its mysteries, of course."

While he was speaking—his choice of words and subject leaving me more or less bewildered, making little or no sense in the context of a first meeting and the customary initial discourse between total strangers—I had found myself once again drawn to look at the peculiarities not only of his face but his entire person. For I had begun to form the vague fancy that, head to toe, this unfortunate man might be horribly deformed . . . Why else wear that grotesque, stifling garment if not to hide from view a yet more unseemly body?

But his face, *his face!*

For now as then, when I was trying to avoid looking at him too openly or curiously, still I find myself shrinking from describing him or . . . or *it*. By which I mean his face—I think. For even the memory is disturbing.

However, it was a long time ago, and time and the healthy mind have ways of reducing or entirely eliminating the unthinkable or unbearable. And so I shall persevere.

His head, despite being large, appeared rather small in comparison with the outward-flowing vastness of the shoulders that must lie directly beneath it under his cloak; and the ugly face upon that head bore a flattish nose, little or no chin worth the mention, and eyes that were more than slightly protuberant. As in many fish species, those eyes in their deep-sunken orbits bulged unblinkingly and the leprous, flaky, grayish-blue flesh around them was deeply pitted. His neck at both sides—or as much as I could see of it where the cowl failed to shroud it—was scarred by deep parallel creases or horizontal, gouge-like flaps. I believe that at the time I thought they were cicatrices, resulting from tribal or cultish acts of self-mutilation. That at least was my initial impression—in support of which there was the tortured flesh of his cheeks.

For from his cheekbones under the orbits of his eyes down to his mouth, and from his lower lip down to that round blob of an atrophied chin, further evidence of this self-abuse seemed indisputable. It was there in the form of eight coiled bas-reliefs, somewhat similar in design to the tightly wound fossils of common ammonites.

Then there was this unfortunate creature's froggish mouth, with fat yellowish lips so long they almost reached the sides of cheeks which in turn supported a pair of stunted, distinctly rudimentary ears, again mostly in the shade of his garment's cowl. A disk of metal—an earring of sorts, depending on little more than an inch of golden chain from the meager lobe of the underdeveloped or deformed ear on the right—glinted dully with each slightest motion of its bearer's head.

As for the rest of him, his limbs and presumably prodigious body: all was hidden beneath the peculiar tent-like canopy of his strange garment . . . a circumstance for which I felt unaccountably, or rather not yet justifiably, thankful.

But however I had tried to hide my revulsion of his looks and especially his *smell*—for it was becoming increasingly obvious that those loathsome waves of stench were indeed issuing from him—he had not failed to notice my reticence. As a direct result of which:

"You find me repulsive!" he choked, coughed, finally spat the accusation out. "I am too *unlike* for your tastes . . . is it not so?"

"Why, I don't even know you!" I protested. "You're a complete stranger and we've barely spoken. I haven't said more than a word or two to you since finding you here."

"But you have *looked* at me—and in such a way!" His cloak trembled with the agitation or restless anger of the figure beneath it.

"Then if I have somehow offended you," I replied, "though I assure you any such offense was unintentional, I am sorry. And as for the matter of the disturbed privacy of this place: that can very quickly be put right. You say you'll be leaving soon? Please don't trouble yourself, for I'll be leaving even sooner—indeed right now!"

"Do you deny that you have gazed at me? And such an *intolerable* examination at that?" His words were thick as bubbles on a black swamp, gurgling from that awful mouth. "'No offense intended,' you say . . . which is *not* to say that you don't find my . . . my changeling *countenance* unnatural, unpleasant, even hideous to your inalienable land-born eyes!"

I was on my feet by then, moving toward him. And why not? Even if he intended me harm, I didn't actually fear him; I felt sure he would be incapable of any sort of rapid physical exertion; he was—he *must* be—simply too huge under that purple-rippling cassock-like cloak. Besides which, I wasn't closing with him directly but more properly reaching for my belongings, that little heap of casual clothing and my equipment bag where I had left those items on the huge bench-like slab of rock . . . items which to my discomfort I now saw were closer to him than I had previously thought, and much *too* close for comfort.

Then, holding my breath rather than suffer the full extent of his dreadful smell, as I took up my things and backed away again, I saw the golden glinting of the disk dangling from his shrunken ear where his swiveling head as it followed my every move was causing it to sway. Being that much closer now, I recognized the earring's distinctive style and recalled where I had seen jewelry of its like before. And in that same moment I remembered what little I knew of its somewhat esoteric origins.

But then, before I could further gather my thoughts on that subject—as I once again took my lesser seat opposite the other and began to dress myself—the oh-so-peculiar stranger leaned toward me in what was an aggressive, almost threatening manner to babble and cough a further guttural accusation:

"What? And is my aspect so fearsome . . . so fascinating . . . so freakish, then? You continue to *stare at me*, damn you!"

Well, of course I did, keeping an at least wary eye on him! And indeed, who wouldn't have? But now I saw what I hoped was a way to more surely excuse myself, a way to "explain" my obviously unacceptable interest in him, and protested:

"But it isn't *you*! And I'm very sorry if you find my curiosity disturbing and offensive. It's simply that I'm fascinated by the earring or pendant, that ornament you're wearing in your ear. It's that, I'm sure, which has caused me to seem so disrespectful!"

"My earring?" he gurgled, leaning back to regain his previous posture. "This golden bauble of mine?"

"Gold?" I repeated him. "Is it?"

He at once narrowed his eyes—but before he was able to reply I quickly went on: "But of course it is! Indeed, since it's the same as other pieces I've seen, including a few items I've been fortunate enough to acquire for myself, then it must be gold—well, gold of a sort—albeit impure and strangely alloyed stuff."

"Stuff?" He in turn repeated, and finally nodded. "Well, yes, but exceptionally rare *stuff*—I can assure you of that! And you've seen similar pieces? You even own some? Oh, really? Well, now you've interested me and must tell me more. And if I have seemed a little too brusque or overly aggressive, perhaps you'll forgive me? But let me explain that among my own people, while I admit to being, how to put it: a *deviation*?— yes, even among my own—a changeling of sorts, still to them I am completely acceptable. Which tends to make me very sensitive to the gauche opinions of certain ill-bred others and causes me to shy from them. And because I value my privacy so highly, I occasionally come to this favorite place of mine where I'm unlikely to come into contact with anyone else—especially toward evening, as now. But even so, my privacy cannot always be guaranteed, as witness your presence here."

"Ill-bred others"? A rather poor choice of words, I thought. Or there again, perhaps apt when applied to himself. For I now found it not in the least unlikely that—*physically*, at least—he might well be the product of just such ill or impure inbreeding. But on the other hand, which is to say *mentally*, he appeared highly intelligent, despite that in his reasoning he seemed oddly wandering, and in his discourse more than a little obscure. (But of course, while I was given to *think* and consider such things, I hardly intended—or dared—to communicate them by allowing my uneasiness to get the better of me, perhaps becoming too obvious; for with regard to his strange appearance he had already made his sensitivity to the reactions of other, presumably normal persons perfectly clear—and anyway, common decency alone would forbid my showing signs of revulsion.)

So once again I tried to appease him. "I quite understand the value you put on your privacy," I said. "Why, I'm a private person myself, which is why like you I find this place so very much to my liking." (Which had been true enough—until now, at least.) "But, you see, my interest in coins and medallions, especially when they're minted in precious or rare metals, is almost an obsession. In fact I've made it both my hobby and my work; it's how I earn my living."

He suddenly stiffened, sat up straight and seemed to gaze far out over the reef. And: "Look at that!" he said. "Directly behind you, out there! Are those dolphins I see in the bay?"

I at once turned, looked and saw nothing: just a splash in the water, maybe, where a fish—but only a very small one—might have jumped and soared aloft for a single moment. So I narrowed my eyes, squinting in order to focus more intently on the calm surface out beyond the reef. And still there was nothing to be seen . . .

But there was something to be *felt*!

I felt it on the towel that covered my thighs where I had draped it for modesty's sake while removing my swimming trunks and pulling on my shorts: the soft *thump!* of something landing there. And I immediately snatched my head around to see what it was, never for a moment thinking it might be the ornament from the stranger's shriveled ear. But that's exactly what it was: the golden medallion on its inch of fine chain.

Then as I switched my gaze to the man himself, I saw the disturbed motion of his robe: purplish ripples spreading over its dense, singular surface. So then, it seemed I wasn't alone in my concerns about modesty. But still I had to ask myself: What harm would there have been in letting me witness the action of hand and arm as he plucked the ornament from its anchorage and tossed it into my lap? Why the obvious red herring—the pretense and distraction—of a nonexistent leaping dolphin?

And then there was another thing: from what I could make of it, there were no openings in his robe, which appeared to be fashioned in a single piece. More truly like a monk's cassock, it lacked buttons or an overlap in front; neither were there sleeves nor any visible armholes! But while I would later remember and think of these things, at that time my interest was more especially centered on the medallion.

It was indeed of a kind with those two or three items I had managed to collect over the years; it had the same silvery luster. But I had long since had my specimens tested and there was nothing of silver—or platinum, or any other easily identifiable alloy—in them. As for the ornament I now held in my hand, trying to keep it from reflecting the odd beam of failing light: for all that it was scarcely two inches in diameter, still the intricacy and marvelous quality of its almost cabalistic, minuscule designs—not to mention their otherworldly, often as not sub-aquatic themes—imbued it with an appearance that was in short completely weird and indeed alien. And these were the qualities which had attracted me to this anthropologically esoteric strain of art in the first place. Even as they continued to attract me now.

The craftsmanship, as I have mentioned, was of an amazingly high quality. But despite that it looked stamped, almost to the "proofed" degree of fine precious-metal coinage, still the otherwise undeniable beauty of its reliefs was spoiled by their depiction of awesome, indeed sinister monsters. This was hardly surprising: the specimens in my personal collection were adorned in a like fashion with grotesque ichthyic high reliefs where lesser fishlike or batrachian figures—including several that appeared to be hybrid varieties of both types—were not only extraordinarily humanlike in their postures and attitudes but were also very bizarrely attired in late eighteenth- or nineteenth-century-styled clothing! These lesser figures were pictured as the servitors, even the worshippers, of greater, far more horrifically alien beings or creatures.

As for the source of such ornaments and the queer alloys from which they were fashioned, who could say with any degree of certainty? Among my friends back in England were several so-called experts who at various times had hazarded opinions that ranged from Cambodia or perhaps Papua New Guinea to the South Sea Islands, in particular Hawaii; yet despite my contacts abroad I knew of no outlets in such foreign parts and had purchased my own specimens from salesrooms and numismatic sources in towns in the English southwest, which is to say Exeter in Devon and Penzance in Cornwall.

With regard to the latter: that should not be considered especially surprising, for in the day there were indeed "Pirates *in* Penzance," and examples of their booty—the foreign plunder they brought back with them from many a blood-soaked voyage—may still be discovered, albeit increasingly rarely, at small-town auctions, or for sale in antique curiosity shops across the counties of the far southwest . . . always assuming of course that one knows where to look.

Moreover, in comparatively recent to modern times there has been no lack of legitimate eighteenth- and nineteenth-century commercially venturesome seafarers, ensuring that ports such as Plymouth and Falmouth have been ever astir with vessels returning from afar full of foreign produce. And among the crews of those vessels were those who came home with other than typical goods— even a few who brought back to British shores "companions" in the form of dusky tropical-island ladies, some of whom were as "wives" to their sailor "husbands."

According to rumors passed down the decades by word of mouth from old salts—tales that may still be heard to this day in certain wharf-side taverns—at least a handful of these *kanaka* women were known to have worn outlandish, cold but seductive golden jewelry.

That stories such as these were not so much rumor as factual, reasonably accurate contemporary reports and accounts had always seemed self-evident to me, which my personal possession of those several aforementioned items had, to my satisfaction, amply served to corroborate.

And now, as I gave my attention to the stranger's earring, all such facts were passing in short order through my mind; so that it was probably my expression as I handled the thing—an expression that displayed less of surprise or amazement than of definite familiarity, perhaps strengthening in the other's eyes my claim of ownership— which decided the course of the rest of this unconventional encounter.

For now it seemed he accepted all that I had said, though so far there had been little enough of that, as a result becoming far more conversationally reasonable. And thus:

"Interesting, are they not?" he said, all signs of enmity gone as quickly as that from his voice and attitude. "The tiny reliefs on the disk, I mean."

"Very," I agreed, albeit stumblingly. "Indeed fascinating . . . if less than entirely unique." Then, remembering his alleged sensitivity, I hoped that I had said the right thing. But I need not have worried.

"Apparently"—he nodded—"for I note from your expression that you have indeed seen such before; which is to say the several items that you profess to possess. But may I inquire where you obtained them? Not that I doubt you, you understand, but it may perhaps explain something of how an Englishman such as yourself comes to own such ... well, such rarities ... not to mention your obvious interest in them."

I saw no harm in answering his inquiry, and so as I finished dressing and bundling my things, without making a meal of it I told of my beginnings: my young, earliest years as a math teacher in a school in Newquay; my interest, living so close to the sea, in all aspects of oceanology, but more as a hobby than a career; my later obsession with numismatics that came with my father's lifelong collection of precious coins and medals when he had passed on, and which in my early thirties replaced teaching as my career of choice. And yes, indeed there had been just such coins or medallions as the earring among the many hundreds of items the Old Man had left to me.

More, I went on to speak of my discoveries and theories—mainly the lack of such—regarding the source of these peculiar, oddly repellent yet fascinating ornaments: that I believed they had arrived in England around the 1820s and '30s along with the South Sea Island women; and finally I described as accurately as I could remember them the samples in my collection and how and where I had come across them.

Then, when I was done, he who had remained silently attentive in the ever more swiftly deepening dusk—the sun having by then gone down behind the rim of the cliffs at the western curve of the bay—at last cried out, or rather choked, gasped and gurgled:

"*Ahhh!* In the southwest! But of course! Taken to England by ... by my people. It all fits, yes. But the only thing that doesn't fit is you yourself! I mean, why your obvious *affinity* with these golden baubles? For that is all they are—or were—to them that fashioned them. But you don't have the eyes for it, or the chin, the lips—the general *otherness*—that results from the changes. Nor for that matter do you seem to have the *additions*—or, to your way of thinking, the 'anomalies'—necessary for any sort of prolonged ... of prolonged survival *out there!* So that for your part the connection must be circumstantial, entirely coincidental, including your coming here. Quite remarkable!"

I had no idea what he was talking about—or perhaps only the faintest idea, as yet half-formed in the back of my mind—and made as if to rise. For coming to me from nowhere I sensed a need more urgent than any I had known so far to be away from that no longer idyllic place, and from him, both of which were suddenly and utterly alien to me. But while the urge to depart was very strong, so was my . . . my *desire* to know whatever else there was to know, which I had not yet learned or understood.

In any case, before I could get to my feet:

"Ah, but wait! Don't be in such a rush!" he said. And his words, while gutturally formed, sounded at least reasonably normal when compared with what had gone immediately before, as he almost visibly attempted to exert a measure of control over himself. And in the next moment, as I surrendered to my natural curiosity and remained seated—for I still couldn't allow that I was in any way actually threatened by the other, whether he was entirely sane or indeed suffering from some kind of sorely disordered intellect— he said:

"Perhaps to explain something of my own presence here, which I had mistakenly thought might in some way apply to you also, perhaps I should relate . . . perhaps I might *tell* you a story, yes? One that I heard a long time ago and which has for origin those same counties of southwest England where you say you discovered your own—er, should I call them exotic, even though they are scarcely that to me?—but your own *specimens* anyway. And then, in payment for your patience, your audience, you must allow me to make you a gift of the one you hold in your hand, hopefully to enhance your collection."

And before I could protest or immediately offer to return the thing:

"No, no!" He shook his head. "For when my . . . my *story* is done you may be sure I shall feel compensated for the bauble, if only by virtue of your company for a few extra minutes."

And now there was no way out but to sit still and listen, and suffer his stench, as the light in that cliff-shadowed bay grew dimmer by the minute and the air cooler but no less vile; until after a longish pause—I assumed to gather his thoughts—finally he continued:

"There was in Cornwall a young man who loved the sea. An orphan, found as a babe on the shore where the tide could not reach him, he had grown up on the charity of others until, in recognition of his superior intelligence, he secured a grant which permitted him to attend a university. There he obtained excellent grades that guaranteed him later work in a suitable occupation—as a theoretical physicist—which in turn made him completely self-reliant.

"He lived alone, earning a more-than-adequate living from his work, and just like you spent much of his free time beachcombing or swimming, but mainly thinking, which I am sure you will appreciate is the way of men of his persuasions. And in a bay similar to this one—though more dramatically in keeping with the craggy Cornish coastline—he would don his mask and snorkel to go exploring on and just below the surface of the water. Which is where any comparison with yourself would seem to end.

"One day, a little further out at sea and in deeper water than usual, while observing a great but entirely harmless basking shark, he failed to notice the storm that was suddenly brewing as the wind picked up and the sky began to darken over. By the time he became aware of the danger the waves were beginning to throw him about and his swim-fins were inadequate against powerful surges and a tide driven by the wind.

"Well, to cut a long story short, he quickly found himself in trouble; indeed he was sure it was the end as his strength gave out and his lungs filled with brine, and he began to sink beneath an increasingly turbulent surface . . . and the land so seemingly close and yet so far away.

"And then for a while no more . . .

"Except it wasn't the end but in fact the beginning of a very different life—or existence!

"He regained consciousness in a fisherman's ancient cottage, in a tiny village close to the Devon-Cornwall border, where he was tended by just such a dusky female—the fisherman's wife—as your research shows was brought to England from the South Sea islands all those many years ago as the common-law 'wife' of a sailor . . . or she was at least descended from such. And in time it transpired that this was indeed the case, mainly because of the evidence which was apparent in the . . . well, shall we say the nature? . . . in the *nature,* then, of her son; which at first seemed anything but natural in the opinion of our very slowly recovering protagonist.

"But enough of that; rather than slow the story down, let it suffice to say that this lone child of the fisherman and his exotic wife was a changeling creature, not so much a freak as a mutant, and less of a mutant than a protean . . . But there again, even that is not entirely correct, for the word 'protean' is more the definition of an ability to assume different shapes, while the youth of the story had no such ability but was *fixed* in his changeling guise or form.

"And if I may for a moment digress: as a man of learning, indeed a teacher, I am sure you will recognize the source of that word 'protean.' It derives, of course, from 'Proteus,' the name of an ancient Greek sea god with the power to readily change his shape to whatever was desired. Ah, those remarkable Greeks and their yet-more-remarkable mythology! But which sea god were they in fact referring to, eh? The Philistine sea god Dagon, perhaps? Or possibly something much older than him? For, like the Romans, they were inclined to adopt willy-nilly the so-called gods of other lands and civilizations. Or was this Proteus some even greater power: one that Dagon himself might have worshipped, for example? And despite the name they'd given him, was he really so variable, so instantly inconstant? Or was that in fact his skill in . . . well, in bringing about changes—sea changes—in others?

"But there, I must relate the tale as I, er, *heard* it, and not get too far ahead of myself. And, to return to the subject of the only gradual recovery experienced by our protagonist—not to mention the constant care, peculiar physiotherapeutic and other esoteric treatments provided by the fisherfolk, or more properly the fisher*wife*—here was a mystery indeed. For apart from his near drowning, before being rescued and taken aboard the fisherman's boat, details of which he recalled little or nothing, he did not appear to have suffered any especially threatening injury. In short, from the moment he regained consciousness he seemed entirely intact, if weak from prolonged inactivity, but in every other respect 'as sound'—as they are wont to say—'as a bell.'

"So why, then, all of this dusky lady's tremendous efforts on his behalf? And why had he not been visited or seen, and his treatments overseen, by a properly qualified physician? But on the handful of occasions when he thought to ask such questions they were never satisfactorily answered—at least, not for quite a long time . . .

"But it was not *too* long a time before certain changes began to manifest themselves, when at last his nurse, the dusky lady of the house, became more voluble as to his specifics.

"She did not wish to shock or frighten him, she said, but now that his condition was—how to put it?—in flux, it was time he knew the truth: that he hadn't merely *nearly* drowned in that storm but had very *certainly* drowned; in short he had been dead, albeit recently so, when her menfolk snatched him from the raging sea. Thus her first efforts on his behalf were performed in order to revitalize him . . . She had quite literally brought him back to life!

"Well of course he found that difficult to believe. He was a learned man of science, albeit mainly theoretical, but metaphysics was not within his scope! On the other hand, however, the changes I have mentioned—subtle and not-so-subtle alterations in his physical being—were similarly incredible however self-evident. Indeed, and if he was not losing his mind, they were utterly impossible. And yet they were real!

"But the dusky lady, this descendant of a heterogeneous people from far foreign parts, was also able to explain at least something of these transformations: knowledge or understanding that had been passed down to her by her ancestors. For it was in her blood, her very genes—which were not entirely human! It was why her son was the way he was, though he would and did pass for human: a throwback, however malformed! And the freakishness that our protagonist had noted in him corresponded in part, if only a small part, to greater changes that he could sense were even now taking place in him!

"For the ungainly youth was certainly a kind of reversion, one that showed some of the characteristics of an earlier developmental type. A throwback, yes . . . *but to what?* To those monstrously alien creatures on the disk that I have given you? Or, if not them, to their protean creators, then? For that disk is nothing less than a sample of several items which the dusky lady would later entrust into the keeping of our horrified protagonist . . . !'"

Horrific, yes: a fitting description of this extraordinary, indeed incredible story. And now, as its narrator paused to take great gulping, wheezing, powerful emotional breaths, I became aware of his growing agitation: the way he seemed to *wobble* where he sat, like some enormous, freshly set jelly. Then, as I tried to gather my own more-than-mildly-disturbed thoughts, he said:

"But look, it's getting late and we must go our separate ways . . . soon. For though I promise that I shall not keep you too much longer—and I can see how very eager you are to be on your way— still the tale is not yet told. Not in its entirety . . ."

He was of course right: the shadows in the little bay were almost visibly creeping now, and likewise my flesh as the—the person?— opposite me, where I sat shivering, prepared to continue the telling of what could only be *his own* fantastic story; a tale which I had no doubt he believed in every detail, despite that it was obviously the figment of a warped imagination.

And because of that, and also because of the *disturbances* which now appeared to be affecting him physically—the way the movements of his gross, still-unseen body caused his cloak to heave and shudder with some deep inner passion as he swayed from side to side and began to toss his awful head, and the way his glutinous voice had been growing more and more coarse and phlegmy— because of these things I once again made as if to rise.

For I needed to be away from there, from that once but no longer idyllic place, that strange Greek bay, and away from *him*, both of which were now so utterly alien to me. But my legs were weak—from the swimming or the chill of a perfectly understandable dread that had risen in me, I couldn't say; probably from both. For by then I more than fancied I was in the company of a raving madman, and in a way that I could barely explain to myself I found myself hoping that this was so! But I tripped as I attempted to rise, stumbled and at once sat down again. And, helpless to stop my jaw from falling open, I gaped in frozen astonishment, completely petrified as the changes in my stranger's weird appearance continued to take place, evolving more monstrously yet.

I had seen motion in that robe or cassock, that garment of his, before—seen it move when he seemed angered or agitated—but now its entire surface was moving, *rippling* like the small waves on a pool when a pebble strikes the water. The color of the ripples was a translucent purple similar to the faded pastel shade or living flush that I had seen in certain jellyfish, in the ichor of various tropical conches, and in the fascinating color-changing displays of cuttle-fishes . . . as if in some fantastic way the garment was reacting to its owner's excitement, his passions! But as for what those emotions were doing to the man himself:

Beneath the robe's cowl—which was also horribly mobile, flut-tering away from the stranger's face as if trying to turn back on itself—his great head was a mutable mass of blurred, vibrating flesh. His eyes, bulging even further from their sockets, glared at me as he leaned forward; and it dawned on me that I had not once seen those eyes blink! But the rest of his face . . . those puls-ing slits, or overlapping flaps of flesh in the sides of his neck . . . the wobbling and apparently boneless blob where a chin should be . . . his obsolete nose and rudimentary or atrophied ears . . . and worst of all his cicatrices—or those coiled bas-relief shapes which I had *assumed* were cicatrices—which appeared to be twisting and twining, pulsing and throbbing, shrinking and bloating! It was all far too much, too terrifying. And the thought occurred that I was actually looking at an alien, a thing from some far world—which in a sense he was—or at best something that might once have been a man! And:

"Ah, see!" He burst in on my thoughts and nightmarish conclusions. "You are doing it *again!* I can see it in your face . . . your fear . . . your intense loathing! But myself, I knew no fear or horror when I saw that poor, faltering youth . . . that stumbling travesty that a handful of local dimwits believed was some sort of retard or imbecile, for I felt an indisputable kinship! His mother, dusky descendant of strange islands and liaisons that she was, she had seen it in me, too . . . she had *known* immediately, instinctively, that my blood was the same as hers, the legacy of an elder race . . . It was why she had saved me with her cold saltwater massages, her eel and octopus oils and myriad other exotic balms, potions, poisons and even prayers to the protean gods of ocean.

"But alas, she told me in her own blunt and uncultivated, mainly unschooled fashion, in order to save my life and revitalize me, she had found it necessary to accelerate my . . . my *transformation.* Unfortunately, in so doing she had overstepped herself, had gone too far. And now there was no going back.

"I tried to deny what she was telling me; I was and always had been a wholly human being, a man, I told her . . . until she inquired: Had I known my parents? No, I was obliged to answer; I had been found in the wild, wrapped in seaweeds and abandoned on a beach at the tide's reach. 'Ah!' she said then: abandoned by my mother, or perhaps my father, or possibly both, who had known . . . *known* what they had brought into this world and couldn't face it, and perhaps in their way had hoped the sea would take it back where . . . where *I* belonged! For this dusky lady knew that she was not the only being from distant lands—not the only one come down from ancient stock—who walked the sands at England's ocean's rim and felt not only the tide's surge but also the surging of her changeling blood.

"But I asked her, what of me now? And what of your son who goes to sea with his father to lure the fishes?

"'He can go no further,' she replied. He had to remain as he was, where he was, suffering the loneliness in silence. For he was incomplete, ill-equipped, and if he tried to take to the sea it would kill him. But as for me—

"Yes, I again urged her. What of me?

"'You are even further, *much* further down the road to the sea! And if you would survive you may not stay here. Before you are seen to be . . . to be *different*, you must move on. For there are places in all the many oceans that are suited to you, as you are destined to be.'

"And she also told me of a place she knew of in the middle sea, a place that was deep and completely unknown to men, whose dwellers would accept me while I lived out my life . . . the oh-so-long life that she had bequeathed me. Thus I came here to complete my change. And now the tale—*my* tale, as I am sure you know—is told."

With which he arose and approached me. But when I say that he "arose," that hardly says it all. For while he had been telling me his story, during all that time he had not really been seated, or only half so. No, he had been merely resting, leaning against the slab of fallen rock, which now became apparent as he straightened and stood a little taller, but not too tall, before *slithering* toward me.

Still frozen as if hypnotized, incapable of any meaningful movement of my own, with my mouth gaping, trying to utter some incoherent thing, but lost for words and failing, I sat there with my equipment bag over my trembling knees, my impotent speargun still propped against the rock; impotent because I just couldn't find the strength to reach for it, and I didn't want to disturb this mad creature any more than he or it was already disturbed.

"But see"—he coughed the words out as, bending a little, he thrust his face close to mine and enveloped me in that awful rotting-weed foulness—"even now I cannot help myself . . . I am still drawn to this land that calls to me mockingly yet is forbidden to me. For I cannot—I may not—stay here in your world, in this world, which men accept as their birthright. For my world is out there . . . out there in the deeps!"

"I—I—" I somehow managed to gulp, almost choking on that pointless stuttering and in effect meaningless repetition. But:

"No, no—don't you 'I—I' me!" he blurted. "Say nothing—but only watch! For while I have told you all, even paying you to listen, still I have proved very little. The proof lies in what remains. And so farewell . . ."

With which he smiled—if I may call what he did with his hideous face a smile—and I saw that the teeth behind his fat fish-lips were small, razor-sharp triangles like those of a piranha! Then, gurgling with mad, viscous, sobbing laughter, finally he turned away.

At last, capable of movement, I did as he had requested of me, turning my head to follow his movements as he squirmed away from me and made for the now sullen sea. And just exactly as he had stated, the proof was there in what remained.

He *squirmed,* yes, and I then saw how completely mistaken I had been. I had thought that he wore some kind of cloak or cassock. Wrong, for his all-enveloping, purple-tinted canopy was in fact a part of him: a mantle, most definitely, but in no way an article of clothing. It was more properly a *mollusk's* mantle—the flexible outer-layer or "skin" of an octopus's or sea snail's protective sheath. And its hood, drawn back so revealingly now, was a part of that sheath; while beneath the hood a misshapen head . . .

. . . was frog- or fishlike, a bulging warty blob . . . and the neck with those throbbing gill-slits . . . and *that face* when he turned his head to look back . . . those eight tightly coiled raised markings which I had believed were cicatrices or self-inflicted scars, except they were no such thing but twelve-inch, suckered tentacles, writhing as they now *uncoiled*! But the worst came as his mantle lifted like a skirt, shaking itself to be rid of the damp, clinging sand at the sea's rim . . . the sight of his huge, bulbous, however truncated body, itself supported by—but I simply can't say by how many—fat, blue-black tentacles like a great convulsing nest of rubbery, alien snakes. And above what passed for lower limbs, the purple-glistening softness of upper parts, with never a sign of normal human arms!

I saw all of that, and also the trail left by the heaving propulsive contractions and expansions of those massive nether members: the way the sand was sculpted into a swirling, zigzag pattern, much like the earlier impressions those youths had made in dragging the weathered limb of a waterlogged tree back down to the sea—and *exactly* like the track this creature had carved into prominence on leaving the sea to make his way here while I was swimming!

And now finally he was returning to the sea, leaving me alive, entire and uninjured, however shaken and in doubt of my own five senses. But then, at the very end, there came the occurrence that brought everything else I had experienced into horrific focus, burning itself into my brain so intensely that I know I shall never forget it. It was simply this:

That as this protean thing sank into the water, he turned and waved a last farewell. But how, with no arms to wave? The answer is this: *that he waved with his terrible face!*

I do not remember escaping from that place, climbing the cliff-hewn path and returning to the resort, but my dreams have been inescapable. Perhaps I should have hurled that golden medallion into the sea, but I did not. Along with the other specimens in my collection, the thing has this unmentionable attraction all its own. And it seems possible, however much I try to resist admitting it, that there is a reason.

For now I ask myself these questions:

What involuntary impulse—what images of a weird paradise— had drawn me to that lonely bay in the first place? And what was it in the monstrous being's tale that continues to haunt me despite that I refuse to accept its relevance? For the fact is that while I grew to adulthood in the keeping of loving, watchful parents, they were *not* my natural parents. Having been adopted from an orphanage, I had no knowledge of my real mother and father, though the man I had *called* Father had once told me that he was the brother of he who sired me. So much he told me, and then no more. But keeping in mind such an alleged relationship, then there are those coins he left me, those now sinister disks with their own fateful attraction. Did he perhaps inherit them from his brother, my real father?

Moreover, despite my nightmarish experience in that little Greek bay, I still have this love of the sea and dream of deeps I can only describe as Elysian, however alien.

But there, none of my fancies or fears may be real, and in both heart and mind I strive to convince myself that I was born of and for this earth, the ground under my feet, and not the surging ocean. At times I feel certain of this, yes—

But still I know that for the rest of my life, no matter how long, I shall continue my daily ritual of examining myself—my entire body head to toe—oh-so-very, very carefully . . .

BRIAN LUMLEY started his writing career by emulating the work of H. P. Lovecraft and has ended up with his own highly enthusiastic fan following for his worldwide best-selling series of Necroscope® vampire books. After discovering Lovecraft's stories while stationed in Berlin in the early 1960s, he decided to try his own hand at writing horror fiction, initially based around the influential Cthulhu Mythos. He sent his early efforts to editor August Derleth, and Arkham House published two collections of the author's stories, *The Caller of the Black* and *The Horror at Oakdene and Others,* along with the short novel *Beneath the Moors.* Since then he has published numerous novels and collections and won the British Fantasy Award for his short story "Fruiting Bodies." More recent works by Lumley from William Schafer's Subterranean Press include *The Möbius Murders,* a long novella set in the Necroscope® universe, and *The Compleat Crow,* reprinting all the short adventures and longer novellas in the saga of Titus Crow. He is a recipient of the World Horror Convention's Grand Master Award and World Fantasy Convention's Lifetime Achievement Award.

The Nixie of the Mill-Pond

THERE WAS ONCE upon a time a miller who lived with his wife in great contentment. They had money and land, and their prosperity increased year by year more and more. But ill-luck comes like a thief in the night. As their wealth had increased so did it again decrease, year by year, and at last the miller could hardly call the mill in which he lived his own. He was in great distress and, when he lay down after his day's work, found no rest, but tossed about in his bed, sorely troubled.

One morning he rose before daybreak and went out into the open air, thinking that perhaps there his heart might become lighter. As he was stepping over the mill-dam the first sunbeam was just breaking forth, and he heard a rippling sound in the pond. He turned around and perceived a beautiful woman, rising slowly out of the water. Her long hair, which she was holding off her shoulders with her soft hands, fell down on both sides, and covered her white body.

He soon saw that she was the nixie of the mill-pond, and in his fright did not know whether he should run away or stay where he was.

But the nixie made her sweet voice heard, called him by his name, and asked him why he was so sad.

The miller was at first struck dumb, but when he heard her speak so kindly, he took heart, and told her how he had formerly lived in wealth and happiness, but that now he was so poor that he did not know what to do.

"Be easy," answered the nixie. "I will make you richer and happier than you have ever been before, only you must promise to give me the young thing which has just been born in your house."

What else can that be, thought the miller, *but a puppy or a kitten?* and he promised her what she desired.

The nixie descended into the water again, and he hurried back to his mill, consoled and in good spirits.

He had not yet reached it, when the maid-servant came out of the house and cried to him to rejoice, for his wife had given birth to a little boy. The miller stood as if struck by lightning. He saw very well that the cunning nixie had been aware of it, and had cheated him.

Hanging his head, he went up to his wife's bedside. And when she said, "Why do you not rejoice over the fine boy?" he told her what had befallen him, and what kind of a promise he had given to the nixie.

"Of what use to me are riches and prosperity," he added, "if I am to lose my child? But what can I do?"

Even the relatives, who had come thither to wish them joy, did not know what to say.

In the meantime prosperity again returned to the miller's house. All that he undertook succeeded. It was as if presses and coffers filled themselves of their own accord, and as if money multiplied nightly in the cupboards.

It was not long before his wealth was greater than it had ever been before. But he could not rejoice over it untroubled, for the bargain which he had made with the nixie tormented his soul. Whenever he passed the mill-pond, he feared she might ascend and remind him of his debt.

He never let the boy himself go near the water. "Beware," he said to him, "if you do but touch the water, a hand will rise, seize you, and draw you down."

But as year after year went by and the nixie did not show herself again, the miller began to feel at ease.

The boy grew up to be a youth and was apprenticed to a huntsman. When he had learned everything, and had become an excellent huntsman, the lord of the village took him into his service.

In the village lived a beautiful and true-hearted maiden, who pleased the huntsman. And when his master perceived that, he gave him a little house. The two were married, lived peacefully and happily, and loved each other with all their hearts.

One day the huntsman was chasing a roe dear. And when the animal turned aside from the forest into the open country, he pursued it and at last shot it. He did not notice that he was now in the neighborhood of the dangerous mill-pond, and went, after he had disemboweled the roe dear, to the water, in order to wash his blood-stained hands.

Scarcely, however, had he dipped them in than the nixie ascended, smilingly wound her dripping arms around him, and drew him quickly down under the waves, which closed over him.

When it was evening, and the huntsman did not return home, his wife became alarmed. She went out to seek him, and as he had often told her that he had to be on his guard against the snares of the nixie, and dared not venture into the neighborhood of the mill-pond, she already suspected what had happened.

She hastened to the water, and when she found his hunting-pouch lying on the shore, she could no longer have any doubt of the misfortune.

Lamenting her sorrow, and wringing her hands, she called on her beloved by name, but in vain. She hurried across to the other side of the pond, and called him anew. She reviled the nixie with harsh words, but no answer greeted her. The surface of the water remained calm. Only the crescent moon stared steadily back at her.

The poor woman did not leave the pond. With hasty steps, she paced around and around it, without resting a moment—sometimes in silence, sometimes uttering a loud cry, sometimes sobbing softly.

At last her strength came to an end, she sank down to the ground and fell into a heavy sleep.

Presently a dream took possession of her. She was anxiously climbing upward between great masses of rock. Thorns and briars caught her feet, the rain beat in her face, and the wind tossed her long hair about. When she had reached the summit, quite a different sight presented itself to her. The sky was blue, the air soft, the ground sloped gently downward, and on a green meadow, gay with flowers of every color, stood a pretty cottage. She went up to it and opened the door. There sat an old woman with white hair, who beckoned to her kindly.

At that very moment, the poor woman awoke. Day had already dawned, and she at once resolved to act in accordance with her dream.

She laboriously climbed the mountain. Everything was exactly as she had seen it in the night. The old woman received her kindly, and pointed out a chair on which she might sit.

"You must have met with a misfortune," she said, "since you have sought out my lonely cottage."

With tears, the woman related what had befallen her.

"Be comforted," said the old woman. "I will help you. Here is a golden comb for you. Tarry till the full moon has risen, then go to the mill-pond, seat yourself on the shore, and comb your long black hair with this comb. When you have done, lay it down on the bank, and you will see what will happen."

The woman returned home, but the time till the full moon came passed slowly. When at last the shining disk appeared in the heavens, she went out to the mill-pond, sat down and combed her long black hair with the golden comb. And when she had finished, she laid it down at the water's edge. It was not long before there was a movement in the depths, a wave rose, rolled to the shore, and bore the comb away with it.

In not more than the time necessary for the comb to sink to the bottom, the surface of the water parted, and the head of the huntsman arose. He did not speak, but looked at his wife with sorrowful glances.

At the same instant, a second wave came rushing up, and covered the man's head. All had vanished, the mill-pond lay peaceful as before, and nothing but the face of the full moon shone on it.

Full of sorrow, the woman went back. But again the dream showed her the cottage of the old woman.

Next morning she again set out and complained of her woes to the wise woman. The old woman gave her a golden flute, and said,

"Tarry till the full moon comes again, then take this flute. Play a beautiful air on it, and when you have finished, lay it on the sand. Then you will see what will happen."

The wife did as the old woman told her. No sooner was the flute lying on the sand than there was a stirring in the depths, and a wave rushed up and bore the flute away with it.

Immediately afterward the water parted, and not only the head of the man but half of his body also arose. He stretched out his arms longingly toward her, but a second wave came up, covered him, and drew him down again.

"Alas, what does it help me," said the unhappy woman, "that I should see my beloved, only to lose him again?"

Despair filled her heart anew, but the dream led her a third time to the house of the old woman. She set out, and the wise woman gave her a golden spinning-wheel, consoled her and said, "All is not yet fulfilled. Tarry until the time of the full moon, then take the spinning-wheel, seat yourself on the shore, and spin the spool full. And when you have done that, place the spinning-wheel near the water, and you will see what will happen."

The woman obeyed all she said exactly. As soon as the full moon showed itself, she carried the golden spinning-wheel to the shore, and spun industriously until the flax came to an end, and the spool was quite filled with the threads.

No sooner was the wheel standing on the shore than there was a more violent movement than before in the depths of the pond, and a mighty wave rushed up, and bore the wheel away with it.

Immediately the head and the whole body of the man rose into the air, in a water-spout. He quickly sprang to the shore, caught his wife by the hand and fled.

But they had scarcely gone a very little distance, when the whole pond rose with a frightful roar, and streamed out over the open country.

The fugitives already saw death before their eyes, when the woman in her terror implored the help of the old woman, and in an instant they were transformed, she into a toad, he into a frog. The flood which had overtaken them could not destroy them, but it tore them apart and carried them far away.

When the water had dispersed and they both touched dry land again, they regained their human form, but neither knew where the other was. They found themselves among strange people, who did not know their native land. High mountains and deep valleys lay between them.

In order to keep themselves alive, they were both obliged to tend sheep. For many long years they drove their flocks through field and forest and were full of sorrow and longing.

When spring had once more broken forth on the earth, they both went out one day with their flocks, and as chance would have it, they drew near each other. They met in a valley, but did not recognize each other.

Yet they rejoiced that they were no longer so lonely. Henceforth they each day drove their flocks to the same place. They did not speak much, but they felt comforted.

One evening when the full moon was shining in the sky, and the sheep were already at rest, the shepherd pulled the flute out of his pocket, and played on it a beautiful but sorrowful air. When he had finished he saw that the shepherdess was weeping bitterly.

"Why are you weeping?" he asked.

"Alas," answered she, "thus shone the full moon when I played this air on the flute for the last time, and the head of my beloved rose out of the water."

He looked at her, and it seemed as if a veil fell from his eyes, and he recognized his dear wife. And when she looked at him, and the moon shone in his face, she knew him also. They embraced and kissed each other, and no one need ask if they were happy.

The Silken Drum

REGGIE OLIVER

Fly, fiend! Over the Western Sea
Followed by cries of hate from the Afterworld
—*Aya no Tsuzumi (The Silken Drum),*
Japanese Noh play, origin and author unknown.

"SHE'S JAPANESE," SAID Karen from the estate agent's. I noticed a hint of apprehension in her voice, as if she had felt compelled to warn me.

"Fine," I said. I had no particular prejudice. It was my father who had suffered at their hands in the war, not me, and my father was dead.

"So, shall I bring her round to view the property about ten tomorrow morning, Mr. Weston?" Karen sounded relieved. I agreed on the time and put down the phone. When I told my wife that we might have found a Japanese tenant for the cottage on our land, she seemed mildly interested.

"I suppose she'll keep the place nice and clean," she said.

Karen brought her at the appointed time in her car. My wife, Danielle, was content to watch her arrival from her wheelchair through the window. She did not want to meet the lady just at the moment. Danielle was not shy, but increasing disability had enhanced her natural social reticence.

I went out to meet them. Karen introduced her to me as Mrs. Naga. Mrs. Naga said: "I am Yukie," and so she became Yukie to us—or, more familiarly, Yuki.

She was tall, I thought, for a Japanese woman: about five foot eight, slim, with a narrow waist and an almost absurdly perfect figure. Her features were small and delicate, her lips were the color of raspberries, unaided by lipstick. I am not sure whether I would describe her as beautiful—we all have our personal criteria, which are far from objective—but she immediately gave an impression of charm and allure. When she smiled it was with her whole face, and her exquisite almond-shaped brown eyes shone.

Her only unattractive feature to me was her hair. It was jet-black and lustrous but somehow too fine, hanging limp over her forehead, so that the exact contours of her skull could be discerned beneath. The top of her head was somewhat flat, a black lake over which a single streak of white shivered like a water snake, swimming away from her left temple. It could have been the work of a hairstylist, but I thought not. She had the most perfect skin, magnolia-colored, smooth and unblemished as an unused bolt of silk.

Was I attracted to her? This is a subject that is still oddly painful. I can only say that when she was in the room with my wife I always avoided looking at her for too long. My wife, Danielle, was a very observant woman.

That first time I met her I noticed that she was very well dressed in tones of black but with a bright crimson shawl draped elegantly over one shoulder. I was not surprised when she told me that she was connected to the fashion business. She said she was a designer, but whether of fabrics, clothes or accessories was not made clear.

She had come to this country so that her nine-year-old son, Lee, could go to school here. According to her, education in Japan was a very rigid affair and she had decided that Lee needed a freer approach. She had heard of a school in Suffolk called Springfields which is only a few miles away from us. It was founded in the 1920s by an educationalist of extreme libertarian views and had acquired a worldwide reputation for its eccentric, antiauthoritarian ethos. Pupils could go to classes or stay away as they chose, rise and go to bed when they wanted, all that sort of thing. Needless to say, rumors of more scandalous happenings on its premises abounded.

At any rate, Yuki had decided to send Lee there. Evidently the father, whoever or wherever he might have been, had no say in the matter. Yukie Naga was someone who did nothing by halves.

I took Karen and Yuki down the drive to show them the cottage. It is a converted barn of brick and black weatherboarding, essentially a bungalow, but with a bedroom and bathroom in the roof space. I am not sure if it was particularly Japanese in aspect but its open planning, its use of wood and its plain white walls would perhaps appeal to the Japanese sensibility. Yuki seemed to approve, but she was particularly charmed by the fact that, adjoining the cottage, there was a small pond presided over by a weeping willow which trailed its long fronds in the mirror-still surface.

I suppose there was something Japanese about this, especially as there was also a flowering cherry nearby. Yuki observed it with pleasure, though she would not go very close to the water's edge. Having made this inspection, Yuki smiled and nodded at Karen, the estate agent, and that, I gathered, was that. She had taken Manor Farm Cottage at the rent we were asking.

She and Lee moved in the following week and on their first night there I invited them up to supper with us. Danielle by this time had expressed some curiosity about our new neighbors.

It was the first time that I had met Lee and I was impressed. Danielle and I had no offspring of our own and I am not in the habit of rhapsodizing over children, but Lee was exceptional. He was extraordinarily like his mother, with a perfect oval face and unblemished silken skin. His hair was as fine as Yuki's and he wore it rather long so that, at a distance, he might have been mistaken for a girl. He was exquisitely polite and obliging, and seemed almost unnaturally self-possessed for a nine-year-old. That was the only aspect of him that made me uneasy.

He said little because his English was even more rudimentary than Yuki's, but one small exchange I do remember. I had been telling Yuki that I had been an actor, which she conveyed to her son. Through her, he asked me:

"Were you a *waki* or a *shite*?"

The Japanese theater, Noh drama in particular, is very formal, and you are, I understand, either a *waki*, or a *shite*, pronounced "shté." They have certain prescribed traits, and the *shite* is generally thought to be the player of more important roles. I replied that I had in my time been both *waki* and *shite*. This puzzled Lee, but no more was said on the subject.

Though Yuki's English was patchy she was very charming and, in her way, good company. She showed enormous interest in our house and pictures and was very good at quietly attending to Danielle's needs when this was required. Both she and Lee were quite unselfconscious in the presence of her disabilities and for this I was grateful. I began to feel that I could invite her to dinner parties and introduce her to our small circle of friends.

Despite being of necessity left out of much of our conversation, Lee seemed at ease, particularly as our black and white cat, Laura, took a fancy to him. After supper they played together contentedly while Yuki, Danielle and I drank coffee in the sitting room.

Above the fireplace in the sitting room is a large Regency mirror, and though I had indicated a place for Yuki next to my wife's wheelchair and opposite the looking glass, I noticed that she took a seat very deliberately with her back to it. It was no more than slightly puzzling, as was the fact that Laura the cat, though very much enamored of Lee, seemed to take pains not to come too close to Yuki.

When they had gone I made some general remark to Danielle about Yuki, to the effect that we were lucky to have such a delightful tenant. Laura jumped onto Danielle's wheelchair and began eagerly purring and nuzzling her as she was stroked.

"Yes, she's charming," said Danielle in that deliberately neutral tone of voice she adopted when she wanted to imply something but was in no mood for a discussion. I said nothing and took note.

My days, when I am not looking after Danielle, are relatively idle. Because I cannot leave my wife, I no longer work as an actor but do some PR work for a firm from home, so I was able to indulge my natural curiosity by watching Yuki.

During the week, while Lee boarded at Springfields, Yuki was mostly away, but she would appear at odd times. On one occasion I noticed that her door was open and so I strolled down to the cottage and knocked. My ostensible purpose was the traditional landlord's excuse of asking if everything was all right. Yuki was hanging a picture and I offered to help. She smiled and invited me in.

I was surprised by the way in which she had transformed the cottage into something Japanese. The Turkish rugs had gone and the polished floorboards were now covered with Japanese matting. The padded furniture had been covered by plain white or off-white throws. All Western ornaments and pictures had been cleared away. It was not something to which I objected—she had asked my permission, even though she had taken the cottage furnished—but I was surprised by the extent of the transformation.

I hammered in the hook for her picture. It was a Japanese print depicting an old man sweeping leaves beside a pond fringed with laurel and other vegetation. The sky was dark and in it hung a large moon across which a bat flew. Despite this there were no shadows or darkness in the main part of the picture, which gave it a strange surreal effect, like one of Magritte's paintings of bright skies and dark lamp-lit streets, only in reverse. The effect was rather beautiful, I thought, except for the face of the old man, which was riddled with wriggling lines. He looked like a soul in torment. In one of the trees beside the lake hung a flat, disk-like object, resembling a tambourine. Yuki thanked me when I had hung the picture, then said:

"How come your wife, Danielle, is in a wheelchair?"

The question took me aback. It came without preliminary or excuse. I explained as briefly and coolly as possible, knowing how much my wife (and I for that matter) detested expressions of sympathy, but she offered none. She merely smiled—rather inappropriately, I thought—and nodded her head, as if the cause (multiple sclerosis, as it happens) was the diagnosis she had expected.

"How soon will she die?"

I was so startled by the baldness of this second question that I did not think to be offended. I stuttered out a very vague answer, feeling somehow guilty that I had given any answer at all.

Then Yuki said: "Please, may I ask something else?"

"Carry on." I braced myself for more personal probing.

"In your garden, there is a lake. May I walk beside it if I wish?"

"Of course." Besides the small pond next to her cottage, there is also a lake, fed by springs, in our grounds.

"Thank you very much, Weston-*san*." She bowed formally.

I took this to be the politest form of dismissal from her premises, so I went. I reflected for a while on the curious behavior in which she had unashamedly asked about my wife's condition and yet had sought permission to walk by the lake in my grounds. Another instance of: "Oh, East is East, and West is West, and never the twain shall meet," I suppose. The other odd thing I had noticed was that she had removed the large mirror in the main room and, in the wall space left vacant, had hung a number of Japanese theatrical masks, exquisitely modeled and painted. One of them seemed to me identical to Yuki's face, just a little whiter in complexion. The smile was hers to the last dimple, but the emptiness of the eyes gave it a disconcerting ambiguity.

I did not like myself for having her constantly on my mind. Whenever she came into my head I would drive her out, but there were so many unanswered questions about her. I even picked up a Japanese phrase book in a secondhand bookshop so that I could get the rudiments of her language. I hid this from Danielle, knowing that she would disapprove. I would often catch myself looking out of the window from which Yuki's cottage could be seen, but most of the time her curtains were drawn.

The lake in our grounds lies at the bottom of a slope in our garden and is fringed by alders and willow. It is plainly visible from our house, though not from Yuki's cottage. I have mown a pathway around it, along which, on fine days when the ground is dry, I wheel Danielle.

I often rise early so that I can find time to be with myself before I have to help Danielle. In these quiet moments I walk about the house, feed Laura the cat and open the curtains to let in the day. I can feel unconstrained by the limits of Danielle's disability, as can she, in her own way, in sleep.

One morning I remember standing at the sitting room window, which has a fine view down to the lake. The sun was just up and had not yet burned the dew off the grass, which glistened grayly. A few tendrils of mist were suspended over the lake. A figure of a woman, her back to me, was standing by the water. She was naked and her skin in that morning glow was as white as a sheet of paper, so that for several moments I doubted my senses. A long fall of lustrous black hair with a thin white streak in it came straight down her back to the top of her buttocks, almost obscuring that absurdly narrow waist. It was Yuki.

With a steady, slow walk, like a priest performing a ritual immersion, she descended into the water. Barely a ripple flowed out from her wading thighs. Then the water touched her hair and began to splay it out in a black fan. When it was above her waist she launched herself gently into a swimming position and began to navigate the lake with a gentle breaststroke, still barely disturbing its surface, except with a few fine undulating rings of water.

I watched avidly, telling myself that, since the lake was on my property, I was entitled to the spectacle. Besides, I imagined that my feelings in those moments were not predominantly sexual. I was filled with the desire to possess her, but in the way that one longs to possess some exquisite little object—an ivory statuette, perhaps, seen in the window of an antique shop.

The still of the morning was utterly noiseless, so that I seemed to hear the blood running through my veins and my heart drumming. Laura the cat, having had her fill of breakfast, came over and began to nose my legs. I continued to watch, motionless.

Presently Yuki dived down into the depths of the lake, leaving the surface a dark, unblemished mirror. Her absence stretched from fifteen to thirty seconds, so that I began to be concerned for her, then to wonder if my vision of her had not been some kind of illusion.

Thirty seconds stretched to a minute and my concern became a fever. I considered running down to the lake to rescue her. Then at last she broke the surface and was swimming toward me. Strangely she had allowed her hair to fall over her face so that I could barely see her features, and what I could see was blurred by the water that dripped over it.

As she walked up the bank the water seemed to cling to her like a viscous veil. There was a moment when she stopped abruptly and lifted her head, still partially covered with her hair. I was reminded of an animal in a forest suddenly scenting danger and felt sure that she had somehow become aware that I was watching her. With instinctive quickness—again I was reminded of an animal—she crouched down and turned her head away from me.

When she rose again she had her back to me and was clutching something white. It was a robe of some kind—toweling, perhaps—and when she had put it on she began to run up the bank and across the grass in the direction of her cottage as if seven devils were behind her. I turned away from the window, not wanting to be seen and feeling obscurely guilty. I had seen her breasts: they were small but perfectly formed and the nipples, like her lips, were the color of raspberries.

In the next few days I tried to avoid all contact with Yuki. I occupied myself with the small amounts of work to which I had been delegated: writing articles for trade magazines and the like. Danielle, whose powers of observation had been enhanced rather than dimmed by her condition, noticed at once that I was in an odd, distracted state. Of course I tried to conceal it from her, but it was no use. Her oblique, intuitive intelligence devised a plan to shake me free of my neurosis. She proposed that we should have a dinner party, and that our pretext should be that we were inviting friends and neighbors to meet our charming new tenant, Yuki. I agreed, knowing that any reluctance on my part would immediately invite further suspicion.

In the country one can become extremely attached to rather dull people simply because they live nearby and are pleasant and kind. So we invited the Havards and the Spences. I say they were dull, but, to be as objective as I possibly can, I can't really say they were any duller than Danielle and I had become over the years. They were almost inevitable choices because, apart from anything else, we owed them hospitality. The difficulty was to find a spare man to partner Yuki, and Danielle was oddly insistent that we should sit down to table as four couples. Eventually, for want of anyone more suitable, we invited Justin.

Justin lived in a small cottage in our village and was an artist. That is to say, he painted and called himself an artist, though I have never heard of anyone buying one of his paintings. His means of subsistence was a small inherited private income. I found his choice of lifestyle on the whole rather admirable. He never complained, as some artists do, about the neglect to his genius, perhaps because he never did anything to inflict it upon others; at the same time I did wonder how he found purpose in life. He was a tall, lean man in his fifties, not unattractive, but too diffident to be a charmer. He had about him the slightly wistful, neglected air that you find in many unpartnered middle-aged men. He was not dull; at any rate his form of dullness was peculiar to himself, which, in our part of the world, counts as being interesting.

Yuki was the first to arrive for the dinner party. It was a warm July evening, so we had decided to have drinks on the terrace over-looking the lake. Danielle and I noticed at once that in the fortnight since she had come to us her English had improved enormously. Paradoxically, this only served to make her seem more Japanese, since she had managed to translate the formal conversational patterns of her native language into equally formal English. On arrival, having first presented Danielle with a bonsai tree in a pot, she handed me something wrapped in black tissue paper.

"Because you a famous and popular actor interested in theater," she said.

I had come across this penchant for meaningless flattery in the Japanese before and knew that it required no denial from me that I had ever been famous or popular. We both understood it was nonsense, just part of the game.

I opened the tissue paper and found that it was a book called *Noh Plays of Old Japan Translated by A Lady*. The edition, dated 1867, was bound in Hessian cloth and printed on what looked like handmade paper. There were full-page illustrations too, in black and white. I thanked Yuki profoundly for this strange rarity and she bowed in acknowledgment. She told me she had discovered it in a local secondhand bookshop.

The next person to arrive was Justin, carrying an untidy bunch of flowers plucked from his garden, which he presented to Danielle. It was typical of him that the shirt and jacket he had decided to put on for the occasion were almost smart, but his jeans were clearly the ones he had worn all day and were smeared with countless dabs of paint. Yuki seemed bewildered at first by this vision of British eccentricity.

Egoists like Justin can occasionally deliver bursts of enormous charm, and for about twenty minutes he showed his best side, but as soon as the Spences and the Havards arrived he began to devote his attention exclusively to Yuki. From then until the end of the evening he monopolized her. It was difficult to say whether he had captivated her or she him, but there was clearly a mutual fascination. I have to say that their relationship bothered me from the first, but I did nothing at all to hinder it. It was partly that any interference would have aroused Danielle's suspicions; in any case, I could never decide whether I should warn Justin about Yuki or vice versa.

That night, after our guests had left, I said to Danielle: "That seemed to go all right." Usually this rather banal opening was the prelude to a discussion about the social interactions that had just taken place. It was a process which both Danielle and I were still able to share and enjoy, but on this occasion Danielle was not in the mood for postmortems. Rather abruptly she asked to be put to bed. I wanted to ask what was the matter, but was afraid of a rebuff.

Having settled Danielle, I went to my own study to drink a final glass of whisky on my own. I often feel that the best thing about exercising hospitality is the stillness that follows it. Outside in the darkness an owl shrieked. I started violently and was a little alarmed by my reaction. My nerves were unexpectedly on edge. I picked up Yuki's gift and leafed through it.

Noh plays are not really dramas as we would understand it. They consist mostly of narration and comment. To the Westerner they are more like cantatas or liturgies with responses and lyrical interludes, and yet, though the tales they tell are often vanishingly slight, they have a compelling quality. Events pass as if in a dream; delicate atmospheres are invoked. There is sometimes a harshness and cruelty about them which may even enhance their beauty.

I turned the pages dreamily and was surprised to find that one of the illustrations was similar to the print I had hung on Yuki's wall. It was in severe black and white as opposed to color and the lines were more crudely engraved, but the image was the same. An old man is sweeping leaves beside a pond. His face is a serpentine wriggle of black lines that simply but effectively convey the man's age and the torture of his soul. In the trees that fringe the pond hangs an object like a tambourine.

On the page facing the picture was the beginning of a play that announced itself as *Aya no Tsuzumi, The Silken Drum.* After a list of characters came the first speech of one designated as COURT OFFICIAL (*Waki*):

"You have before you an official at the Palace of the Moon in the province of Chukuzen. Let me relate to you the history of this place. There was once a beautiful Princess who lived in the Palace of the Moon which was surrounded by a lovely garden. The garden was tended by an old man who regularly came to sweep the leaves by the Laurel Pond. There one day he saw the Princess and fell in love with her. He was a very foolish old man because one day he could not prevent himself from declaring his love for the Princess, but she was born of a water spirit and had no heart, and when she was alone she had no face. The Princess appeared to take pity on the old man and hung a drum in the tree beside the Laurel Pond telling him that every time he beat it, she would hear the drum in the Palace of the Moon and come to him. But when the old man beat the drum he found that she had mocked him by stretching silk instead of skin across the drum so that it made no sound. The old man would beat the drum in vain and in the end he went mad with despair and threw himself into the Laurel Pond. And now his angry ghost haunts the Laurel Pond with his endless torment and those who come to it at night hear inside their heads the beating of the silken drum."

The rest of the play seemed to me to be a simple working out of this strange little story, and not very impressive save for a few stray lyrical fragments from the chorus:

> "A silken drum, hung in a laurel tree,
> Beats out the autumn of his lust,
> As rainfall on withered leaves,
> As the fall of a dragonfly into a moonlit lake."

I found it hard to sleep that night, possessed by the sheer strangeness of what I had read. The story stuck in my mind, despite its cruel pointlessness, or perhaps because of it. In my fitful dreams I seemed to discover a meaning which, when I woke, evaporated. Eventually I could stand it no longer and decided to get up.

Laura the cat was pleased to be fed so early. She nuzzled my hand tenderly before attacking the sachet of food I had opened for her. I wandered about the sitting room, idly clearing up after the previous night's party. I pulled open the curtains.

The dew was heavy on the lawn. The sun had only just risen above the horizon behind a thin veil of cloud. Over the lake hung mist like a congregation of specters, twisted into strange shapes. I had hoped—yes, I admit it—that I might have seen again the naked form of Yuki dipping in those waters, but she was not there. Of course not! Why should she have been? It was a shameful idea.

A figure stood on the far side of the lake, but it was fully clothed and male. I could not tell immediately who it was because of the mist. The figure was pacing around, hands in pockets with slightly hunched shoulders. He was an odd sort of trespasser. Was he waiting for someone? I found a pair of binoculars and looked again. This time I could see that it was Justin.

It angered me to find this artistic deadbeat making free with my property at such an early hour. I decided to go down and challenge him, firmly but politely, of course, but just then Danielle called out from the bedroom. Once I had attended to her needs I came back into the sitting room to look again, but Justin was gone.

There was no doubt, however, that something was happening between Yuki and Justin. I would often see Justin walking down the drive to pay a call on her. If I waved or called out to him he would often ignore me, or offer the most perfunctory of salutes. Frequently he would be carrying a brush and a tin of paint or a box of tools, presumably with a view to making some minor adjustment to Yuki's domestic arrangements. I might have told him that any repairs or alterations were my responsibility, not his, but somehow I did not. When Lee was at home Justin could be seen out on the lawn with the boy, bowling to him with a tennis ball or catering to some other childish whim. He seemed to me to have become a slave to Yuki and her son.

I remember on one occasion watching Justin as he wheeled Lee around the lawn in a wheelbarrow which had been lined with cushions for the boy's comfort. It was a hot August afternoon and Justin was sweating from the exertion. Every time he stopped, Lee would yell at him and insist on one more circuit of the lawn. Dimly through the window of the cottage I could see Yuki looking out. Her face was expressionless, the eyes dark. It was as if she had placed a mask at the window instead of her own face to look out on the scene.

As time went on, my concern—you might say my obsession—with Yuki and Justin's relationship increased. Even now I cannot fully explain it. I even voiced it to Danielle, though I knew I would get no sympathy there. In the last few weeks Danielle had begun to withdraw into herself. Acute illness and disability sometimes take people in this way. When I mentioned Yuki and Justin almost light-heartedly to her, saying something like "I just can't make out their relationship," she looked at me with that unnervingly penetrating gaze she had.

"Why on earth are you bothering about them?" she said. "Just thank your stars she hasn't got her little hooks into you." In other words it was none of my business, and of course she was right.

I tried not to think about it, but it was difficult. One evening in mid-September, just as autumn was beginning to encroach on us, having settled Danielle in front of the television with a light supper, I went out for a walk. I went down the road to the stream which divided us from the next village and lingered at the ford, watching the light drain from the sky behind the black trees. By the time I was returning it was darker than I had expected. At the top of the drive I looked down toward Yuki's cottage.

The curtains of one of the windows to her sitting room were open and the interior was bathed in the yellow glow of a standard lamp. In the background on the opposite wall I could make out the array of white theatrical masks that had replaced the mirror. In front of them were two people. Yuki was standing up and Justin was sitting or kneeling in front of her, I could not tell which.

Yuki's face was almost entirely obscured from me by her long black hair. I could see her figure down to just below the thigh and she was naked. Though half turned away from me, I saw the contour of her breast and its raspberry-colored nipple. Justin's face was clearly visible and his expression gave me a shock. He was gazing up at her and his look was one of perplexity and terror. I could not help approaching for a closer look.

Yuki lifted up one arm and from a cup began to pour a liquid over Justin's head. His expression turned from one of fear to acute agony and he covered his face with his hands. I heard her laugh. It was a terrible laugh, high-pitched, like an animal's shriek—a laugh of pure vicious mockery without a trace of humor or humanity in it.

I stepped forward, half-minded to intervene, but then something was in my hair, fluttering and screeching. Glancingly I touched it, and there were no feathers, so not a bird. It was only a second or two, but I believe that I had touched the fur and leathern wing of a bat. I turned and ran back to my house.

After that I became still more distracted and out of touch. Fortunately—or perhaps unfortunately—Danielle did not notice. She was by that time too involved in her own physical deterioration. I had begun to hire carers for her on a more regular basis, and this in turn gave me more time for my own obsessions.

A few days later I was taking a walk through the village when I happened to pass Justin's cottage. Morbid curiosity had been growing in me and I decided to satisfy it.

His was one of a row of workmen's cottages, barely large enough for one, of the two-up and two-down variety with a kitchen extension at the back. His front door was not open, so I concluded that he must be in his studio, a brick outhouse at the end of his garden. Its door was standing open and I could see him within, his back to me, attending to one of two canvases, both of which were on easels. Not wishing to extend the period of my unobserved scrutiny of him, I knocked tentatively at the door.

He started violently and turned round. "Christ, where did you spring from?"

I was shocked to see how he had aged in a few short weeks. His lean face was now scribbled over with lines that I had not seen before. Deep grooves creased his cheeks and curved around his mouth from the nostrils; the eyes were puddled in grayish-purple sleeplessness. His sparse hair was in wild confusion over the top of his head, with more gray in it than previously. It broke like a storm over the shore of his temples. I thought I saw madness on him, but this may be the product of hindsight or wishful thinking.

"I'm sorry," he said, with an effort to control himself. "I don't really like to be disturbed when I'm working." *Working*, he called it: a small vanity, I suppose.

"Looks interesting," I said.

Justin's paintings were vaguely reminiscent of the sloshy semiabstract style of Willem de Kooning, an artist whom he admired. The two canvases before me seemed more controlled and less abstract than his usual work. Both showed roughly the same scene: a woman standing beside a pond fringed with trees. The woman was wearing a traditional Japanese kimono, sketchily done, but well enough to create a clear impression. In one painting the woman was bent over the pond so that her long black hair, blazoned with a single streak of white, streamed over the front of her head, obscuring her face. But there was no reflection of her in the water. In the second she was standing upright and her face, fringed by the black hair, had no features; it was a smooth white oval, like an egg. Hanging in the bushes behind her was a tambourine-like object covered with patterned cloth.

"Is that meant to be Yuki?"

"Piss off! Look, just . . . piss off!"

I did as I was told. I had seen the anguish on Justin's face and knew that it was no use arguing. As I left the cottage an autumn wind sprang up and began to snatch leaves from the trees. Later that afternoon from the windows of my house I caught sight of Justin again. He was raking dead leaves from the lawn in front of Yuki's cottage. A white face seen dimly through a windowpane indicated that she was watching.

One morning, about a week later, I found a woman wandering about in our driveway. She had evidently been down to the cottage and was returning from it, somewhat indecisively. Her car was parked across the road. When she saw me she flinched slightly, but seemed reassured when I smiled and asked if I could help.

"I'm Leonie," she said with a downward emphasis on the second syllable. "I'm the deputy head of Springfields. In charge of pupil welfare."

She was in her late thirties, a shapeless woman dressed mostly in handwoven garments of sage green. She had a long, sagging face and wore a necklace of hand-beaten copper disks. Rather naïvely, perhaps, I thought she looked somewhat careworn for an employee at a supposedly "free" school.

"I rang up yesterday to make an appointment to see Mrs. Naga this morning, but she doesn't seem to be there."

"Her car isn't in the drive. She must have gone out," I said.

"I'm sorry. You are . . . ?"

"I'm John Weston. Her landlord. I live here at the main house."

"I see," said Leonie. There was a faint note of disapproval in her voice. "Do you know when she will be back?"

"I'm afraid I have no idea. Mrs. Naga is a law unto herself."

"Yeah," said Leonie. My last words seemed to have struck a chord. "Look, I think I should wait here a little in case she does turn up. Is that all right?"

"Of course," I said, and invited her into our house for a coffee. Leonie seemed very awkward at first, but when she met Danielle in her wheelchair she relaxed a little. While I made coffee, Leonie began talking earnestly to my wife. Danielle still liked company in small doses, but became easily tired, especially when she had to address herself to strangers. Every now and then Leonie would go to the window to see if Yuki's car was back in the carport beside the cottage.

When we were finally settled with our coffee, Leonie said: "Look, Mrs. Weston—Danielle, if I may—can I be frank with you?"

"Please do," said Danielle, throwing me a quizzical glance. She was beginning to tire.

"It's about Lee, Mrs. Naga's son."

"Oh, yes. Sweet boy." My wife's bland words troubled Leonie.

"Yeah, well . . . He can be difficult. I mean, it's not his fault or anything. We don't play the blame game at Springfields, but there must be some sort of trauma there. Perhaps abuse by the father. This is why I made an appointment to see Mrs. Naga. Lee is a bright boy, but he is being quite a disruptive influence. I have to think of all the kids, not just one. As you know, Springfields has a very nonauthoritarian ethos. There are no rules as such, but there are, well, like, lines in the sand. You know? Lee can behave very inappropriately, especially around the girls."

"But he's barely nine!"

"I know! I know! But that's not all. There are other things. Worse. I can't say, obviously. And he has this thing about fire. Twice he's tried to burn down the tree house in the grounds. When there were kids in it too! And he put dead frogs in our vegetarian food—at least they were dead when we found them. The fact is, in all the eighty or so years of Springfields we have never had to ask anyone to leave. It looks as if we may have to. I'm sorry to burden you with all this, Danielle." Leonie's hand was trembling as she put down her coffee cup.

"That's quite all right, Leonie," Danielle said, with obvious weariness.

"The fact is, I don't want to be judgmental, but the boy is a fucking little devil—oh, I'm so sorry, Mrs. Weston! I shouldn't have said that—"

In her embarrassment Leonie got up and went to the window. Yuki had still not come home. When Leonie turned back from the window she saw that my wife had suddenly dropped off to sleep in her wheelchair, as she sometimes did toward the end.

"I'm sorry," said Leonie, and fled from the house. Soon after she drove away.

Yuki did not come back until after six o'clock. I heard her car enter the carport by her cottage as I was preparing the supper. I thought it was necessary for me to tell her of Leonie's visit, so when we had had our meal and Danielle was settled in front of the television, I went down to the cottage and knocked on Yuki's door. The curtains were drawn and the lights were on, so she was obviously in, but there was no response. Perhaps she had not heard. I knocked louder, but there was still no reply. Then I walked around the cottage and rapped on one of the sitting room windows. Almost immediately the curtains were drawn and Yuki's face was looking at me, her eyes black with fury. Then I saw a look of recognition in them and she indicated to me that she would go to open the front door.

The Yuki who met me there was smiling demurely, though I could not dispel the impression that this was only a mask that concealed other thoughts. She wore a peach-colored silk kimono that trailed round her feet and over it hung her lustrous black hair. Gone was the Western chic of her designer clothes; she had reverted to a more ancient archetype.

"What is it you must say, please?"

I gave her a brief résumé of what Leonie had told us that afternoon. Yuki listened impassively, the mask-like smile still on her lips, then she said:

"It does not matter. I am taking Lee away from Springfields in any case. It is a stupid school and he hates it. We will go back to Japan, I think."

"When?"

"Soon. Very soon."

I reminded her that, as her landlord, I needed at least a month's notice of her departure.

"That will be no trouble," she said carelessly. Her indifference was infuriating. I wanted somehow to smash the mask.

"And what about Justin?" I asked. "Have you told *him* you're going?"

For a brief moment I saw surprise on her face. *I have broken the mask*, I thought. Then she began to laugh, that high-pitched bat-screech of a laugh that was barely a laugh at all. Her mouth opened enough for me to see her perfect little sharp teeth and the bright red interior of her head. The laughter went on until I could not bear it, so I got up and left.

Outside the cottage it was dark and a full moon hung in a clear night sky. Yuki had stopped laughing and I could hear nothing but a faint squeaking that came from the guttering of the cottage. There, almost on the corner of the building, an object like a black leather bag was suspended. I stared at it for some time, not daring to approach, let alone touch it.

A slight quiver told me that it was alive and then the lower part of it began to raise itself. Soon I would see its head. It was a bat, of that I was now sure. We had had them roosting in our roof and I was well-disposed toward the creatures, but this was so much larger than the pipistrelles to which we were accustomed. Soon I would see its deep brown Pekinese face and bulging black eyes. I wanted to move, but could not. Then I saw its face. It was not black at all, but white, almost like a mask, almost human, but through it the black eyes gleamed with senseless, feral hatred.

Up at the house, when I reached it, Danielle was calling to be taken to the bedroom. The tasks of a carer helped to wipe away some of the confused horror of that night. I began even to believe consolingly that I had been the victim of an illusion or a practical joke.

The following morning I rang Karen at the estate agent's and asked her to deal with Yuki's departure from the cottage. I wanted as far as possible to distance myself from her and the whole business. It was a relief to me that during the next few days I saw neither Yuki nor Lee nor Justin.

I live in a quiet lane of a quiet village in a quiet part of Suffolk. Apart from the occasional hooting of owls or the shriek of a vixen, the nights are virtually noiseless. That night, five days after my last interview with Yuki, was still and quiet. The sky was clear and the moon only just past its fullness. Danielle and I had retired early. Since her illness we had had separate bedrooms: it was easier, we were both agreed on that. Her room was at the front of the house, mine at the back, closer to Yuki's cottage.

At about three o'clock I was woken by what my confused brain first told me was thunder. Yet I heard no rain to accompany it. The sound was rhythmical, almost like the banging of a drum. That was even more absurd. But the noise persisted: it was real.

I rose and put on a dressing gown and slippers. In the sitting room Laura was running about fearfully and clawing at the carpet. I looked out of the window and down to the cottage. I could just make out a dark figure at the door, banging at it. A faint light glowed from behind the drawn curtains; the figure went on banging. This was intolerable.

I picked up a flashlight and ran out of the house, down to the cottage. My flashlight shined onto the face of Justin. It was he who was standing at the door and banging on it with his fists. His face was ruined. Dark circles surrounded his eyes; his mouth was set in a rictus of pain. He looked like a soul in torment.

He did not stop when he saw me. He gave me one fleeting, agonized look, then returned to his drumming on the door, as if he were compelled to continue his work, regardless.

I shouted at him: "For God's sake, stop that!"

"Go away!"

"Stop that at once."

"Leave me alone!"

"No, I will not! This is my property. We can't get to sleep with that racket."

"All right, I'll stop." He stopped. "Now go away."

After getting an assurance that there would be no more noise, I did. There was nothing I could do for him. The man was in Hell.

For the next hour or so I lay in bed waiting for the drumming to return, but it did not. I heard nothing more that night except, when my mind was just on the edge of sleep, a shrill, thin cry—like a beast in agony. That may have been an illusion.

I woke early. My mind was still unrested and I took my time with the simple pleasure of feeding Laura. When I looked out onto the garden, mist was coming up in strange spirals from the lake and I saw something dark floating on its surface.

I think instinct told me what I would find before I did. I unlocked the French windows and ran down the grass slope to the lake. The body of a man was lying face-downward on the still water. I waded in and pulled the thing out. Of course it was Justin. Of course he was dead. His mouth gaped madly.

I ran back to get to a telephone in the house, passing as I did so the little pond beside Yuki's cottage. There I saw on its bank another body, again facedown, dressed in a kimono of peach-colored silk. The silk was torn and sprayed with blood. The body was battered and bruised, but when I turned her over I saw that the head was undamaged.

This was odd, but not so odd nor so horrible as the fact that her face, framed by the familiar shiny flat black hair with its lightning streak of white, was not only without a wound but completely featureless. Across the oval space where her eyes, nose, mouth and chin should have been was a flat expanse of bare magnolia-colored flesh with not a mark on it. The skin appeared to be stretched tightly, like that on a drum.

REGGIE OLIVER has been a professional playwright, actor, and theater director since 1975. Besides plays, his publications include the authorized biography of Stella Gibbons, *Out of the Woodshed,* published by Bloomsbury in 1998, and five collections of stories of supernatural terror, of which the latest, *Mrs. Midnight,* won the Children of the Night Award for Best Work of Supernatural Fiction in 2011. Forthcoming is a new collection, entitled *Flowers of the Sea.* Tartarus Press has reissued his first and second collections, *The Dreams of Cardinal Vittorini* and *The Complete Symphonies of Adolf Hitler,* with new illustrations by the author; his novel *The Dracula Papers I—The Scholar's Tale* is the first of a projected four, and an omnibus edition of the author's stories, entitled *Dramas from the Depths,* is published by Centipede as part of the Masters of the Weird Tale series.

The Robber Bridegroom

THERE WAS ONCE upon a time a miller, who had a beautiful daughter, and as she was grown-up, he wished that she was provided for, and well married. He thought, *If any good suitor comes and asks for her, I will give her to him.*

Not long afterward, a suitor came, who appeared to be very rich, and as the miller had no fault to find with him, he promised his daughter to him. The maiden, however, did not like him quite so much as a girl should like the man to whom she is engaged, and had no confidence in him. Whenever she saw, or thought of him, she felt a secret horror.

Once he said to her, "You are my betrothed, and yet you have never once paid me a visit."

The maiden replied, "I know not where your house is."

Then said the bridegroom, "My house is out there in the dark forest."

She tried to excuse herself and said she could not find the way there.

The bridegroom said, "Next Sunday you must come out there to me. I have already invited the guests, and I will strew ashes in order that you may find your way through the forest."

When Sunday came, and the maiden had to set out on her way, she became very uneasy. She herself knew not exactly why, and to mark her way she filled both her pockets full of peas and lentils.

Ashes were strewn at the entrance of the forest, and these she followed, but at every step she threw a couple of peas on the ground. She walked almost the whole day until she reached the middle of the forest, where it was the darkest, and there stood a solitary house, which she did not like—for it looked so dark and dismal. She went inside it, but no one was within, and the most absolute stillness reigned.

Suddenly a voice cried, "Turn back, turn back, young maiden dear, 'tis a murderer's house you enter here!"

The maiden looked up, and saw that the voice came from a bird, which was hanging in a cage on the wall. Again it cried, "Turn back, turn back, young maiden dear, 'tis a murderer's house you enter here!"

Then the young maiden went on farther from one room to another, and walked through the whole house, but it was entirely empty and not one human being was to be found. At last she came to the cellar, and there sat an extremely aged woman, whose head shook constantly.

"Can you not tell me," said the maiden, "if my betrothed lives here?"

"Alas, poor child," replied the old woman, "whither have you come? You are in a murderer's den. You think you are a bride soon to be married, but you will keep your wedding with Death. Look, I have been forced to put a great kettle on there, with water in it, and when they have you in their power, they will cut you into pieces without mercy, will cook you, and eat you, for they are eaters of human flesh. If I do not have compassion on you, and save you, you are lost."

Thereupon the old woman led her behind a great hogshead, where she could not be seen. "Be still as a mouse," said she, "do not make a sound, or move, or all will be over with you. At night, when the robbers are asleep, we will escape. I have long waited for an opportunity."

Hardly was this done than the godless crew came home. They dragged with them another young girl. They were drunk, and paid no heed to her screams and lamentations.

They gave her wine to drink, three glasses full, one glass of white wine, one glass of red, and a glass of yellow, and with this her heart burst in twain. Thereupon they tore off her delicate raiment, laid her on a table, cut her beautiful body into pieces and strewed salt thereon.

The poor bride behind the cask trembled and shook, for she saw right well what fate the robbers had destined for her.

One of them noticed a gold ring on the finger of the murdered girl and, as it would not come off at once, he took an ax and cut the finger off. But it sprang up in the air, away over the cask, and fell straight into the bride's bosom.

The robber took a candle and wanted to look for it, but could not find it. Then another of them said, "Have you looked behind the great hogshead?"

But the old woman cried, "Come get something to eat, and leave off looking till the morning. The finger won't run away from you."

Then the robbers said, "The old woman is right," and gave up their search, and sat down to eat. And the old woman poured a sleeping-draft in their wine, so that they soon lay down in the cellar, and slept and snored.

When the bride heard that, she came out from behind the hogshead, and had to step over the sleepers, for they lay in rows on the ground, and great was her terror lest she should waken one of them. But God helped her, and she got safely over.

The old woman went up with her, opened the doors, and they hurried out of the murderer's den with all the speed in their power.

The wind had blown away the strewn ashes, but the peas and lentils had sprouted and grown up, and showed them the way in the moonlight. They walked the whole night, until in the morning they arrived at the mill, and then the maiden told her father everything exactly as it had happened.

When the day came for the wedding to be celebrated, the bridegroom appeared, and the miller had invited all his relations and friends. As they sat at table, each was bidden to relate something. The bride sat still, and said nothing.

Then said the bridegroom to the bride, "Come, my darling, do you know nothing? Relate something to us like the rest."

She replied, "Then I will relate a dream. I was walking alone through a wood, and at last I came to a house, in which no living soul was, but on the wall there was a bird in a cage which cried, 'Turn back, turn back, young maiden dear, 'tis a murderer's house you enter here.' And this it cried once more. My darling, I only dreamt this.

"Then I went through all the rooms, and they were all empty, and there was something so horrible about them. At last I went down into the cellar, and there sat a very, very old woman, whose head shook. I asked her, 'Does my bridegroom live in this house?' She answered, 'Alas poor child, you have got into a murderer's den, your bridegroom does live here, but he will hew you in pieces, and kill you, and then he will cook you, and eat you.' My darling I only dreamt this.

"But the old woman hid me behind a great hogshead, and scarcely was I hidden, when the robbers came home, dragging a maiden with them, to whom they gave three kinds of wine to drink—white, red, and yellow—with which her heart broke in twain. My darling, I only dreamt this.

"Thereupon they pulled off her pretty clothes, and hewed her fair body into pieces on a table, and sprinkled them with salt. My darling, I only dreamt this.

"And one of the robbers saw that there was still a ring on her little finger, and as it was hard to draw off, he took an ax and cut it off, but the finger sprang up in the air, and sprang behind the great hogshead, and fell into my bosom. And there is the finger with the ring."

And with these words she drew it forth, and showed it to those present.

The robber, who had during this story become as pale as ashes, leapt up and wanted to escape, but the guests held him fast, and delivered him over to justice.

Then he and his whole troop were executed for their infamous deeds.

By the Weeping Gate

Angela Slatter

SEE, HERE?

This house here in Breakwater, this one, by the Weeping Gate where men and women come to wait and weep for those lost to the sea. This house is very fine, given the notoriety of the canton in which it resides—indeed, given the notoriety of its inhabitants.

The front stairs are swept daily by the girl who tends to such things (more of Nel later); the façade is cleverly created, a parquetry of stones colored from cream through to ochre; some look as red as rubies, all creating a mosaic of florals and vines (the latter use malachite tiles). There is nothing like it anywhere else in the port city and there are uncharitable souls who whisper its existence is owed solely to the artisans' truck with magic. The windows are always clean and shine like crystals, but none may see inside due to the heavy brocade drapes hung within.

Come to the door, look at its intricacies, all carved from ebony, bas-relief mermaids and sirens, perched upon jagged rocks with the sea throwing itself against those ragged angles. The knocker is surprisingly plain, as if some tiny attempt at good taste was made; it's merely brass (highly polished, of course), with a slight ripple pattern so it looks something like a piece of rope. The house was not built by its current occupants—they have shifted into it, grown like a kind of hermit crab into a new shell—but by a sea captain who quickly made and then lost his fortune to the ocean and its serpents and pirates, its storms and violent eddies, its whirlpools and deceptive coasts with rocks sewn just beneath the surface. After that, another man purchased it, an ill-famed prelate with no flock, who spent his days delving into dark mysteries, talking to spirits and trying to create soul clocks so that, if he might not live forever, he could at least access another lifetime. His departure from the city was encouraged by a nervous populace. The abode lay dormant and lonely for several years until *this* woman came along.

Dalita.

Tall and striking with jet-black hair, skin the color of wheat, and eyes like brown stones. She dragged behind her three small daughters, their features enough like hers and distinct enough from each other's to say they had different fathers. No one knew whether she bought the property or simply set up shop there—a lawyer did descend a few weeks after her presence was noticed, but by then her business was well-established (it took only a week).

The solicitor rapped the knocker peremptorily, a look of displeasure on his face, and entered when the door was whisked open. He came out some time later, features quite changed and set in what seemed an unfamiliar arrangement of happiness. He walked somewhat stiffly now, but this did not seem to bother him at all. He became a regular visitor and was content to leave Dalita to her affairs (and her offspring, who continued to increase in number), and if his wallet was a little heavier and his balls a little lighter each time he left, then so much the better.

For all its decorative glory, the house does not have a delightful marine aspect. Perhaps that is unfair. By peeking out one window, inching one's body sharply to the left and pressing one's face hard against the glass, one might see, through the tight arch of the Weeping Gate, a sliver of water. It is, it must be said, a strip of the peculiarly unclean, slightly greasy liquid that lines the port, infected by humanity and its waste. But then, no one who ventures this far comes for the sea view.

The house has no wrought-iron fence, nor tiny enclosed garden; it simply sits cheek by jowl with its street, which is muddy in times of rain, dusty in times without. The cries of the gulls are not faint here, nor is the smell of fresh, drying or dying fish.

Once inside, however, incense and perfume, a heady opiate mix, negates any piscine odors (and others more personal, leisure-related), and anyone setting foot in the spectacular red entrance hall will immediately lose hold of their fears or concerns. The richness of the decor and the beauty of the girls, their charm, their smiles, their voices (coached to pitch low and light), combine to wash away all imperatives but one. After a single visit, even the most nervous trader, wheelwright, tailor, sailor, princeling or clergyman—in short, anyone who can scrape up Dalita's hefty fee—will be content to wander the requisite dark alleyways to the house by the Weeping Gate.

And in truth, with time the locale became strangely safer— mariners keen to earn extra coin were easily recruited to run interference in the streets. Thieves and ruffians learned quickly not to trouble those walking in a certain direction with a particular gait, lest they find themselves faced with consequences they did not wish to bear. The longshoremen were known on occasion to shift some of the more inconvenient street-side debris further away from the house. No need to scare the punters.

Gradually, Dalita's clientele increased, and soon enough she took fewer *habitués* herself, becoming fussier, more miserly, with her favors. But as each daughter came of reasonable age, so the number of employees of the house grew; firstly Silva, then the twins Yara and Nane, then Carin, next Iskha, then Tallinn, and finally Kizzy.

Asha was kept aside, held back for finer things.

And Nel, too, was kept aside, banished to the kitchens.

Iskha, taking her fate in her own hands, ran away and should not have been seen again.

Nel has never feared the streets. They always felt more welcoming than the woman's house—she does not think of Dalita as her mother, possibly because she has never been encouraged to do so.

Nel is plain, astonishingly so. Perhaps Dalita might have forgiven her if she had been ugly, for that would have been one thing or the other, but as plain as she is, Nel seems almost . . . nothing. A blank upon which looks did not imprint. Perhaps this causes the most offense—the other daughters all have some version of their mother's allure, enhanced cunningly with pastes and powders, dresses and corsets, all to make the best impression in the eye of the beholder.

But Nel . . . on the occasions her sisters tried to make her up, make her *over*, it seemed as if the colors they layered upon her face had no effect at all, merely sat on her skin effecting no more of an impression than the merest hint of a breeze. The lacy pink tea gown dangled listlessly on her as if it, too, could find nothing on which to *take*. Her hair, similarly, would neither kink nor wave even after a full night wrapped tight in rag curlers. When let loose, it simply hung to her shoulders in thick straight lengths, neither brown nor black nor blond, but an unremarkable mix of all three. Of middling height, with middling gray eyes, she was a middling sort of girl and blended into her surroundings as well as a chameleon might.

She'd found in the avenues, the alleys, the seldom-used thoroughfares, the hidden ways *through*, a kind of home and a kinship with those who inhabited those places. Similarly invisible, they recognized a fellow shadow. Some took the trouble to help. Not attracting the eye meant not attracting attention, and there was safety in this. Mother Magnus, the cunning woman, showed her smidges of magic to help dampen the sound of her footsteps, to make darker shades cling to her as camouflage. Lil'bit, the cleverest thief, taught her how difficult locks might be encouraged to open, even though she did not indulge this newfound talent for nefarious purposes. Every little bit of knowledge was stored away, if not used immediately.

But the streets had become less welcoming in the past few months, the gloom seemed darker and deeper, the night silences heavier, and she was never sure now what she might find when she went abroad, either on ways of packed earth or cobbles.

Nel had found the first girl.

She'd gone to buy the week's coal, dragging the newly cleaned little red tin wagon behind (Dalita always insisted it be pristine no matter that the coal filthed it up within moments). Nel was always there earlier than Bilson's Coal Yard opened, but she knew how to subvert the lock on the rickety wooden gates and Mr. Bilson was happy for her to leave the small bag of brass bits and quarter-golds in a tiny niche beside the back door of the building.

Nel let herself in, every bump of the wagon on the ground making a loud protest against the quiet of the dawn, but it kept her company. She made her way over to the huge scuttle (the height of one man, the length of two and the width of three) with its metal lid and rolled the thing open to find a face staring back at her. As she looked harder into the dim space she could see a body carelessly laid across a bed of black, bare but for its dusting of coal, an expression of eternal bewilderment on the dead girl's face.

The Constable, fat and red-faced, was terribly upset with Nel because she couldn't tell him who had done this thing, which was going to make his job difficult. He normally dealt with nothing more than theft and drunk-and-disorderlies. He studiously ignored runaways, vowing that they would return whenever hungry enough. He quietly took his bribes from those who ran the underbelly of the city—they were terribly good at self-regulation, which he appreciated. Any bodies that were the result of the criminal machinations tended to disappear. *He* did not have to deal with them. This . . . this was something new.

"I didn't see anyone," she said for the third time. "I just found her."

"And what are you doing out so early?" he demanded.

She rolled her eyes. "Buying the coal for the house; and Madame Dalita will be looking for me by now."

At the mention of her mother's name, the Constable realized that he didn't need to detain her any longer.

Everyone hoped this murder was simply an aberration, but no. There had been five others since—or, at least, five who had been *found*. Nel had seen two of them, but only from a distance as they were hastily taken away to avoid public panic. One from the fountain in the city square (which was round), one from the garden at the bottom of the old Fenton House (deserted for many years), another in the orchard belonging to the Widow Hendry on the outskirts of the city, yet another on the steps of the city hall and the final one tied to the prow of the largest ship in port, a caravel belonging to the Antiphon Trading Company. The young woman was wrapped around the figurehead as if holding on for dear life.

The girls were all poor, mostly without family, but all very, very lovely, once upon a time. It didn't matter, however, when they were lifeless and lying on the marble slabs of the Breakwater Mortuary, all wrapped in black cloth so their souls couldn't see to get out, all waiting for the coffins paid for by the city council—penniless girls, yes, but nothing puts more of a fright into folk than the idea of the restless dead. Those who in life had been destitute and dispossessed, when improperly buried, seemed to be more disagreeable, disgruntled and disturbing as revenants. So the council of ten, made up of four members of the finest families, three of the richest traders, two of the most vociferous clergymen and the Viceroy, reached into their deep pockets and stumped up for properly made coffins and decent burials.

The Viceroy began to make noises after girl number two, found in the fountain—*People drank that water!*—and so the Constable was given two helpers to aid in his investigations. Unfortunately, the need to spend time in taverns asking questions also meant the under-constables found themselves unable to resist the temptation of drinking while working and managed, by sheer effort, to not help very much at all. The Constable traipsed daily to the Viceroy's office, a hangdog expression on his face, his head sinking lower and lower into the setting of his shoulders, so much so that people wondered if it might simply disappear and he would cut peepholes in his chest so he might see out. He stood quietly while the Viceroy yelled.

Nel had watched with interest some of the Viceroy's performances.

He was in his seeming midthirties, a handsome blond man with a poet's soft blue eyes. Tall and well-made, he dressed with care and splendor, which set him apart from the previous Viceroy. He raged at the Constable. He ranted at the council members. He looked splendid doing it. He spoke gently to those who had lost daughters and paid out a blood price to those who asked, even

though, as people commented approvingly, it was not his place
to do so. And he attended at the funerals of the murdered girls,
eulogizing each and every one, warmly praising the power of their
youth and beauty, and lamenting their loss.

When Nel had first appeared at the door to the council chamber
bearing her mother's initial missive, he had paused in his tirade at
the Constable and given a vague smile. Now he did not bother, as
if her plainness made his eyes slide away and he could no longer
notice her. She wondered if he thought the notes floated to him all
by themselves. Indeed, her approach excited so little attention that
she often watched him unheeded, caught his unguarded expressions and was surprised by those times when it seemed his face was
not his own but a mask set loosely atop another. Nel would shake
her head, knowing her eyes deceived her.

She would clear her throat and he would stop what he was doing,
stretch forth his very fine hand with its manicured nails for her to
place the letter onto his pale, lineless palm. That fascinated her, the
blank slate of flesh, as if he had neither past nor future. As if he had
simply appeared in the world as he had appeared in Breakwater, six
months prior, bearing all the right letters with all the right seals.
Accompanied only by two potato-faced men, who spoke seldom
and then in monosyllabic grunts, he tidily ousted the incumbent
Viceroy—a man known for his indolence, drinking and fondness
for young flesh and payments made under the table—in a coup that
had delighted and surprised the citizens.

He was terribly good at organizing things and wonderfully
talented at shouting down opposition, so the city began to run
smoothly for the first time in many a year. Grumbles about his dic-
tatorial style gave way to admiring nods as the mail began to arrive
in a timely manner, purveyors were obliged to clean up their kitchens, and slack or shoddy workmanship incurred painfully large
fines.

When Dalita initially sent her on this errand (having waited in
vain for the new Viceroy to attend her establishment), Nel wondered at the woman touting for business. She thought perhaps Dalita

feared the man's next target would be to root out moral corrup-
tion and the like—he seemed the type. How else could one explain
his absence from the house by the Weeping Gate? Dalita's product
spoke for itself, attracted buyers and created its own momentum,
and would have done so even without the little bewitching touches
such as enchanted whispers blown across a crowded marketplace,
and tiny ensorcelled chains of love-daisies slipped into pockets and
baskets.

Eventually, though, Nel realized that this was something more
than a simple marketing ploy; this was higher stakes. Dalita was
offering something for a more permanent purchase, not merely a
short-term *rental*.

Dalita was planning to move *up* in society.

At the outset, Nel simply waited for the Viceroy to sniff and snort
and send her out of the chamber with laughter echoing in her ears;
but he did no such thing. He read the note, opened the locket which
had weighted down the billet-doux and stared at the miniature por-
trait of Asha for a while, then gave a nod, and the words, "I will
consider this proposition."

She duly reported to her mother, who sat back on a padded
chaise with a well-satisfied look and a gleam in her eye. The speed
with which this businesslike courtship has proceeded surprises
no one.

Now Nel visits the Viceroy every second morning or so with
some wedding-related query. He does not give her a direct answer,
but sends one of his men back with a written reply in the afternoon.

What he *does* give Nel are his traditional sennight gifts for his
bride-to-be (whom he has never met), one for each day of the week
before the wedding.

These are strange, gaudy things that seem to have begun life as
something else. A rusty iron coin, set in a fine filigree and hung
on a thick gold chain. A rag doll dressed up in a robe of impossible finery and carefully crafted miniature shoes, but the doll itself
smells . . . wrong, musty, a little dead. A bracelet of old, discolored
beads, restrung on a length of rope of wrought silver. A brass ring

with a piece of pink coral atop it. A shard of green, green glass set in a gilt frame as if it is a painting. A mourning broach dented and tarnished, the hair inside ancient, dry and dusty, but a new stout pin has been affixed to the thing so it won't fall away. And finally, today, the earrings.

They are large, uncut, dirty-looking diamonds, stones only an expert would recognize (and Dalita is such a one).

They hang from simple silver hooks.

They are ugly and the Viceroy insists his bride wear them for their upcoming wedding.

The attic stretches the length of the house. It is populated by six beds, narrow wooden things, but with fat, soft mattresses and thick eiderdown duvets, satin coverlets and as many pillows as might be accommodated on the sparse space. To one side of each bed is a freestanding wardrobe, plain yellow pine, lightly lacquered, barely able to be closed for the wealth of attire stuffed within: day frocks, evening gowns, costumes for clients with more particular needs, wisps of peignoirs for those who prefer fewer hindrances to their endeavors. To the other, bedside tables stuffed with jewelry, hair decorations, stockings, knickers, protective amulets, random votives, powders, paints and perfumes. Nel's thin pallet is in the kitchen, piled high with her sisters' cast-off quilts.

There is a space, too, where bed, 'robe and table no longer reside, but the marks of their feet are still visible. A gentle reminder of Iskha, who always talked of running away and one day did. A space haunted by the glances the other girls give it, and by the presence of one whom they now speak of rarely and then only in whispers for fear their mother might hear. A space filled with yearning.

The wooden floors are covered with rugs of thickly woven silk— only naked feet may tread on these, so all the footwear for the ladies of Dalita's establishment is kept in the room, which takes up half the tiny entry hall to the attic (the other half is a curtained-off bath- room), and is lined with shelves stashed with rows and rows of all manner of shoes: slippers, boots, heeled creations, sandals of gold and silver leather, complex constructions of ribbons and bows that must be applied to the foot using an equally complex equation of order and folds to ensure the wearer can walk.

Against the back wall of the long room is the sacred space: one large bed with four posts, big enough to accommodate three fully grown adults, and hung with thickly embroidered tapestries to cut out the light when beauty sleep is a must. On either side of the bed rests a wardrobe, mahogany, also tightly packed. To the left of this suite is a dressing table, complete with a stool, cushioned lest the buttocks of the chosen one be bruised. On the tabletop, rows and reams and streams of necklaces, bracelets, droplets of earrings and finger rings, all a sparkle like a tiny universe of stars carelessly strewn. And amongst this are pots and bottles (carved of crystal in various shades), palettes and brushes to apply all the colors required to highlight eyes, emphasize cheekbones, give lips more pout than Nature intended, and an oil (expensive, rare) to make black hair shine like wet obsidian.

This is the space laid out for Dalita's special darling, her most beautiful child, the loveliest of them all; the one, Dalita believes, who most resembles *her*.

Asha's mane falls below her waist, its ends tickling the tops of her thighs when she stands; Nel, when she is not in the kitchen, spends many hours washing it, rubbing oil into it, washing it once more, then brushing it, brushing it again until it glistens.

Asha's eyes are just a little too large (like a doll's), and hazel, and in the company of men, frequently cast down as Dalita has taught her. Her skin is the color of butter with a marked sheen—again, Nel spends many hours rubbing this skin with creams that contain tiny flecks of gold and silver. Asha's face is the shape of a heart, her nose pert and straight and her mouth an inviting purple blossom, lips always moist. She is secure in her position, in the knowledge that she's destined for something *more*. It does not make her unkind.

She is Dalita's gem, her pearl, her sole unspoiled child, for Dalita has greater plans for this daughter. Asha remains untouched and unbroken, a prize to go to the highest of highs. And at the moment, she is not in the room, which is awash with the noise of young women waking and dressing, bickering and bonding.

"Don't pull so!"

"Oh, hush."

"You're never so rough with Asha," whines Nane.

Yara, sitting opposite her, nods, "No, never so rough."

"I'm not rough," protests Nel, "but you will let clients mess up your hair like this. Honestly, it's a bird's nest—what do they do?"

"Naught you'll ever know about." Nane laughs and pokes her tongue out. Nel catches sight of it in the mirror and tugs harder on the black tresses, smiling when her sister howls. Yara sniggers and earns a kick from her twin.

From one of the beds comes a growl. Silva sits up and glares. "Shut up, you lot. Some of us are trying to get our beauty sleep."

"Some need it more than others," replies Tallinn silkily, and a barrage of giggles and pillows explodes from Silva's bed. Her aim is excellent and her ability to throw in more than one direction is impressive. Only Nel is safe. As if the sisters know Dalita's treatment of the plain one is more than enough torment for anyone, they are always tender to their kitchen sister.

"There." Nel draws the silver-backed brush through the now-smooth locks one last time, smiling at their luster with content-ment. "Hurry, Yara, you're next, before Asha comes."

"Oh, yes, Asha's big entrance. Gods forbid she ever slip *quietly* into a room." Kizzy rolls out of bed and slides to the floor, a look of discontent painted on her porcelain face. She is rounder than her sisters, scrumptious and cuddly, and the youngest; as such she instinctively knows she should be the one who is spoiled, but Asha's preeminence has deprived her of this and she resents it daily.

Yara slips into the spot vacated by her twin and lets her eyes close, feline, as the brush begins its work. Yara is as *neat* as Nane is untidy; with their faces so alike it's hard to believe that their natures are so different. Nane is robust, hoydenish; Yara is sleek, almost virginal (something truly precluded by her occupation, but the impression is more than enough to satisfy a particular kind of client).

"Someone help me with these stays," howls Carin. "Gods, Nel, can't you be more careful when you wash these things? You've shrunk my corset!" She struggles with the garment, tugging it this way and that, pulling on the tying ribbons until they threaten to snap. Nel puts down the brush and makes her way over to the wildly struggling sister.

Calmly, she bats Carin's hands away and adjusts the corset, shifting a fold of fabric here, straightening a caught-up hem there, and finally pulling the ties into alignment and deftly doing them up. She pats her sister's face and kisses her cheek.

"I think you'll find the corset is the same size and you're the one who's changed. How long since—"

"Oh, no!" Carin wails. "Not again."

"You're so careless," says Tallinn, rippling a frilly green day dress over her head. "Mother will make you keep this one—she said so last time."

Carin slumps to her bed, head hung low, face covered with her hands. But she doesn't cry—none of Dalita's girls are given to tears, for they redden eyes, puff up faces, coarsen complexions and fill sinuses with unpleasant fluids; no one looks charming thus.

"Maybe," she mumbles through her fingers. "Maybe it wouldn't be so bad?"

"And what life for it?" snarls Kizzy. "What life?"

Nel looks at the youngest and frowns, putting a finger to her lips. "Hush now, hush, Carin. We'll take care of it, don't worry. Dalita doesn't need to know."

"Maybe," says Carin, "Maybe I could find Iskha?"

Carin's expression of hope hurts Nel's heart. She wonders if her other sisters suspect that she helped Iskha.

"I could go to stay with her? Do you think, Nel? Could we find her?"

"I *think* I'll make the appointment for next week. Mother Magnus will take care of it. Just keep your food down for a few more days, and give me one of those brooches the fat little Constable gave you last week."

"What for?" demands Carin, affronted that any of her trinkets might be taken. Nel rolls her eyes.

"You have to pay for her services somehow and what money do you think I have?" she asks tartly.

Carin subsides and reaches into the top drawer of her bedside table to pull out a square mother-of-pearl container stuffed with things that shine. She hands Nel a cameo engraved with the head of a Medusa, lovely and serpentine, then insists, "Could *you* find her, Nel?"

"I think she wanted to get away and if she doesn't want to be found, she won't be."

Nel pats her shoulder and returns to Yara's hair, which she gives a final cursory brush and twists into a tightly elegant chignon. "Now, all of you, neat and tidy—lest *she* come looking and find you wanting."

As if summoned, Dalita appears, with all the imposing poise of an empress. Her eyes sweep the room, finding nothing to complain about, all daughters dressed and coiffed, paints applied to faces, potions and perfumes to skin. In her hands (strangely square, mannish, very capable, ruthless—what might those hands not do?) is a box, ancient, highly polished, yet with its wood cracking under the weight of years, a gold clasp holding it shut. It is almost four of the afternoon and the clients will soon come a-knocking, but first there is this to be done, this important thing before tomorrow.

Behind her stands Asha, quietly dignified, her wedding dress a great white confection glowing in a ray of last sun pouring through the skylight above. Carefully taught by her mother, she knows how to always present herself in the best possible way; she knows everything there is to know about lighting, position, composure, posture, how to dominate a room from the moment you entered to the moment you left.

One senses, however, that she is not at full power, that she has dimmed herself for this moment, which is a practice run; she conserves her energy until she needs to *glow*.

The dress—the result of seven seamstresses sewing sleeplessly for seven nights—is rather like a wedding cake, with its lace and frills, its layers and embellishments. Shiny white, reflecting with so many hand-sewn crystals it almost hurts the eyes. It is the first time she's seen it, and Nel thinks it looks like a suit of armor.

No one but Dalita is to have the honor of preparing Asha for her wedding day, for Dalita trusts no one but herself. She certainly knows her craft: Asha is breathtaking; her sisters, even Kizzy (slightly green), stare in admiration and longing, and not a little envy.

Upon Asha's hair—which has been carefully coiffed, bouffed, backcombed, woven, braided, twisted, tied and knotted and sculpted like spun black sugar—is a fringe tiara, a framework of gold-wrought wire. From it flows a veil of silk gossamer, spider-spun, almost to the floor, but somehow incomplete. The headdress fans across the crown of her head like a peacock's tail, with seven fine hollow spikes as part of the structure, yet there is no adornment, none of the gems one might expect.

Dalita looks over her shoulder, gives Asha leave to move into the center of the attic so she is encircled by her sisters (not Nel, though; Nel falls back, knowing her place is not *there*, and stands against a wall, quiet as a shadow-mouse). Dalita's fingers clutch at the casket, fumble with excitement as she flicks the clasp.

"This box," she says, pauses, struggles. "*This* has not been opened for forty years, not since your grandmother wed. What is inside is a gift to the bride that only a family can give: protection and a dowry against the future."

She lifts the lid and offers the contents to Silva, then Tallinn, then Yara, then Nane, then Kizzy, and finally Carin; she herself takes the last item. Apiece, they hold what looks like a very long hatpin (the length of a hand), topped with a gemstone, each a different color. Dalita takes her diamond-tipped pin and approaches Asha; carefully she inserts it into the middle spindle of the headpiece. "Long life to you, my daughter. Bring your family prosperity and pride."

All the sisters do the same, and soon a rainbow arcs across Asha's tiara: blue, red, green, purple, orange, pink and the diamond, clear as light.

The earrings from Asha's betrothed hang like clumps of dirty water at her ears. Dalita adjusts her daughter's hair, just a little, to try to cover the offending ornaments. She frowns, making mental note to ensure the 'do is tweaked *just so* on the morrow.

Dalita surveys her other daughters, does not speak, but merely waves a hand.

To a woman, they traipse out of the attic and down the stairs, past the two floors of the house where each bedroom is equipped with a sturdy bed, themed decorations, and a discrete bathing corner, down to the three parlors on the ground floor, where they will drape themselves over chairs and long sofas. Yara and Nane will pull back the curtains in the front windows and settle themselves on the padded seats to watch for oncoming visitors, and smile and wave, welcoming the regulars and drawing new customers in. Kizzy and Tallinn will ensure the drinks trolley in each room is fully stocked and all the heavy crystal glasses of varying shape and sort and size are ready. Silva will hover to open the front door upon the third knock (always the third, any less is too hasty, any more too tardy—three is just enough to sharpen a client's anticipation, but not enough to stretch his or her patience). Carin will wait with her, ready to take coats and hats and canes and carefully put them away in the walk-in cupboard by the door. Tomorrow, they will have the day off, but not tonight.

"You," says Dalita, pointing a finger at Nel, but not looking at her. Nel wonders if the woman suspects. "Take this to the Viceroy."

Nel nods, pocketing the letter.

"But first help your sister out of that dress." Dalita's need to control extends only to the construction, not the deconstruction, of an illusion.

Nel nods again, although she knows this is neither required nor expected.

Dalita turns, her burgundy gown whispering, and lightly touches Asha's creamy cheek. She catches sight of herself in one of the mirrors hung on either side of the doorway and pauses, struck. Nel wonders how many nights the woman spends before her own reflection, watching the years converge upon her skin and begin to decay her beauty. Dalita shakes her head, closes her eyes for a moment, then leaves. Both girls let their breath go as soon as they hear her heels on the stairs.

"Is it heavy?" Nel asks. Asha nods carefully so as not to dislodge the work of art on her head. Nel begins with the headdress, unclasping the veil first of all and tenderly draping it across the nearest bed. Then the tiara, laid beside it.

"Is he handsome? Up close?" Asha asks unexpectedly.

Nel pauses in the task of unbuttoning the two hundred tiny pearl buttons running down the back of the gown. Nel wonders if she should tell her about the times when she fancied the Viceroy seemed *other*, but decides against it. "Yes. You've seen him from the window."

"But that's not close up. Is he nice? You've spoken with him."

"No, I've delivered things to him and that's different." She considers. "He seems . . . determined. He knows what he wants. He is polite."

Asha sighs. "I suppose it's the best I can hope for."

Nel hugs her sister, pressing her plain pale cheek against Asha's butter-rose one. They are silent then, knowing that Asha has already had the best that can be hoped for in the house by the Weeping Gate.

Mother Magnus works and lives in a long narrow room, a forgotten roofed area, a lacuna between two larger buildings. Her bed and washroom are at the back, her workshop and store at the front; a ramshackle kitchen punctuates the middle. To look at, Magnus is anyone's idea of a witch, hunchbacked and bent, a shuffling gait, one side of her face a mess of scars, the other still quite smooth. Her hair, though, defies expectation; it is silver-white, long, soft, luxuriant, and hints at a different past. She smells like lavender.

Nel picks up bottle and jars, then puts them down. She flicks through the handwritten yellowed recipe and spell pages Magnus sells, stacked in boxes on a bench. She shifts back and forth impatiently while waiting, batting at the dried ingredients hanging from the low ceiling.

"Stand still before I hex you, child." The woman's voice is sweet, mellifluous and deep.

"I'll be late. Yet another letter to the bridegroom."

"Can't hurry magic, girl. Hurried magic is messy magic. Messy magic is dangerous magic." Mother Magnus points to the corrugated side of her face, then turns back to the mortar and pestle, attending to the task of grinding herbs with a particular intensity. Nel will ask her, one day, what happened, but she knows that now is not the time. The cunning woman's back is eloquent in its deflection of inquiries. There is a dry rustling as the crushed ingredients are shepherded into the neck of a small bottle, then a *glug* as a purple liquid is poured in after. Magnus stoppers the flask and seals it with black wax. She hands it to Nel, who, in return, counts five quarter-golds in her wrinkled palm.

"My thanks, Mother," says Nel. A tisane for Asha, to help with conception. Dalita is determined that her daughter will be *embedded* in the Viceroy's life as soon as possible.

Nel finds herself staring at the ruined side of Magnus's face and, without thought, she blurts, "Does my mother ever come to you?"

Magnus shakes her head. If the question surprises her she does not show it. "Never. Although if ever there was a woman I thought would seek me out, it's her."

"Why?" Nel thinks she knows the answer.

Magnus grins. "Why, for a cure against a woman's mortal enemy."

"Time." Nel nods, smiles a little, is thankful she doesn't have to worry about having beauty to lose.

"If ever I thought there was a woman who would want potions—if ever there was a woman I thought would seek a soul clock or some such . . ."

"A soul clock?"

"Steals the life—the youth more particularly, and all that goes with it. Done right, it will give you another lifetime, perhaps."

"Perhaps?"

"I've never seen it done right." Magnus rubs at her own face and turns away. She will not say more. "Night, Nel."

Nel is out of the street and heading up toward the finer part of Breakwater, where the houses rest at the feet of the mountains, when she remembers she neglected to mention Carin and her needs. No matter. There will be plenty of time after tomorrow.

The Viceroy, in preparation for his wedding, is not at the council chambers this day. Running of the city has been suspended as the townsfolk anticipate the celebration to come and no one has any complaint. The taverns have opened their doors and libations are free—courtesy of the Viceroy's fat wallet—and the brothels similarly are offering their services gratis (not Dalita's girls, though—there is no promise of a change of life for them). There is much laughter in the streets and good-natured camaraderie; petty arguments have been suspended, debts and obligations forgiven and forgotten, at least for a few days. A carousing city relaxes, lowers its guard.

As the afternoon shades to an evening lilac, Nel finds the iron gate of the Viceroy's mansion secured. From her pocket she draws out a lockpick (a gift from Lil'bit), and has the lock clicking merrily in a trice. She slips in and wanders along the path, which rises slightly as it makes its way toward the white plaster-and-granite edifice. A mansion of twenty bedrooms for a single man and his two menservants. And soon, Asha; and soon Asha will have children. Nel dreams that she might leave the house by the Weeping Gate and look after Asha's babies.

The trail winds its way through the overgrown grounds of the house, which are somewhat tropical; the air here is hot and damp. There is the smell of rotting vegetation and something else. Nel thinks the garden needs work and wonders that a man who so generously spreads his fortune across his citizens, who is so concerned with an organized and tidy city, takes no such care in his own home. In the foliage, behind the trees and bushes, things move and her spine twitches with the weight of gazes she cannot see. Nel picks up her pace.

The stone stairs of the mansion are off-white (no one washes and sweeps *this* stoop) and in places cracks make deep veins where dirt has infiltrated, looking like black blood. Nel tiptoes over them, and toward the front entrance. She raises her hand and knocks, which causes the door to swing open.

"Hello?" she calls.

There is only silence. She steps into the wide entry hall. The floor is covered with a black-and-white chessboard pattern of tiles; dual staircases climb the walls, to the left and right of a strangely placed fireplace, where only cold ashes shift in the slight breeze that has snuck in behind her. To her left and right are double doors, ornately carved, painted dove-gray with gold filigree decorations around the handles. Nel chooses the left. The parlor is empty, silent and filled with stale air. She wanders through and finds another door, a single one this time. She pushes it open: a room lined with books and at the far end two chairs (with curved armrests, slender legs and threadbare cushioning) wait, each with a large silver pan in front. In the pans is dust: two heaped piles of gray particles. On closer inspection, there is dirt, too, and what look like flakes of snakeskin. On a delicate table between, two pewter ewers, filled with water, and beside the chairs, a pile of clothes: the livery worn by the Viceroy's two attendants.

Nel slips a hand into her pocket and rubs at the thick paper of Dalita's note. Her heart does not hammer, but its rhythm has become more certain, like a punctuation of every second she remains here. She backs away, turns, and sees something she missed before: a curtained alcove. There is the sound of a latch rattling, a handle turning, and now her heart kicks like a startled horse. Without a thought, she slips behind the hanging and holds her breath.

The space is small, containing only her, a slim crowded shelf and a chest, a sea chest, not closed, with fabric spilling out. Nel reaches down and pulls at one of the rags; it's a dress, aged, dirty, with smears of coal dust across the skirt. Another dress, and another. All old, well-worn, as if by someone who could not afford to replace it; eleven in all. On the shelf, bottles. Phials half the length of her hand; she counts twelve and only one is empty. The others swirl with a roiling red-gray mist that seems to push against the glass as if to get out.

Her attention is drawn away by footsteps. Footsteps and muttering; nothing intelligible, but determined. She puts an eye to the split between the curtains and watches the Viceroy pace, his back to her, to the chairs and their cups and pitchers. He kneels, grunting and groaning like a grandfather, and pours, carefully, the contents of a jug into a pan, whispering all the while.

A mist rises, swirling into a tall tower that takes on the shape of a man. The Viceroy moves to the other pan and, while the first thing is coalescing, firming, begins the process anew. He lifts his head and Nel sees his face: the Viceroy, yes, with all the peaks and valleys of the features she knows, but old, so much older than he has presented himself. Furrows in a skin blotched with age and malign intent. Nel, understanding her time is short, slips out of the alcove and through the open door.

Her mouth is dry as paper, her throat closed over, as she sneaks from the house. A sudden breeze pulls the door from her numb grip and slams it. Nel is used to little magics, the tiny enchantments to help things along, the harmless brushes of conjuring; what the Viceroy has done—is doing—is beyond her understanding. She runs down the cracked steps; behind her she hears the front door pushed back against the façade of the house, and two sets of stumbling feet, as if their owners have just woken. Nel darts into the undergrowth; fear of what she knows is chasing her greater than that which she imagines might be lurking in the garden. She tiptoes through dank detritus, glances behind her, and in the process trips over an ill-covered lump, wrapped in a moldering blanket.

The smell of *something else* is worst here, right by this thing, this cylinder-shaped thing that feels soft and giving beneath her shaking hands. Before she summons the courage to unwrap it, however, the sound of footsteps grows louder, more confident, rushing through the leaf-litter, following her tracks. The moment before they appear, the Viceroy's golems, there is a whisper and a sigh—no, *whispers and sighs*—and Nel is surrounded by gray, wispy women, made wan by death. Through them she can just make out the potato-faced minions, their heads moving back and forth, back and forth, like confused bloodhounds. They cannot see her; the women have shielded her. The menservants shuffle off, back toward the path and the house.

Nel soughs her thanks, but the girls do not reply, merely watch her with sad, sad eyes. She glances at them, at the swirling number of them, trying to fix their faces in her memory, until her eye lights on a face she knows too well. One for whom she packed a knapsack with warm clothing and food and drink; for whom, not six months since, she'd silently unlocked the door and watched as she disappeared into the fog of the early morning. One she'd thought *free* of Breakwater and the house by the Weeping Gate.

She runs to her mother, not to the Constable, not any of the other council members. She runs to her mother, with the specter of Iskha at her heels. To Dalita because she is the most powerful being Nel has ever known. No matter that there is no love there, Dalita loves Asha and Dalita will not allow her chosen daughter to be harmed.

Nel, propelled forward by the force of Dalita's large hands, keeps her balance until the final few steps. Then she trips and sprawls.

Her fall is broken by damp fabric; felt, soaked with water. There is the sharp, briny smell of salt.

"You will not ruin this for me!" Dalita howls like a cat impaled upon a hot poker. Her rage, her disbelief, when Nel told her what she had seen, what she feared, was something to behold.

At first Nel thought it was directed toward the Viceroy, then a ringing blow to her head and a second to her face made her reconsider. While she was disoriented, her mother grabbed her by her hair and dragged her, half-crawling, half-walking, through the house, then into the kitchen and down into the cellar. Nel was unsure what enraged the woman most: the idea that Nel might endanger the wedding or that she had helped Iskha flee.

"Liar! Ingrate! Knave! Bitch!"

Dalita threw open another door, in the floor—a sub-cellar.

And the terrible truth of this place is becoming clear, after Nel's drear hours in the dank, dark room: this place is *tidal*.

There is a gap at the base of one wall, she can see, where the sea comes in, but there's no hope of escape: there is a crosshatch of bars across the opening. The water is rising, rising, rising.

Wailing and shouting have not helped—no one can hear her through the cold, thick rock of the walls and ceiling. Anyway, her sisters are all a-flap with celebrations—there was no pause for them in the evening, business as usual, but today they wear wedding finery and act the dutiful daughters, even though the streets will be filled with people who sneer and laugh at them behind their backs.

The hours have done nothing but make Nel colder, to bring her closer to despair; her teeth chatter and she shakes so badly she can no longer stand and beat at the wood of the trapdoor, which is sodden but not soft, not rotten. Her hands are bruised and her fingers bloody from that hopeless endeavor. There is no lock which she might finagle into compliance.

And the water has continued to rise, mercilessly; inevitably; inexorably.

A wash of waves pushes Nel and her bluish lips and nose scrape against the rock-carved ceiling. She tastes salt and metal; she smells mildew and death. In moments, the sea will replace the last tiny pocket of air and she will drown. It doesn't matter.

It doesn't matter anymore.

With this realization she feels her body suddenly become very heavy, her spirit suddenly very light. She ceases to fight, ceases trying to stay afloat, gives herself up to the water, and she bobs about, heedless as seaweed. The tide pushes against her again, once, twice, thrice, and she feels this is the end.

Hands.

Hands, strong and insistent, many of them; and voices, crying, angry, relieved. Many voices, all at once, and Nel is hauled upward. Behind her the trapdoor is slammed back into place, the bolt shot as loud as a lightning strike.

And her sisters, all her sisters but one, gather around her, clamoring, demanding, groaning with fear and relief, wanting to know what happened, where has she been, was this why she missed the wedding?

And she tells them, choking on seawater and bile and vomit; shivering and shaking and desperately trying to pull her soul—which she so recently was preparing to let go—back into her body.

And they believe her; they believe her because she has never lied and because they *know* their mother and the length, breadth and height of her ambitions.

Nel hopes Asha is safe, that there is *time*.

"The Viceroy insisted they pay their respects to the morgue dead after the ceremony, while the city feasts."

The mortuary, thinks Nel, so full of lost souls and spent lives, of untapped *power*.

And as they sit there, the seven of them, they hear in the distance the sonorous clang of the death bell. Not a rhythmic beating, but a desperate clamor, a cacophony: a cry for help. It stills them, voices, faces, hands trying to dry Nel off. It stills their hearts and their minds for precious seconds. And then they run, all of them, even Nel, in a halting, stuttering fashion.

They run up the stairs, through empty rooms. They tumble down the front steps like kittens released from a box; they process through the cobbled streets, fast and fleet and trailing diaphanous fabrics and long tresses behind them like banners. They run through the night streets like glorious, terrified ghosts, flashing past windows and open doors, glowing in the lamplight as they pass from shadow to light and back again.

Not far from their destination they are almost run over by a black carriage and four, ebony plumes waving in the air. In a blinking moment, Nel glimpses the Viceroy slumped inside, his white wedding attire bloodied and torn, his true age writ large upon his face. Then the conveyance is gone, on toward the city gates, and the sight gives wings to Nel's feet.

The sisters run until they merge with the gathering crowd outside Breakwater's black marble and cardinal brick mortuary, threading their way through folk who were so recently celebrating, all unawares.

Upward the girls rush, pushing past the fat Constable and his slack-jawed deputies, along corridors embedded with the smell of death: mortification and preservation. Finally they crowd into a room, the room where all will one day go, lined with alabaster tables, each bordered with gutters and silver tubes leading to channels in the floor, stained rusty with all the years of bodily fluids. A room laid out not unlike their own attic sanctum. A room with windows set very high in the walls so no gawkers might peek at the frailty of the dead.

A room with a roughly drawn scarlet circle laid out before them, a star etched inside it with bottles at eleven of its twelve points. Bottles filled with a churning red-gray mist, some fallen on their sides as if collateral victims of a struggle, but none of them broken; none but the empty one lying beside Asha, who is draped across one of the tables.

Her wedding gown is worse for wear, and her tiara is askew and missing some of its pins. As the sisters approach, they notice her makeup has smudged and run, the lip wax is smeared, the kohl and mascara lie in lines across her face, her eyes seemingly bruised by the mess of dark smudges. One earlobe is torn and bloody, its earring gone.

The others stop; these are steps they cannot take. But Nel continues, her feet bare and muddy (her shoes lost in the depths of the sub-cellar), her dress saturated and still dripping on the cold marmoreal floor. She notices that her sister still breathes laboriously, crimson vapor traveling on the exhalation. Nel gathers her up, heedless of the heart's blood spilling from the tear in her chest. Nel leans close and catches Asha's last words, "I can see Iskha."

As her sister relaxes into death, Nel lets her lie back down. She arranges Asha's limbs and clothing, gently closes her lids over staring eyes, tries to tidy the wildly disheveled tresses. Clenched in Asha's right hand is one of the missing pins, the diamond-tipped one. Its long, thin shaft is covered with rapidly congealing blood.

Nel does not believe this is her sister's and she wraps the spindle in a piece of fabric torn from the wedding dress and buries it deep in her own pocket.

She then notices around Asha's body an aura, a silver shimmer that pours off the dead skin; a voice in her head says *No* but she ignores it and touches once more the morbid flesh.

There is nothing. No bolt of lightning, no arching pain, neither scream nor shout nor moan. Nothing but a kind of itch across her scalp and her own skin, her own face. Nothing that hurts, nor is even uncomfortable, but simply the sensation of a change creeping on, slowly.

"A soul clock," says Mother Magnus, her voice tunneling through the dim front parlor of the house by the Weeping Gate. All the rooms have been dark for some weeks, all business dealings postponed, all noises hushed. Nel stands, staring out through the gap in the thick curtains. The view of the street has not changed, although there is a carriage waiting, not too fine, not too ordinary, simply one that will draw no attention. She lets the old woman reel out her explanation. Nel occasionally asks questions and wonders if the cunning woman should have noticed—or did notice—the signs.

"Why girls? Why not boys?"

"Vanity? Convenience? Soft skin? Who looks for lost girls of suspect morals?"

"And Asha? Why Asha?" Nel's voice trembles but does not break.

"Who was more beautiful than Asha?"

Nel realizes she is wringing her hands; she shakes them, stills them.

"He was ageing—I saw him. I think he was getting desperate. He was getting sloppy, stopped bothering to hide them." Nel rubs her face, still getting used to it. "I wonder what he'll do now, where he'll go."

"Like I said, hen, you can track him with *this*, if it's his blood."

Nel nods, because she is sure. She *wants* to be sure. She takes the item from Magnus.

"*He* won't recognize you, but it will be harder for you to hide."

"I know," says Nel, skin all goose bumps at the thought of being seen.

"What about the other ones?" the old woman asks.

Nel turns. Mother Magnus is pointing to the eleven bottles, now empty. Nel had taken them to the harbor and let the contents free. The wisps of souls had flown, each in a different direction to, Nel hoped, the right body, the right resting place. She prayed Iskha found where they'd laid her body, exhumed along with the others from the Viceroy's overgrown garden.

"Home," she says. "They went home."

Upstairs, Nel can hear her mother's ruckus and she takes her leave of the cunning woman. Dalita, having disappeared after being given news of her darling's demise, was found hours later screaming at the Viceroy's mansion, yelling obscenities at the top of her lungs, banging at the doors and breaking the windows with anything she could find to hand. She has been abed ever since.

The first time she opened her eyes and saw Nel, she recoiled, gibbering. Now she will take food only from this daughter's hands.

For it is Nel, but not Nel alone.

The plain daughter is transformed. She is not the great and terrible beauty Asha was, but something of the dead sister has passed over to her.

Her hair is now a decided black, her eyes are larger, but still gray. Her mouth has blossomed into something that demands attention and her figure has filled out, hips and breasts growing wider, just a little, and waist pinching in without the aid of a corset. She is dressed in Asha's clothes, for her own no longer fit.

She is a different girl, touched somehow by the magic left on Asha's skin. She is no longer a girl who can live in the shadows, and she feels this loss. Nel no longer feels safe, for there is nowhere she can hide from the eyes of those who would drink her in.

This morning, dressed in a gray velvet traveling dress (once Asha's favorite), a beaded purse hanging from one wrist, and a black lacquer fan which, when open, shows mermaids and sailors, on the other, she gives instructions to Carin, who insists upon interrupting.

"And what do we do," asks Carin (now rounder than she was and determined to become rounder still), "when she asks for you? When she refuses to eat?"

"Mix a little of the valerian in her food, it keeps her calm. Tell her I am doing what I must and she needs to be patient." Nel pulls on gray kid gloves with jet buttons at the wrists.

"When will you come home?"

"When it is done."

Her single carpetbag waits by the doorway. When she is in the shadowy confines of the carriage, when she can feel the rock and sway of the vehicle and knows they are beyond the city's boundaries, Nel will take the diamond-topped spindle from her reticule. She will place it on her palm and wait to see which way it spins, until it finds the direction she must follow.

Nel takes a deep breath, steeling herself to step outside, to move through the world and be *seen*.

See here?

See this girl?

She is a very fine girl indeed.

ANGELA SLATTER is an Australian writer of dark fantasy and horror. She is the author of the Aurealis Award–winning *The Girl with No Hands and Other Tales,* the World Fantasy Award short-listed *Sourdough and Other Stories,* and the recent collection/mosaic novel *Midnight and Moonshine* (with Lisa L. Hannett). She has a PhD in Creative Writing, and won a British Fantasy Award for her story "The Coffin-Maker's Daughter" (from *A Book of Horrors*). Her work has also appeared in Australian, British, and American "Best of" anthologies, along with *Fantasy Magazine, Lady Churchill's Rosebud Wristlet, Dreaming Again,* and *Weirder Shadows over Innsmouth.* In 2014 she will take up one of the inaugural Queensland Writers Fellowships.

Fräu Trude

THERE WAS ONCE a little girl who was obstinate and inquisitive, and when her parents told her to do anything, she did not obey them, so how could she fare well?

One day she said to her parents, "I have heard so much of Fräu Trude, I will go to her someday. People say that everything about her does look so strange, and that there are such odd things in her house, that I have become quite curious."

Her parents absolutely forbade her, and said, "Fräu Trude is a bad woman who does wicked things, and if you go to her, you are no longer our child."

But the maiden did not let herself be turned aside by her parents' prohibition, and still went to Fräu Trude.

And when she got to her, Fräu Trude said, "Why are you so pale?"

"Ah," she replied, and her whole body trembled. "I have been so terrified at what I have seen."

"What have you seen?"

"I saw a black man on your steps."

"That was a collier."

"Then I saw a green man."

"That was a huntsman."

"After that I saw a blood-red man."

"That was a butcher."

"Ah, Fräu Trude, I was terrified. I looked through the window and saw not you, but, as I verily believe, the Devil himself with a head of fire."

"Oh-oh," said she, "then you have seen the witch in her proper costume. I have been waiting for you, and wanting you a long time already. You shall give me some light."

Then she changed the girl into a block of wood, and threw it into the fire.

And when it was in a full blaze she sat down close to it, and warmed herself by it, and said, "That shines bright for once in a way."

Anything to Me Is Sweeter Than to Cross Shock-Headed Peter

BRIAN HODGE

CONCERNING THE BROWNSTONE building where they were housed, it was said that the sun had never once shined on the place in all the days and decades it had stood, and whenever the rain pelted it, it was always Arctic cold. And this was fitting, for it had been a terribly long time since the sun had shined on their lives, if ever the sun had blessed their unhappy countenances at all.

They were not children for sunny days and parks, for paddle boats and picnics. God, no. These were children for hailstorms and the roughest of back alleys, for shipwrecks and for plagues.

They still had their uses, of course. To visit them was to see the future, a destination at the far end of an ill-advised road, and know that all was not too late. To look at them was to know that for most any other child in the world, not nearly so far gone as these, there was time to turn around and mend their wayward ways.

And so, dim and dreary though the place may have been, people found their way there. Eagerly. By the car-full, sometimes even by the busload. Tours ran once in the morning, once in the afternoon, and—all the better for sending a child to bed with fresh nightmares—once in the evening. Pay your admittance to the stern-faced Mr. Crouch at the door, or more likely the even sterner-faced Mrs. Crouch, and the tour began. You could linger as long as you liked, anywhere you wished—sometimes extra minutes were needed to drive a point home for a particularly stubborn or stupid child—although tarrying too long was likely to mean missing part of Mr. Crouch's helpful comments further along the way.

Peter had been listening to the man's spiel for such a long time that he figured, should Mr. Crouch take sick, or better yet take a tumble down some creaky stairs and snap his wretched scrawny neck, Peter himself could take over without missing a beat.

He listened now—his ears were exceptionally keen—and hardly a word differed from the time before, and the time before that.

"This sullen little fellow's name is Caspar," Mr. Crouch's voice floated up from below as the tour began with Caspar's room. "And you'll not find a more fitting name for the likes of him, because if he keeps up his habits, he'll waste away to a ghost, just you wait and see."

"What's wrong with him?" asked some faceless woman. "He looks acceptable."

"Decided he was too good for the food he was being served. His poor parents had such a time trying to get a morsel down him, he might as well have bolted his own mouth shut. So what could they do but bring him here, eh? He was a healthy boy once. A plump boy, you might even say. But look at him now." There was always a pause for drama here. "Show 'em your ribs, boy. Show these nice folks your ribs."

And here there always arose a gasp.

"Like to try and feed him, would you?" Mr. Crouch asked someone.

"No, no, that . . . I don't think that'll be necessary," the someone demurred.

"Nonsense. Here you go, just try and offer him this. See what it gets you."

Now there was a clatter and a clang, the door within the door opening, just wide enough to admit something that was too big to fit between the bars. Like, for instance, a bowl.

Peter knew what was to come. Only it didn't. Not today. It happened like that sometimes.

"Say your line, boy," growled Mr. Crouch. *"Say the line!"*

"*'Take that nasty soup away!'*" cried Caspar, but his heart wasn't really in it. It happened like that, too, sometimes.

There was another clang as Mr. Crouch chuckled. "See? Told you. Incorrigible, that one. He'll be dead within the month, I give him."

Mr. Crouch had been giving Caspar a month for years.

"Which brings us to Pauline," said Mr. Crouch, amid a shuffling of feet, then came another great swelling gasp that didn't even wait for a prompting from the sour old man. "Liked to play with matches, she did. Even the kitties knew better, but not her. And you can see what it's got her. Looks more like lizard than girl now, what with all the bits the flames took."

At this point, Mr. Crouch would toss her a matchbox containing a single wooden match, no more than that, lest she get up to old mischief and give everyone much more than they'd bargained for.

"That's it, dearie," he would say. "Let's see that trick of yours."

A scratch, a pop, and then a hiss. Sometimes another collective gasp, other times a group groan.

"Now, don't you folks fret none," Mr. Crouch soothed. "She can't feel a thing. If that blackened lump of tongue has got any nerve endings left, I'm the king of Siam."

The herd moved along, as herds always do, clumping up the stairs to the next floor, and as often happened, as they gathered around the next door of the tour, people began to complain that the room must be empty, that they couldn't see anyone.

"Is that so?" said Mr. Crouch. "Look harder, why don't you."

Slowly, slowly, came murmurs of recognition and approval.

"Them three there, they don't stand out much anymore. Thought it was grand fun to have a mean little laugh at folks with skin, let's say, a few shades darker than their own. Well, darker than their own *used* to be." Mr. Crouch always treated himself to a mean little snicker of his own here. "Dunk these lads in ink, and about all you can make out of 'em now is the whites of their eyes. I expect you could see 'em better if they'd smile, too, but we're still waiting for that to happen." He banged on the bars of the door to their room. "Don't got much to smile about these days, do you, you miserable lot!"

The tour proceeded along the halls and up more stairs, and by now somebody was usually crying, maybe a great number of young visitors taken over by weeping and sobs, and the promises, oh, the promises— Peter had heard every promise a frightened child could make, a thousand times over. Promises to be good, promises to be better. Promises to never do it again, or to remember to do what was expected.

Next there was Philip, a fidgety boy who couldn't sit still, and banged around his room until he was a mass of bruises almost as dark as the Black Boys, post-ink.

And there was Flying Robert, who'd foolishly gone out with an umbrella during a frightfully windy storm, and was swept away. Even more foolishly, he'd refused to let go of the umbrella, until up up up he'd been carried, aloft among the rooftops, then dumped back to the hard streets when the wind tired of him as surely as his parents had tired of caring for such a feeble-minded lad.

"Bet you good people didn't know arms and legs could bend that way," Mr. Crouch, ever helpful, pointed out.

Then came Frederick, liked by nobody, even among the otherwise friendless few beneath the roof of this place where the sun never shined and the rain was always cold. Frederick was mean and cruel, spiteful and vicious, to every living thing on four legs and two. With anyone else, Peter would've felt the greatest of pity every time he heard Mr. Crouch turn the dog loose to harass him, and fight for the sausage that the wailing boy never got to eat . . . but with Frederick, Peter made an exception.

At last the tour arrived next door, one room over, almost done.

Here Mr. Crouch turned sly. "Wave to the nice folks, Conrad. That's it, lad. Give 'em a nice big wave. Both hands, now."

Coming from next door as they did, the gasps and cries belonged to people now, not a crowd. They came from fathers and mothers, from girls and boys, in voices high and low. There was always at least one tyke screaming by now. Always.

"What happened to him?" some pushy mother begged to know.

"You can't hold it against babies that they suck their thumbs. But there comes a day when a youngster's got to give that up. Not for Conrad, though. His parents said they practically had to take a crowbar to pry his hand from his face," said Mr. Crouch. "In a case this bad, best to remove the temptation altogether."

Some grim father muttered as if he couldn't decide whether he admired this or not. "Whoever would do such a thing?"

"Snip-Snap, he's called. You don't want a visit from *him*."

And then, a most unexpected thing, almost certainly the most unexpected thing that had ever happened here. Up piped the voice of a young girl, betraying no more than honest curiosity: "What kind of scissors did he use?"

"Jenny!" barked a voice, dripping with a mother's shame and scorn. "What kind of question is that?"

"What?" Jenny sounded plainly ignorant of her crime. "I just wanted to know!"

Mr. Crouch grumped and grumbled the way he did when he seemed to feel he'd lost control. "Sharp ones," he said, and made a few quick shearing sounds. "That answer your question, you nosy thing?"

"You'll have to forgive her," the mother begged. "But she's paying attention, and that has to be good, right? Most of the time she doesn't even notice what's in front of her at all."

"You don't say," mused Mr. Crouch. "I know the type, all right."

Order was restored, and all was well with the tour again, with just enough tears and blubbering to confirm that points were getting across and lessons being learned, but not so much so that people couldn't hear what Mr. Crouch had to say next.

"And now we've saved the worst for last . . ."

On the other side of the bars, they came into view: a herd of staring eyes and craning necks, knees and shoulders and stamping feet jostling for position, grim-faced grown-ups shoving their progeny forward to look and learn. And though he supposed he should've, long ago, Peter had never wholly grown accustomed to the first wave of revulsion that rippled over their faces. It was the same every time—they peered in, then recoiled—and every time, it stung.

"Hard to believe, I know, but that's a boy there, under all that mess and tangle," said Mr. Crouch. "Just look at him! Guess he had better things to do than take care of himself so that he was the least bit presentable. Yep, them there are his real fingernails. Got so long by now the grimy things are starting to curl. And if his hair's ever once met a comb, I don't know of it. Shock-Headed Peter, we call him. The most slovenly boy that ever was. Even I can barely stomach the sight of him. Anything to me is sweeter than to see Shock-Headed Peter. And don't get me started on the stink between hosings."

Through the bars they stared and pointed, and he glared right back at them, and for as much as he hated the place, he couldn't imagine leaving. Because in all the time he'd been here, and the innumerable visitors who'd filed past his door, not once had he seen a father or a mother who looked like someone he would want to go home with. Even if they'd have him.

"Let's be moving along, now. Children need their rest. You've seen what you've seen and I don't imagine you'll be forgetting it anytime soon," Mr. Crouch said as he began to sweep the herd toward the stairs. "But just in case the little ones do, I couldn't live with myself if I didn't tell you responsible folks about the pretty little picture books we've got down where you first came in. Guaranteed to bring it all back again. For their own good, of course. Just see my lovely missus about that and she'll get you fixed right up."

Peter turned his back on them as they clomped along the scarred wooden floor, to wait until they were gone. More often than not, he wondered how they would react if they knew that the sight of them disgusted him probably every bit as much as the sight of him revolted them.

"Pssst." A hiss of sound, soft enough to go unnoticed by grown-up ears in the thunder of their ponderous feet. *"Psssst."*

He turned and the day changed yet again, for now *this* was the most unexpected thing that had ever happened here.

No one had ever stopped to talk. Never.

"You don't scare me," whispered the curious girl, Jenny, as she peered in, pressed against his door, her fingers curled round the bars. "You don't scare me at all."

Then she was swept along with the rest, out of sight and out of hearing. But not out of his thoughts, because he had the feeling that he'd be seeing her again.

And so it was, and so he did. Jenny was back in less than a week.

But this time she was not here to learn. Someone must have decided it was too late for that. Instead, she was now here to teach. She was, same as the rest of them, here to be the horrible example of her very own self. She was here to *stay*.

Mrs. Crouch brought her up in the middle of the night. The cold, wee hours of darkness were when new arrivals were brought in, and those who were no longer working out taken away. Night, after all, was an informal time, between tours, when room doors were unlocked, and they all had the run of the residence . . . although not the lobby below, and the separate rooms down there they'd never seen, which Mr. and Mrs. Crouch called home.

The only spare rooms Peter knew of were across the hallway from him, and that was where Mrs. Crouch brought her. Because they were free to roam, and because this was an event that did not happen very often, the children from below followed the pair up. Lots of feet on lots of stairs, but still, Mrs. Crouch, her feet as wide as waffles at the end of her elephantine ankles, was the only one who made much noise. They'd all learned to tread quietly here, even Cruel Frederick.

"I would like to introduce you to Jenny," whinnied Mrs. Crouch, as red-cheeked and stout as her husband was whey-faced and lanky. "Some of you may remember her for her unconscionable interruption of one of last week's tours. What kind of scissors, indeed! But the most appalling thing of all is that she doesn't yet appear to recognize that a *tragedy* has just befallen her. Can you imagine?"

She always had a look of distaste about her, did Mrs. Crouch, as though some invisible prankster were holding a stinky finger beneath her recoiling nose.

She was, however, telling the truth. With neatly combed dark hair and curious dreamer's eyes, not only was Jenny quite clearly *not* scared, not of Peter nor of anyone else here, but she looked like a girl who believed she was on a great adventure.

"So I trust that the lot of you will waste no time in setting her straight on the matter," said Mrs. Crouch, then checked her watch and tut-tutted about the time. "Sleep well, good urchins! Or don't. It's all the same!"

With that she was gone, flights of stairs protesting in her formidable wake, until at last they heard the final clang of the great barred door down below and the jangle of keys.

They all gathered around Jenny, this pristine new arrival whose crimes and sins against grown-up sensibilities were in no way obvious.

"What's wrong with *you*?" Conrad, whose absence of thumbs marked his misfortune at a glance, was first to ask. "You don't look wrong."

"Yeah," sneered Cruel Frederick, and gave her shoulder a poke. "You don't belong here. You're not one of us."

Jenny frowned at her shoulder, then at Frederick. "Don't poke me again. If you do," and here she pointed at Conrad, "you're going to draw back a hand like his."

A hush descended over the hall. No one had ever stood up to Frederick. *Ever.* They'd merely learned to live with his insults and bullying until he tired of them and went away.

"And then where will you be?" Jenny said, not nearly through with him yet. "Just an imitation of Conrad, only not as good. So what use will they have for you then? Because you can't even make a proper fist anymore."

Confusion knit itself all through Frederick's thick and sullen features, until he seemed to realize he had no choice but to wave her off with a grumble and another sneer, and retreat back downstairs to his room.

Unheard-of.

"I don't know," Jenny said, returning to Conrad and his query. "I don't know what's wrong with me. I didn't think anything was. I just know what my family thinks is wrong with me."

Peter found himself crowding closer. They all were. Conrad and Caspar, the Black Boys and Pauline, and even Fidgety Philip had calmed down. All but Flying Robert, who'd never made it up here in the first place, because his poor smashed legs didn't handle stairs well, or walking in general, for that matter.

"Jenny-with-Her-Head-in-the-Clouds . . . that's what they'd call me. They only *thought* I wasn't ever paying attention."

"Oh," said Pauline, solemn and grave. "They don't like that. They *hate* that."

"They never stopped to think if maybe it wasn't their own fault that the clouds were more interesting than they were."

Pauline may have looked rather dreamy then. But because she had no eyebrows, it was hard to tell. "Like the flames," she whispered.

Caspar sucked a gasp past his gaunt cheeks. "You didn't *tell* them that, did you?"

"I may have let it slip," Jenny confessed. "It's why they brought me here the first time. I don't know why they thought it would do any good. They told me you were dreadful, but you looked plenty normal to me. I thought you were all brilliant! Well . . . Frederick needs some work. But even he's not entirely hopeless."

This was even stranger than her standing up to Frederick. No one had ever spoken to the rest of them this way, either.

"Even you, under all that ratty hair," she told Peter. "But do tell me you speak. It'll be so much better living across the hall from someone who speaks."

"*I* speak," Conrad said, more eagerly than he'd perhaps intended.

"And it's good you do. Because I don't think you'll play catch very well."

If this had come from Frederick it would've been horrible, but the way Jenny said it, it just made him laugh. Because it was true. He was an inveterate ball-dropper.

She got settled in then, not a process that took long, pacing her room to get a feel for its limits and bouncing on the bed and sniffing the bar of soap she'd been allotted. The rest drifted away to their rooms because it was night, after all, and they were starting to grow sleepy, and it was good to get away from the place for a while, if only during their dreams.

Peter, though, lingered in her doorway awhile longer.

"One thing," he said. "When they feed us? Save a little aside, if you would. We all do, except for Frederick. Just don't let them catch you doing it." He checked the hallway even though he knew no one could be listening. "It's for Caspar, right? They only feed him enough to barely keep him going. He's got to have the look, you know?"

"Consider it done," Jenny said.

"And . . . you don't mind coming here?" he said. "You really don't?"

"Well, I didn't like ballet and wasn't much on sports, and I didn't like being told *how* and *what* to sing," she said. "According to them, I don't fit in anywhere. So maybe giving it a go here won't be so bad."

"Let's see if you can say that in a month." Again Peter checked that this was just between them. "You're not *supposed* to like it here. Nothing good can come of it if they think you do."

"Then I'll work on just the right expressions of misery and woe," she said. "You know, for a kid who can pick his nose without getting his actual finger anywhere near it, you're really quite nice."

Peter had no idea how to answer that, but it sounded like a compliment and he wasn't used to those.

Before he left for his room, he noticed that she'd wandered over to one wall and tipped her head toward the ceiling. He watched her watch it, expecting something to happen next, only a peculiar long time passed and nothing ever did.

Finally he was forced to ask: "What are you looking at?"

"The stars, of course."

"But you've got no window."

"They're still there," she said.

And now he knew, really knew, why they'd called her Jenny-with-Her-Head-in-the-Clouds, and why they'd feared her. She could see stars where everybody else saw old wallpaper. How were you going to cure *that*?

And that was why, one morning a couple of weeks later, Peter didn't know anything was any different about her at first. There had been some bumbling and fumbling in the halls during the night, and the sound of whimpering, but he'd not thought much about them, because as sounds go, they weren't unusual, not here, and so he'd rolled over and gone back to sleep.

It was early yet, long before the first tour of the day, before breakfast even, and Jenny was late in coming from her room, and when she finally did, she had eyes only for the ceiling. Peter watched her grope her way through the doorway and into the hall, and thought, all right, perhaps she was carrying this head-in-the-clouds business just a little too far.

"What?" he said. "You can't even look at me to talk to me anymore?" Saying this, yes, but thinking worse, that maybe she'd decided she couldn't stomach the sight of him either, finally.

"I can't," she whispered.

"I'm down here. Just drop your nose toward your chin and you'll find me."

"Really," she whispered, and now he heard the distress in her voice. "I *can't*." She wiggled a finger over one shoulder. "It's back there."

Peter stepped behind her. Nothing looked any different at a glance, so he used his fingernails to sweep aside the shiny dark fall of her hair—wishing, with a sudden thrill, that his nails were not such talons, and he could feel her hair with his fingers.

His breath caught in his throat for grimmer reasons. "What have they done to you?"

"I don't know." Now she sounded impatient with him. "You're the one who can see it, not me."

He held her hair aside as he scrutinized. They'd sewn her up where nothing was wrong to begin with. They had yanked her head back so far she could only look straight up, then made sure she stayed that way, with no mobility left at all. A great mass of thick black stitches bunched together the skin at the base of her skull and webbed it to the skin where her neck met her shoulders. It looked excruciatingly uncomfortable, and when he told her what he'd found, she uttered a sob that tore out the heart he wasn't even sure he had anymore.

He let her hair fall into place again and promised her that he wasn't leaving her, even though it might look like it for the moment—that he would be back and that if she needed help eating when breakfast came, he would help her do that too.

Then he ran, ran down the stairs, fourth floor to third to second to the landing on the first floor, the point beyond which none of them could venture. Here he was stopped by the greatest barred door of all, not just up-and-down bars like the ones that confined them to their rooms during tour hours, but side-to-side bars as well, so close together that even children couldn't quite reach through them.

With his nails so long, he couldn't pull together a true fist, but he made the best one he could and banged on the door, banged and kicked and banged, and hollered a few times on top of that, until a door opened down the hallway and out stormed Mr. Crouch.

"Here, now, here, now!" he shouted. "What's all this fuss and racket?"

"Why'd you do a thing like that to her?" Peter shouted back, another act unheard-of for such a long time he'd forgotten it could be any other way. "She was already herself when she came here! You didn't need to do that to her!"

Still wearing a faded purple bathrobe that hung over his pajamas like a sail, Mr. Crouch drew up to the other side of the bars with a squint and a glare, and then a mean little chuckle. "Gone a little sweet on her, have you?"

"It's not right!" Peter shouted. "It's not fair!"

"You'll want to watch yourself, boy. Don't make me call Snip-Snap on you, eh? You don't want a visit from *him*," Mr. Crouch said in a low voice full of menace and threat. "It's not just thumbs he likes to snip, so you mind that tongue of yours."

Peter clamped his mouth shut. He'd never considered such a thing. But backing down felt worse than contemplating the loss of a tongue he hadn't ever had much need for anyway, because nobody cared what he had to say.

Until now, perhaps.

And he thought it a shame that there was so much hair tumbling down over his forehead and face that Mr. Crouch couldn't see him smirk.

"What kind of scissors would he use for *that*?" Peter asked.

Mr. Crouch rumbled with a growl deep in his wattled throat and finished with a weary sigh. "Ain't you figured out your place yet? All this time, have you not noticed where you stand in the grand scheme, boy? You, the rest of your miserable rabble up there? You don't know what you are?"

He waited for Peter to think about it.

"You're what's left behind when there's no more hope. When there's nothing more for your poor parents to do but throw their hands in the air and give up." He spat the words, each and every one. "Don't like it? Too bad. You should've thought of that before. So now you're here. Not fair? Not right? I'll tell you what's not fair and right. Decent folks not getting their money's worth when they bring their own young ones here to show them *you* lot and scare 'em back to rights again."

Mr. Crouch drew himself up straighter, taller, and looked at Peter down his long nose.

"You're not boys and girls anymore. You're just something to look at, and if you need a little adjusting, then so be it. It's not for no reason." He rolled his eyes. "Who's going to learn their lesson from a Jenny-with-Her-Head-in-the-Clouds when she's not even looking at the silly clouds? When she's looking right straight at you?"

Peter began to back away from the bars.

"So you keep mouthing off, and we'll arrange a little visit from Snip-Snap. It's what we do here. We smooth off the rough edges." He was very full of himself now, leaning against the bars and leering through. "Let me let you in on a little something. I told you there was no more hope? There can be . . . it just doesn't happen that way very often. But our Snip-Snap . . . ? He's proof that an incorrigible boy like yourself has still got a chance to grow up and make something of himself. Even a boy who liked to run with scissors. So you keep that in mind . . . and hold your tongue."

Tours came and tours went, an endless passage of shuffling feet and pointing fingers and staring eyes, and through it all Peter tried to convince himself that it was not such a bad lot in life. But there was no selling this one anymore. They all seemed to feel it, even Cruel Frederick, who'd rather liked having a captive audience to torment.

There had to be more than this.

Early mornings and late nights, and sometimes during the day if he thought he could get away with it, Peter crept down the stairs to the first floor, as far as he could go, until stopped by the great barred door. Not to bang, nor to kick, nor to holler, but only to look, staring at the door at the opposite end of the hallway.

There was daylight there, and it wasn't very bright, but still, it spoke of fearless days and open skies. There was rain, too, and it felt cold even from here, but Peter imagined how clean it might feel. There was a street out there, and beyond it, more streets, and beyond them, roads, then fields, and beyond all that . . . well, who rightly knew?

Was it his longing that made the next unexpected thing happen? Or had even sour old Mr. Crouch tired of the game? Not likely, that, but perhaps time had made him careless.

The last tour was not entirely gone yet, the stragglers lingering endlessly in what Mrs. Crouch called the gift shop, buying up picture books and tut-tutting about the sorry state of children today, when Peter, his room door newly opened once more, crept down to stare after them. He'd been there several moments when his gaze dropped, and he could not believe his eyes.

There, on the other side of the door, the great barred door, lay the key.

In his haste to sell more picture books, the careless oaf had missed his pocket.

A chance like this would never come along again.

Peter squatted and reached, but no matter how he twisted and turned and contorted his hand, it wouldn't fit through the openings, none of them. There were all the same, all too tight, too small, and he nearly squealed with the frustration of it.

Until, frantic, he realized he was going about this all wrong. His nails, his long, hideous fingernails—*that* was sure to do it.

The longest of them grew from the index finger of his left hand, so he curled the rest back along his palm, then reached through like a wizard with a wand, and no no *no no no!* It *still* fell short, the tip of his nail scritch-scratching the tiled floor not half an inch from the key, even as he ground his hand against the door until his knuckles were bloody.

He pulled back his hand in defeat and licked away the blood.

In sorrow, in despair, he trudged back upstairs, and was at the third floor before realizing he'd *still* been going about this the wrong way, and launched himself to take the rest two steps at a time.

Conrad protested and struggled, as you do when what seems like a crazy boy has seized you to drag you down flight after flight of stairs, and clapped his hand over your mouth to keep you quiet. But it all made sense when they got to the door, the great barred door, and Peter pointed.

The reach through the bars was not nearly as difficult for a boy whose hands were so unencumbered by thumbs.

He waited a week. He waited two.

A thing like this could not be rushed. A thing like this had to be planned. And courage, too, it took, for some matters Peter could only guess at and hope that he was right. As well, Mr. Crouch was on his guard. Undoubtedly he knew he'd lost a key, or more likely blamed the gelatinous Mrs. Crouch for it, yet if he was in any way logical, he had to know he'd lost it on *his* side of the door. It was bound to turn up eventually, and in any case, there were spares.

In the meantime it was Peter's secret, his and Conrad's alone. What the others didn't know about they couldn't look suspicious about, and while Mr. Crouch was by nature a suspicious man, there wasn't much of Peter's face that he could even see, the smelly hair like another set of bars between them. As for Conrad, well, what did anyone have to fear from a boy without thumbs?

And, in time, Mr. Crouch settled back into being his usual petulant self.

Meaning the time had come.

Peter had chosen to begin in the evening, for that was when the most hours stretched ahead of them before the daily routine began all over again. He returned to his spot at the great barred door and, as never before, banged and kicked and banged some more. Predictable as gravity, out stormed Mr. Crouch, shirttails flying as he stalked toward the door.

"Here, now, what's all this fuss and—" He stopped short with a glare fit to curdle milk. "You again. Didn't I warn you, boy?"

"I don't think there *is* a Snip-Snap," Peter said with the greatest confidence. "I think you made him up."

Mr. Crouch's eyes narrowed to a wrathful squint. "You keep at it, you flea-bitten little gutter rat, and you'll find out what's real and what isn't."

There was nothing more to say. Peter lifted both hands before him, grubby knuckles out, and fired both his middle fingers at the ceiling.

Given the length of his nails, the insult cut doubly deep.

In case this next part went badly, he told the others they might want to hide, especially Conrad. For him, the mere sight of Snip-Snap was bound to bring back memories best unstirred. Peter sat on the end of his bed then, and hadn't long to wait.

There sounded a clang of the door from far below. Next came footsteps, up the stairs, floor after floor. This was someone who did not walk like the other grown-ups. He didn't clomp, he didn't shuffle. His pace was measured and full of purpose. It never once varied, like the sound of an enormous clock, ticking away each moment until the moment of reckoning.

His stride took him down the hall, then he filled the doorway and was through it, immensely tall and frightfully thin, his legs in particular, sweeping past each other like . . . well, like scissors. His top hat gave him scarcely an inch of clearance with the ceiling, and his face was all sharp bone and sallow skin, although he didn't look to be terribly old.

It was the glasses he wore that Peter was glad to see—an odd pair, with brass frames and round lenses, one clear and one dark. *Yes*, Peter thought as he breathed relief. *I knew it.*

Snip-Snap studied him a moment, and his hands were elegant as spiders as he peeled open the left side of his frock coat to reveal a gleaming assortment of scissors and shears, all hung just so. He regarded them but a moment, and chose. He clicked the pair in the air, *snipsnipsnip.*

"A middle finger, it's to be," he said. "Mr. Crouch was good enough to allow you to choose which one. He finds them equally offensive."

Peter offered both hands, splayed wide. "Make it all ten. Just the nails, though."

Behind the clear lens, Snip-Snap's eyebrow lifted nearly to the brim of his hat. "The nails?"

"And then my hair. And then another last thing, but one at a time, right?"

Snip-Snap may not have been capable of an entire smile, but he could manage half a one. "You do realize who I am, and why I'm here. Do you not?"

Peter rested his hands in his lap. "Actually, I've thought about that quite a lot. You were one of us once, weren't you? They put you away here, too, didn't they? For what—because you wouldn't stop running with scissors? That's all?"

"Ancient history."

"Maybe so, but I bet even right this minute you'd still like to have that eye back."

Snip-Snap lowered the scissors and held his head at a curious tilt.

"I'll bet it wasn't even an accident, was it? Oh, everyone kept telling you a thing like that was going to happen, only it never did. Because you kept your feet under you and you never fell. But that made them wrong, and they couldn't have that, could they? They had to be right, and for that, they had to make it *look* right." Peter pointed at the dark lens. "*They* did that to you, didn't they? *They* took your eye."

Slowly, contemplatively, Snip-Snap slipped the glasses from his head. It was not a pretty sight. True, Peter had no experience with missing eyes, only missing thumbs, but he was expecting that they might have sewn the whole thing shut, stitched the eyelids together like a window shade over the empty socket. Instead, the ruin was still prominent: folds of raw pink over a spongy, dry mass.

Snip-Snap opened his coat again and replaced the first pair of scissors on their little cloth loop. In their place, he took a dull, stained pair that were lesser in every way—a short pair, a child's first true scissors after graduating from blunt tips.

"I've kept this pair all these years," he said, and gazed at them with his good eye. "It still fits."

He slipped his heirloom tip-first into the center of what remained of his eye, not an act that appeared to cause him pain. It hurt to watch, though, and Peter's stomach rolled. When Snip-Snap left them there, content to wear them as in days gone by, Peter forced himself to look.

Snip-Snap leaned forward and down, to make sure Peter missed nothing. "Say the right thing," he whispered. He *urged.* "Tell me just the right thing."

Riddles now? Peter's confidence sank. He could only speak from the heart, and when he did, for the first time his voice shook. "What did you want to do to them right after they did that to you?" he said. "Whatever it was . . . that's how all of us are now."

Snip-Snap drew back to his full imposing height. He crossed his arms for a long moment's thought, then withdrew the scissors from his eye and, mercifully, put his glasses back on. He opened his coat and exchanged scissors once more.

"Right enough," he said.

And, for Peter, shock-headed and slovenly no longer, what a strange thing it was to sit on the edge of his bed and watch these bits and pieces of him drop away to the floor. Nail after long, grimy nail; lock after lock of springy, serpentine hair. It was not as welcome a feeling as he'd thought it might be, nor as freeing, for what had they been if not the identity of him, and a shield behind which to hide?

Who would he be without them?

Snip-Snap stepped back to appraise his work and seemed to find it done. "One last thing, you said?"

"Right. Not for me, though."

Peter led him across the hall to Jenny's room, where she sat gazing at stars through the ceiling because she had no choice. He patted her on the shoulder, then swept aside her hair, touching it with his fingers now, his fingers and nothing but, to reveal the ugly black thicket of stitches.

"I know you can get through those," said Peter. "The thing is, can you do it without hurting her?"

"I'm right here, you know," Jenny huffed. "Don't stand there talking about me like I'm not."

Snip-Snap folded at the knees, bracing his hands on his thighs as he levered down for a closer look. He went "Hmmm" a lot. When he stood tall again, he did not appear discouraged. Only resolute.

"This one will cost," he said.

Peter had been afraid of that.

Although he still got to choose the finger.

A key goes into a lock, the lock goes click, a door creaks open . . . These were such small things to be the end of all that was past and the start of all that was new.

He let the Black Boys through and gave them time to get into position, although it was still night and dark, with only the dimmest of lights burning in the first-floor hallway, where one shadow was likely to be as good as another. Then he shut the door after them.

"Good and loud, and don't stop," Peter told Cruel Frederick. "Like you mean it."

Frederick looked at him with a sneer, but after all this time, he couldn't help himself. "You don't have to tell me how to beat on something and make a row."

Peter stepped aside to let him at it, Frederick banging and kicking and bellowing with such ferocious enthusiasm that surely no greater racket had ever been heard here in this brownstone where the sun never shined and the rain was always cold.

The apartment door flew open and out stormed Mr. Crouch, for the last time.

"See here now, you shock-headed little beast!" he shouted. "If you're so sick of being attached to those other nine fingers, there's something we can do about it, there is!" He stopped abruptly when he saw that it was Frederick. "*You*, now? What's got into you?"

The Black Boys were on him then, ink-dyed skin out of ink-black shadows, and Mr. Crouch never saw them coming. They swarmed over him and took him to the floor as Peter once more used the key to let Cruel Frederick through this time, so that Frederick could do what he did best.

It was better that the hallway need as little cleaning as possible, so once Mr. Crouch was subdued, they dragged him back into the apartment he shared with his lovely missus, and the dog that had bedeviled Frederick every day of his life. There was more racket and fuss, muffled now, coming as it did from behind closed doors, and this was just as well, for the sounds were unpleasant in the extreme.

It didn't take long . . . although it still might have taken a good deal longer than was strictly necessary.

Hours later, they were open on time for business as usual, with Peter out front to greet the gloating grown-ups and nervous children who'd come for the morning tour, and Jenny seated in the ticket office window to smile brightly and take their money.

If unexpectedly young, perhaps, Peter still looked the part. Snip-Snap was by trade a tailor, and with a little cutting here and sewing there, it took not much work to fit him with one of Mr. Crouch's old suits. The feel of it made his skin crawl, not so much the fabric as the history, but he would not have to wear it for long.

"If you've paid us a visit before, I'm sure you've noticed a change in routine already," Peter told his audience, taking care to keep his left hand down, and hide the bandage where his littlest finger once was. "It's only temporary, you'll be pleased to know. Sometimes even such formidable good folks as my Uncle Eben and Aunt Lizzy can be no match for a dose of ague. No worries, though! You'll still see what you came for!"

And he was right. He'd overheard it all so many times that as he led them up the stairs, he was able to take over Mr. Crouch's spiel without missing a beat.

"Now, this sullen fellow's name is Caspar," he told them as the tour began on the second floor. "And you'll not find a more fitting name for the likes of him, because if he keeps up his naughty habits, he'll waste away to a ghost, just you wait and see."

"What's wrong with him?" asked a horse-faced woman. "He doesn't look sick."

"Decided he was too good for the food he was being served. His poor parents had such a time trying to get a morsel down him, he might as well have stitched his own face together. So what could they do but bring him here, right? He was a healthy boy once. A plump boy, you might say. But look at him now." He paused for the usual drama here. "Show 'em your ribs, kid. Show these fine people your ribs."

When Caspar tugged up his shirt, this time he inspired only confusion.

"Why, he looks positively gorged!" a father protested. "What's he been into?"

"Whatever it was, we'll see to it he never has a chance to get into it ever again," Peter promised . . . leaving unsaid, for the good of all, that Mrs. Crouch hadn't weighed so little in many, many years.

He unlocked Caspar's door and flung it open, barging in and bristling with so much umbrage he could scarcely keep a straight face. Caspar was no better, even as Peter grabbed him by the ear and pretended to drag him out into the hall.

"Get a move on, you crumb-snitching cur!" Peter shouted. "Turn your prissy nose up at the fine food we provide, will you, then stuff your face with junk?"

Solemnly, sternly, the good parents made way, and understood. They knew the type, all right. He continued to drag Caspar through the parting crowd, shouting as they went.

"A thing like this, you can't very well let it go unpunished, can you? How's our Caspar going to learn, eh?"

A father nodded vigorously and wet his lips. "Make it good. Make it *hurt*."

"Oh, I promise you it will, sir. But I couldn't live with myself if I didn't invite the young ones along to watch it happen. Watch and learn, we always say." Peter looked from child's face to child's face and beckoned them to follow. "The rest of you can stay right here and we'll be back in five. Consider it a bonus! You're getting more for your money today, and who'd argue against that?"

And with the children down the stairs and past the great barred door, Peter locked it behind him, and hurled the key where no one was likely to find it ever again.

They all gathered across the street then, everyone who'd called this hateful place a home, kept for so long on the wrong side of cold bars and staring eyes by crimes so petty he wondered who was *not* guilty.

To Pauline, Peter gave a box of matches taken from the Crouches' kitchen, a giant box whose matches she'd been getting one at a time, thrice a day. No one, girl or boy, could've been happier to now get them all at once.

"Pretty," she said, past her blackened lump of tongue, then dashed back into the building without another look behind.

They waited five minutes. They waited ten.

"She's not coming out again, I don't think," Jenny said.

But when he started across the street after Pauline, Jenny caught his arm and shook her head no, sorrowfully no, and while he didn't like it a bit, she was right. No matter how much you wished to, you could not save everyone from themselves.

Caspar and Fidgety Philip were the first to go, led away by Snip-Snap, who thought it best to leave before the fire grew visible. Philip, who'd only ever needed something to focus his energies on, had ably assisted in resizing the suit for Peter, and as Snip-Snap could always use help at his tailor shop, he offered Philip an apprenticeship. There was no apparent reason why he should have offered Caspar one too. But given the gusto with which the starved boy had partaken of his most recent meal—a prodigious fillet of Crouch—there seemed something a bit monstrous in him now, and so perhaps Snip-Snap, who knew more than a bit about being monstrous himself, thought it bore watching.

The rest? Cruel Frederick and Conrad watched until the flames were showing in the windows, then slipped away as well, together, for even Frederick had to admit that life on one's own would never be easy for a boy devoid of thumbs. With his arms and legs left twisted by his fall, Flying Robert needed help and always would . . . but the Black Boys had been the ones to bring him down from upstairs, and weren't giving up on him now, and soon they, too, disappeared with the morning.

At last the smoke and flames were enough to start drawing a crowd, and the children brought for lessons were certainly getting one. They all watched as if they couldn't quite believe what they were seeing, some wiping their eyes and rubbing their noses, but they got over it, resilient to the core, then even they began to drift away from the scene . . .

Until it was just the two of them left, Peter and Jenny-with-Her-Head-in-the-Clouds, who was looking nowhere near the sky.

"I liked you better the other way," she said. "You look like anybody else now."

He understood. "But I don't *feel* like anybody else."

He gazed down the street and beyond it, toward more streets, and beyond those, to the roads leading everywhere but here, and there were so many they could take that it made his head spin.

They could be anything now.

So he would be what the grown-ups had made him.

Or be something better, in spite of it.

Time would tell.

BRIAN HODGE is the award-winning author of eleven novels spanning horror, crime, and historical. He's also written more than one hundred short stories, novelettes, and novellas, plus five full-length collections. Recent works include *No Law Left Unbroken,* a collection of crime fiction; *The Weight of the Dead* and *Whom the Gods Would Destroy,* both stand-alone novellas; a newly revised hardcover edition of his early postapocalyptic epic *Dark Advent*; and his latest novel, *Leaves of Sherwood.* He lives in Colorado, where more of everything is in the works. He also dabbles in music, sound design, and photography, loves everything about organic gardening, except the thieving squirrels, and trains in Krav Maga, grappling, and kickboxing, which are of no use at all against the squirrels.

The Elves #2

THERE WAS ONCE a poor servant-girl who was industrious and cleanly and swept the house every day, and emptied her sweepings on the great heap in front of the door.

One morning, when she was just going back to her work, she found a letter on this heap and, as she could not read, she put her broom in the corner and took the letter to her employers. And behold, it was an invitation from the elves, who asked the girl to hold a child for them at its christening.

The girl did not know what to do. But, at length, after much persuasion, and as they told her that it was not right to refuse an invitation of this kind, she consented.

Then three elves came and conducted her to a hollow mountain, where the little folks lived. Everything there was small, but more elegant and beautiful than can be described. The baby's mother lay in a bed of black ebony ornamented with pearls, the covers were embroidered with gold, the cradle was of ivory, the bath-tub of gold.

The girl stood as godmother, and then wanted to go home again; but the little elves urgently entreated her to stay three days with them. So she stayed, and passed the time in pleasure and gaiety, and the little folks did all they could to make her happy.

At last she set out on her way home. But first they filled her pockets quite full of gold, and then they led her out of the mountain again.

When she got home, she wanted to begin her work. She took the broom—which was still standing in the corner—in her hand and began to sweep. Then some strangers came out of the house, who asked her who she was and what business she had there.

And she had not, as she thought, been three days with the little men in the mountains, but seven years. And in the meantime her former masters had died.

The Artemis Line

PETER CROWTHER

"A certain mother had her child taken out of its cradle
by the elves, and a changeling with a large head and
staring eyes, which would do nothing but eat and
drink, lay in its place."

—The Brothers Grimm ("The Elves #1")

"Fairies are magical . . . and they'll just kill you
before you can kill them."

—Karen (from *Outnumbered*)

Prologue

CHARLES CAVANAGH PULLED the car off the main
road and onto what amounted to little more than a neat track
barely wide enough for one car. They had visited the house twice
before. Turning a sharp right onto the tiny bridge that led to the
wide gates and the little orchard beyond it, Charles stopped the car
and shifted into park. He whistled and shook his head.

"Are we there?"

Geraldine Cavanagh pulled off her headphones and slapped her
brother on the arm. "Does it look like we're there?" There was no
answer so Gerry followed it up with "Lame brain."

Tom looked over and saw his sister carefully writing the name
"Julien Tibbets" and drawing little hearts all around it. He fashioned
a pretend cough around the word "whore" and Gerry hit him again.

"Geraldine!" Trudy Cavanagh snapped from the front seat.

"He called me a *name.*" Gerry hid the notebook under her arm so that her mother wouldn't see what she was doing.

"Yeah," Tom sneered, "Hortense."

Gerry took a wider swing this time and caught her brother on the cheek.

"Ow!" He split the word into two, giving it multiple syllables— "Ow-whirr"—and rubbed his arm.

"Gerry, I will not tell you again."

Good, that'll suit me, she thought. "Okay, sorry," she said.

"Not to me, to your brother."

"Sorry, *Brother,*" she said. There was no conviction there at all.

"I need to pee," Tom said.

"Tom!" Now it was Tom's father's turn to get in on the debate.

Tom shrugged and in what he considered to be his most reasonable voice said, "Just tell her not to look."

"We'll be there in a minute, sweetie," Trudy said. "Just nip the end and you'll be fine."

Tom already had his right hand clasped tightly around his crotch, and when his sister saw it she made a face and turned to the window. "Totally gross."

"'During the whole of a dull, dark and soundless day in the autumn of the year, when the clouds hung oppressively low in the heavens, I had been passing alone—'"

"Sweetie?"

"Dad, are you okay?"

"It's from 'Fall of the House of Usher,'" Charles said. He turned back to the window and lowered it.

"Dad," Gerry bleated. "*Cold.*"

"'I had been passing alone on horseback,'" Tom Cavanagh continued, "'through a singularly dreary tract of country, and at length found myself, as the shades of the evening drew on, within view of the melancholy House of Usher . . .'"

Charles shook his head and watched the house across the fields as though it was about to do something spectacular.

"Isn't it wonderful?"

Nobody answered.

"Poe had it right."

Trudy reached her right hand across and patted her husband's knee affectionately. Tom, who was now leaning against the back of his mother's seat, saw the gesture, and though he was not able to articulate what he had seen, saw something there, in that smallest of exchanges, that he was to remember all of his life . . . with the memory coming back when he least expected it. Or, indeed, wanted it.

"There's sadness there, sure." Charles pointed a hand, jabbing his index finger repeatedly at things of which nobody else was aware. "But there's solidity and there's history, and there's—"

"There's shelter, sweetie." This time the pat suggested it was time to move. "And Tommy wants to go wee-wee."

"Mom! That's even worse than 'pee.'"

"Tom, I told you al—"

"But you told me . . . Oh, forget it." He pushed himself back into the Jaguar's seat and made a face. He was astonished when Gerry leaned over and whispered, "Two minutes and we'll be there." And then she patted her brother's leg, just the way her mother had patted Dad's.

"Looks like it's going to rain," Trudy said as they passed over the bridge and headed up the track for Grainger Hall.

And it did. The sky stretching across to the west looked like a bruised knee, purple and a strange greeny-yellow.

Tom jiggled the hand holding his crotch, the urgent need to release the flow growing with every few yards they came closer to the pebbled forecourt and main doors.

Way over in the distance, Tom saw a lone scarecrow standing just to the side of a copse of trees. As the car swung to the right, Tom reached for the door handle and picked up his comic books. When he next looked out of the window the scarecrow had now shifted behind the trees, out of sight.

Minutes later he was upstairs in the toilet, whistling as the pent-up flow hit the stagnant water in the bowl.

"Remember to wash your hands, young man," Trudy called from a kitchen that was—like all the rooms they had passed from the front door—piled high with boxes. She leaned against the sink and stared at the countryside. It looked so lonely.

Up on the first floor, Tom was just turning toward the basin when the floorboards outside the door creaked and there was a noise as though something heavy was being pulled along the corridor. The sound, albeit very soft, was growing slightly louder. So whatever was causing it was coming from the west side of the house toward the east . . . and right past the small room where Tom was standing.

"Ger?"

Tom could hear voices downstairs, but he was too far away to tell who they were.

A sniffing noise came from just outside the door now. It had to be Gerry.

"Gerry, you're not funny, okay? You are so not funny."

Sniff . . . sniff sniff . . . sniff . . .

"Gerry, could you quit it now?"

The noise stopped suddenly. Tom stood very quietly and watched the two glass panes in the toilet door. The corridor on the other side of the door was dark—the light had gone very quickly since they had arrived. How long ago was that? Five minutes? Seven?

"Gerry, would you quit fooling around?"

No answer.

"*Please*, Ger." Still no reply. It could be that she was still pissed off at him, but no, that didn't make sense; after all, she was—

What was that?

Tom turned his head so that he could hear better.

There it was again. He turned his head swiftly to face the door just in time to see the round handle move back into place.

Then something splashed in the toilet bowl. And that's when the door handle started to move again.

* * *

Gerry struggled into the house and took the heap of coats straight to the cloakroom.

Charles dropped the car keys onto a thick wooden table that looked as though it had been there for centuries. He stepped into the kitchen, threw his arms around his wife and turned her around to face him.

"Happy new home, sweetie."

Trudy wrapped her own arms around Charles and stood on her tiptoes to give him a kiss. "Happy new home to you, too, Charlie-mine."

"You happy?"

"Happy? Oh, dear Charlie-mine, I am happier than you could imagine."

He nodded.

"Don't I look happy?"

"You looked a little sad."

"When? When was that?"

"When I came in, just then." He pointed at the window. "You were looking outside."

"Oh, I was just thinking. You know . . . about the past."

"But happy thoughts, yes?"

Trudy nodded and hugged him tight. "Happy thoughts, yes . . . But those memories . . ." She let her voice trail. "Where would we be without them, huh?"

"Ah, so nice to hear my parents saying nice things about their children," Gerry said as she came in from the cloakroom.

"In your dreams, Gerry," Charles said. It was more of a snort.

Gerry didn't respond. "I'll go get changed. My boxes in my room?"

"They should be, pooch."

As Gerry started up the stairs, Trudy said to Charles, "That stuff in the car."

"Stuff in the car?"

"The 'House of Usher' stuff. How'd you remember all that? I mean— you were quoting word for word. You were like . . . like an actor."

"You know how much I love Poe's 'stuff,' as you call it. I've only learned a few bits by heart—that, the opening part of 'Fall of the House of Usher'—bits of 'The Raven' and 'The Premature Burial' . . . and 'The Masque of the Red Death,' of course—"

She smiled and assumed a shocked expression. "Of course!"

Charles pulled his head back and studied her face. He reached out and ran a finger through the single tear running down her cheek.

"You're tired," he said.

"Yes, I am tired—fucking knackered, if the truth be known—" She chuckled and then her face grew serious again. "I was just thinking about—well, stuff, really. Things from our past, memories I just couldn't do without now."

"Like what? Give me an example."

She took a deep breath and then let out the air through clenched lips. "Remember when Mo and I—Maureen, yes? From college?"

Charles nodded and looked around to make sure Gerry wasn't standing on the staircase, listening.

"Remember when we came to see you at the bank, where you were working that summer?"

He groaned. "Yes, a nightmare."

"And you were really sweet—I think that was the first time I thought that maybe we could make a go of it, you and me. You know?"

He didn't say anything, just blinked and smiled.

"You bought us lunch—Mo was having a heavy time at home—and then afterward, she and I went into Austicks and bought you—"

"*The Town and the City,* Jack Kerouac's first novel."

"You remember!"

"Of course I remember. I didn't know of the book at all, even though I'd read *On the Road* back when I was thirteen or fourteen. I still remember how it starts—it's a remarkable book." He held Trudy by the shoulders, arms locked straight, and looked at her face, saw the moisture forming in her eyes. "If anyone were to ask me if I could name the moment that I fell in love with you, that would be it. When you and Mo came back into the bank and gave me Kerouac's *The Town and the City* in one of those striped paper bags that Austicks used to use."

Trudy took hold of her husband's face tightly between her hands. "See," she said, "and now imagine if that memory were removed from . . . from your memory bank. Your storage device. Think how you'd feel."

Charles took hold of his wife's right hand and kissed it. "I can tell you how I'd feel right now."

Trudy frowned.

"I wouldn't give a damn. I know. I know. It sounds like sacrilege . . . but the fact is that if it were removed from my memory, then I wouldn't remember the book nor would I remember the circumstances in which I received it."

He looked at her. "You're thinking about your mom now, aren't you?" he asked.

"Yes. But I'm thinking about us as well. *Our* memories. When I was at university, we had a lecture one morning and we were asked to pick a sense you could do without."

"Do without?"

"Yeah . . . like, if we were to have a choice—I know it sounds crazy, but if someone said to you, 'Okay, you can keep only one of your senses—your sense of smell, your sense of taste, your hearing or your eyesight—which—'"

"Kind of like a *Sophie's Choice* of the senses."

Trudy nodded. "*Trudy's* choice."

Charles gave her a kiss on the cheek but, for a few seconds, Trudy straightened away from him, thinking he was being patronizing. He pulled back and nodded.

"And I was having a real hard time thinking about whether to get rid of my hearing—and not being able to listen to Carole King's *Tapestry* ever again—or ditch my eyesight, which would mean I wouldn't be able to see your face ever again." She swiped hair back from her forehead and shifted her weight to her right foot.

"And suddenly, Jeremy something or other—I forget, but we all called him Jem . . . Roberts! It was Jem Roberts!—he waves his hand and asks if the lecturer was including memory.

"And the lecturer waits a minute and then he says—a real smart-ass, this guy was—'That's not a sense, it's a function.'"

"What? That's bullshit."

Trudy nodded vehemently. "Yes, total bullshit."

Then she paused.

Charles asked, "So what happened?"

Trudy shrugged. "Nothing else happened—or I just don't recall what happened. But he had made the point. Jem Roberts, yeah . . ." Trudy gazed along the darkened hallway that led to the main drawing room. She gave a weak smile.

"And from then on, I've dreaded losing my memory of you or the places I've been. Because, you see, I could lose my eyes and my ears, my smell and my taste buds—it would be traumatic and devastating, yes, particularly when it comes to bacon sandwiches—but in my memories . . . like right now"—and she closed her eyes—"I'm thinking of your face and I can see it. I'm thinking about Carole singing 'Will You Love Me Tomorrow' and I can hear it. You know what I mean."

"Yes, I do."

"And, yes, dammit, when I try, I can smell bacon sandwiches. I mean, I know I can't, but I have this memory locked away and I can . . . I can just call it up." She snapped her fingers. "Just like that."

"And taste?"

"Taste would be Indian food. Doing without that would be agony. But I believe I can experience at least some of how it tastes simply by accessing the memories I've got stored of all the fantastic meals I've eaten." She reached out and rubbed his bare forearm. "Most of them with you, dear Charlie-mine."

The silence following intruded the way silences sometimes can and it was Charles who decided that perhaps it should be he who broke the spell.

"Well, sweetie . . . there but for the grace of God and all that."

"Mommy doesn't remember one thing to another in the same day . . . sometimes in the same sentence."

"But she's happy."

"Like a pet," Trudy said and there was a sharpness to her tone. "Like a dog that doesn't know it's going to die. Doesn't know its doggy friend has died."

"Your dad?"

"Yes, Dad. She doesn't even know his name."

"And that's fine, sweetie. She's fine. She doesn't know about what she's lost. It's hard for you to grasp, I know."

"Emily Dickinson said that 'parting is all we know of Heaven and all we need of Hell.'"

"Boy, she surely had *that* right, didn't she?"

Tom went to the sink and ran the hot tap—but there wasn't any hot water. All the time, he kept his eyes on the door handle.

Footsteps sounded along the hallway, getting louder. Before he could even think of saying anything, the handle turned and his sister walked in.

"Jesus Christ, Tommy," she said. "Lock the door next time."

"Why didn't you answer me," he asked her, looking around for something to dry his hands on, "instead of messing with the doorknob?"

"I wasn't messing with the doorknob. I just came—"

"Have you got a towel?"

"Do I look like I have a towel?"

"Could you get me one?"

"Get it yourself."

Tom looked at the window, but there were no curtains.

"Hey, can you leave the bathroom, please? I need to go."

Tom sidled out and Gerry closed the door.

"Well, somebody was outside the door," he said. "Sniffing." He crossed the corridor and ran his hands across the uneven wall. "I thought it was you."

The toilet flushed, the tap ran and Gerry opened the door, shaking the water off her hands.

"Hey, this wall . . . there's a piece of board across it."

"Later." She strode past Tom. "I think we're going out to eat."

Tom clapped. "Yay, I'm starving."

* * *

"Are we going out to eat?" Tom asked as he bounded into the kitchen.

"There was a Pizza Express in town," Charles said. "How about that? Pizza and pasta—sound good?"

"Sounds good to me, Mister Poe," Trudy said as she turned right around and marched for the door.

Tom frowned. *Mister Poe?* He shrugged and followed with a skip. Adults were strange creatures, and parents the strangest of all.

As Charles retrieved his keys, Gerry called out, "Hey, wait for me."

Charles put his arm around his daughter and pulled her close.

"Where are we going?" she asked.

"Town."

"To eat?"

He nodded. "Pizza. And pasta," he added as he pulled the door closed, rattling it to make sure it was locked.

A minute later the Jaguar roared to life, and soon the noise of it had faded away, leaving only the sound of the wind in the trees.

Inside, the house got to work.

I: A Little Cupboard

Just before Gerry called out, a loud crash sounded from outside. Trudy thought someone had broken something.

It was their second day at Grainger Hall, their new house—well, not new in age terms but new to them. So here they were, out on the coast of the North Sea after twenty-five years as landlubbers in York and a four-month spell in Manchester. It had been a full day, and here it was getting toward dusk and still so much left to do.

Gerry had announced her discovery—"There's a little secret cupboard in here!"—although her words were almost drowned out by the sound of the rain lashing against the windows of the new house. "Come see!"

Tom broke off from unraveling a confusion of aerial, telephone and cable leads, dropping the lot noisily to the dusty bare boards and setting off for his sister's room at a gallop. Tom went everywhere at a gallop. Even when he had broken his ankle swinging into a backflip from the basketball hoop attached to the garage roof at the old house back in Harrogate, the eleven-year-old had continued to propel himself and his plastered leg across house floor or paved pathway with something approaching unnatural speed. "He's got a pain threshold that will work against him one of these days," was how Charles always evaluated his son's "ability."

"Let's see!" Tom yelled as he skidded to a halt beside his sister.

"Thomas, just calm down," Trudy called from downstairs. She had been trying to arrange a visit from the local odd-job man suggested by the estate agent. Essie was a big woman—she tipped the scales at more than twenty stone—and boasted a formidable gap-toothed overbite with a space so wide she could surely have been able to suck in sausages like another person could clear a plate of spaghetti.

Trudy listened to the ringtone in the town about five miles away and was about to give up when a voice snapped, "Yes?"

She was caught unprepared by the rudeness on the other end of the phone as she struggled to gather her thoughts. "Is that Mr. Blamire?"

"Do I sound like a 'mister' to you?" the voice—now clearly that of a female—said, and then chuckled. "I'm Charity Blamire. You want Carol."

"Don't pull on it," Trudy heard her daughter shout, and just for a second she wanted to giggle.

"Carol?" she said.

"Yeah, my husband's name is Carol." The laugh that followed was without any humor. "Like the song, you know?"

"The song?"

"God, it's tight," she heard Tom say, sounding like it was through clenched teeth.

"Country music feller? Singing about a boy called Sue?"

"Ah," Trudy said as she edged into the hallway to hear better what was going on, "Johnny Cash."

In the silence that followed that, Trudy sensed the woman shaking her head and staring at the phone with a mix of pity and frustration. But all the woman had to say was "Whatever," and then "He's not here; he's away on—"

"When will he be back?"

Tom emerged from one of the upstairs rooms and took the stairs two at a time.

"No matter," Trudy said, glaring at her son to keep the noise down. "I'll call back later." She killed the call and took a deep breath before holding a hand up in front of her son. "Whoa, slow down there, hoss."

"There's nothing to see," Tom explained, ignoring his mother's frown. "I stood on my tiptoes and leaned nearly all the way in but—"

"All the way in where? Nothing to see where?"

He turned around and started back up the stairs. "It's a cupboard. In the wall," he added, so excited that he had notched down his voice to almost a whisper.

When Trudy stepped into the bedroom—was this Geraldine's or was it Tommy's? She couldn't remember—Tom was already standing at the wall and trying desperately to clamber into a large cupboard about five feet from the ground.

"Give me a leg up, Ger," Tom said as he scrabbled at the wall, trying to get a foothold so he could pull himself up.

"There's nothing *in* there."

"Just let me have another look!"

Gerry sighed and hoisted her brother up so that he could rest his elbows and forearms inside the cupboard on a narrow lip of wood.

"It's still empty," he said after just a few seconds, his voice back to its usual level.

"I did tell you."

He sniffed loudly and pulled a face. Turning to Gerry he said, "Smells like you've farted."

Gerry thumped him in the side, causing Tom to move his right arm. He slid back down the wall into a crumpled heap below the opening.

"I think we'll have less of that, thank you, both of you," Trudy said. She stepped across the room and studied the opening before running her hands along the edges of the square aperture.

"It's Tom," Gerry explained, nodding at the heap of eleven-year-old nursing his side.

"She does do farts," Tom countered.

"I did *not* fart!"

"But you *do* do them. Don't you?" He turned to Trudy and whined, "Make her answer, Mum."

"Let's have less about farting and more about trying to sort stuff out. Your father will be home in—" She broke off and pulled back from the cupboard, gagging. She waved a hand in front of her nose and pulled a face. "My, it *does* whiff a bit in there." She glanced across at her daughter and raised one eyebrow questioningly.

"Moth-*er*," Gerry complained, but Trudy had already moved on to other things. She picked up a bunch of papers and started sorting through them, frowning.

"Hmm. Oh well, it's been closed up a while. Maybe that's it."

His "injury" forgotten, Tom got to his feet and looked first at his mother and then up at the cupboard.

Trudy placed her papers on a chair. She slid up the lip of wood at the bottom of the cupboard and magically, as she raised it, a similar piece came down to meet it.

"Hey, look at *that*!" Tom exclaimed. "Little doors . . . and up and down instead of side to side—cool."

"It's a dumbwaiter," Trudy said.

"What's a dumb waiter?"

"It's like a little elevator between floors. It's designed just to carry food from the kitchen to the upstairs rooms." Trudy looked at the piece of wallpapered plywood standing against the wall to the side. "Was this over it?"

Gerry nodded. "I was banging the wall and I noticed that this section"—she pointed to the cupboard—"sounded hollow. And it moved."

"Moved?" Tom's eyes widened.

"Not by itself, soil-brain. It moved when I pressed it."

"How did you get the plywood out?"

Gerry looked down at her feet. "I ran a coin along the gaps that I felt behind the paper."

"Hmm, well, there's some immediate decorating needed before we even start." The words were sharp but the delivery was soft, so Tom and Gerry skipped further comment, and anyway, Trudy was now dialing a number on her cell.

"I'm going down to the kitchen," Tom announced.

As she listened to the phone ringing on the other end of the line, Trudy stared at the dumbwaiter and the piece of plywood leaning against the wall. That certainly was a big dumbwaiter just to carry food. Bloody hell, it could carry an entire—

"Hello?" a voice said in her ear and she turned away.

Geraldine was checking her texts.

Neither of them noticed the two thick ropes that ran through the roof of the dumbwaiter and continued down through its floor.

II: The Scarecrow

Tom turned quickly and rushed out of the room. His two-steps-at-a-time descent could be heard dwindling away into the distance. As he reached the downstairs hallway his feet clacked on the tiled floor they had exposed beneath the threadbare carpet. He called up to his sister, "I'll shout up to you. Stay there. By the dumb waiter."

Gerry *tut-tutted* and shook her head at her mother.

Such exasperation, and still only fourteen years old. Trudy smiled and rolled her own eyes before turning away quickly. "Yes, hello. It's Trudy Cavanagh here, Grainger Hall?" She waited. Then: "On Honeypot Lane, just off Clifton Road?" Another pause.

A distant voice called up to Gerry, "I'm in the kitchen, but I can't find the dumb waiter."

Trudy stepped out of the bedroom, explaining to the person on the other end of the line that she was still expecting delivery of their new wardrobes even though it was now almost dark and night was fast approaching.

As her mother left the room, Gerry glanced out of the window across the field toward the main road behind Kindling Wood. A solitary figure stood in the middle of the field, one arm raised and stretched out, with the wind clearly blowing its clothes. She leaned forward, shielding her eyes from the reflected glare of the room lights behind her. Just for a moment, it seemed as though the figure was doing exactly the same—copying her.

"Ger, come *on!*" Tom shouted.

"Yes, I'm still here," Trudy was saying into her cell as Gerry passed her on the landing. "No, I'd rather wait."

"There's a scarecrow in that field," Gerry said as she started down the stairs.

"Hmm?" Trudy moved back into the bedroom and looked out of the window. "Whatever's that doing there?" she muttered. "That's a grazing field, so why—Yes, hello?" She moved away from the window. "Yes, it's Mrs. Cavanagh. Grainger Hall. Honeypot Lane? Off the old Clifton Road?"

In the kitchen, Tom was running a hand over the section of kitchen wall that was directly below the opening to the dumbwaiter on the floor above, but he couldn't feel anything. He rapped on the wall repeatedly, listening to the sounds his small knuckles made. "There's deffo a shaft behind here," he said, emphasizing the statement with three echoing knocks followed by a trio of dull raps on a section of wall that was clearly concrete or brick. "But I don't think there's a way to get into it."

"Let me see," Gerry said, pushing her brother out of the way. She ran her fingers slowly over the smooth wall, searching for the tiniest hint of something hidden beneath the painted-over wallpaper, but there was nothing.

Trudy appeared at the kitchen door, her face a mask of frowns. She saw the children with their heads against the wall by the sink and leaned over for a listen.

"What are we listening for?"

"Oh, God," Gerry said, rolling her eyes as she straightened up.

"I suggest you employ a little respect, young lady. Or you'll be spending the evening listening to the walls in your room."

Gerry grunted and glared at Tom when he stuck out his tongue at her.

"Tom?"

"Sorry, Mom."

"I saw that."

"I know. Sorry, Mom."

There was a brief moment when the three of them stood their respective ground at the kitchen entrance and then Trudy gave a sigh. "Okay, shall we have takeaway?"

"Yay!"

"Not fish and chips," Trudy said. She was riffling through the pile of papers the estate agent had left them, looking for the menu for the only Indian restaurant in town.

"Boo," Tom countered, adjusting his expression accordingly.

Trudy found the menu and asked for requests.

"Chicken tikka," Gerry said, "and a portion of tarka dal."

"And Bambie potato," Tom added excitedly.

"*Bombay,* not *Bambie,*" Gerry whined. "Philistine," she added under her breath.

Tom ignored her. "Mustn't forget the Bambie potato," he said.

"You haven't said what you want for your actual meal yet," Trudy replied. She was still frowning, though the exasperation in her voice was pretend.

"Korma," came the response. "Chicken." He rubbed his stomach and made *yum yum* sounds as he walked across to the high stool by the breakfast counter. Clambering up, he looked out into the darkening sky. "Hey," he said.

Trudy finished pressing the buttons on her phone and almost immediately started to speak. "Oh, good evening, I wonder if we might order a takeaway? Do you deliver?" She moved away from the children as Gerry reached the counter next to her brother and hissed, "What?"

Tom pointed at the field across the road that ran between Cherryfield Road on the right and Kindling Wood on the left. "The field," he said.

"What about it?"

"Grainger Hall," Trudy was saying. "Yes—oh?"

"I thought you said there was a scarecrow in it," Tom said.

Gerry watched her reflection lean forward in the window glass and she shielded her eyes. "There was," she whispered.

"Whatever for?" Trudy wanted to know.

"Someone's taken it, then," Tom said.

"Well," Trudy was saying, "I'm very much obliged to you, in that case."

"Why would anyone want a scarecrow?" Gerry wanted to know.

"How odd," Trudy said as she killed the connection, speaking to nobody in particular. "They didn't want to deliver."

Tom groaned.

"So what are we going to—"

"It's all right; they're delivering now, after I expressed my disappointment. But they didn't want to."

"Why?"

Trudy tousled Tom's hair. "Too far out, maybe," she said.

Tom didn't answer his sister for a few seconds and then he said, "Well, it didn't just stand up and walk away, did it?"

The front door opened with a crash, and everyone jumped.

"Sorry," Charles said, bending down to retrieve the papers strewn on the steps between the pillars on either side of the double front doors. "Bloody wind took it out of my hand." He kicked it closed with his foot and started along the hall.

"I'm starving," he said, dropping the papers and briefcase on the counter.

"Hello, Charlie-mine," Trudy said. "Indian food is on the way. Busy day?"

III: The Doorbell

While they were waiting for the food to arrive, Tom worked out in foot-lengths just where the dumbwaiter elevator should open up in the kitchen. Only it wasn't there.

"It's not here," he informed his mother again.

Outside, gloom had stolen what little remained of the daylight. Inside, the house sat somnolent and apprehensive, secretive even . . . with the susurrant whisper of floorboards settling. Rain lashed the windows in sheets.

"What's not where?" Trudy asked.

"The dumb waiter thingy. It's not in the wall, where it should be." He frowned and chewed his lip. And then: "Hey, do we have a cellar?"

"More than one." Charles was putting the finishing touches to his paper on Nathaniel Hawthorne. "Door's over in the corner." He gestured toward the pantry door.

Trudy didn't say anything at first—she was busy poring over a newspaper—but then she remembered that her son was waiting for a response, for she suddenly looked up directly at him and removed her glasses from the bridge of her nose. "I'm sorry, sweetie. What?"

"The dumb waiter," Tom whined. "It's not there."

"Dumbwaiter," his father corrected. "One word. We've got a dumbwaiter?"

"*I* found it," Tom said proudly, adding, "and now it's *gone*."

"It can't have gone, Thomas," Trudy said, getting up from the table.

"Actually, *I* found it," Gerry announced. She had spent the past few minutes jiggling the keys of her phone, oblivious to what was happening around the dinner table.

"Hey, why don't you go and get ready for bed?"

"But we haven't eaten!" Tom protested, his right hand on his hip. "And nobody has explained where the dumbwaiter goes to." He hung his head in disappointment.

"I didn't mean you were going to bed before you ate. Just trying to save time."

"Are we still having a story?"

"Of course!" Charles placed his own hands defiantly on *his* hips, smiling at his son. "As though you wouldn't have a story." He *tsk*ed. "The very thought."

"Don't be too long, sweetie," Trudy said. "I want you to give me a hand looking through some of the boxes and at least putting them into the correct rooms."

"Can we have a grim story?" Tom wanted to know.

"He means one of the fairy stories in that Brothers Grimm book," Gerry said. "I think I'll pass."

Charles stood up from his chair and stretched. "Don't you like them?"

"She's *scared*," Tom said with a sneer.

"I am not scared."

The doorbell chimed.

"The food's here, the food's here!" Tom did a dance. "I'm ravishing."

Trudy turned from the sink and reached for a towel. "I'll get it."

"Ravenous, stupid." For a second, Gerry wanted to tell her little brother to piss off but she felt it might impact on her life for the next few days, so she bit her tongue and pulled a face. Tom pulled one back.

A blast of cold air ran along the corridor.

Charles walked to the door of the kitchen and shouted, "Is it the food at last?"

Trudy leaned out into the darkness. As Charles reached her, money at the ready, she said, "Nobody here."

Charles lifted his wife's hand from the doorjamb and sidestepped her out into the night.

"I hate that," Trudy said, not to anyone in particular.

The children reached her and pushed past onto the step. Charles had replaced the money in his pocket and was already at the gate. He leaned over and looked each way along their lane. There were no streetlights, but the moon was full so they could all see quite easily.

Charles shrugged as he turned around. "Nobody there," he said.

"Well, I heard it ring. Did *you* hear it ring?"

"I thought it was a little fast for the food," Gerry said. "They said half an hour and it's barely been fifteen minutes."

"Hey, look." Tom pointed. "Your scarecrow's back."

The moth-eaten hat on the thing's head ruffled in the slight breeze, and just for a second it looked as though it had been caught in the act of spying on them . . . standing there in the field directly across from them, its arms outstretched, glove-fingered hands hanging from the ends of its jacket sleeves.

Gerry backed away from the step and knocked over the umbrella stand, the one Mrs. Finch had given her parents when they left Manchester. "That wasn't there," she said, shaking her head.

Tom looked at his sister and then back at the scarecrow, which stood proudly in the field across the lane, about ten or twelve yards from a rather straggly hedge.

Charles frowned, not sure what to say.

"It wasn't there," Gerry repeated.

"I did hear the bell," Trudy said.

They all stared at the scarecrow.

It looked as though nobody was going to say anything—in fact, Tom wondered whether his family would ever speak again. His sister could be a total pain at times, but seeing her cowering in the hallway made him feel sorry for her. But then, watching his mother pulling the collar of her blouse together as though it were some kind of armor suddenly made him feel a little nervous. Somebody had to deal with the situation.

"I heard it," Tom said. "I heard it—the bell."

Charles turned to look at the scarecrow. He looked sideways, trying to keep the moonlight from his eyes. Then he stepped forward.

Tom followed that step and quickly moved alongside. "Go and stay with your mother."

Your mother! Things must be bad. Tom started to protest, but the next instruction clinched it.

IV: Not Exactly Sartorial

"You heard me, Tom. *Back in the house,*" Charles snapped. He was not a man given to flights of fancy, but there was something that did not feel altogether right. The lane itself looked strangely deserted, though why the lack of movement and cars on a country road at night should give cause for alarm or suspicion was beyond him.

He kept hold of his son's shoulder and glanced back. In his wife's eyes he saw concern and the unspoken plea for him to turn around and flee back to the house, back to where lights shone through windowpanes, and a politician was locked in civilized argument with one of Radio 4's finest.

He pushed at Tom. "Go on now," he said, neatly stopping just before adding: *and why the hell don't I come with you, keep you company on your journey?*

"Tommy, come back to the house," Trudy called in the no-nonsense voice that she had skillfully developed over fourteen years of parenting.

When he saw his son reach the doorstep and get unceremoniously bundled into the house, Charles felt dual senses of relief and isolation. With a deep breath, he turned to face the road, the hedge at its side and the peering scarecrow, still standing slightly askew and angled in the field, those dangling glove-fingers moving slightly with each small gust of wind.

He stopped at the hedge, now a mere two or three feet from the scarecrow's upper torso and be-hatted head (a head which he now saw to be a pair of tights jammed with rags). Two buttons were stitched in the place of eyes, a strip of black felt for a slightly wrinkled mouth and a clothes peg affixed to the center of its "face." He almost laughed, but managed to stop himself. Why, there was not the slightest thing strange about this "creature of the night." What had he—

And then he caught sight of the field in which the scarecrow had been planted. It was grazing pastureland: no need whatsoever to scare birds from this piece of land, because there was nothing planted there. There probably had never been anything planted there.

As his eyes scanned the field behind the scarecrow, he had a sudden sense that he was being watched. He turned quickly so that, instead of being on the periphery of the vision in his right eye, the scarecrow was now in the same position with regard to his left. Charles squinted. What he was about to ask himself was so totally ridiculous that he wanted to dismiss it entirely. But he asked it anyway, silently, deep under his breath where none could scoff behind their hands: *Is the scarecrow watching me?*

He turned to face it full on.

"Are you all right?" Trudy called.

"Dad, come back into the house," Gerry shouted.

Tom didn't say anything. There was something about this night, he knew, in that way that all children know there really is someone or something hiding under your bed when the lights go out; or something that relishes the closing of the bedroom door after parent-checking so that they might silently step into the quiet room, tiptoeing (if, indeed, they have toes the way we have them) across the moonlit carpet, casting wrong-shaped shadows.

Charles reached the hedge and moved sideways so that he was straight in front of the scarecrow. He pushed his way through the hedge so that he was standing in the pasture.

The scarecrow was spindly, listing to one side as though caught doing a pirouette. The thing was tied up on a simple cross, the stake jammed hard into the packed grassland. It wore a tweed jacket, a collarless shirt and a battered fedora whose edges were crinkled and misshapen. Not exactly sartorial. Perhaps it was the wind that set the thing to moving slightly, but Charles saw now, instead of buttons for eyes, little furrows of black—a careless slash of dark crayon that seemed to have the tiniest flick of moisture on the lower corner. How, he wondered, could he have mistaken that for a button?

And in the middle of this ruin of a face—a face, truly, that only a mother scarecrow might love (or even bear to look at for too long)—a protuberance held malignant sway: a veritable knuckle-joint thrust through the material and twisted itself at odd angles to the gash of mouth below, a gash that sloped up to Charles's left and down at its other end.

"Sweetie?"

"It's okay," Charles shouted back. "It's just a scarecrow."

Was it? Was that what it was? A simple scare-device to send birds winging off into the sky? He leaned on the hedge and pulled himself up so that he might see the ground behind. It was as he had already surmised, simple grazing land. There was no sign of any animals . . . and none when they had first arrived.

"And no scarecrows," he said softly. "There were no scarecrows."

"Come back to the house," Trudy called.

Charles turned to walk back, and that was when he noticed it. Over by the other hedge that ran at ninety degrees to the one that bordered the roadside was a long block of some kind—a feeding trough, Charles assumed, though there were no animals visible. What was visible, however, was another scarecrow, almost identical to the one immediately in front of him. He did a double and then a triple take, flicking his eyes from one to the other. Yes, the two of them were *exactly* the same.

"There's another one," Charles said, immediately regretting the unease that he had allowed to infiltrate the statement.

"What? What did you say?" Trudy shouted.

"Dad . . . will you—"

"I said, there's another one. Another damned scarecrow."

A wind flurried and the scarecrow turned creakily on its stake. When Charles looked over, he saw the scarecrow by the trough list to the right, as though hunkering down in preparation for something.

Charles turned, sweeping his eyes over the field behind the hedge, and at first it looked okay. But then, on a second glance, as he clapped his hands together after grappling with the hedgerow,

Charles could make out a solitary figure standing just below the drop where the field ran down toward Kindling Beck.

Another scarecrow.

Three scarecrows—at *least*, he thought; there could well be more—and all of them standing in a field that didn't appear to be growing anything at all.

"Dad?"

Should that bother him? *Scarecrows?*

"Charlie, come back to the house."

"I'm going back to the house," Charles whispered to the scarecrow immediately in front of him. For a few seconds he half-expected it to lean forward conspiratorially and, with a gloved hand of wood and old clothes, whisper in a soil-smelling hoarse voice: *Think I'll join you all . . . We'll have ourselves a little party.*

But it didn't.

Charles took a deep breath and turned on his heel. Anyone watching might have concluded that he was some kind of dancer, this man who faced up to scarecrows by a nighttime hedge, pirouetting in the cold.

Something rustled behind him and he hunched his shoulders, waiting for the inevitable contact. But nothing came.

"The scarecrow fell over!" Tom shouted. There was a tone of wonder in his voice, that could easily have worked just as well if he had simply called out, *It's alive!*

Charles turned around and, sure enough, the scarecrow behind the hedge had gone. It had fallen over, of course . . . the wooden stake had given in to the pressures of gravity and taken a tumble. It was nothing more sinister than that. *'Tis the wind and nothing more!* a voice in Charles's mind hissed. *Quoth the raven . . .*

"Come on," he announced, clapping of hands. "Supper, and then story-time."

V: Up the Stairs to Bedfordshire

It was a little before nine o'clock when the food finally arrived, delivered in a large brown bag by a youth of maybe nineteen or twenty who boasted a thick thatch of coal-black hair and smiled all the time while he chewed on what appeared to be a piece of root.

"Very good," the boy had said repeatedly in a singsong fashion as Charles counted bills into his proffered hand. And when, following careful thought, Charles had added three extra pound coins, the young man clasped his hands tightly together as if in prayer and bowed. "Very good," he had told Charles once more, still smiling. "I am very grateful to you."

"You're very welcome." Charles had to fight not to mimic the man's tuneful speech, but as he closed the door, he let loose a smile.

Tom stood by the little window at the foot of the stairs and watched the deliveryman straddle his aged Honda and kick-start it. The machine leapt and for a minute Tom thought he was going fall backward while the Honda reared into the air and shot forward toward the old barn by the side of the house. But he got it under control. He gave a wave to the house and shouted something that sounded like "Very good!"—though Tom couldn't be sure—then set off along the side of the building.

Charles pushed the dead bolt across the door. "Where's he going?" he asked.

"Back to work? Wh—Tom! No!" Trudy slapped her son's hand as he tried to fish a piece of chicken from Trudy's masala.

"His fingers are in that now, Mom," Gerry said.

Tom mimicked his sister's whine, jiggling his head from side to side: "Oh, his fingers are in that now, Mumsy-wumsy . . . his—'"

Charles shook his head. "Doesn't matter." And he joined in the chaos of what always served as mealtime for the Cavanaghs as everyone took their places at the large table, shifting boxes across the kitchen floor.

"I'll put some music on," Gerry suggested, but her mother laid a hand on her arm and smiled tiredly.

"Not right now," Trudy said.

On any one of a thousand other occasions, Gerry would have thrown a tantrum, complaining that her mother hated her music and then storming up to her room, only to allow herself to be coaxed back to the family hearthside a little later, when the point had been made. But not this night.

"Radio?" Tom suggested around a folded wedge of garlic and coriander naan bread.

"Mmm." Trudy nodded gratefully. "Radio 3? Classic FM?"

He took another bite of naan, dipped it into his chicken korma and walked across to the counter. Soon soft music swirled through the air and everyone began to feel more normal again.

The food had been devoured, and the whole house smelled of an intoxicating blend of warmth and exotic spices.

Tom's Captain America clock registered 21:22 when he finally pulled the bedclothes up around his chin.

"Do we have to have a fairy story?" Gerry wanted to know. When Charles turned to her he was momentarily sideswiped by the fact that his little girl was fast becoming a woman. *No, forget that,* he thought, *Geraldine Cavanagh is a woman—a fourteen-year-old one, admittedly, but a woman nonetheless. Jesus, how did that happen?*

"Don't you like fairy stories?" Tom asked.

"Hey," Charles said, rubbing his daughter's shoulder, "don't get too old for fairy stories—not yet, anyways."

Gerry sighed and hunkered down on the spare bed.

"You want me to come read to you in your own room?"

She thought for a few seconds and then shook her head. "No," she said, "'s okay. I'll stay."

"Okay," Charles said, "then I'll begin."

And he did.

"'A certain mother's child,'" Charles recited, "'had been taken away out of its cradle by elves, and a changeling with a large head and staring eyes, which would do nothing but eat and drink, lay in its place.

"'In her trouble, the mother went to her neighbor, and asked her advice. The neighbor said—'"

And there followed the Grimms' tale about boiling water and eggshells, and the imp protesting that, despite being as old as the Wester Forest, he had never seen such a thing. Whereupon he began to laugh, and in so doing he brought his situation to the attention of the elves, who returned the stolen child and took the changeling away with them.

"'And so the mother and her child were reunited,'" Charles said in conclusion.

"How did the elves hear? The laughter, I mean."

"Elves can hear anything from any distance at all," Charles said. He felt that pretty well tied everything up neatly.

Gerry did not agree. "That doesn't make any sense." She thought for a few seconds and then added, "Nor does it make any sense that I should be listening to fairy stories at my age."

Charles thought about that for a moment and decided not to respond. He considered bringing Tom into the discussion, but only a tufty top of his hair was visible on the pillow and the slight sawing sound that his son was producing made him decide against it.

"Come on," Charles whispered, "let's leave him to it." The day was taking its toll on him, too, and he simply couldn't control a yawn so big he half-expected his head to split in half and the top half flip over, like one of the Muppets.

Charles gave his daughter a big hug. "You okay?"

"Of course I'm okay." She shrugged. "Why wouldn't I be okay?"

Somewhere in the bowels of the house a pipe clunked and a floorboard creaked.

"What was that?" Although she was putting on a brave face, Gerry had been spooked by her father's tale. She glanced at the window and was pleased to see the sky was clear and the moon shining.

"Hey, you scared?"

She shook her head emphatically. *"Nuh uh."*

Once she had climbed into bed, Charles said, "It's okay to be scared sometimes, you know."

"I'm. Not. Scared."

"Okay." He held up his hands for a few seconds and then let them drop to his side. "I guess it's okay not to be scared too." He looked down at her and smiled.

Gerry's face softened and she pulled the top sheet over the bottom of her face so that he couldn't see her mouth.

She was smiling as well.

VI: Neither the Sand nor the Sea

Tom had been in that lazy free fall that existed between wakefulness and sleep, those magical seconds when the mind is aware of what's happening, but is either unable or unwilling to do anything about it.

"Neither the sand nor the sea," Tom's paternal grandfather used to say. The expression fascinated Tom, but for some reason, it scared his sister. On this night he was very aware of the two areas: the wet ocean spreading around his feet, advancing and then retreating, always playfully, and conversely, the feel of the sand, not soft but not hard either, forcing itself between the toes of his right foot while the left relished the cool wetness.

But then, just as he started to feel a slight lean toward the endless waves, something outside in the hallway made a sound.

Tom's eyes opened wide and, without moving his head, he stared at the doorway. The bedroom door was slightly ajar. Was someone out there? He strained to hear. His mother and father were still downstairs; he could hear them muttering to each other and he could hear the strains of music from the radio.

He sat upright in his bed, pulling the sheet tightly around him, and tried to listen some more. This time he attempted to separate the noises.

There was the music—strings, French horns, oboes, cymbals—he recognized these sounds and felt comfortable with them, safe. In his head, Tom moved those to one side. Keeping his eyes trained on the slightly open door, he listened to the two voices, his mother and father . . . split them up in his mind: his dad's West Yorkshire twang, all flattened vowels and lazy *t*'s and his mother's singsong Midlands brogue. He yawned—and almost missed the noise out on the landing.

His eyes were more acclimatized to the darkness now, but even so, he couldn't make out anything that could have made the sound. The more he concentrated on the doorway, the more he wondered if maybe he had made a mistake. Maybe the noise had come from outside and not from the landing at all.

Moving very slowly, Tom swiveled around so that he could reach the windowsill and lean on it so that he could see outside.

What a lot to see in the nighttime country . . .

The door behind him creaked open.

"Ger?" Tom whispered. Perhaps she was playing around, the way she'd done yesterday, messing with the door handle.

But you don't believe that, do you? Tom's inner voice reasoned. *You're not stupid. You might* want *to believe it, but you* know *it wasn't your sister's hand on that handle.*

Something shivered down his spine. Without turning around, Tom knew that his inner voice was right: he was no longer alone in his bedroom.

He suddenly grew very cold and he wanted to curl up in bed again, but he was too busy watching a line of scarecrows *walking* across the horizon—he counted eight of them, each one strapped to its own stake, which it dragged along behind it. Clouds scudded from right to left, obscuring the moon one minute and then allowing the countryside to be bathed in silver light for a few seconds. Above the scarecrows, birds wheeled and whirled. *Birds? You know they're not birds*, the voice whispered in Tom's inner ear. *Those are bats.*

Bats! Tom had never seen a bat, not up close anyway. He had seen them on TV, natural history programs, but that was it.

Whatever it was that had come into Tom's bedroom now knocked over something just inside the doorway. Tom desperately wanted to turn around, particularly when he heard more things crash over. Something rolled along the bare floorboards under the bed.

"Gerry?" Tom said. He could just shout right out and Gerry and Mom and Dad would come blustering in here, asking what the hell was the matter, and he would be there, half-standing on his bed like a baby, eyes wide-open and having no answer for them. Because there wouldn't be anything there.

But what about the scarecrows? the voice in his head asked.

Yes, that was a very good point. What about the scarecrows?

Something was touching his bed now. He could feel the slightest of movements on the bedclothes. He started to moan very softly, and at the first sound he made, there was a noticeable cessation of anything moving on the bed.

Way over on the horizon, where the land dropped away into Kindling Woods, the scarecrows were now turning around to face the house fully, the bats still wheeling above their heads. But were they actual heads? No, of course not. He could see that from here, a hundred or more yards distant—

(The mattress sank on one side: now something was trying to get onto it.)

—that they were not heads at all . . . they were simply pieces of fabric and old clothing, off-cuts from long-abandoned dresses and shirts, old blankets and the like, pegs for noses, small flaps of make-up sponges, the sort his mother used to apply her foundation, cut clean in half like half-moons for the mouths. And those were not eyes—

(Had something just brushed Tom's bare left ankle?)

—those were sewn-on buttons . . . and he must not allow the tiny glints of moonshine reflected from the scarecrows' button eyes to check his resolve—

(A resolve? You've got a resolve, Lame-brain? he imagined his sister saying to him. *You don't even know what a resolve is.)*

—his resolve not to allow this thing, whatever it was—

(This thing now fully on his bed; he can feel the pressure of it, can feel it tilting the mattress.)

"Gerry, if that's you . . ." he whispered to the room, even though he knew that it was not.

The touch on his ankle was gentle, almost loving. At first he allowed his foot to respond. The touch wasn't unpleasant, not forceful nor aggressive, but then it felt a little slimy. From nowhere (but it must have come from somewhere . . . even though his window was almost twenty feet up in the air), a scarecrow's head appeared and flopped fully against the pane. The head turned slightly, so that it was almost in profile. A battered trilby hat sat askew on the scarecrow's head and its arms stretched out to either side. The stitching of the thing's mouth was a little uneven, so that it looked like it was sneering at him, and the eye-buttons were not straight, which made it look as though it was about to chastise him for some wrongdoing.

It's a hand, he thought as the scarecrow's head slowly fell from view, the hat dislodging, pushed up and back by the brim until it fell off completely, exposing a material dome beneath, sprinkled with dry straw.

It's a hand grasping at my foot, he thought.

Then:

Tom, it's me.

Gerry? But he didn't actually speak his sister's name. Her voice sounded different. But now the touch of her hand on his foot (it was her hand, wasn't it?)—even that, the touch of his sister's hand—felt . . . loving and warm. And his sister was not—and never had been—loving and warm . . .

He started to turn his head, slowly, while the hand—

(Please God, please let it be a hand—those fingernails feel ever so sharp.)

—continued to massage his ankle.

He tried to ignore the scarecrow's face at the bottom of the window-pane, clothes-peg nose pressed against the glass . . . and that was cool—the black button eyes blinked at him, almost like a friendly, *You okay, pal?* and in so doing they revealed a blackness far greater behind the rough stitching.

At last he could stand it no more. He turned his head so that now he was looking at the wall beside the window. As his eyes acclimatized, he saw shadows moving amidst shadows, a darkness on top of the muted darkness of things caught in relief. He tilted his head slightly more, now almost oblivious to the massaging of his ankle.

Then at last he turned fully around.

VII: Who's Gerald?

"They tucked up?"

Charles nodded and slumped onto the sofa. "I can't face much more tonight." He saw the pot of herbal tea and immediately fancied one for himself.

"That's okay, Charlie-mine. Where're you going?"

He pointed at Trudy's pot. "I'll get a cup." He poured, then slurped. A little tepid, but good.

"What about the scarecrows?" Trudy asked.

"What about them?"

"That land is not arable. You know that, right?"

"Have we got any chocolate? I need a fix."

She pointed at the pile of boxes still to be unpacked. "Top box." She sighed and stretched. "I'm going to be unpacking all day tomorrow—oh, I just remembered: I'm getting a visitor."

Speaking around a thick wedge of Snickers bar he asked, "Who's that?"

"Carol Blamire."

"Who's she when she's at home?"

"He. It's a 'he.'"

Overhead something made a drawn-out rattling sound. It rolled right over them, directly above their heads.

"Carol Blamire is a man?"

"That's what his wife says, and I guess she should know. What's in a name, dear Charlie-mine?"

"Amen to that," Charles said.

He could hear the sound of his own munching. But there was something else. Other noises.

Something was moving behind the wall.

They both turned, raising their heads to follow the path of whatever it was.

"Geraldine . . ." Trudy whispered.

They turned back to the pile of boxes and listened to the sound of flicking papers, things clattering and bouncing and thudding inside the boxes.

"What did you just say?"

Trudy frowned. "What?"

They heard a screeching sound, like nails on a blackboard, coming from the next landing.

"You said something. What was it?"

"I don't know—"

"'Is Gerald in?' you said. Who's Gerald?"

Something fell onto the landing. It sounded like a side of beef, sloppy and big . . . and heavy.

Whatever it was started to move.

"Sounds like—" she began.

Charles turned to his wife and saw her frown.

"Sounds like . . . the kid," she said, looking bemused.

"The kid?"

"Mmm," she whispered slowly. "Tommy—"

"Tommy—" Charles repeated.

Something crashed above them. Maybe a glass knocked off a side table.

"Time to go to sleep," Trudy said.

Charles scrunched up the chocolate wrapper and tossed it into the hearth. When he looked across at his wife, Trudy was already asleep.

He slouched back and stared at the window.

A door was opening upstairs. He couldn't hear it, but he could sense it.

He closed his eyes and thought again, *Gerald? Who's Gerald?*

Someone was coming down the stairs, slowly . . . *Tom,* he imagined. Not Gerald. "Who is Ger—" he started to say, but then he simply could not keep his eyes open any longer.

The last thing he heard before the drawing room door creaked open was Trudy's snore.

VIII: A Late-Night Caller

Half-sitting on the edge of Tom's bed was a bulbous object that looked like a gigantic Muppet gone wrong. Folds of pasty-looking flesh sat one on top of the other as it held out its wattled arms. The hand at the end of one was firmly clasped around Tom's ankle.

Behind him, something clacked against the windowpane. Tommy wanted to turn around—he wanted desperately to take his eyes away from the thing in front of him, its belly puckered and creased, one leg gashed down the thigh, the blood congealing. As Tom had turned, the thing had ceased its strange attentions to Tom's ankle and now appeared to be frozen, like a gigantic ugly rabbit trapped in the headlights of an oncoming car.

In that single instant two things amazed Tom.

The first was that he neither screamed nor yanked his foot away. He just knelt there, hands still on the windowsill and his body twisted around toward the open bedroom door. In the hallway beyond, he was aware of a group of four tiny people, all of them naked. They all had wings. He could see them in the shifting moonlight . . . could see their pallor and their skeletal faces; could see long genitals (all of them seemed to be male, though he could not help but notice that some of them also had pendulous breasts dangling almost all the way down to filthy feet ending in blackened, cracked toenails).

The second thing—and, God help him, Tom almost laughed—was that the bulbous creature looked almost exactly like Tom himself. It was as though he were looking into a fairground mirror, at the rheumy eyes, puffed-out cheeks, spots and craters, discolored bags under the eyes, jowly neck. He blinked as the things in the hallway backed away from the door. He thought he could hear one of them starting down the stairs.

He felt a sharp stabbing sensation in his ankle, but still he refrained from shouting out. He just had to keep concentrating. He kicked out and felt his foot hit the creature in the chest. As the thing staggered backward, Tom pulled his leg back, grimacing in pain. Something clattered against the window again, but still he did not turn; he did not dare take his eyes away from the bizarre tableau just inside the doorway, a grisly parody of one of Rupert Bear's adventures on the wilder paths to be found around Nutwood forest.

Two of the winged creatures tried to push the bloated monstrosity forward again, hissing as they did so. The thing lifted arms that looked like a sequence of thick rolls, running from underneath the armpits all the way down to the wrists and gnarled hands with long fingers.

"Oh, God," Tom gasped. The pain in his ankle was like fire.

The things in the doorway craned their faces forward, mouths pulled perilously wide as though they were greatly amused by the boy's discomfort. But though they hissed threateningly, still they maintained their ground. In that moment, Tom made what he considered to be a startling discovery: the things—both the winged creatures and the bulbous shape by his bed—appeared to be as wary of him as he was of them.

All of this was a dream anyway, wasn't it? (*Wasn't* it?) So anything—

Clatter . . .

—so anything he did now had little consequence.

The bulbous thing snarled and straightened up. It shifted its body sideways and knocked the bedroom door against a pile of boxes. *That should do it,* Tom thought. *That should bring Mom and Dad up the stairs, even though this whole thing is some kind of mad dream.*

The creature shifted its head and wiggled it, as though trying to relieve the pressure of a too-tight collar. The thing's features had been slowly taking clearer shape, but since Tom had kicked it in the chest, the head and arms were losing their form.

Tom felt a strange pulling sensation around his stomach, as though something were—

. . . Clatter . . .

—tugging at him. As he carefully raised his right arm and pressed the palm against his stomach, he was suddenly aware of reality stretching around him, in front of him . . . He suspected the same thing was happening behind him, too.

"Gerry," Tom called. He didn't want to shout too loud; he didn't really want his parents to hear and then come upstairs, because that would clinch his suspicion that this was not a dream.

He eased himself into a standing position on his bed and immediately felt vulnerable. The bed was too springy. If he fell down, then that thing—plus the other creatures, the ones with the wings—would be all over him like a rash.

"Ger-ry." This time he tried to make his voice—

. . . *Clatter* . . .

—be more singsong, not concerned in any way; just matter-of-factly calling out for his sister.

The bulbous creature had now retreated all the way to the bedroom door and joined the four winged things that were huddled half inside Tom's room and half in the hallway. The quintet pushed their faces forward and snarled loudly, waving filthy hands with fingers frozen into claws.

Tom edged to the side of the bed and—

. . . *Clatter* . . .

—and what the hell *was* that?

Tom turned toward the window just in time to see something move past him, a few inches above the floor of his room, but when he looked, there was nothing to be seen.

Outside, a pebble clattered against the window.

. . . *Clatter* . . .

Tom spun around quickly and the five creatures suddenly withdrew again, snarling and spitting and clawing.

He turned sideways so that he could check both the room and the window at a glance without too much difficulty. But he had to push himself up onto his tiptoes to see outside onto the gravel driveway.

There was a man standing down there in the wind and rain—it wasn't torrential, Tom noticed, but it was probably uncomfortable—and he was waving to Tom.

"Can I come in?" the man shouted up through cupped hands.

Something moved past Tom again, this time higher up the wall . . . *scampering*. He glanced back at the doorway and the creatures were still there, only now their attention was no longer solely upon him. Perhaps they had noticed the scampering thing too.

"*I said—*" the man was shouting, but Tom didn't hear the rest of it. He had seen the scamperer, and so, too, had the things in the doorway. It was not something moving across the wall that he had seen, but rather—

"Can I—?"

—the walls themselves.

Tom could not contain himself. "Mom! Dad!" And, when there was no answer, "Gerry! Somebody . . . *please!*"

Tom's bedroom appeared to have doubled in size several times over, and that ballroom-proportioned space was still stretching and moving. Tiny tornado twisters of masonry and plaster-dust could be seen between the bed and the door, like small fog wraiths swirling and hovering—the very image of steam-ghosts from the manhole covers that lined every New York street on the TV shows.

Tom considered the doorway from his bed, but it was now too far away. He had no idea what he might encounter in between. Instead, he leaned up onto the windowsill and looked down at the man still standing in the drive.

The figure was wearing a waterproof jacket, a dark hat—black, Tom supposed—with earflaps, and he carried a tall staff. But strangest thing of all was that he was flanked by several scarecrows, which seemed to be standing with their arms held almost straight by their sides, like bizarre gunslingers about to draw. The man removed his wet cap and slapped it against his free hand before returning it to his head. "So?" he asked.

"So?" Tom turned quickly to see that his bedroom doorway was empty again . . . but it was still so very far away. And now he noticed that thick clumps of grass were growing along the walls and out of floorboards which had been partially pried open.

"So can I come in?"

"Come in?" Tom couldn't hold back the sigh of total relief. "Yes, oh, God, yes. Please. I'll come down—" He was about to say that he would go downstairs and open the door, but then he realized he didn't want to walk through the alien darkness.

And then the man was suddenly there, standing in Tom's room, while alongside the bed, four scarecrows propped themselves against the wall, unmoving.

IX: What Do You Know About Fairies?

"So," the man said, "that wasn't too hard, was it?" He smiled. "Tom, isn't it?"

Tom nodded. "Tom," he repeated, still wondering how the man had arrived in his room. He closed his eyes and grimaced.

"Are you hurting?"

He nodded again and lifted his leg. His eyes went so wide that he feared for a few seconds that his eyeballs were going to topple out of their sockets. The flesh on the ankle, the one the thing had been holding, was flayed off in strips, exposing cartilage and bone.

"Ah, unfortunate," the man said. "Tom . . ." He turned the name over in his mouth, as if testing it, trying to find its taste suitable.

Somewhere outside the bedroom door a growl echoed. It sounded like a huge animal lost in the forest, bemoaning its hunger and loneliness.

"I figured as much from the smell." The man sniffed loudly.

"Smell?"

The stranger sniffed again, louder this time. "Don't you get it? Shit and vanilla."

"Shit and vanilla?"

"Yes, indeed. Fairies. And where fairies have been, there's always a mess." He pointed to Tom's leg. "Right there, for instance."

"What's happening to me?" Tom asked. He glanced around the room just in time to see the bulbous thing reaching its pudgy arms out to take hold of the bedsheets while one of the winged creatures—its filthy body was clearly visible in the rain-washed moonlight coming through the window—was crawling up (yes, *up*!) the wall toward the top of the wardrobe.

"Just a second," the man said. He looked quickly around the room and spotted an old window-hook on a long wooden pole. He stepped forward, lifted the pole and swung it with all his might into the winged creature's back, managing to hit the bulbous thing at the same time, knocking it across the room. The winged thing emitted a strangled howl and fell to the floor, whereupon the man kicked it out through the doorway,

"Who are you?" Tom wanted to know. "And what is going on?" Then he opened his eyes wide. "Gerry!" he cried and jumped off the bed. "My sister, Gerry." Even as he said it, the words felt wrong. Gerry was surely a boy's name—was he mistaken? In fact . . . in fact, was he absolutely sure he even *had* a sister?

The man said sadly, "She's already been taken, I'm afraid." As another plaintive howl echoed he added, "That's her."

"Let's go and get her, then," Tom said, though he suddenly felt a little halfhearted about the idea. In fact, this whole dream was getting a little too much. And he still wasn't totally convinced that he had ever had a sister.

"Not so easy." The man crouched down to face Tom. "To get your sister, I mean." He patted the bed. "Particularly with that leg."

The stranger was right—his ankle was not improving. In fact, it was deteriorating by the minute. The muscle of the entire calf had atrophied and the leg itself now looked like the man's window-pole.

"Okay for me to sit?" And when Tom made space, he said, "I want to tell you a story."

As the two of them sat on the edge of a bed the size of a small lake in a room as cavernous as a twelfth-century cathedral, he began: "My name is Carol—a hell of a name to give a boy, don't you think?"

Tom wasn't sure what to think, so he didn't say anything.

"Carol Blamire. Doesn't exactly trip off the tongue." He sniffed and for maybe a whole minute he sat looking at Tom. Then he said, "What do you know about fairies?"

Tom frowned. He knew about elves and their like, living in the greenwood, flying like moths encased in gossamer gowns sprinkled with stardust, but he suspected that that wasn't what the man sitting in front of him was talking about.

"Christ," Tom sighed, even though his father would have grounded him for a week for the curse. But he couldn't think of anything else to say; all he could feel was the pain, coursing up his leg and into his belly.

Something crashed out in the corridor. It sounded far, far away and yet the house, though spacious, was not exactly huge. The sound continued for a few seconds, and then a determined grunting noise started, coupled with stamping feet, all still a long way away.

"What's that?" asked Tom.

"Trolls," Blamire replied calmly. "It's an Artemis Line."

"What's an Art—"

"Artemis Line."

"What is it?"

"It's a line of trolls stretching from down in Fairyland and up into your house."

Tom started shouting for his mother and father.

"They can't hear you, I'm afraid."

"Are they . . . are they de—"

"No, they're not dead. They're just asleep."

"In bed?" A surge of pain across his stomach caused Tom to pull back his T-shirt. His belly was rippling as though something had actually got beneath his skin and was moving around.

"We need to get that fixed for you."

Tom winced and pulled down his shirt again. "Where are they? My mom and dad?"

"Downstairs."

The tromping sound was interspersed with a crash of something breaking. It sounded to Tom like an Irish dancing troupe, all of them clicking and clacking their metal heels together.

"What's a troll?" Tom had watched a DVD, some foreign movie with subtitles (Geraldine always teased him about how he always avoided subtitled films—Geraldine? Who was Ger—?—and then something tugged at the walls of his stomach and he cried out), and the troll there was as big as King Kong, so he wasn't sure how one troll could get into their house, never mind a whole dancing parade of the things.

"It's a kind of fairy, but lacking any brains at all," said the man.

Carol Blamire—what a stupid name.

"And they cannot move far away from water. That's why they tend to live under bridges."

"If they can't move away from water, what are they doing"—Tom pointed to his bedroom door—"stomping around inside the house?" He pulled down the neck of his T-shirt just in time to see something ripple across his ribs. He felt a dull stab of pain and something sharp upended itself beneath his skin before moving away to his side. He writhed and fell back onto the bed.

"That's the Artemis Line," the man said. He reached over and laid a hand on Tom's forehead. "One of them is standing in water while holding on to another. He, in turn, is holding another . . . and so on. And one by one, the trolls manhandle their way up the line, still holding on to the flesh of the trolls on each side of them and—"

"Mom! Dad!"

"I told you, they're asleep. Your sister, too."

"What sister?" he shouted out again, then added, *"I don't have a—"*

"Gerry," Blamire said. "Her name is—*was*—Gerry. As in Geraldine."

"This isn't making any sense. But what about her . . . What about my sister—the one I don't have? What about Gerry?"

"Gerry has been taken." The man glanced briefly toward the open doorway. "She was the one who opened the portal, so she is the one they came for."

"The trolls already came for her? I would have heard—"

"No, the trolls are coming now. They're the heavy gang. Think of them as the fairies' bouncers." Blamire frowned and considered that for a moment. "Do you know about bouncers? You know, night-clubs and so on?"

"Yes . . . I know about bouncers. Sometimes they're bullies hired to hurt people," Tom suggested, and the man's face lit up.

"Absolutely," he said, almost cheerfully. "Spot-on. The bouncers maintain order—their version of order—while the fairies and the elves, they're the ones in charge."

They turned in unison to stare at the bedroom doorway.

"Is it my imagination, or is the noise getting louder?" asked Tom.

"It's getting louder."

"You're really going to have to help me here, because I have absolutely no idea of what's going on, what's happened, what's—"

"There are four of them left," the man said, sounding for all the world as though he was settling in and there was no possible cause for concern. Across the room, out into the hallway and then, down down down that suddenly impossibly long corridor a bestial grunt rang out, as though from a herd of cows so large that the sun never completely set on it . . . fighting for dominance against a thick chorus of clacking shoe-heels . . . getting louder by the minute. "Four portals," he continued.

Ahoooum!

"What was that?"

"They're coming." Blamire didn't add anything else.

Tom waited for a few seconds, then asked, "Portals? Like doorways?"

"Yes, doorways. Ways to get into—and *out* of: we must never forget getting out once we're in—ways to get into and out of Fairyland."

The howl that followed amidst the clatter of stamping hooves struck a chill down Tom's back. When he spoke, he had unconsciously increased his own volume.

"Where are they? Is one of them here?"

Blamire nodded. "Of the four that are left, one is along a dirty blind alley that runs off a fluctuating street market in Zhejiang province, just south of Shanghai and the Yangtze delta. Another is in a backroom broom cupboard in a disused and boarded-up brownstone on Bleecker Street in New York City. The third is the entire acreage of Chesuncook woods in Maine, and the fourth and final one is—"

"Here," whispered Tom.

"Here, yes."

"The little cupboard."

"The dumbwaiter. Yes."

"You said that"—he waved a hand and winced at the pain in his leg—"what's-her-name? See, I'm already forg—"

"Geraldine. Gerry. You called her 'Ger.'"

"You said that she discovered the dumbwaiter. I don't remember that, but I do remember the little cupboard."

"It's because the fairies have her. We'll have to deal with your sister another time. And probably not here."

Tom hunkered down on his bed and rubbed his shin in an attempt to ease the pain in his ankle and the calf. He glanced around again at the door. It was now the length of a football pitch away. When he looked back at his guest, Blamire looked momentarily sad.

Ahoooum!

"We don't have much time," said the stranger. "And we have a long way to go."

Tom leaned forward and allowed himself to rest against Blamire's shoulder. The man placed a protective arm around the boy.

"Where . . . where are we going?" he asked.

"Downstairs. To your mother and father."

Tom grunted and closed his eyes. "I thought you said it was a long way."

"It's further than you think."

"What's happening to me?"

"The changeling—the thing we saw right at the start of all this . . . that was holding your leg—the changeling is *stealing* you in the same way that it, or one just like it, stole your sister."

"Am I going to die?" Tom asked suddenly.

The man didn't immediately answer. Finally, he said, "The changeling is stealing your flesh . . . your body."

"Why? What have I done to—"

"You've not done anything, young Tom. There is no tit-for-tat at play here, far from it. It is simply a matter of survival. When a fairy wakes up, its mind is a blank slate. There is nothing there. Everything that happened to it the previous day and the day before that and the one before that and so on . . . everything that happened, no matter how small, how trivial . . . it's gone. Erased. Rubbed out. They can have anything they want, just like that." Blamire snapped his fingers, then paused.

After a moment, he went on, "But they can't have memories. They don't know their name. Don't have a favorite smell or sound, a longed-for taste or a book in which they might lose themselves. They have nothing. They don't recall how to wash or how to wipe their filthy asses, don't know how to speak. And that first few seconds of a morning, they have to discover all over again how to breathe. And that is why they—" He searched for the right word. "That's why they seek to *consume* you . . . to eat and drink in every tiny thing about you."

He held out his hands, palm up. "For what is the complex tangle of sinew and blood, bone and cartilage, except a complicated compendium of memories . . . things getting older, things getting bigger, things growing and things shrinking. We are rich pickings to them."

"Rich Pickens," Tom grunted. He had never heard of the fellow.

The trolls howled *Ahoooum!* and stamped and howled *Ahoooum!* and stamped some more.

"They're like animals, aren't they?"

"They smell blood. They don't mean anything by it."

If that had been intended to make Tom feel a little easier, it failed. Truth was, Tom felt a little spacey. He was losing consciousness. It wasn't falling asleep—it was more than that, though he would not have been able to put it into words. It was a growing sense of not belonging. Of not *existing*.

Unable to keep his eyes open, Tom could only sense the movement around him, though he could feel rough-gloved stick-hands guiding his body as though it were the slenderest roll of greaseproof paper, like the stuff that his mother used when she was cooking.

"I think . . ." he began, surprised at the matter-of-factness about what he was about to say. "I think I'm going to die."

Way outside in the corridor, the sound of stamping feet and the bestial chorus of pained grunts seemed to have receded. As though reading Tom's thoughts, Blamire said, "The house is getting bigger.

It's becoming the one true borderland . . . the cusp of faerie and humanie."

"Humanie . . ." Tom said with a soft chuckle as a shaft of pain shot up from his belly to between his shoulder blades.

One of the brittle twig-hands stroked Tom's hair and lifted him onto somebody's shoulder: Blamire's? He didn't know. And he could not face the sheer exertion of opening his eyes to see. He breathed in against the pain and felt straw brush against his face . . . and the smell *was* of vanilla and shit. He couldn't have explained why that was what he could smell, it just was.

"Scarecrows . . ." he sighed. "Who'd've thought?"

As far as last words were concerned, he thought it was a pretty good line.

X: Lilac Time

Sometime during the third day since the group left Tom's bedroom, the boy relaxed his tenuous hold on life and drifted away without ever opening his eyes again.

They had seen many things already, and there was a promise—like the smell of sweet-scented stocks in the night air—of more to come.

The scarecrows took it in turn to carry the boy's body (now very light indeed) and the man called Carol Blamire led the way. Along the bedroom floor corridor, the light was suffused with a violet hue. And still they heard the sound of the Artemis Line, sometimes soft and sometimes loud . . . but it was always there if they paused to listen for it. But they didn't have time to stop; instead, they simply plowed on through the memories.

"This is a bad one, Rintannen," Blamire eventually said. They had paused for a minute to switch the boy from one scarecrow to another. Blamire looked around where they were standing. The scenery and topography changed constantly.

"I wonder who all this lot belonged to?" he asked no one in par-ticular. The scarecrow hoisted Tom's body over its shoulder and waited for instructions. The man slapped the scarecrow's back. "Onwards, Rintannen!" he cried.

The next time they stopped was outside a white-goods shop called Vallances. It was evening time and three steps led up to the locked doors—these were bygone times, when shops closed well before six o'clock. Blamire sat on the top step next to the scarecrows and held the unmoving boy on his lap.

Ahoooum!

Blamire ignored the chant, the first one he had heard for some time.

It's curious, he thought as they all watched the comings and goings of young people out on dates, *how the males gravitate to the left side of the shop entrance and the females congregate on the right.*

A man sat down on the step and rested his head on Blamire's shoulder.

"I asked Sylvia to meet me for lunch today," the man said. "I shouldn't have done that."

It didn't sound as if the man was expecting a response, so Blamire kept quiet.

"We were about to lose the house," he said, and then burst into a fit of uncontrolled sobbing. "So I phoned her and asked her to meet me for lunch. Sylvia, I mean."

"Sylvia," Blamire said. "Nice name."

"We lost the house," he said, his voice soft and even now. "I couldn't do that to her."

Nobody said anything then for a minute or two. The four scarecrows propped against the huge windows of Vallances, the two men on the step and the emaciated bundle on Blamire's lap all stared emptily across the busy road to the endless deserted field on the other side. There were ravens out there, circling over something. Blamire could not see what it was from where he sat.

"It's just a memory," Blamire said at last. "Not necessarily *your* memory and not even necessarily something that did or even *will* happen."

Without turning around, the man started sobbing again. "I killed her," he said, "with this." He reached into his jacket pocket and removed a thick-handled hammer. "I left her on the train tracks."

"Maybe you did, maybe you didn't. Maybe she's at home right now, waiting for you."

"I killed her." The man took a deep breath and, suddenly sitting up very straight, he hit himself in the face with the hammer. It struck the bridge of his nose and lodged itself in his eye socket. He shook as though an electric current was being passed through his body.

Blamire closed his eyes and clasped his hands tightly together. "It's just memories, glimpses of the past or the future. None of it needs to happen."

When he opened his eyes again, the man was gone. The boy was curled up beneath a wooden bench-table on which the four scarecrows were playing a game of Find the Lady.

A woman's voice shouted, "Why? I don't understand."

Blamire got to his feet. Rintannen stood with him. They were in what appeared to be a back garden, looked down upon by houses and apartments on every side. He moved across to a low wall and peered over into the garden of another house. The garden path ran from a child's swing just over the wall to the rear door, which was ajar. A woman was walking around, holding her head and muttering.

"But what have I done?" the woman wanted to know. "Just tell me that."

One of the other scarecrows had moved alongside Blamire, its gloved hand resting on his shoulder. A playing card—the four of spades—fell from the scarecrow's sleeve.

"She got up this morning and life was just fine and dandy," Blamire said to himself. "And then everything went to hell in a handcart."

Ahoooum!

The woman had seen them and had come up to the door, pulling it wide.

"He won't tell me what I've done!" the woman shouted.

"Go back to bed," Blamire whispered. "Try again."

Then he turned around and the four scarecrows were standing on a snow-covered road. One of them held the boy in its arms and appeared to be saying something to him. Or singing.

As he got closer, Blamire heard, ". . . to tell him all I can, about the plan, for lilac time . . ."

"How long have we been walking?" Blamire wanted to know as he reached the group of scarecrows.

The scarecrows remained motionless and didn't say anything. They never said anything. In fact, Blamire wondered if they could actually speak at all. *Perhaps that was just in my head*, he thought. And then: *Who is "he?" And what's lilac time?*

Ahoooum!

They set off along the road, occasionally spotting wallpapered walls in the constant wind-blown flurry of fine snow. Blamire reached over and felt the boy's forehead. It was gray-colored, like the rest of his skin, and he was completely rigid. *Completely* rigid? Were there degrees of rigidity, or was "rigid" a finite term?

He looked up from his school desk and saw Mr. Jones, his English language tutor, staring at him and repeatedly tossing a small piece of chalk into the air and catching it. He had apparently written on the blackboard a sequence of names—DICK DEWY, WILLIAM DEWY, REUBEN DEWY, FANCY DAY, GEOFFREY DAY, FREDERIC SHINER, VICAR MAYBOLD—and was partway through saying, "What do we think might have been Fancy's 'secret she would nev—'"

"You ask too many questions, Master Blamire," Mr. Jones was saying.

"Sir?"

"I said, you ask too many questions."

He nodded. "It was the Vicar, sir. Vicar Maybold." He looked around a sea of faces staring at him while the teacher continued to toss the chalk. "That was Fancy Day's secret."

They were crossing a steep bridge. The traffic was driving on the wrong side of the road—and the drivers were in the wrong side of the cars—and Blamire felt out of breath. Two of the scarecrows were ahead of him, but the boy wasn't to be seen. He turned around and looked straight into the stitched button-eyes of Rintannen, who was carrying the boy.

"Nearly there," he said to the scarecrow. The scarecrow called Rintannen nodded. And when Blamire turned back to face forward he saw that the descending slope of the bridge had morphed into stairs that led down to the hallway beneath the bedrooms.

And he was almost at the bottom.

Above him, far off but getting closer, he could hear the sound of the Artemis Line . . .

Ahoooum!

He stepped down into the hallway and made for the open kitchen door.

XI: Memories

It was almost six o'clock by the big clock over the back door, and Charles Cavanagh must have been surfacing from sleep because he jumped up as soon as Carol Blamire entered the room.

"Who are you?" Charles asked.

Trudy Cavanagh snorted herself awake and stared wide-eyed at the intruder.

"My name is Carol," Blamire began.

"Ah, Mr. Blamire," Trudy said as she tried to straighten out her hair. "My, but you certainly start early in these parts. Remind me never to—"

"Mrs. Cavanagh, we don't have much time. I suggest—"

"Are those yours?" Charles was asking, pointing at a shambolic-looking quartet of raggedy scarecrows propped up against packing boxes and cupboards alike. The one at the front wore a battered trilby, a thick woolen scarf with several large holes in it, a collarless shirt (that Charles momentarily thought that he recognized), a bow tie, and a grease-stained Barbour jacket. The thing's two button-eyes appeared (Charles thought) to be pleading with him. Suddenly, the thing fell sideways and landed on the floor in a heap. "I don't really think we want—"

Ahoooum!

Trudy frowned and looked toward the door just behind Blamire. "What's all that? The noise, I mean."

Blamire took a deep breath, visibly filling out, before releasing all of that air and just as visibly deflating. "We need to talk."

Trudy sniffed and pulled a face.

"And what on earth is that smell?"

"It's—" Blamire paused, then said, "—vanilla, I believe. And—"

"It smells more like sewage," Trudy said.

"As I said, we need to talk."

"Talk?"

And so it began . . . Blamire spoke mainly, though Trudy and Charles Cavanagh were not without questions, not least:

"Children? We don't have any children."

Charles flipped the switch on the kettle and walked across to his wife, placing a hand on her shoulder.

Blamire reached into his jacket pocket and produced a dog-eared brown packet from which he removed a quantity of photographs—old ones, judging from the condition. Blamire flicked through; then, grunting with some satisfaction, he picked one and handed it across to Trudy.

Charles was staring at the bundle on the floor. It looked like some kind of papier-mâché model of a small man—a child, perhaps—who was folded up in a semblance of deep sleep or even death.

"What *is* that?" Charles wanted to know.

He was starting to lean over the bundle of rags that Blamire had deposited when Trudy said, "Where did you get this?"

Charles asked what it was again.

Ahoooum!

"Where did you get it?" repeated Trudy.

Blamire blinked in an almost foreign way—*Ah, comme ci, comme ça, madame*—and gave a little shrug.

"Isn't that our house in Bramhope?" Trudy continued. She turned to her husband, but Charles had turned back to look at the bundle . . . against (or even onto) which one of the scarecrows had toppled, giving an almost protective or defensive air.

"Who's the little girl?" Charles wanted to know. He looked first at Blamire and then turned to Trudy. "Who's that little girl?"

Trudy felt a sudden flutter of palpitations. "Little girl," she said, repeating the words coldly and barely above a whisper. "I have no idea."

"She's your daughter," Blamire said. His voice was very soft.

"I never saw her in my—"

"Sweetie . . ." Charles was pointing at a vague outline partly visible in the open door behind the girl.

Trudy leaned forward just as the loud clomping sound had apparently reached the head of the staircase.

Nobody turned around at the noise, but Blamire said, without moving his attention from the photograph, "We have to speed up a little here. They're coming for your son."

Trudy looked up. "Who are 'they'?"

Blamire shrugged, his patience wearing a little thin. "Trolls . . ."

Ahoooum!

"That's them," he added, jerking his head in the direction of the noise. "Plus fairies—you smelled them before?"

"The sewage?"

"Shit and vanilla, if you'll pardon my saying. Plus changelings. The whole lot. They have your daughter and now they're coming for your son."

Ahoooum! A howl rang out and reverberated amidst the fevered clomping.

"Is that them?"

Blamire nodded.

"Fairies . . ." Trudy said. "Shit and vanilla." She turned back to Blamire. "Why do I feel so calm?" Here she was, in her new house— the house they had been in for barely a couple of days—and they had both of them slept in chairs (she presumed, because she was pretty sure she had not been to bed) and here was a complete stranger telling her that she had two children and there was some troupe of trolls and fairies grunting and stamping their way down to them from God-only-knew-where and . . .

"I think you should leave," Charles said, getting to his feet.

Trudy reached over and grasped her husband's arm. "No, Charlie-mine," she said. She turned the photo around and held it up, right in front of him, and pointed to the blurred face at the doorway in the photograph. "Look. It's me," she said. "Me laughing at some . . . some child I've never seen before."

Charles looked at the photograph and then at his wife, then back at the photo. She reached across the table and lifted another one from the pile. She turned it over and saw the same girl, a little older now. She had her arms folded and was determinedly looking to the side as a younger boy was apparently attempting to push her over. And again, the same face was watching it all, apparently whooping with laughter, barely holding on to a glass of what looked like white wine. (*God,* Trudy thought, *how I wish I could have a glass right now*). The three of them were in the garden at Bramhope.

And there was a shadow on the grass, holding what was clearly a camera, recording the whole thing.

"That's you," Trudy said, stroking Charles's arm and smiling up at him. "You taking the photo."

Charles snatched it from her hand and stared openmouthed.

"Now, Mr. Blamire, tell me one more thing." Trudy gestured at the wrapped-up bundle of skeletal remains against the wall. As she did so, a wind must have blown across from one of the windows (though she could not see if one was even open), because the scarecrow that was slumped against the remains slipped sideways as though preparing itself for some kind of confrontation. "Is that my—"

Blamire nodded and moved away from the table. "They're getting close now," he said, but not to Trudy. "We need to prepare ourselves, Rintannen."

The bigger of the scarecrows got to its feet and the others followed, arms stretched out to their sides like rickety marionettes. Was it Trudy's imagination, or were the scarecrows' faces now sterner—their eyes slanted, their flat chests more solid, their legs firm and fixed in place?

"Oh, Jesus!" was all Charles could say.

Trudy could not manage even that. She held her hand to her mouth as if trying to hide her sudden, sheer delight, for suddenly the world that had lost its sheen had now regained its childhood excitement. Yes, there were dangers in this brave new world, and things she did not understand . . . but there was magic here, too.

Ahoooum!

The grunt from outside the kitchen door was louder now, shaking the crockery that littered the breakfast-bar counter.

The door pushed open.

"They're here," Blamire announced.

XII: The Battle in the Kitchen

Blamire scooped up the photographs and handed them to Trudy and folded her hands around them as though they were the most precious of jewels. Trudy began to shake, her body jerking as though pummeled by a thousand fists.

"Concentrate on the boy," Blamire said, his voice little more than a whisper.

The convulsions took Trudy's body, but it wasn't just the physical exertion, it was the barrage of images and pictures.

"My . . . my d-d-daughter" was all she could manage. "Umm . . . uh . . . umm . . . ummm—" Each utterance sounded like her reaction to a fierce blow to her solar plexus.

Blamire patted her shoulder. As she started to turn, one of the scarecrows scooped up the boy's rigid corpse and laid it on the kitchen table, pushing aside cutlery and crockery.

"Concentrate on the boy," Blamire said again as he turned to face the kitchen door.

This cannot be happening, Trudy thought. She could hear a faint, far-off moaning. She watched the other scarecrows get to their feet and shuffle penguin-like to stand around Mr. Blamire. She clamped her teeth hard and swallowed . . . and was then both surprised and concerned that the moaning had abruptly ceased.

"Sweetie," Charles whispered, "none of this is happening. *Is* it?"

She looked at the shrunken figure on the table and placed a hand lovingly on its face. "I think it is, Charlie-mine," she said. "This is our son."

"Our son . . ." He could have made it into a question, but there didn't seem to be any point. That was the reality—*this was reality?*—they now faced.

"Say hello to Tom," she said. "Tell him all you know."

Blamire shouted, and Trudy looked up in time to see a thickset bald man push open the kitchen door. As the man grunted, another appeared, climbing over the line of odd-looking men, all grasping each other tightly.

Charles looked across in a daze, one hand on the body on the table and the other held palm-up as though to ward off evil spirits.

But the things coming through the doors were not spirits, at least not as they understood the word; rather, they were like a multitude of Three Stooges look-alikes: some were tall, some small; some were skinny, others like little barrels on legs; some had slender faces with dark rings around the eyes, while others had rotund moon-shapes, slashed with thin-lipped mouths bereft of humor or softness.

Ahoooum! the figures chorused, their long brown coats swirling like cloaks as they turned and grappled, hands upon arms, while clog- and boot-encased feet clacked on the wooden floor and mingled with the more muted sound of even more feet on the hallway carpet.

"Look in the drawers," Blamire suggested.

More of the figures spilled into the kitchen, hands grabbing as—

Ahoooum!

—the doorway filled up.

"The Artemis Line," Trudy said.

Two scarecrows had moved over to the kitchen units and were pulling open drawers, mostly to no avail, as Trudy had not yet unpacked, and anyway, she had absolutely no idea what her visitors were looking for.

"Anything that could be used as a weapon," Blamire snapped.

"You can read minds?"

Blamire ignored her and instead cried, "Yes!" when one of the scarecrows turned around brandishing a large carving knife.

"So you need to find the one in the water and sever his—or 'its'— connection to all the others that followed?" Trudy asked.

"Well, you can—"

Ahoooum!

"—gain some time by just going back down the line to the dumb- waiter and make the split as close to that as possible."

"And then what happens?"

Ahoooum!

"They'll still keep coming, but it'll give us some time."

"To do what?"

"To bring the boy back."

Charles had been listening as he flicked through the photo- graphs. He was frowning. Could it be that these pictures captured a life he might have had in some other variant of the world? Because he was starting to believe that was the case. He looked at Trudy.

Ahoooum!

"He said for us to concentrate on the boy," she said.

Flicking through more photographs (which seemed to be repro- ducing all the while, for he was sure there were considerably more than when he started), Charles said, "What should I do?"

"Tell him some stories," Blamire said. "They're in the photo- graphs . . . lots and lots of stories. And after all, that's all any of us wants or needs when it comes right down to it: stories."

Charles leaned closer to the figure on the table.

"Hey, Tom"—the name sounded right in his mouth, like pop- corn at the cinema. (Had he and Trudy been to the cinema with this boy? He imagined they would have done that, many times.) He flicked through the photos, turning them toward the boy's face one by one. But the boy's eyes were closed . . . weren't they? Were they really closed? Charles felt he could see a crack, like a light shining beneath a door. And then, just as he was about to turn over another one, he froze—for there was the boy, the very boy right now in front of him, hugging Charles's legs as tight as only a father's legs can be hugged by a son. "This is you . . ." he started to say.

Tom, his name is Tom, a small voice wanted him to know.

"You were standing next to me. You were upset," Charles said. He said it because he *remembered* it.

"I *do* . . . I *do* remember it!" he cried, and turned back to the photograph. He had no idea who was on photo duty because Trudy was in the shot, looking crestfallen.

Trudy looked over at him and—

"The hamster," Charles said, as though he were reminding her of the most obvious piece of information. But Trudy—

Ahoooum!

—looked blankly at the photo.

"Tom," Charles whispered, and he stroked the corpse's forehead, leaning over as far as he could. And he reminded the boy about Ray and Jean coming to visit and Tom wanting to show off his new hamster to their two girls, Rebecca and Laura. But in his excitement, as he was lifting up the wooden run, he—

Charles shook his head in denial. "I never did this," he said. "I never made a . . . I never made a hamster run in my life."

"Finish the story," Trudy whispered. "Look."

She pointed and—

Ahoooum!

—the boy was fleshing out. There could be no doubt about it. And color was slowly returning to his cheeks.

"And you dropped the wooden run onto the hamster's neck—"

"Sleedo," Trudy interrupted. "It was called Sleedo . . . your hamster."

Charles stared at his wife in wonder.

Ahoooum!

He looked around and saw one of the scarecrows swinging a small shovel it had found by the coal bin near the back door. The shovel connected with two of the trolls and sent them spinning away from the Artemis Line—and best of all, they were from well down the line, and so every troll after them fizzed out in a spray of sparks.

Trudy leaned over and ran a finger along the boy's cheek. Was it her imagination, or was that a tear?

And did the boy's face feel softer?

"Keep going," she said.

The next picture showed the boy sitting on Charles's knee.

"Oh my God," Charles said.

"What is it?"

Ahoooum!

From memory, he began to recite, "'First of all, it was October, a rare month for boys . . .'"

Behind them, Blamire took hold of the head of one of the trolls and yanked it around until there was a loud crack. Still listening as the troll lifted its hands and burst into a green fountain-spray, Trudy thought that where wrestlers and boxers had cauliflower ears, these things had cauliflower-entire-faces.

All around the kitchen Blamire and the scarecrows were swinging things they had found in boxes or in the cutlery drawer.

"June," Charles said as a troll fell against the table, its mouth twisted into a grimace of obvious pain before it, too, disappeared in a crimson cloud of gas bubbles. "No doubting it," he continued.

An eyelid flickered.

Ahoooum!

"'June's best of all, for the school doors spring wide and September's a billion years away . . .'"

Trudy reached out and grasped her husband's hand. "He's *remembering*, Charlie-mine."

Ahoooum!

This time, the war cry sounded more feeble.

And then *Ahoooum!* came again, and once more, *Ahoooum!* Each more feeble yet.

Blamire and the scarecrows wielded chairs at the trolls, breaking necks and knocking them out of the Artemis Line until, though the chant and the clacking feet could still be heard, the noise was not actually in the kitchen but further away, down the hall.

Blamire looked around in a sudden panic. "Rintannen!"

A lonely howl rang out, and Blamire ran for the door, spinning it wide-open.

"*Rintannen!*"

"'So they went off together,'" Charles was saying as he stroked the boy's hand.

Out in the corridor—a surprisingly long corridor, she noted—Trudy could see one of the scarecrows down on the floor, having its arms and legs pulled free of its body by two of the trolls, who had managed to keep their own arms free while their fellow creatures held on to their heads and necks. The scarecrow howled again and tried to move its arms, but they wouldn't work. The trolls had interlocked their arms and, before Blamire could reach Rintannen, the things pulled in unison and yanked the scarecrow's head from its body. One of them plucked out the sewed-on button-eyes and flicked them against the wall.

Blamire reached out and jammed two fingers into the troll's own eye sockets and *yanked*. The thing grunted, and as its link with its fellow was broken, it exploded. The second troll fared the same; just seconds later it, too, was nowhere to be seen.

"'But wherever they go,'" Charles was still quoting, "'and whatever happens to them on the way . . .'"

Blamire lifted the discarded head of the scarecrow and held it to his own face. Trudy could not hear what he was saying.

"'. . . in that enchanted place on the top of the Forest, a little boy and his Bear will always—'"

"'—will always be playing.'" Tom said, completing the story's closing line. "Hi, Dad."

Epilogue

It felt to Blamire as if the land itself were moving at the same pace in the opposite direction to the one he was traveling, thereby doubling the distance he covered with each step.

Ahead of him stretched an apparently endless forest.

Behind him stretched the same view.

It was identical on either side, too.

There was just one blip on the landscape, a way off, but he knew what it was. Blamire lifted the binoculars that Trudy Cavanagh had given him. *I'll bring them back,* he had told her. And then he had left.

"It's there," he said. The scarecrows remained silent, although they at least did him the courtesy of looking in the direction of his pointing arm.

Blamire had no real idea if the things rationalized information the way humans did; he had never seen excitement or fear from them . . . just swaths of loyalty and honesty. He fought back the recurring image of Rintannen's head and arms being unceremoniously wrenched from the scarecrow's torso.

"Come on." He set to walking again, and the scarecrows took up his easy pace.

He had promised the couple—Charles and Trudy; nice people, he thought—that he would find their daughter. *And I'll bring her back, too,* he had assured Trudy. *Whatever,* her eyes had said, though her face had feigned interest, even gratitude. The truth was that neither of the Cavanaghs had appeared to be particularly bothered. But then, Blamire thought, would most people when a strange man comes around to your house with a bunch of walking scarecrows and tells you about fairies and changelings, and an Artemis Line of noisy trolls plus *Oh, and by the way, you have a daughter*—well, you could see that might be rather hard to swallow.

To his left, two of the remaining scarecrows trudged, swaying from side to side the way they always did, stick-arms flicking.

On his right was the third one, and in the knapsack on Blamire's back—*I'll bring it back, too,* he had assured Trudy Cavanagh; *Whatever,* she had said with a gentle smile—was all that was left of Rintannen.

He didn't know whether he would be able to do anything about the deceased scarecrow (did scarecrows die? He didn't know; come to think of it, he didn't know many things), but he would give it a try.

Whatever, he imagined Trudy Cavanagh saying.

A gloved stick-hand rested on Blamire's shoulder and he stopped. One of the scarecrows was looking at a piece of wood—a way-marker—that had been driven into the ground a few feet in front of them. The wood had been hand-carved into a pointing hand. The fingers were emaciated to the point of being skeletal, and the nails cracked and split. On the hand's palm, just under the bent-around fingernails, were the words:

THIS WAY TO FAIRYLAND

"Anyone wants to change their mind, now's the time to do it," Blamire said.

The scarecrows started up again, walking. Ahead of them, now clearly visible, was the side of a wall. It was an interior wall, partly polished wood paneling, partly wallpapered in a kind of William Morris rip-off. As they got nearer, Blamire stopped and closed his eyes. "Charity?" he said.

The response in his head was immediate, as he had expected it to be. "You there?"

"Nearly."

There was a pause and then Blamire said, "They still there, the Cavanaghs?"

"Settling in. Just three of them now, mind. That what you're aiming to set right?"

He nodded, though he knew she couldn't see.

"You need to recover the dumbwaiter is what you need to do," said his wife.

Blamire opened his eyes. Just a few feet in front of him, the wall with the dumbwaiter was forming itself out of thin air. "Well," he said, "maybe so."

Another pause and then the other voice said, "It's there, isn't it?"

"Yes, it's here."

"And you're close to it?"

"Yes, we're close to it."

One of the scarecrows tapped his shoulder. The two doors to the dumbwaiter were shuddering in their mountings.

As Blamire removed the knapsack from his back, the rest of the corridor began to take shape, walls and ceiling and floor, with other doors appearing every few yards. As he watched, several of the doors were starting to open, very slowly. He unzipped the bag, took out the axes and handed one to each of the scarecrows.

"I'm going to have to go," he said as he shrugged himself back into the knapsack straps.

"Be careful," his wife said, and she chuckled. "I always say that, don't I?"

"Yes, you always say that."

"I'll be back."

"You'd better." And then she was gone.

As the dumbwaiter's doors started to move apart, Blamire hefted his ax, jammed his foot into what remained of the soil and took a deep breath.

"Mmm," he said, "stronger than usual."

"Shit and vanilla," the scarecrow by his side said.

Blamire turned in shock. "So you *can* speak!"

And then the doors fully opened.

PETER CROWTHER is the recipient of numerous awards for his writing, his editing, and, as publisher, for the hugely successful PS Publishing imprints. As well as being widely translated, his stories have been adapted for TV on both sides of the Atlantic and collected in *The Longest Single Note, Lonesome Roads, Songs of Leaving, Cold Comforts, The Spaces Between the Lines, The Land at the End of the Working Day,* and the upcoming *Jewels in the Dust.* He is the coauthor (with James Lovegrove) of *Escardy Gap* and *The Hand That Feeds,* and author of the *Forever Twilight* SF/horror cycle and *By Wizard Oak.* Crowther lives and works with his wife and PS business partner, Nicky, on the Yorkshire coast of England. He is currently writing a sequence of novelettes set against a background of alien invasion and the implosion of the multiverse.

The Old Woman in the Wood

POOR SERVANT-GIRL WAS once traveling with the family with which she was in service through a great forest. And when they were in the midst of it, robbers came out of the thicket, and murdered all they found.

All perished together except the girl, who had jumped out of the carriage in a fright, and hidden herself behind a tree. When the robbers had gone away with their booty, she came out and beheld the great disaster. Then she began to weep bitterly, and said, "What can a poor girl like me do now? I do not know how to get out of the forest. No human-being lives in it, so I must certainly starve."

She walked about and looked for a road, but could find none. When it was evening she seated herself under a tree, gave herself into God's keeping, and resolved to sit waiting there and not go away, let happen what might.

When she had sat there for a while, a white dove came flying to her with a little golden key in its beak. It put the little key in her hand, and said, "Do you see that great tree? Therein is a little lock. Open it with the tiny key, and you will find food enough, and suffer no more hunger."

Then she went to the tree and opened it, and found milk in a little dish, and white bread to break into it, so that she could eat her fill. When she was satisfied, she said, "It is now the time when the hens at home go to roost. I am so tired I could go to bed too."

Then the dove flew to her again, and brought another golden key in its bill, and said, "Open that tree there, and you will find a bed."

So she opened it, and found a beautiful white bed, and she prayed God to protect her during the night, and lay down and slept.

In the morning the dove came for the third time, and again brought a little key, and said, "Open that tree there, and you will find clothes."

And when she opened it, she found garments beset with gold and with jewels, more splendid than those of any king's daughter. So she lived there for some time, and the dove came every day and provided her with all she needed, and it was a quiet good life.

Then one day the dove came and said, "Will you do something for my sake?"

"With all my heart," said the girl.

Then said the little dove, "I will guide you to a small house. Enter it, and inside it an old woman will be sitting by the fire and will say, 'Good-day.' But on your life give her no answer. Let her do what she will, but pass by her on the right side. Further on, there is a door, which open, and you will enter into a room where a quantity of rings of all kinds are lying, amongst which are some magnificent ones with shining stones. Leave them, however, where they are, and seek out a plain one, which must likewise be amongst them, and bring it here to me as quickly as you can."

The girl went to the little house, and came to the door. There sat an old woman who stared when she saw her, and said, "Good-day my child."

The girl gave her no answer, and opened the door.

"Whither away?" cried the old woman, and seized her by the gown, and wanted to hold her fast, saying, "That is my house, no one can go in there if I choose not to allow it."

But the girl was silent, got away from her, and went straight into the room.

Now there lay upon the table an enormous quantity of rings, which gleamed and glittered before her eyes. She turned them over and looked for the plain one, but could not find it. While she was seeking, she saw the old woman and how she was stealing away, and wanting to go off with a bird-cage which she had in her hand.

So she went after her and took the cage out of her hand. And when she raised it up and looked into it, a bird was inside which had the plain ring in its bill.

Then she took the ring and ran quite joyously home with it, and thought the little white dove would come get the ring. But it did not. Then she leaned against a tree, determined to wait for the dove.

As she thus stood, it seemed just as if the tree was soft and pliant, and was letting its branches down. And suddenly the branches twined around her, and were two arms. And when she looked around, the tree was a handsome man, who embraced and kissed her heartily, and said, "You have delivered me from the power of the old woman, who is a wicked witch. She had changed me into a tree, and every day for two hours I was a white dove. And so long as she possessed the ring I could not regain my human form."

Then his servants and his horses, who had likewise been changed into trees, were freed from the enchanter also, and stood beside him. And he led them forth to his kingdom, for he was a King's son, and they married, and lived happily.

The Silken People

JOANNE HARRIS

ONCE THERE WAS a little girl who lived in a village by a wood. She was very curious and always asking questions. She asked her nurse: "How did you lose your eye?"

The nurse, who had a porcelain eye as blue and white as a china plate, said: "Oh, I don't remember. Maybe I left it lying around, and the Silken People stole it away."

"The Silken People?" said the girl.

"The ones our kind call insects. They have as many tribes as there are people in our world. They're everywhere: in the food you eat; in the fruit you pick from the orchard; on the path you tread; in the air you breathe; in your house; in your bed; under the eaves; and when you die, they'll be there still, feeding on what's left of you."

"That's horrible!" exclaimed the girl.

"That's life," said the nurse. "Learn to live with it. And never hurt an insect, child—not a bee, or a wasp, or a butterfly—or the Lacewing King will get you, for sure."

The girl said: "Who's the Lacewing King?"

"Some call him Lord of the Flies," said the nurse. "Some call him King of the Faërie. He lives under the mountain, and in stagnant water, and in the trees, and his people have always been in the world, even before First Man and First Woman."

"Have you ever seen him?" said the girl, her eyes wide.

"No one sees him," said the nurse. "Not unless he wants to be seen. But you'd know him, if you did. And you'd live to regret it, too."

You notice how the nurse didn't quite answer the question. The girl noticed too, but for once, didn't push for an answer. Instead, she said: "What does he look like?"

"Sometimes he looks like a man," said the nurse. "Tall, with hair like a moth's wing. But sometimes he is a swarm of bees, or wasps, or a dancing cloud of gnats. Sometimes he comes into our world, but no one knows he's there. He has a million million spies, and no one can ever hide from him."

"Can I see him?" said the girl.

"No," said the nurse. "But he sees you. The Silken People see everything."

After that, the girl spent a long time watching the insect world. She learned how ants can carry loads a dozen times heavier than themselves; how butterflies spend one life as a grub and then grow wings for a life in the air; how bees make honey; how wasps fight, gnats bite and even the cheery ladybug is a predator fiercer than a wolf, biting the heads off aphids as they travel up the flower stems. She watched how the mantis dines on her mate, wringing her hands in silent prayer, and how the termites shape their nests into great underground cathedrals. She watched them all attentively, but she never saw the Lacewing King, or the Silken People.

"Well, of course you didn't," said the fat nurse, when the girl complained to her. "The Silken Folk walk in disguise. They never cast a shadow. No one sees their true shape, except when—"

"What?"

"Well, sometimes you can glimpse them just as you're waking from a dream. Or from the corner of your eye, when you're looking at something else. But they know how to move among us. They've been doing it ever since our kind began to take over the earth. They're quick—and clever—and they only move when they know we can't see them."

"How?" said the girl quickly, having already decided that *she* was going to see them, however long it took her.

"They wait until we close our eyes," said the nurse. "The Silken Folk have no eyelids. They don't have to blink like you and me, or dream, or sleep the way we do. So, every time you blink, they move, faster than a dragonfly's wing. And by the time you open your eyes, they've disappeared."

After that, the girl watched more closely than ever. But, this time, she watched from the tail of her eye, spending hours in the woods, or by the bank of the river, staring, trying not to blink. Once or twice she even thought she saw a flicker of movement— and often, there were clouds of gnats, or tiny green-and-brown butterflies, or summer swarms of bees that came to circle in the sleepy air.

The nurse became anxious. "It isn't good for you," she said, "to be spending so much of your time in those woods. It isn't healthy. And besides, why do you even *want* to see the Silks? They're dangerous, and cruel, and cold, and the Lacewing King is the worst of them all. Better to leave them well alone."

But the girl didn't listen. She wanted to see the Lacewing King. She already saw him in her dreams, with his waistcoat of bees and his honey-dark eyes. Sometimes, as she was waking up, she even thought she'd caught him watching her from the foot of the bed, but she could never be quite sure.

And then, one day in the summertime, when the girl was fifteen years old, she went to her secret place in the woods and found a stranger sitting there, a man with hair like a moth's wing and eyes the color of honey. In the dappled light under the trees, she saw that he cast no shadow, and her heart began to beat very fast as she greeted him with a brave, bold smile.

"You're one of them, aren't you?" she said. "One of the Silken People."

He grinned. "You're very curious."

The girl nodded. "My nurse always says I ask too many questions. But if I don't ask them, then how will I *know*?"

"Know what?" said the stranger.

"*Everything*," said the girl.

The stranger laughed. "That's the spirit," he said. "No compromise. No surrender. Well, little girl, I can't promise to teach you everything. But there are things I *can* teach you, as long as you can trust me. Will you do that? Trust me?"

Once more she nodded. "I promise," she said.

"And don't tell anyone I'm here. You'll never see me again if you do."

"I promise. Now teach me!" said the girl.

That summer, she came to the woods every day, and every day met the stranger. He told her stories, taught her songs, and they kissed in the shade of the beech trees. The girl was so happy that she barely knew how to hide her excitement, but she knew she mustn't speak of it to anyone in the village. If anyone found out that she was seeing the Silken Folk, that would be the end of her—and the end of her lover, too.

Her nurse was the only suspicious one. She saw the roses in the girl's cheeks, and the sparkle in her eyes, and she wasn't so old that she didn't know Love when it was staring her in the face. One day she followed the girl to the woods, and saw her, sitting on the ground, talking to someone who wasn't there. She knew at once what was happening, and she leaped out from her hiding-place, croaking out a warning—

The man without a shadow turned at the sound of the woman's voice, and for a moment the girl thought she saw his face change; his skin darken; his body twist like a curl of smoke as he fell to his knees on the forest floor. She remembered how the Silken Folk could change into a swarm of bees, and cried out in alarm as her lover's skin began to crawl, vanishing under a doublet of bees that covered him like a living suit, swarming out of his shirt-cuffs and from the turn-ups of his boots. Soon it seemed to the girl that there was no man standing there at all, just a multitude of bees, streaming away into the air, leaving only his discarded clothes and the distant sound of humming.

The old nurse said to the girl: "Well, that's the last you'll see of *him*. Good thing, too."

The nurse was right. The girl went back many times, but her lover never returned to the glade. She *sometimes* thought she saw him, fleetingly, from the tail of her eye, or when she awoke from deep sleep, but although she begged him to give her a sign, to show himself or to talk to her, he never replied, or gave her any indication that he had ever been there at all.

"It's for the best," said the old nurse. "You'll soon get over him, you'll see. Those Silken Folk are dangerous, and you had no business running after them, or wanting to see things that shouldn't be seen."

But the girl didn't get over him. Months passed, and still she did not forget. She lost her bloom, which had once been so bright, and her rosy cheeks grew pale and wan. People in the village began to call her crazy because she was always talking to herself, and because she so seldom blinked.

The nurse grew increasingly worried. "What are you trying to do?" she said.

"I have to see him again," said the girl.

"Silly, stubborn child," said the nurse. "What is he to you, anyway? You don't even know who he is. He never told you his name, did he? Why do you think that was, eh?"

The girl looked at her wearily with eyes that were red from not blinking. "Why?"

The nurse shrugged. "The Silken People have no names, just as they have no eyelids. Just as they have no shadows, and some might say they have no souls. That young man you met in the woods? That was the Lacewing King, that was: the cruelest and most terrible of all the Silken People. Didn't I warn you when you were small, to beware the Silks and their sweet talk? They feed you honey, but they sting. Never forget that, child. They sting."

Well, the girl had been stung, all right. And now the poison ran deep in her veins. Nothing the nurse said made any difference, or changed the way she went every day to the little glade in the wood, and sat there, tearless, unblinking, waiting for her lover's return.

And then one day she didn't come home. She went to the glade as usual, but when night fell, and the girl still had not returned, the old nurse went to look for her. By the time the old woman reached the glade, the moon had risen above the trees, and its light filtered down through the branches, illuminating the figure of a girl, sitting weeping on a stump. The tears ran darkly down her face, and as the old woman came closer, she saw what the girl had done, and cried out in horror and dismay.

For the tears that ran down the young girl's face and dripped onto her white dress were tears of blood, dark in the moonlight. She turned toward the old nurse then, her expression a mixture of madness and calm, and now the old nurse understood.

The girl had cut off her eyelids.

The nurse fell to her knees in shock, as her heart gave way at that instant. No one saw her alive again, and no one saw her as, shadowless, the girl stood in the moonlight, looking down at the old nurse with her huge, unblinking eyes.

"I see clearly now," she said, and walked away into the night. No one ever saw her again. No one human, anyway.

JOANNE HARRIS is best known as the author of the international best-selling *Chocolat,* which was made into an Oscar-nominated film starring Juliette Binoche and Johnny Depp. However, her first book, published in 1989, was the vampire novel *The Evil Seed.* It was followed by a Victorian Gothic ghost story, *Sleep, Pale Sister.* Since then she has published ten further novels, including the fantasy volumes *Runemarks* and *Runelight,* and her stories of horror, fantasy, and magic have appeared widely. Forthcoming is *The Gospel of Loki,* a fantasy novel based on Norse mythology.

Rumpelstiltskin

ONCE THERE WAS a miller who was poor, but who had a beautiful daughter. Now it happened that he had to go and speak to the King, and in order to make himself appear important he said to him, "I have a daughter who can spin straw into gold."

The King said to the miller, "That is an art which pleases me well. If your daughter is as clever as you say, bring her tomorrow to my palace, and I will put her to the test."

And when the girl was brought to him he took her into a room which was quite full of straw, gave her a spinning-wheel and a reel, and said, "Now set to work, and if by tomorrow morning early you have not spun this straw into gold during the night, you must die."

Thereupon he himself locked up the room, and left her in it alone.

So there sat the poor miller's daughter, and for the life of her could not tell what to do. She had no idea how straw could be spun into gold. And she grew more and more frightened, until at last she began to weep.

But all at once the door opened, and in came a little man, who said, "Good evening, mistress miller, why are you crying so?"

"Alas," answered the girl, "I have to spin straw into gold, and I do not know how to do it."

"What will you give me," said the manikin, "if I do it for you?"

"My necklace," said the girl.

The little man took the necklace, seated himself in front of the wheel, and *whirr, whirr, whirr,* three turns, and the reel was full.

Then he put another on, and *whirr, whirr, whirr,* three times round, and the second was full, too. And so it went on until the morning, when all the straw was spun, and all the reels were full of gold.

By daybreak the King was already there, and when he saw the gold he was astonished and delighted, but his heart became only more greedy. He had the miller's daughter taken into another room full of straw, which was much larger, and commanded her to spin that also in one night if she valued her life.

The girl knew not how to help herself, and was crying, when the door opened again, and the little man appeared, and said, "What will you give me if I spin that straw into gold for you?"

"The ring on my finger," answered the girl.

The little man took the ring, again began to turn the wheel, and by morning had spun all the straw into glittering gold.

The King rejoiced beyond measure at the sight, but still he had not gold enough, and he had the miller's daughter taken into a still larger room full of straw, and said, "You must spin this too, in the course of this night. But if you succeed, you shall be my wife."

Even if she be a miller's daughter, thought he, *I could not find a richer wife in the whole world.*

When the girl was alone the manikin came again for the third time, and said, "What will you give me if I spin the straw for you this time also?"

"I have nothing left that I could give," answered the girl.

"Then promise me, if you should become Queen, to give me your first child."

Who knows whether that will ever happen, thought the miller's daughter. And, not knowing how else to help herself in this strait, she promised the manikin what he wanted. And for that he once more spun the straw into gold.

And when the King came in the morning, and found all as he had wished, he took her in marriage, and the pretty miller's daughter became a queen.

* * *

A year after, she brought a beautiful child into the world, and she never gave a thought to the manikin.

But suddenly he came into her room, and said, "Now give me what you promised."

The Queen was horror-struck, and offered the manikin all the riches of the kingdom if he would leave her the child.

But the manikin said, "No. Something alive is dearer to me than all the treasures in the world."

Then the Queen began to lament and cry, so that the manikin pitied her. "I will give you three days' time," said he. "If by that time you find out my name, then shall you keep your child."

So the Queen thought the whole night of all the names that she had ever heard, and she sent a messenger over the country to inquire, far and wide, for any other names that there might be.

When the manikin came the next day, she began with Caspar, Melchior, Balthazar, and said all the names she knew, one after another. But to everyone the little man said, "That is not my name."

On the second day she had inquiries made in the neighborhood as to the names of the people there, and she repeated to the manikin the most uncommon and curious. "Perhaps your name is Shortribs, or Sheepshanks, or Laceleg?"

But he always answered, "That is not my name."

On the third day the messenger came back again, and said, "I have not been able to find a single new name. But as I came to a high mountain at the end of the forest, where the fox and the hare bid each other good night, there I saw a little house. And before the house a fire was burning, and round about the fire quite a ridiculous little man was jumping. He hopped upon one leg, and shouted: 'Today I bake, tomorrow brew, the next I'll have the young Queen's child! Ha, glad am I that no one knew that Rumpelstiltskin I am styled.'"

You may imagine how glad the Queen was when she heard the name. And when soon afterward the little man came in, and asked, "Now, mistress Queen, what is my name?" at first she said, "Is your name Conrad? No. Is your name Harry? No. Perhaps your name is Rumpelstiltskin?"

"The Devil has told you that! The Devil has told you that!" cried the little man, and in his anger he plunged his right foot so deep into the earth that his whole leg went in. And then in rage he pulled at his left leg so hard with both hands that he tore himself in two.

Come unto Me

JOHN AJVIDE LINDQVIST

Translated by Marlaine Delargy

I

FOR THE SECOND time in less than a month, Annika was walking up the aisle of the church with Robert. This time they didn't continue as far as the altar but turned aside and slipped into a pew at the front of the chancel. The spot where they had exchanged their wedding vows was now occupied by a black coffin.

Inside the coffin lay Albert, Robert's father, who was the former managing director of Axryd's, Sweden's largest bread manufacturer. The church was packed. There were few friends, but on the other hand plenty of interested parties had turned up—people whose welfare was linked to Axryd's successes in a variety of ways: representatives from overseas branches, shareholders, directors of subcontractors . . .

People kept looking at Robert, exchanging glances, murmuring among themselves. He was the only child and the sole heir. Everything depended on him now. Robert's soft fingers drummed on the cover of the hymnbook and Annika stroked his wedding ring; she took his hand in hers and squeezed it gently.

She couldn't say that she knew him. A dating website had brought them together on the basis of their mutual interest in literature in general and Selma Lagerlöf in particular. They had clicked. They had found plenty to talk about: books they had read, films they had seen, countries they had visited. They shared the same opinions, and they laughed at the same things.

He was forty-five, she was forty-one. They had both picked their way through a number of doomed relationships, including marriages, and were afraid of a lonely old age. They had a great deal in common, including this fear. When Robert proposed after six months, Annika saw no reason to turn him down. They had such fun together.

Robert was reluctant to talk about either his family or the company, and it wasn't until they announced the wedding that Annika realized how rich they actually were. Robert's father paid for everything, with no expense spared—the bus drawn by four white horses, the symphony orchestra, the castle, the reception catered by chefs with a national reputation for excellence, five hundred guests. It was a fairy-tale wedding, where Annika felt like an uninvited guest.

Albert's generosity hadn't done him much good. During the reception he had embarked upon the journey that would eventually lead him to the black coffin.

"Far beyond the starry skies . . ."

The cantor's voice echoed desolately beneath the vaulted ceiling as the congregation mimed the words. Maintaining one's dignity, keeping one's distance: these were the watchwords in the alien world into which Annika had married. Robert stood there with his lips firmly clamped together, staring at the sea of extravagant wreaths before the altar, the final farewells to a powerful man.

It was difficult to make a connection between these accolades and the skinny little old man who had stood up to make a speech at the wedding reception. Albert had to cling on to the table with both hands just to get to his feet, and he managed only a few sentences before he collapsed.

A collective gasp passed through the magnificent room, and Robert fell to his knees by Albert's side, supporting his father's head in his hands as he shouted, "Call an ambulance!"

Albert grasped Robert's wrist and whispered, "No."

"Dad, we have to get you to hospital."

"We need to talk first."

"We can talk later, Dad. We've got—"

"Now!" the old man hissed. "We need to talk *now!*"

He was intractable, and eventually Robert picked up his frail body and carried him to a nearby room, where he laid him down on a sofa. Annika fetched a glass of water and placed it on a chair by his side.

"So," Robert said to his father, "what was it you wanted to tell me?"

Albert waved impatiently at Annika. "Not her. Just you."

"Dad," Robert said, "Annika is my wife now, and if you have anything to say to me—"

"Out. I want her out of here."

Robert sighed and made a move to walk away, but Annika placed a hand on his shoulder. "It's okay," she said. "You two talk. I'll go."

She kissed Robert gently on the cheek and left the room. As she closed the door behind her she was surrounded and whisked away by wedding guests, wanting to know how Albert was. That was when she began to realize how important the company was to those present.

Annika heard stories about Axryd's. How a simple miller, Robert's great-great-grandfather, had started baking bread, and soon came to dominate the market in Tingsryd. Under the leadership of Albert's grandfather, the firm had conquered half of the province of Småland with bakeries in many different locations, and had then gone on to spread both north and south.

A series of wise strategic decisions, combined with a certain element of ruthlessness, had led to the expansion of the company during subsequent generations. Was Robert the right man to take up the reins?

The door opened and Robert slipped out to inform the paramedics that they could take his father. His shoulders slumped as he walked, his head was down and he didn't even look in Annika's direction.

People flocked around the stretcher, trooping after it on the way to the ambulance, then waving good-bye as if they were bidding farewell to a ship embarking on a long voyage, its destination far from home. Robert stood there with his hands in his pockets, staring down at the gravel drive.

Annika went over and tucked her arm beneath his. "Hello, you."

Robert looked up. The skin around his eyes was taut, and his lips trembled slightly as he said, "Oh. Yes. Hello."

"How are you doing?"

He swallowed and looked at her as if he was about to say something. Then he shook his head, changed tack and said, "I think I need . . . a little time out."

With those words he left her and headed toward an arbor at the back of the castle. Annika watched him walk away, but had to go back inside with the guests, since it wasn't really acceptable for both bride and groom to disappear from the celebrations.

Half an hour later she made her way to a window overlooking the arbor. Robert was sitting motionless on a stone seat. His hands were resting on his knees, and his face was frozen in an agonized expression.

Annika touched her wedding ring. *What have I let myself in for?*

She hadn't known then, and she still didn't know now. Albert had passed away a week later, and from then until the funeral Robert had been constantly involved in meetings with solicitors, accountants and advisers. Annika went to work on the Lancôme counter at the Åhléns department store as usual, but every day she came home to an empty five-room apartment on Strandvägen.

She had fallen in love with a playboy, but now she was married to a company director who must be quickly tempered in the fire in order to fulfill his role. Robert had had a privileged upbringing. He had been given whatever he wanted; anything he asked for had been done. While Albert was still alive, Annika had accompanied Robert on a number of occasions to the mansion in Djursholm where he had grown up. It was just over ten kilometers from the rented apartment in Råcksta where she had spent her childhood, but it might as well have been in a different country. Or on a different planet.

As long as Robert had been a carefree *bon vivant*, their shared interests and preferences had fooled Annika into thinking they were alike. With the death of his father, a deep-seated aspect of Robert's character had been forced to the surface, one that was all about blood, family, tradition and responsibility. The problem was that Annika was now a part of this family and this responsibility. She had no idea how she was going to handle that.

And there was something she hadn't told Robert. Something closely linked to family and bloodlines. She was unable to have children. Ever since Albert's death she had been dreading the day when the topic would arise. Perhaps today would be that day, now that Robert's predecessor had been laid in his grave, and it was time to think about his successor.

With a lump in her stomach, Annika got to her feet in the pew to mime along with the final hymn, after which the congregation began to file past the coffin in order to pay their last respects. Annika took Robert's hand. It was ice-cold; she raised it to her lips and breathed warm air onto it as she smiled at him. His expression didn't change one iota; he just kept on staring darkly in the direction of the coffin.

Annika followed his gaze and saw the most handsome man she had ever set eyes on. He hadn't attended their wedding; she would have remembered. She had plenty of time to look at him, because he spent an age standing at the head of the coffin. He stood perfectly still, his fingers resting on the wood, his lips moving as if he was whispering something to the deceased.

Annika glanced around. Many of the guests were murmuring to each other, their heads close together. Some of the women were sitting openmouthed, staring at the man with a dreamy look in their eyes.

In spite of the fact that her question might be taken the wrong way, Annika just had to ask Robert, "Who's that?" In order to sound more indifferent, she added, "I haven't seen him before."

Robert's expression hardened and his lips narrowed. Then he said, "His name is Erik. He was my father's . . . right-hand man."

Erik had now left the coffin and was walking down the aisle toward his seat near the back of the church. As he passed Robert and Annika he nodded a greeting and smiled. Annika smiled back with some difficulty, since every drop of saliva had dried up and her tongue was stuck firmly to the roof of her mouth.

She wasn't the kind of woman who fell head over heels for a good-looking guy; over the years she had enjoyed the attention of several men who could have been part of the Clooney or Pattinson families, but she had never reacted like this.

It wasn't just the fact that Erik had a masculine beauty, with something of the Greek statue or a Paco Rabanne model about him; no, it was also the way he wore his beauty, the way one wears a favorite jumper that is far too big and faded from washing: totally relaxed, totally without pretension. He was probably about Annika's age or a few years older, and the lines on his face served only to add character.

Several women stole a glance at Erik as he walked past, but Annika controlled herself and didn't turn her head one millimeter.

That evening, when Annika and Robert were sitting on the sofa with a glass of wine, he took her hand.

"Darling," he said, "I know I've been terribly busy, but it will be better now. Most things have been sorted out and you'll be seeing more of me. If you think that's a good idea, of course."

"How can you say such a thing? Obviously it's a good idea!"

"I might not be the most entertaining companion in the world. If you've changed your mind, then I won't—"

Annika grabbed hold of the front of Robert's shirt and pulled him close with such force that a few drops of wine spilled on the very expensive sofa. She kissed him fiercely and said, "Be quiet, you idiot. I married you because I want to *be* with you, okay?"

She put down her glass. He put down his. Then they subjected the expensive sofa to further depredations.

As they lay naked in each other's arms afterward, Robert said, "This business of children . . ."

Annika tried not to stiffen, or to give any other indication that the topic terrified her. She merely nodded and said, "Yes?"

"I don't know what your position is with regard to having children."

In spite of the fear lurking in her breast, Annika couldn't help smiling at Robert's formal approach to such a personal matter. She turned the question back on him in the same format, "What's your position?"

"I think . . ." he said as Annika held her breath. "I think it's a bit overrated."

Annika exhaled slowly. "Are you sure?"

"Yes. I'm sure. Absolutely sure. How about you?"

Robert seemed genuinely disinclined to have children, so after a moment's consideration Annika decided to tell him the truth: that she couldn't have children anyway.

Robert's reaction was somewhat unexpected. His face lit up as if it had been struck by a sudden ray of sunlight; he held her tight and whispered, "That's wonderful. Terrific. In that case we can . . . do as we please, without—"

He frowned, seemingly bewildered by his own sudden lack of formality.

Annika laughed; they kissed and cuddled, but just before they got carried away, a serious look came over Robert's face. "There was one thing. We're going to have to move. To Djursholm."

"Okay," Annika said, "fine by me. It's a lovely place."

"Yes," Robert replied. "It is. It's just that—"

"What? Do you think it's too big for just the two of us?"

"No," Robert said. "The thing is, Erik will be living there too."

He explained the situation to Annika. On her brief visits to Djursholm she had seen very little apart from the drive and certain parts of the house. In fact, the property was quite extensive. There was a large garden, with a wide variety of trees and shrubs, a small lake teeming with imported carp, a barn housing six horses and an adjoining paddock. Annika would have recognized the names of two of the stallions if she had been interested in the sport of harness racing; they were now much sought after for breeding purposes.

All of this was Erik's responsibility, and he also took care of other minor tasks as they arose.

"So he's some kind of odd-job man?" Annika asked.

"Well, sort of," Robert replied, refusing to look her in the eye. "He does lots of different things. And then there's a cook and a cleaner too. Although they don't live in."

"But Erik does."

"Yes."

"And where exactly does he live? Has he got a place of his own?"

"No, he lives in the main house. He has a room."

At some point in her life Annika had no doubt toyed with the idea of having *staff*. Now that the fantasy was about to become a reality, she discovered she wasn't very keen. The thought of having someone around all the time, someone sleeping in the same house who could pop up at any moment . . . Plus the fact that this someone happened to be Erik . . . No, she wasn't keen at all.

"Couldn't we arrange things differently?" she said. "I mean, if it's such a big place, then surely we could—"

She broke off as Robert shook his head. He cupped her face gently in his hands, and she heard a faint tremor in his voice as he said, "No. We can't change things. It has to be this way."

Robert's final pronouncement was so definite and so serious that it remained hanging in the air between them and they fell silent; they lay there on the sofa, distractedly caressing each other's skin. Annika gazed at her husband, whose expression had altered; he almost looked as if he might be on the verge of tears. She didn't understand it. She really didn't. "I was just wondering," she said, "does this have anything to do with what your father wanted to talk about? At our wedding?"

Robert looked away. "Yes," he said, "you could say that. Yes."

A couple of days later, they started packing. Robert's books alone filled fifty boxes. A removal firm came and collected household appliances and furniture. Some was going into storage, some was going to Djursholm. Annika and Robert followed the removal van to oversee the unloading, and they began by taking a closer look at the corner of the world that now belonged to them.

Annika may have had reservations about Erik, but no one could deny that he was a conscientious worker. It was the middle of July, and the garden was the very definition of "glorious." Wherever they turned there was something new and beautiful to bring joy.

Flowering shrubs had been planted singly and in entrancing combinations, and fruit trees were placed apparently at random, yet in harmony with the garden as a whole. Clusters of showy annuals and perennials shared the space with meadow flowers in well-thought-out proportions, and climbers created lines that led the eye between the different areas of the garden. Not one fallen leaf could be seen on the ground.

"Do you like it?" Robert asked.

"I love it. Don't you?"

"I suppose so."

Presumably Robert was so used to the garden that he had stopped noticing it. Perhaps it was also linked to some painful memory, because he looked very gloomy.

"And what about the horses?" Annika asked.

"The horses," Robert said, with a vague wave of his hand. "The horses are over there."

They set off along a gravel path leading through a tunnel of rhododendron bushes. On the other side lay the lake, and Annika was just able to catch glimpses of the slow movements of large fish beneath the surface. The barn was beyond the lake, with the paddock extending down as far as the water's edge. A familiar smell of hay, manure and animals drifted across to Annika, and she said, "Did I tell you I can ride?"

Robert sighed and shook his head. "No, you never mentioned that."

"I used to go riding fairly regularly between the ages of ten and thirteen, but then we couldn't afford it anymore."

Whenever the difference in their financial circumstances during their childhood and teenage years arose, it led to an uncomfortable silence between them. It was as if Robert didn't know how or what to ask. Annika had chosen to regard this as a charming ineptitude, but this time it annoyed her. His melancholy mood was casting a shadow over what should have been a sunny day, so she added blithely, "Mom was on benefits for a while after Dad left us."

"Right, yes," Robert said, opening the door.

The barn Annika walked into had very little in common with the scruffy metal structure in Råsunda where she had learned to ride. This place was more like a church. Huge windows had been inserted in the high ceiling, which was supported by a high wooden cruck frame. There was a small indoor school, and a hayloft. Both planking and beams were beautifully aged, with no trace of mold or rot. Bridles and reins shone as if they had just been oiled.

Annika looked around and shook her head. "Does one person look after all this and the garden?"

"Yes," Robert replied. "Why do you ask?"

"How on earth does he manage it?"

Robert gazed around the barn, raising his eyebrows as if the thought had never occurred to him. "I suppose he works hard."

Annika walked across the sawdust toward the horses' loose boxes, inhaling deeply through her nose. It was so long since she had been inside a stable, and she had forgotten how much she loved it.

She was halfway across the school when the door of one of the loose boxes opened and Erik emerged. He had a body brush in one hand, and he was dressed in jeans and a red checked shirt. Annika's footsteps, which had been confident and expectant, suddenly became a complex combination of poorly coordinated muscle movements and she stumbled over a nonexistent obstacle.

In the hope of avoiding further embarrassment, she stopped and pretended to admire the architecture, pushing her hands deep into the pockets of her pants. Erik came toward her, and if he had looked handsome in his suit, he was now incredibly attractive. His jeans hugged his muscular legs, and his chest was broad beneath the fabric of his shirt. Annika blinked and swallowed. Something jelly-like was trying to take over her body.

Enough! She clenched her fists in her pockets as Erik came closer. *Enough!*

What the hell was she thinking? A bit of a tumble in the hay with the stable lad while the master was away on business? Callused hands caressing silky soft skin, and *Would madam care for a ride today?* Had she turned into a character in some cheap, trashy novel? *Enough.*

She took her hands out of her pockets and walked toward Erik, holding out her hand. He slipped off the grooming brush and shook hands. Touching him was nothing special. Nothing at all. One of the horses whinnied as Erik said something.

"Sorry?" Annika said, leaning closer.

"I said welcome home."

"Thanks," she said, letting go of his hand and taking a step back. Two things bothered her, and she hid the fact by looking over at Robert, who was ambling across the sawdust-covered ground.

First of all: *Welcome home.* Wasn't that rather a strange thing to say? Secondly: if she had been harboring any fantasies concerning Erik, the smell of his breath had certainly put a stop to them. It was disgusting: a combination of rotting flesh and excrement that had almost made her retch when she leaned closer to him.

The visit to the stables was a short one. Annika declined the offer to take a closer look at the horses. She needed to get outside into the fresh air, and she made the excuse that they still had a great deal of unpacking to do.

As she and Robert were walking away from the stables, she said, "I don't know if it's just me, but . . . his breath."

Robert sniggered, and at last something about his demeanor seemed to lift. "You're right," he said. "I don't know how the horses stand it."

They laughed together, and it felt good. Annika tucked her arm beneath Robert's, and at long last they strolled as man and wife through the paradise that had been given to them. As they approached the house, Robert stopped and turned to Annika.

"I was just wondering," he said. "Are you thinking of going riding?"

"I don't know. Why?"

Robert interlaced his fingers and began to twiddle his thumbs, which he had a tendency to do when he was nervous or ill at ease.

"I'd rather you didn't visit the stables," he said. "And I'd prefer it if you didn't spend time with Erik, to be perfectly honest."

"Why? Are you jealous? He *is* very good-looking . . ."

"No," Robert said. "I don't think that's something you would be . . . *capable* of. But can we agree that you'll stay away?"

Annika shrugged. "I do love riding, so I might well go over to the stables. With a clothes peg on my nose."

Robert didn't even smile at her little joke. Instead he shook his head sadly and said, "It's your life. I've said what I wanted to say."

He walked toward the house without taking her hand.

II

It was three months before Annika went back to the stables. There was a great deal to do in the house in order to awaken it from twelve years of slumber since the death of Robert's mother. The furniture was shabby and worn, the rugs frayed, the wallpaper impregnated with cigar smoke.

One of Annika's first tasks was to find a new cleaner. The old one hadn't done her job properly, and the neglect contributed significantly to the general air of decay. Every single surface that was not in daily use was sticky, and drifts of dust covered shelves and cupboards. The kitchen was a haven for bacteria, and the toilets were so ingrained with filth that the only solution was to rip them out and install new ones.

Annika felt it necessary to resign from her job so that she could devote herself entirely to the house. It didn't matter: working on the perfume counter had always made her feel slightly brain-dead, while refurbishing the house stimulated her creativity and brought concrete results from one day to the next.

It was a happy period. Robert didn't spend too much time at the office, allowing them plenty of opportunities to work and play together. By this stage they had had sex in each of the fourteen rooms in the house apart from one: Erik's room.

Annika's unease at the thought of having someone around all the time had proved unfounded. Erik was very rarely in his room, and when he wasn't there, it was locked. He spent most of his time in the stables or the garden, and Annika had discovered why the grounds were so beautiful, in stark contrast to the state of the house: Erik worked at night as well. On several occasions she had seen him wandering around among the trees and shrubs, guided only by the light of the moon and stars. He would be digging here, tidying there, pulling up weeds or spreading manure on a flowerbed. It was hard to work out when the man actually slept.

In addition to his work in the stables and the grounds, Erik also had a daily meeting with Robert. The two men would closet themselves in Erik's room for a good hour every day, and in spite of the fact that Robert's antipathy toward Erik seemed to have increased rather than diminished, nothing could persuade him to forgo these meetings. They had something to do with the running of the company, Annika had been told.

She just had to put up with the situation, which wasn't difficult. As the renovation of the house progressed and everything lightened around her, she felt as if it was quite intriguing to have a little mystery, something she didn't know about.

So one beautiful October day, when the sky was blue and clear, a perfect day for going riding, she packed a small rucksack with a flask of coffee and some sandwiches, left a note for Robert, who had gone into town, and headed for the stables.

As she opened the barn door and set off across the indoor school, she suddenly felt unsure of herself. Could she even remember how to tack up? She stopped and looked at the two horses whose heads were poking over the doors of their loose boxes. She could hear faint, familiar sounds: someone was cleaning hooves.

Okay. She would have to ask Erik for help; that was all there was to it. She carried on across the school, watched by a cat that was lying on top of a bale of hay, swishing its tail. As Annika came closer it gave a little meow, jumped down and disappeared into a loose box with the door standing ajar.

"Hello?" Annika called out. "Anyone there?"

Erik emerged; he was indeed holding a hoof pick in one hand while the cat rested in the crook of his other arm, like a baby. He walked toward Annika and she steeled herself to deal with the smell of his breath and the sight of him. Today he was wearing a blue checked shirt which made his piercing blue eyes shine.

For the sake of something to say, Annika pointed at the animal. "Lovely cat."

"Yes," Erik said, putting it down on the ground, "I found her a few months ago. She was only half-grown at the time; I assume she'd been left behind by a summer visitor."

He had stopped a meter away from her, and the stench from his mouth was still noticeable, but it was bearable. She gestured toward the loose boxes. "I thought I might go for a ride."

"I see. And is this an activity you're familiar with?"

"I used to ride a lot."

"I see. And when can we expect an addition?"

Annika assumed she must have misheard him. "Sorry?"

"An addition. To the family. When are you and Robert going to have a baby?"

Annika's right arm moved up and stroked her hair. The palm of her hand rested against the back of her head, as if to stop her from falling over backward. "What's it got to do with you?"

Erik didn't reply; he merely stared at her with those shining eyes: a searching, analytical gaze. Then he moved a step closer; he stopped directly in front of her and inhaled as if he were sniffing the air. He nodded to himself, then exhaled. Through his nose, fortunately.

Annika thought his behavior was so scandalous and so inappropriate for someone who was, after all, an employee that she was about to mention *mouthwash, Listerine, toothpaste.*

But the words never passed her lips, because the next moment Erik's hand shot out and grabbed her crotch.

Her eyes widened as a tidal wave of heat surged up through her belly. The walls of her vagina contracted in a spasm so powerful that it was more than an orgasm. Erik brought his face close to hers and the stench of carrion coming from his mouth turned her stomach, while at the same time her insides throbbed with ecstasy, and everything went black.

When she came round she was lying on her back in the sawdust, looking up at the window in the roof as the sunlight was refracted into prisms. The Thermos in her rucksack was digging into her shoulder. She rolled over onto her side and managed to get to her feet.

She remembered what had happened—but what *had* actually happened? A terrible thought struck her, and she checked her pants, her belt. There was nothing to suggest that her jeans had been removed. She pushed a hand inside her waistband and felt her bottom. No sawdust. There would have been sawdust. She carried out several more checks, everything she could think of. Nothing.

Eventually she looked at her watch. Only five or six minutes had passed since she walked into the barn. There wouldn't have been time for Erik to undress her, do the deed and dress her again. She could dismiss that particular fear.

But why did she feel so strange down there, burning and tingling as if she had just engaged in a bout of passionate lovemaking? Had she secretly harbored such a strong, suppressed desire for Erik that his touch had made her explode like this?

The ginger cat was gazing at her with its unfathomable eyes. Annika adjusted her rucksack and left the barn on unsteady legs.

A horse was saddled up outside; Erik was adjusting the final strap on the girth. When he saw Annika, he smiled and made an inviting gesture. She stood there swaying from side to side, then she shook her head and walked back toward the house. When she got past the rhododendrons and was out of sight, she broke into a run.

* * *

That night she and Robert made love twice. It was as if she needed to drive out some alien element, and Robert's thrusting penis did actually succeed in filling her with something else, something she wanted. She loved him for that, and continued to love him during the ensuing days and weeks. She wanted him all the time, to the extent that one night Robert turned her down, laughing as she began to nibble at his inner thigh.

"Stop, Annika. I can't do it. I'm sore."

She ignored his protests and took him in her mouth. By the time she straddled him a couple of minutes later, he had forgotten any soreness.

A month passed in this way, and Annika didn't even allow Robert any respite during her period, because her period didn't come. She was usually as regular as clockwork, and when she was a week late she began to worry. She was only forty-one, and it was much too early for the menopause, unless there was something wrong with her. Something *else*.

She got an appointment with her gynecologist a week later, when her period still didn't come. She had also started feeling nauseated in the mornings. Obviously she knew what that could mean, but it was simply unthinkable. He ovaries were incapable of producing eggs; her gynecologist had made that very clear fifteen years ago.

When that same gynecologist examined her this time, all he could do was shake his head. Yes, she was pregnant.

"But you said that was impossible," Annika said.

"It *was* impossible. And in my twenty years—well, I've never seen anything like it."

"But it *has* happened before?"

"Well, I have heard of cases where . . . But from a theoretical point of view it is impossible, and that was the only prognosis I could give you at the time. I apologize. Congratulations."

"And how . . . how far gone am I?"

"Approximately five weeks."

When Annika returned to the waiting room, she had to sit down for a while. As she stared at a magazine that promised to tell her all about Kristen Stewart's latest excesses, she thought about Erik.

Five weeks.

It couldn't be a coincidence. Her unthinkable pregnancy was linked to whatever had happened in the barn. Her subsequent sexual hunger, the result that had just been revealed . . . Who was Erik?

She needed to find out before she said anything to Robert.

She began to spy on Erik—only in passing at first, by organizing things so that she could glance out of the corner of her eye at what he was up to. That got her nowhere. He carried out the tasks expected of a gardener and a groom. She had to go one step further.

One pleasant day in the middle of November, she hid in the hayloft. Erik was out exercising one of the horses and she had plenty of time to surround herself with hay and dig out a little peephole. She felt stupid. She had ended up in that cheap, trashy novel after all—just in a different genre.

Half an hour went by, and her entire body was itching. The only thing she had to look at was the ginger cat as it padded around the barn. Annika began to feel mildly claustrophobic as she lay there in the enclosed space.

What's the point of this? I ought to just tell Robert and be pleased that—

The door opened and Erik walked in, leading a black mare. He took off her tack, humming something that Annika couldn't make out. Nothing out of the ordinary. In the worst-case scenario she would have to remain hidden beneath the hay for several hours, ending up none the wiser.

Erik said something that sounded like "*Schweitz*" and the horse followed him toward the center of the indoor school. This was followed by a bizarre display.

Erik shouted, "*Maisch!*" and the horse began to turn around and around, rotating at such a speed that it was surprising that she didn't fall down, overcome with dizziness. Erik clapped his hands and shouted, "*Haitch!*" whereupon the horse stopped spinning and started to gallop around as if it were being pursued by a pack of wolves.

Its eyes were rolling, and there was nothing graceful or beauti-ful about the experience; the horse was terrified, and its body was wracked with a series of shudders as it raced around and around. Erik stood in the middle of the school laughing.

Suddenly he yelled, "*Densch!*" and the horse stopped dead, saw-dust spraying up around its hooves. Then it reared up on its back legs and slammed its front legs down with such force that Annika felt the impact all the way up in the hayloft. The terrified animal repeated this maneuver until Erik shouted, "*Gamm!*" whereupon it began kicking out with its back legs, over and over again.

The mare's body was covered in a lather of sweat, and she was barely able to obey Erik as he ordered her into her loose box.

Annika's nose was itching and she moved back a fraction so that she could pinch her nostrils. She was convinced that she had just witnessed something she wasn't meant to see.

She curled up in the hay, bending her body inward to force back the sneeze, and she succeeded. When she looked out again, Erik had disappeared. She held her breath. He wasn't on his way up the ladder to the loft, was he? No, there wasn't a sound inside the barn. She still waited another five minutes before she climbed down, making sure no one saw her before she went back to the house.

That evening she almost told Robert everything. She began by chatting about the horses in general, which was fine, but as soon as she mentioned Erik's name it was as if the atmosphere in the room changed, and Robert remembered that he had a number of calls to make.

Annika remained in the living room, gazing into the fire; a moment ago it had been crackling cozily, but now it made her think of things being consumed by the flames.

Perhaps Erik's behavior toward animals explained why Annika acquired a new friend a couple of weeks later. The ginger cat that had been living in the barn had made herself a home under the steps leading up to the front door of the house. The December days were growing colder and Annika tried to tempt the cat indoors, but she obstinately remained where she was. Annika brought her a blanket, and every day she put down a saucer of milk, which the cat lapped up.

Annika agonized constantly about how and when she was going to tell Robert about her condition. She would soon begin to show, and she wanted to tell him before then. She remembered the occasion when she and Robert had talked about children: not only what he had said, but his immense relief when she told him that it was impossible for her to get pregnant.

Obviously the best thing would be to lay her cards on the table so that Robert could express his opinion. Perhaps that was why she hadn't said anything so far. She didn't want to know what that opinion might be.

What made her feel really bad was that she didn't merely content herself with the sin of omission by not saying anything; instead, she actually pretended that she was having her periods as usual, wearing pads and refraining from sex due to her nonexistent condition.

And the weeks went by.

In January it became clear why the cat had withdrawn. Like Annika, she was in the family way. Her stomach expanded with each passing day, and by February it was huge. There must be a substantial litter in there, waiting to come out.

Annika had begun to see the first signs in her own body, and she grew increasingly concerned about the cat. She used an extension lead so that she could put a heater under the steps, and swapped the blanket for an old duvet.

Robert spotted her as she was making a new nest for the cat; he stroked her back as she crouched on all fours, trying to make the dark, chilly space as cozy as possible.

"You've grown really fond of that cat, haven't you?" he said.

Before Annika had time to weigh up the pros and cons, it just slipped out: "We sisters in misfortune have to stick together."

Robert tilted his head on one side. "What do you mean?"

Annika shuffled out from under the steps and glanced at Robert, who still looked amused. "I mean that we—the cat and I—that we're both . . . Robert, I'm pregnant."

Robert's mouth opened and closed, opened again to say something, but Annika got there first. "I know what I said, and nobody can understand what's happened. It ought to be impossible, but there you go—I'm pregnant."

"And how long—"

"Fourteen weeks."

"No," Robert said. "No, I mean how long have you known about this?"

It would be so easy to lie, but she couldn't cope with trying to assess the consequences of her imaginary periods, her silence, so she told him the truth. By this time Robert was kneeling on the frozen ground. His head was bowed as if he were waiting for the executioner's ax to fall.

The cat was purring as she made herself comfortable in her new nest. Robert raised his head, looked Annika in the eye and said, "You have to get rid of it."

"But why, Robert? It's—"

"Listen to me. You have to get rid of it. Have you told anyone else?"

"No, I thought I'd wait until I'd spoken to you. But you—"

"Annika, get rid of it." Robert got to his feet, brushing fragments of earth off his pants. "There's nothing to discuss, nothing to say. Get rid of it."

With those words he turned away from her and went back into the house. Annika stayed where she was, gazing at the cat, fat and contented in her comfortable haven. Nobody was telling *her* to get rid of her babies. But then, she didn't have a husband.

For fifteen years, Annika had lived with a constant feeling of inadequacy, a sense that she was defective in some way: a woman who was incapable of fulfilling her key function. That was no longer the case.

It couldn't be helped. If she was forced to choose, then she would do so.

*   *   *

The next few days passed in mutual silence. Robert rang and made an appointment for her, and when he was standing there ready to give her a lift, she refused to go. He upbraided her, but gave no reason apart from his repeated assertion that she just had to get rid of it.

A few days before the date when it would be too late for a legal termination, she spelled it out. "Robert, you can stop all that. I'm not doing it. If you don't want me, that's fine. We'll split up; I'll move out. It would break my heart, but that's the way it is."

Robert gazed at her for a long time, and to her surprise she saw tears welling up in his eyes. He shook his head and whispered something that sounded like "That won't help." His voice was thick with emotion.

"What did you say?"

Robert wiped away the tears, got to his feet and said, "Nothing. Nothing." He took her hand and raised it to his lips. Then he nodded calmly and said, "That's that, then."

He left the room and slipped upstairs to his office. It was almost time for his daily meeting with Erik.

Annika went out on to the front steps to get some fresh air. The thermometer was showing minus ten degrees, and a thin layer of snow covered the ground. Her lungs hurt when she took a deep breath. Had Robert finally accepted the situation? "Accepted" felt like the wrong word. Resigned himself, more like.

She had no more time to ponder because she heard a muted howl of pain from beneath the steps. Annika thought she knew what was happening and hurried down to the cat's little home.

The cat was indeed in the process of giving birth. She hissed at Annika and struck out feebly with one paw while her small body was wracked with contractions. Annika ignored her protests and crawled inside the narrow space, drawing her knees up under her chin. She wanted to watch.

The cat was panting rhythmically and her stomach was heaving with the lives that were determined to make their way out into the world. Annika sat with her fingers tightly interlaced, concentrating so hard on what was going on in front of her eyes that she let out a scream when a face appeared in the opening.

Erik glanced from Annika to the cat and back to Annika. "So," he said. "It's time."

Annika swallowed with some difficulty, and managed to hiss, "Yes."

Erik's breath was polluting the small space and even the cat, who seemed to have accepted Annika's presence, paused in her efforts in order to hiss and lash out at him. He smiled and said, "You two seem to be doing just fine," whereupon he knocked three times on the wall and disappeared from view.

The cat relaxed for a moment, then resumed the task of giving birth to her kittens.

She produced a litter of six. Once the first one was out, it was all over in ten minutes. Annika sat looking at the heap of blind, helpless little creatures with a feeling of dread.

Ten minutes to bring six new lives into the world, and already the cat was lying there licking her kittens as if it was the most natural thing in the world. Which it was, of course, even if it seemed like a miracle to Annika at the moment.

She was particularly taken with the firstborn. He or she was smaller than the others, and while it was possible to detect nuances of color in the thin fur of the rest of the litter, the firstborn was completely white and looked almost as if it had no fur at all. Its body was covered with pale, soft down, and Annika wanted to wrap it up warmly, take care of it and protect it from all evil.

She was sitting there lost in thought, wondering how this could be achieved, when she heard noises from the house: raised voices and a dull thud as something fell to the floor. When she tried to crawl out to see what was going on, her body had grown numb from sitting in such a cramped position for so long and she had to spend some time straightening out her stiff limbs. Meanwhile, the voices fell silent.

Grimacing with pain, Annika slowly edged out from under the steps. Erik was standing there, and he held out his hand. Reluctantly she took it and allowed him to help her to her feet. His expression was one of complete calm, and there was nothing to indicate that he had just been quarreling. "You mustn't get cold like that," he said, glancing at her belly. "In your condition."

Annika withdrew her hand and hurried indoors. Erik headed toward the barn, and Annika stroked her belly. There was no sign of a bump when she was dressed, so how could Erik—

Had Robert told him? Was that why they had quarreled?

She found him in his office, sitting at his desk with his back to the door. There was a bottle of whisky in front of him. Unlike many of his friends, Robert was careful when it came to alcohol, and rarely got drunk. She had never seen him drinking during the day.

"Robert?"

He spun slowly around on his chair as he took a gulp from a half-full glass. His face was pale and his mouth twisted into an unnatural smile as he said, "Yes, my darling?"

"What were you arguing about? You and Erik."

Robert took another substantial gulp and shook his head. "Oh, nothing, nothing. Just the same old thing. Same old same old." He spun his chair and turned his back on her.

The next few weeks were difficult to endure. The clear, cold winter moved into an ill-defined period of slush and gray skies which continued day in and day out. Robert went away on a number of business trips, and when he came home he drank whisky and remained unreachable, sitting by the fire in the living room and staring into the flames.

If Annika hadn't had the cat and her kittens to keep her occupied, she might just have said thank you and good-bye, walked away from the house and tried to regard her marriage to Robert as a strange interlude that had at least led to her becoming pregnant.

But now she had the cat; after a few days of resistance she seemed to have accepted Annika as her assistant and nanny when it came to caring for the kittens. Annika set up a lamp under the steps, and the milder weather allowed her to spend a couple of hours each day in the company of the cat and her offspring.

She realized that her behavior was somewhat peculiar. She had a large, beautiful mansion, and yet she chose to spend the best hours of the day in a cold cubbyhole under the steps. She was waiting. Exactly what for, she didn't know. A change.

Her cell phone showed countless unanswered calls from friends, and a couple from her gynecologist. Soon she would have to tackle things, but for the moment she was waiting. She convinced herself that it was because of the little one.

The white kitten, which she had decided was a male, needed additional care. He wasn't growing as quickly as the others, and therefore he was often pushed out as they crowded around their mother's teats. Annika started bottle-feeding him, so the cat ended up with five kittens while Annika had one.

Perhaps she was preparing herself for a maternal role which she had long ago expelled from her system, and which she must now reclaim? She told herself that once the white kitten could manage on its own, she would get to grips with her life.

One gray, slushy day at the beginning of March, when Robert had gone to work, Annika filled the small bottle with milk substitute and placed it in her basket, along with a bowl of cat food and a dry towel.

As usual she knocked before she went in to see the cat. It was a mark of respect, an indication that she knew she was entering the cat's domain, where she was only a guest.

She put the basket down on the floor and took out the bottle. There was no sign of the white kitten. Its five siblings were tumbling around and making life difficult for their mother, nipping at her ears and head-butting her at every opportunity, until she hissed or gave them a swipe with her paw.

Annika looked behind and under the cat; she lifted the duvet. She picked up the lamp and illuminated each corner in turn, softly calling the kitten. After five minutes there was no longer any doubt. Her little white kitten had disappeared.

The door was always left open slightly so that the cat could come and go as she wished. With a growing feeling of dread that made her stomach churn, Annika crawled outside and began searching the garden in ever-widening circles. None of the other kittens had ever left their cozy home, but perhaps her poor little lost, helpless, wonderful boy . . .

She searched, she shouted, she sobbed and swore, but there was no trace of her protégé. She went back to the cubbyhole and looked again, even though she knew there was no point. Then she curled up in a ball and wept.

She felt a faint stirring in her belly. She stroked it and whispered, "It's okay. Everything's okay." She pulled herself together. It wasn't her own child that had gone missing. She was getting things all mixed up. The cat licked her hand.

"Where is he?" Annika asked her. "Do you know what's happened to him?"

At the sound of her voice, the cat pricked up her ears and looked over toward the entrance. Annika crawled over and pushed open the door.

She gazed out across the half-frozen slush. Now that she wasn't trying to spot the kitten, she immediately noticed the footprints. She went outside and bent over them. The tracks were partially thawed and the edges were ill-defined, but she could see the contours of a broad diamond pattern, like the soles of heavy boots.

Erik was busy mucking out. He was just heaving a pitchfork full of straw and dung into a wheelbarrow when Annika entered the barn. She walked quickly across the school, unable to take her eyes off his boots. When she stopped in front of him, he drove the spikes of the pitchfork into the ground and leaned on the handle, smiling at her with his head tilted to one side as if her visit came as a pleasant surprise.

Annika gestured angrily in the direction of the house. "Have you taken the white kitten?"

She didn't know what she had expected him to say, but it certainly wasn't the answer she got.

Erik shrugged and said, "What if I have?"

"In that case—in—" Annika's cheeks were on fire, and the words stuck in her throat. "In that case you can damn well put him back! He doesn't belong to you!"

Erik raised his eyebrows and picked up the pitchfork. He snorted and shook his head. Before returning to the loose box where he had been working, he said, "I think you'd better have a word with your husband. And by the way, it was a female."

One word reverberated through Annika's mind as she staggered back to the house: "was." And by the way, it *was* a female. She didn't understand what Erik was talking about, or what rights he thought he had, but there was one thing she assumed and another that she knew for sure: she *assumed* he had killed her kitten, and she *knew* the bastard had to go.

Without taking off her sodden shoes, she went into the kitchen, opened a drawer and took out a crowbar. She didn't hesitate as she marched up the stairs and inserted the crowbar between the frame and the door of Erik's room. The lock broke with the first wrench and the door swung open.

Annika had never seen a plan of the building, nor had she given the matter any thought, but she now realized that Erik's room was the largest in the house. She clutched the crowbar to give her courage and stepped inside.

Bookshelves, cupboards and photographs covered the walls. Big windows overlooked the garden and the stables. In front of the window stood a desk and a chair. Several armchairs were grouped around the fireplace; no doubt that was where Robert and Erik held their meetings.

There was an unpleasant smell in the room, as if the Persian carpet covering the floor had been damp. Annika tiptoed gingerly over to one of the bookshelves. It contained no books, just files and more files.

AUDIT 2011, EXPENDITURE 2011. Her gaze traveled upward and she saw CONTRACTS OF EMPLOYMENT 1980–2010. On the next shelf along were different, more old-fashioned files and folders with labels such as: INVOICES 1945–1950 and BUILDING EXPENDITURE 1931–1932.

All the labels denoting the contents were handwritten, and the strangest thing was that every single one—even those that were discolored with age—were in exactly the same handwriting.

The ridiculous suspicion that had begun to take root in Annika's mind was confirmed when she turned her attention to the photographs. Erik and Albert stood side by side in front of the stables; Albert was holding the hand of a little boy who was presumably Robert. Then there were older, black-and-white photographs of men with mustaches, wearing traditional hats, and beside them stood Erik in overalls, leaning on a scythe.

Annika found what was probably the oldest photograph in the collection. The paper had begun to turn yellow and the emulsion had cracked; the figures were slightly blurred, as if they hadn't been standing completely still. There was a mill in the background, with two men displaying a hand-made sign: AXRYD'S BAKERY.

That meant the picture must be at least a hundred years old, and it was the only one in which Erik definitely looked younger than in the others. In his thirties, perhaps.

Annika backed away from the bookshelf, shaking her head.

I think you'd better have a word with your husband.

Just as Albert had had a word with Robert at the wedding, just as Albert's father had had a word with him and so on and so on all the way back to—

The back of Annika's thighs collided with the desk; she gasped and spun around. And dropped the crowbar.

A laptop and a telephone had been pushed to one side to make room for the task in hand. Bottles and jars were arranged next to a case containing knives of various sizes. There was a small box of black glass beads, and a larger one containing something that looked like sawdust.

And in the middle of the desk, the skin of the small creature she had adopted as her own. The skull was held open with tiny clamps, and both the brain and eyes had been removed. The skin itself was stretched out on a piece of wood that was exactly the right size for the purpose, and the flesh had been scooped out. If it hadn't been for the white, downy fur, she would never have recognized her kitten.

Annika's hand flew to her mouth and she swallowed hard and closed her eyes tightly a couple of times to force back the tears. She would not throw up; she would not cry. But she would get rid of that fucking psychopath, regardless of who or what he was.

As she picked up the telephone she heard a discreet cough behind her. Erik was leaning against the doorframe, a scornful smile playing around the corners of his mouth.

"And who were you intending to call?" he asked.

Without letting go of the phone, Annika crouched down and picked up the crowbar. She pointed the curved end at Erik. "Don't come any closer!"

Erik raised his hands as if that were the last thing on his mind, then folded his arms.

"Do tell me. I'm interested. Who were you intending to call? The police? And what exactly were you going to say to them? Robert? He already knows. So who are you going to call now?"

She had been going to call Robert and tell him she wasn't staying in his house for one more second unless he came home right now and sacked Erik on the spot.

He already knows.

Annika put down the phone so that she could grip the crowbar with both hands. She took a step toward Erik.

"Move."

"Why?"

Annika imagined her throat as a metal tube to stop her voice from shaking as she took another step toward him and said, "I'm leaving right now. And if you stand in my way, I promise you—"

She raised the crowbar to illustrate exactly what she was promising. Erik shook his head and stood his ground. "I'm afraid that's not possible."

Annika struck small blows in the air with the crowbar in order to wind herself up, to get her hands ready for action. Could she do it? Was she really capable of hitting another person with a heavy object and hurting him, perhaps killing him?

Perhaps she wouldn't have done it if Erik had stayed where he was. Perhaps she wouldn't have been able to walk up to him and strike him. But he helped her along the way by taking a step toward her, and she reacted instinctively. She swung the crowbar at his head with all her strength.

The next moment a shock ran up her arm as if she had struck a thick tree trunk. Erik had raised one hand with lightning speed and seized the crowbar. He snatched it from her and threw it on the floor. His expression was sympathetic as he gazed at her and said, "Don't you realize that you ought to be grateful?"

She barely had time to register what happened next. One minute she was on her feet, then she glimpsed something from the corner of her eye that could have been the palm of Erik's hand and she was thrown to the floor. A gigantic bell tolled once inside her head, and the world disappeared.

III

She woke up in the double bed she normally shared with Robert with no idea of how much time had elapsed. Her head was pounding, one arm was bent at an odd angle and she needed the toilet. Judging by the fading light from the window, a couple of hours had passed, possibly more.

With some difficulty she managed to push her leg over the edge of the bed, but when she tried to get up, it proved impossible. One hand was attached to the bedpost with a pair of handcuffs. Her eyes widened as she stared at the shiny metal encircling her wrist, the short chain and the other cuff fixed to the dark oak of the post. She laughed out loud.

This was ridiculous. This kind of thing happened in isolated cottages deep in the forest; you could read about it in the tabloids, be appalled by the pictures of the terrible rooms, the dirty mattress, the sicko being taken away with a jacket over his head. It didn't happen here.

"Robert! Roooobeeert!" She twisted around and looked at the alarm clock. Just after three. Robert might well be home by now.

"*Roooobeeert!*"

Erik appeared in the doorway. He stood there looking at her for a while, then said, "He's not home yet. Is there something I can help you with?"

"Get this damn thing off me. I need the toilet—what the fuck are you doing?"

"First of all, you have to do me a favor." He produced Annika's cell phone, then sat down on the bed beside her and scrolled through the list of calls. The revolting smell of his breath made her headache even worse.

"Leave my fucking phone alone," Annika said. "Do you think—"

She fell silent as Erik raised his hand to remind her that the bell could easily toll once more. She clamped her lips together and he nodded and said, "Have you told anyone about your condition?"

Annika shook her head, and Erik gazed intently at her for a long time. Then he said, "I believe you. But there are a couple of calls here from what is apparently a gynecology clinic. Is that how you found out?"

Annika nodded. Erik nodded. They understood one another. He clicked a button and handed the phone to Annika. When she looked at the display, she saw that the gynecologist's number had been selected.

"Ring them," Erik said. "Ring and tell them that you had a miscarriage a month ago, while you were abroad. That's why you haven't called until now. You've been away. Do you understand?"

"Why would I do that?"

Erik's shoulders slumped and he sighed. "Does this have to be so difficult? Because otherwise I will kill Robert when he gets home."

Annika looked into Erik's eyes. They were no longer blue, but green: the green of the forest, steady and calm. She had no doubt that he was telling the truth. She pressed the call button and did exactly what he had told her to do.

Her gynecologist expressed deepest sympathy, and said that she ought to come in for an examination. Annika said she'd already had an examination in . . . Italy. Surely that would satisfy Erik and he would let her go? She thanked the gynecologist and ended the call. Erik took the phone off her, slipped it into his breast pocket and said, "Good. Number one or number two?"

"What?"

"The toilet. Number one or number two?"

"One."

He took a thin chain out of his trouser pocket. There was a small key hanging from one end; he unlocked the cuff around the bedpost and pointed toward the door. "You know where it is."

He followed one meter behind as she moved away from the bed. They reached the landing and her eyes darted around the other rooms and the stairs leading down to the front door.

"I wouldn't bother," Erik said. "You wouldn't manage even two steps."

She thought about the speed with which he had parried her blow and delivered his own. With hunched shoulders she lumbered toward the only upstairs toilet. Erik held the door for her, then left it open a fraction and stood outside.

Annika looked over at the window as she sat on the toilet. *Escape route.* At the large ornamental pebbles beneath the washbasin. *Weapons.* At the bottle of sleeping tablets Robert had started taking. *Alternative escape route.* She shook her head as she dried herself. If only Robert would come home, then . . .

She flushed the toilet and Erik opened the door, held out his hand and asked, "Where would you like to be?"

"What do you mean?"

"Exactly what I say. Where would you like to be? Which room?"

"Do I have to decide now?"

Erik's expression made it clear that he was irritated; as if he were speaking to a child, he explained, "I have other things to do. I can't spend all day hanging around like your personal assistant."

"Nobody's asked you to."

Erik's voice dropped to a menacing growl. "Annika, as far as I'm concerned, I'm happy to chain you to the bed and leave you there until you're lying in your own shit, crying for your mommy. Would you be kind enough to tell me which room you would like to be in?"

Annika swallowed and said, "The library."

Erik grabbed the loose handcuff and dragged her down the stairs. When they reached the hall and were heading toward the double doors of the library, a key was inserted in the front door and Annika thought: *Thank God.*

Erik stopped with Annika by his side. Together they awaited the arrival of the owner of the house. The front door opened slowly and Robert walked in. His shoulders were dark with moisture, and Annika could see by the outside light that a steady drizzle was falling. When Robert caught sight of Annika and Erik, he gave a start and stopped dead.

Erik pulled the cuff and lifted Annika's hand to shoulder level, as if he were showing off a hunting trophy, and said, "Unfortunately this is the way things have to be."

Robert nodded wearily and began to remove his boots. He was looking down, and the dark rings under his eyes became black as the light from the chandelier fell at an angle across his face.

"Robert?" Annika said. "Robert?"

He didn't even glance at her; he just carried on fiddling with his boots as Erik dragged her into the library. Annika was dumbstruck, and didn't even protest when Erik hauled an armchair across to one of the radiators that was fixed to the wall and chained her to it. He placed a small table with a pile of magazines on it by her side, and asked, "Is that all right?"

She looked at the magazines and her brain struggled to cope. The only problem she could come up with at the moment was how she was going to be able to read and turn the pages with one hand.

"In that case, I have other things to do, as I said." Erik made a move to leave the room.

"Who are you?" Annika asked. "*What* are you?"

Erik smiled. "Oh, I think you've worked that out by now."
Then he left her.

*   *   *

Annika remained sitting in the armchair for just over two hours.
From time to time, she called out to Robert. She begged, she cursed,
she pleaded with him, but the only response was the faint clink of
bottle against glass from upstairs.

She caressed her belly, whispered that everything would be all
right, *We're going to get out of this mess.* She didn't know whether
she actually believed that anymore.

It was after six when Erik came back and released her. He led her
to the kitchen and placed a microwaved ready-meal in front of her.
He sat down opposite her, his chin resting on his hands.

"The cook won't be coming anymore. Nor will the cleaner. So
this is the way things are going to be for a while, I'm afraid."

"What does 'a while' mean?"

"Haven't you worked it out yet? In that case, I'll leave you to think
about it for a bit longer. I have my rights; that's all there is to it."

Annika took a mouthful of something that was supposed to
resemble cod with mashed potato, but it tasted of nothing but fat
and ashes. She swallowed the hot mush with difficulty, then put
down her fork.

"You're a *tomte*, is that what you're saying? A fucking *tomte*?"

Erik pulled a face. "I prefer 'guardian of the house.' That other
word has such unfortunate connotations."

"*Tomte*," Annika said. "So where's your pointy hat, you fucking
tomte?"

Erik's eyes darkened, and now they were no longer green or blue.
Through clenched jaws he said, "I don't think you've realized that,
from now on, you are entirely reliant on my goodwill."

"Oh, yes I have," Annika said, dipping one hand into the hot food
on her plate so that it burned her fingertips. She flicked the food in
Erik's face. "Eat your fucking porridge."

She leapt up from the chair and ran for the door, but within a couple of meters Erik was standing in front of her with hot mashed potato dripping down his face. Without a word he grabbed her arm just above the elbow and she cried out in pain. It felt as if he was crushing her very bones.

He dragged her up the stairs, threw her down on the bed and handcuffed her to the bedpost. He walked out, slamming the door behind him.

She lay there for three days. Erik came in on a total of six occasions. The first time he threw her a tin of stew and a spoon, and left a bottle of water on the bedside table. The other times he brought only the stew.

Robert never came, nor did she hear the sound of his voice or his footsteps. He had presumably left the house. She stopped calling for him by the evening of the first day.

On the second day she managed to wriggle out of her pants so that she could pee and defecate on the mat by the side of the bed. She wept silently as she did so. When Erik came in a couple of hours later with the third tin of stew and wrinkled his nose at the stench, she apologized for throwing food at him and promised never to use the *t*-word again. He threw the tin at her and walked out.

On the third day she lay apathetically on the bed. The arm attached to the bedpost had gone numb. She lay there in a semi-stupor, no longer aware of the smell in the room. Erik's visits passed in mutual silence.

Toward the afternoon, when she had shoveled down some of the cold, pulpy mess out of the tin, her spirit began to return. During the first day she had gone through the possibilities of escaping and had reached the conclusion that the only thing that would work would be to chew off her own hand. Freeing herself quickly was therefore not an option. Instead she used her newly regained ability to think in order to plan a more long-term strategy.

If she accepted that Erik was a fairy-tale creature, a . . . guardian of the house . . . someone who made animals and human beings fertile and took care of the family's wealth and success . . . It was absurd, of course, but she no longer had the luxury of thinking along normal lines. She was part of the fairy tale.

So what did fairy tales reveal about how to get rid of such a creature? There were tales of wights, *tomtar*, and evil pixies being driven away from homes, but Annika couldn't remember what to *do*. Presumably it involved Christian symbols in some way, but something told her that wasn't going to work in this case.

She sat up and closed her eyes, walking through Erik's room in her mind, scanning the walls, and there it was: an antique crucifix hanging above the desk. So that route was closed.

So what remained?

The option that always remains when everything else has been tried: violence. Erik might have superhuman strength, but that didn't necessarily mean he was invulnerable. What was it Schwarzenegger said in that film? *If it bleeds we can kill it.*

Annika lay down again, gazed up at the ceiling and thought about what she would do to make Erik bleed.

When he turned up that evening with yet another tin of stew, she looked him in the eye and asked, "You want my child, don't you?"

Erik, who had been about to throw the tin at her, stopped in mid-movement. He shook his head, and nothing made sense. She had been wrong.

But then he said, "It isn't your child."

Annika glanced down at her growing bump. "Isn't it?"

"No. It's mine. The firstborn belongs to me."

"Like the kitten?"

"Like the kitten."

Erik had sat down on the end of the bed; perhaps he would let her go if she said the right things. But she mustn't be too accommodating.

"When you say it's *your* child, what do you mean by that? Are you saying *you're* the one who—"

Erik waved away her query as if it upset him. "Out of the question. Don't flatter yourself. Robert is the father, but without me you would never have carried it. I assume you realize that."

Annika nodded. "I'm very grateful. Really."

Erik gazed searchingly at her. He seemed to conclude that she meant what she said. Something in his demeanor lightened, and he gently touched her foot. "You will have more children. You wouldn't have been able to do that otherwise."

"Really?"

"Yes."

"Are you sure?"

Erik gave a wry smile. "You could say that this is my special area of expertise. Yes, I'm sure."

Annika allowed a little while to pass as she contemplated his hand, resting on her foot. Then she said, "Okay."

"Okay what?"

"You can have the child."

Once again he stared intently at her. Then he shrugged. "I'll take it anyway. It's mine. Sooner or later, I always get what is mine. But if you want to make things easier for yourself . . . then it's a wise decision."

"I've realized that."

Erik took out the chain with the key on the end and unlocked the handcuff on the bedpost. Annika rotated her arm to bring it back to life, and Erik said, "This doesn't mean that I trust you. We'll revert to the arrangement that was in place before our little incident. Perhaps you'd like a shower?"

"Yes, please."

"Come along, then."

Over the next two weeks Annika was moved from room to room as her belly grew. She could feel kicks, movements. She had to make a huge effort to stop herself from screaming when Erik came along and wanted to feel the child. She spent her days chained to various objects in the house. Where there were no suitable fixtures such as pipes or posts, Erik screwed heavy metal rings in place so that she could be tethered like a pregnant cow in her stall.

She had heard Erik answer her cell several times, explaining that *unfortunately the lady of the house is on vacation and does not wish to be disturbed.* She had given him her email address and password when he asked for them, so presumably he had set up an automatic reply saying that she was away on vacation. She was cut off from the outside world.

Apart from Robert. Incredibly, he was still turning up every day for his meetings with Erik. A couple of times he had shot her a guilt-laden glance when she happened to be standing in his way, but he hadn't lifted a finger to help her.

She didn't understand it—she really didn't. Her background was a simple one, and she was incapable of grasping how a *business* could make Robert act this way.

She tried to think of all the wedding guests who had been dependent on the success of the company, of the long line of ancestors gazing encouragingly at Robert as he took on the task of carrying the proud tradition of Axryd's into the future, but it just wasn't enough. Not for her. The only thing she could see was a stupid old miller who had been seduced by a *tomte*, bringing a curse on his entire family for all time.

Perhaps Robert was simply afraid. At least that would make sense. She knew he wasn't a courageous person, but now she was learning the extent of his cowardice. She was alone with her child. *Her* child.

One light evening in April, Annika was standing by the living room window when she caught sight of Erik doing something or other among the shrubs. Suddenly he darted forward and bent down. When he straightened up, he was holding a wriggling rat by the scruff of the neck.

He made a sharp twisting movement with his fingers, and the body went limp. He gazed at it for a moment, then brought it up to his mouth, bit off the head and began to chew. Annika could hear faint crunching noises. Then he stuffed the entire body into his mouth so that only the tail was dangling between his lips. He looked up and stared at Annika before swallowing the rat and sucking the tail into his mouth like a strand of spaghetti. Annika gulped and met his eyes; she even managed a smile.

Perhaps that was the wrong way to react; perhaps Erik had wanted to shock or disgust her. When he started digging in the loose soil under the shrubs and found a couple of fat earthworms, dangling them above his mouth before he ate them, Annika pulled a face when he looked at her. Erik nodded and disappeared from view.

The child was kicking so violently that she could actually see a bulge under the loose T-shirt she was wearing. She stroked her belly and whispered, "Don't be afraid. No one is going to take you."

The time had come. She had weighed up the pros and cons of various plans and had finally settled on the simplest of all. It wasn't watertight, and it depended on whether she had the courage to injure or kill when it came to the crunch.

The child moved again.

She could. She would. That very evening.

Apart from in the shower, dinner was the only time when she was not handcuffed. She had studied Erik's routine in the kitchen and found a couple of weak points that she hoped to be able to exploit.

That evening she sat at the table looking amenable as she waited for the first opportunity. Erik set out a plate, a glass and cutlery for her. He had also started to put candles on the table, and lit them with the air of a butler so that she could enjoy her microwaved meal by candlelight like a real lady of the manor.

Then he went to the freezer in the pantry to fetch today's meal. That was the first weak point. As soon as he turned his back on her and crouched down in front of the freezer, she slid out of her seat, holding the loose handcuff pressed against her wrist with her index and middle finger so that it wouldn't make a sound.

Silently she removed the largest knife from the block and returned to the table in a single movement; she sat down and pressed the knife along her forearm just as Erik straightened up and came back into the kitchen, reading the packet.

"Beef Stroganoff," he said. "With noodles. Is that okay?"

Annika shrugged. She didn't want to say anything in case her voice shook and gave her away. She didn't care what he chose. It all tasted the same.

She clutched the handle of the knife and visualized the movement she would have to make, going over and over the course of events as she sat completely still, looking unconcerned. The next weak point was coming up.

Erik had a childish fascination for the microwave. Not every day, but often, it was as if the golden glow and the slowly rotating pack of food exerted some primitive magnetic attraction over him. Annika hoped this was one of those days.

And it was. When Erik had placed the food on the glass plate and set the timer for five minutes, he remained standing there with his back to Annika, his elbows resting on the worktop, gazing at the little window as if he were spellbound.

She closed her eyes and sent up a silent prayer, then got to her feet and raised the knife. With all her strength she drove it into Erik's back to the right of his left shoulder blade. The knife was long enough to penetrate as far as the heart, and she hoped that was exactly what it would do.

One worry had been that bone would get in the way and impede the progress of the blade through Erik's flesh, but it went all the way in with a satisfying, sucking sound, right up to the handle, and Erik let out a sigh. Annika moved back two steps, hoping to see his muscular body go limp and slump over the worktop. To be on the safe side she pulled another knife out of the block; when it was in her hand she saw that it was a bread knife.

She giggled nervously and her teeth began to chatter as Erik turned around. His eyes were black, but nothing in his demeanor suggested that he had a twenty-centimeter-long knife through one lung.

"Annika," he said, and she raised the hand holding the bread knife. He looked at her with an expression that said, *What on earth were you thinking?* then reached over his shoulder with his right arm and pulled out the knife as easily as if he were plucking out an irritating strand of hair. When he pointed the blade at Annika, she saw that there wasn't a drop of blood on it. Erik didn't bleed.

"Do you think that human beings can harm me?" he yelled. "Is that what you think?"

It wasn't a question, and Annika didn't answer. She dropped the bread knife. Erik's lips parted in predatory grin and he pointed the knife at her belly.

"I thought we had an agreement," he said. "But obviously we didn't. How about a C-section? Put an end to all this?"

Annika backed away until she bumped into the wall. There were no weapons; there was no escape route. Nothing. Erik stood in front of her with his jaws working, breathing through his nose. Then he thrust the knife into the wall and left it there.

He grabbed her wrist and dragged her up the stairs.

She thought she knew what to expect, but she thought wrong. When they reached the landing he opened the door of his room and pushed her inside, switching on all the ceiling lights. He forced her down onto the floor so that she was sitting with her back to the side of the desk, and attached her right hand to one of its legs. He took another pair of handcuffs out of a drawer and attached her left hand to the other leg.

A large oak cupboard stood against the opposite wall. Annika was sitting two meters away from its double doors. Erik selected a key from his chain and walked over to the cupboard.

"I'm sure you're curious," he said as he unlocked it. "You must be wondering. I've left you in ignorance so far, but there's no longer any point."

He opened the doors wide and showed her his collection.

Shelf after shelf was filled with stuffed animals: cats, dogs, piglets, lambs and calves. The firstborn. But what Erik really wanted to show her was on the bottom shelf.

It looked unnatural. Newborn human children can neither stand nor walk. After stuffing them and giving them glass eyes, Erik had mounted the four newborn babies on metal stands, enabling them to stand on their chubby legs in spite of their smallness.

The skin of those who had been processed first had begun to contract, turning brown and beginning to resemble parchment, while the child on the far right—the brother Robert had never known—still looked nauseatingly like a normal newborn baby, with the eyes of a ghost.

Erik gazed at his trophies, then pointed to the empty space to the right of his most recent acquisition and nodded in the direction of Annika's belly.

"Unless of course it's a special child," he said. "Which I doubt."

Annika couldn't even manage to feel sick. All she wanted was to be allowed to leave this room and the sight before her eyes. Put an iron collar around her neck and leave her on the stone floor in the cellar, anything. Poke out her eyes.

"Why?" she croaked from a dry throat.

Erik scratched the back of his neck as if he had never even considered the question. "Well . . ." he said, "I eat the flesh, of course. That's the most important thing. And"—he spread his hands wide— "everybody needs a hobby, don't they?"

He left her for the night. Without switching off the light.

He came for her the following morning, and she offered no resistance as he carried her over to the bed and fixed each arm to a bedpost using the handcuffs. When she needed a wee she simply let it run into her pants. Later in the day when she needed to defecate she considered calling to him, but eventually she simply allowed nature to take its course.

She wanted to die. If only there was a button, a switch inside her that she could turn off. She tried to imagine it, to conjure up a clear picture of a black Bakelite switch pointing to LIFE, then making her imaginary fingers flick it to DEATH. Nothing happened.

She tried to hold her breath, but she didn't succeed in fainting. She tried to swallow her tongue. She threw herself from side to side in an attempt to bite the veins in her wrists, but she couldn't reach. She fell back on the bed, a stinking, whimpering receptacle, a vessel containing someone else's property.

She heard the front door open and screamed at the top of her voice, "Robert! Robert! Help me! He's killing me!"

Nothing. And still nothing. The hours passed. The child kicked and she no longer whispered words of consolation. Her last hope was that the fetus would die of malnourishment and poison her from the inside.

The stuffed infants were constantly there in her mind's eye. They came padding across the landing on their dried-up feet and gathered around her bed. They writhed in pain as if knives had sliced into their flesh while they were still alive. When they opened their mouths to scream in pain, worms and half-digested rats came pouring out.

The babies crawled over her body and rested their heads on her belly so that they could get to know their future sibling. They never let her sleep, they merely allowed her to fall into a temporary stupor before they once again began scratching at her eyelids with their fingers, like tiny twigs.

Sometimes she was fed, sometimes water was poured into her mouth and she swallowed. Occasionally she was dragged to the shower and sluiced down. It didn't matter. Time passed, that was all.

"Annika? Annika? Can you hear me?"

With difficulty she opened her eyes. She thought she recognized the person leaning over her bed, holding something in his hands. The light in the room suggested that it must be daytime.

She heard a metallic click, and one arm dropped. This was something new. This hadn't happened before. She watched the person as he moved to the other side of the bed and raised the object that was called a . . . a bolt-cutter. Another click, and the other arm dropped. She moved her arms to cradle her swollen belly, and rolled over onto her side so that she could drift away once more.

"Annika! It's me, Robert. We haven't got much time. Come on."

Robert. *Robert.*

Why did that name give her such a bad feeling? He was tugging at her arm, pulling her toward the edge of the bed.

"Stop it," she mumbled. "Leave me alone."

"Please, Annika. He could come home at any minute. We have to get out of here."

She made an effort to understand what he was saying to her. He. Could come. *He.* That was Erik. *Could come.* Erik wasn't here. Now. But he could come. Erik. The *tomte.* And the child.

Robert.

Annika's eyes widened. Robert. The child's father. Her husband. Selma Lagerlöf and a spillage on the sofa.

"Come on. I'll help you."

She was dragged to her feet. Robert looped her arm around his neck because her legs wouldn't carry her. However, it wasn't long since she had been washed down in the shower, and had walked a few steps. By the time they reached the landing, she was able to stand on her own, and pushed him away.

"You little shit," she said. "You pathetic, useless little fucking shit."

"I know," Robert said. "I know. But right now we just have to—"

"It's not your child. You're not having it."

Robert stopped trying to pull her along. "I don't want it, Annika. I never did. Don't you remember?"

Annika tried to spit at him, but she had no saliva. Instead she staggered toward the stairs, grabbed the banister and began to make her way down, one step at a time. She nodded in the direction of Erik's room. "Do you know what he's got in there?"

She turned her head so that she could look at Robert. He knew. His expression told her that he knew and she raised her hand. "Stay there," she said. "Leave me alone."

Robert took a step toward her, and she made her fingers curl into claws. "I mean it! I'll scratch your eyes out. Stay. Where. You. Are."

Robert's shoulders slumped. When she turned away from him to concentrate on the stairs, she heard him say, "The keys are in the car."

Her legs grew stronger with every step she took. By the time she opened the front door, she no longer needed to lean on something in order to walk. She stank of excrement and would probably soil the upholstery in Robert's BMW, which was parked on the drive. The thought made her smile.

When she reached the bottom of the steps, she heard the sound of Erik's pickup approaching along the avenue. She glanced at the BMW; Erik would have no trouble pushing it off the road.

She mumbled, "Please help me, God," and before the pickup appeared she turned left and slipped around the side of the house. Moving as quickly as she could, she crossed the garden; she heard a car door slam. She passed the tunnel leading through the rhododendrons and carried on along the side of the lake, heading for the stables.

Don't let him see me, please, please . . .

She was only a few meters from the barn door when she heard a tinkling sound, and turned to look back at the house. An upstairs window had broken, and something was being forced out through the gap. It looked so peculiar that she stopped.

Limbs unfolded and a deformed head appeared. Robert was dangling over the window ledge like a broken marionette, and Annika gasped when she realized why he looked so . . . wrong. The bolt-cutter had been forced into his mouth, and protruded through the back of his head. She only had a second to observe the terrifying sight before the figure overbalanced and fell to the ground.

Erik was standing in the window, his arm still outstretched. And he was looking at her. She tore open the door of the barn. One last chance.

"I don't know you. I don't even know your name. But you're the only one who can help me, so please, please help me. Understand what I'm saying. Please understand what I'm saying."

Annika stroked the black mare's chest as she whispered in her ear. The horse snorted and jerked her head, so that the bridle almost slipped out of Annika's hand. She gripped it more firmly.

"Stand still," she said. "You have to stand just here, you see, shhh . . ."

Annika leaned to the side and looked at the barn door three meters away. The mare was positioned with her hindquarters a meter from the door, and Annika tugged at the bridle so that the mare moved ten centimeters further back. She heard Erik's footsteps approaching, and kissed the mare's neck. "Please, sweetheart. Please let this work."

Do you think that human beings can harm me?

Just a hint. And her only hope.

The barn door opened and Erik stepped inside. His hands were covered in blood. When he caught sight of Annika and the horse, he frowned. Before he had time to realize what was going on or to react, Annika shouted, "*Gamm!*"

Erik hardly had time to open his mouth before the horse kicked out backward; its hooves struck him right in the face. He was thrown out through the open door and lay motionless on the ground, legs and arms outstretched.

Annika kissed the horse on the muzzle, then ran outside. Erik still wasn't moving. There was no blood on his face, but one cheekbone and temple had been pushed inwards like modeling clay. She searched his pockets and found her cell.

She had managed to hit one number when something began to happen to Erik. She watched as the concave area of his face began to swell, gradually regaining its shape. She slipped the phone into her pocket and raced into the stable.

Erik had regained consciousness while she was attaching the last chain. Fortunately, it had taken quite some time from the first signs of recovery to the completion of the process. His face was now back to normal, looking exactly as it had for God (or the Devil) knew how long.

He looked at Annika and made a move to get up, but the chains prevented him from doing so. One around each wrist, one around each ankle. Without taking his eyes off Annika, he said, "Do you really think this is going to help you? I'm going to *eat* that child out of your belly now."

"Maybe not, *Herr Tomte.*"

Erik glanced around, and for the first time she saw fear in his eyes. At the end of each chain stood a horse. Annika had had to tack them up very quickly, and had only managed to slip on a simple harness to which she had attached the chains. To compensate for this she had allowed several meters of slack for each horse. So that they would have time to pick up speed. So that there would be a violent jerk.

She looked Erik in the eye. And yelled, "Haitch!"

The horses weren't perfectly coordinated. Only one arm and one leg were ripped off. The other arm looked completely undamaged, while the other leg was bent at an impossible angle. The horses whinnied and increased their efforts; one of the smaller ones fell over due to the sudden stop.

Erik opened and closed his mouth, trying to formulate a command as green foam bubbled out. Annika called the two horses that were attached to his remaining limbs, allowing them to come so close that they almost trampled him.

"*Haitch!*"

The undamaged arm was ripped off. Only the distorted leg was left. The horse chained to that limb took a few steps, and what was left of Erik was dragged across the yard. His head jolted from side to side as Annika stood there watching him.

The green foam disappeared and Erik's black eyes stared at her. "Do you really think—" he managed. "Do you really think—"

From the ragged surfaces where his arms and legs had been ripped off, where grayish flesh was visible through the torn remnants of clothing, new limbs were slowly beginning to grow. Ill-defined lumps pulsated outward, finding their shape. Rudimentary fingers tentatively emerged from the shoulders, and the embryo of a foot pushed its way from the pelvis.

Annika called the mare and led her over to Erik. "Yes," she said. "I really do. *Densch!*"

The mare reared up and her hooves smashed into Erik's forehead. His skull bulged out at the sides.

"Densch!"
"Densch!"
"Densch!"

Only when Annika was certain that there was absolutely no sign of regrowth and Erik's body was completely motionless did she lead the horses back into the stable. She poured oats into their mangers and stroked their necks.

She went outside and saw that Erik had disappeared. His clothes were still there, lying flat on the ground, but where his body had been there were only worms, starting to dig their way into the earth.

Annika was halfway back to town in the car when the first contractions began. She clenched her teeth and bent double over the wheel, screaming with pain. In the interval that followed she put her foot down and tensed her body, as if to ward off the next spasm.

She reached the car park at Danderyd Hospital before it came. She left the car and staggered toward the entrance; she just managed to make it through the doors before the pain brought her to her knees.

"Oh, little one," she whimpered. "Is it time?"

She was lifted up, laid on a trolley and wheeled along corridors. Kind voices spoke to her, and at last she wept. For all the children who had not been allowed to live, for this child who *would* live.

"Goodness me, what's happened to you?"

She was undernourished, smeared with excrement and her body was covered in bedsores. She was washed, put on a drip and ointment was applied to her sores as the contractions came and went. It took many hours, and she gradually returned to the real world before she was hurled into the insanity of giving birth.

It was unbelievably painful. It took a very long time. She was given gas and air while soft hands stroked her forehead, and she screamed in agony as her child forced its way into the world.

And then it was over. Everything slipped out of her body, the world regained its colors and only a sharp, stabbing pain remained as the midwife held up a chubby, slippery little body. A son. Annika had given birth to a son.

A special child.

The midwife jiggled the boy up and down and he opened his mouth to let out his very first cry.

The stench of rotting flesh filled the room.

JOHN AJVIDE LINDQVIST was born in 1968 and grew up in Blackberg, a suburb of Stockholm. He is probably the only Swedish person who makes his living from writing horror. A former stand-up comedian and expert at card tricks, Lindqvist's first novel, *Let the Right One In,* has sold more than half a million copies in a country of nine million inhabitants. The book has been published in thirty countries and been made into two movies, one Swedish and the other American (under the title *Let Me In*). The author's other novels include *Handling the Undead* and *Harbor,* both of which are in the process of being turned into films, and *Little Star.* A collection of his short fiction, *Let the Old Dreams Die and Other Stories* (which includes sequels to both *Let the Right One In* and *Handling the Undead*), was recently published in the UK by Quercus. As the author explains: "A *tomte* is a creature in Scandinavian folklore who is responsible for the care and well-being of animals on a property; he also ensures that both people and animals are fertile and successful. In return, he requires a regular supply of porridge."

The Shroud

THERE WAS ONCE a mother who had a little boy of seven years old, who was so handsome and loveable that no one could look at him without liking him, and she herself worshipped him above everything in the world.

Now it so happened that he suddenly became ill, and God took him to himself, and for this the mother could not be comforted and wept both day and night. But soon afterward, when the child had been buried, it appeared by night in the places where it had sat and played during its life. And if the mother wept, it wept also, and when morning came it disappeared.

But as the mother would not stop crying, it came one night, in the little white shroud in which it had been laid in its coffin. And with its wreath of flowers around its head, it stood on the bed at her feet and said, "Oh, Mother, do stop crying, or I shall never fall asleep in my coffin, for my shroud will not dry because of all your tears, which fall upon it."

The mother was afraid when she heard that, and wept no more.

The next night the child came again, and held a little light in its hand, and said, "Look, Mother, my shroud is nearly dry, and I can rest in my grave."

Then the mother gave her sorrow into God's keeping, and bore it quietly and patiently, and the child came no more, but slept in its little bed beneath the earth.

STEPHEN JONES lives in London, England. He is the winner of three World Fantasy Awards, four Horror Writers' Association Bram Stoker Awards, and three International Horror Guild Awards, as well as being a multiple recipient of the British Fantasy Award and a Hugo Award nominee. A former television producer/director and genre movie publicist and consultant (the first three *Hellraiser* movies, *Nightbreed, Split Second,* etc.), he has written and edited more than 120 books, including *A Book of Horrors, Curious Warnings: The Great Ghost Stories of M. R. James, Horror: 100 Best Books* and *Horror: Another 100 Best Books* (both with Kim Newman), and the *Dark Terrors, Dark Voices* and *The Mammoth Book of Best New Horror* series. A Guest of Honor at the 2002 World Fantasy Convention in Minneapolis, Minnesota, and the 2004 World Horror Convention in Phoenix, Arizona, he has been a guest lecturer at UCLA and London's Kingston University and St. Mary's University College. You can visit his website at *www.stephenjoneseditor.com.*

ALAN LEE studied at the Ealing School of Art and went on to become a commercial artist, illustrating dozens of paperback book covers. With Brian Froud he created the groundbreaking illustrated volume *Faeries* (1978). Lee's other books include *The Mabinogion, Castles,* and Peter Dickinson's *Merlin Dreams*. After illustrating the centenary edition of J. R. R. Tolkien's *The Lord of the Rings,* artist and author became inextricably linked, leading to his Oscar-winning conceptual work on Peter Jackson's acclaimed *The Lord of the Rings*. He is currently working on *the Hobbit* movies for the same director. Alan Lee's work has won him the Kate Greenaway Award and the World Fantasy Award.

Acknowledgments

I would like to thank Jo Fletcher, Nicola Budd, Alan Lee, John Howe, Marlaine Delargy, Sheelagh Alabaster, Peter Robinson (Rogers, Coleridge & White Ltd.), Merrilee Heifetz and Sarah Nagel (Writers House Literary Agency), Mandy Slater, Dorothy Lumley, and all the authors for all their help and support.